The Witch & the Wicked

Kade Patrick

Dust Jackrabbit Publishing

Book Cover by MegKPart

Illustrations by Megkpart

First edition 2024

Published by Dust Jackrabbit Publishing

This work contains references to sex, abuse, and fantastical violence.

To the second-grade girl who chose to be an author for Career Day, to my partner, who walked through the woods with me, and to all the daydreamers:
here's to the stories you haven't crafted yet.

Skevsurvia

Mistum

Colds

Whelms

The Dead
Queendom

Aristus

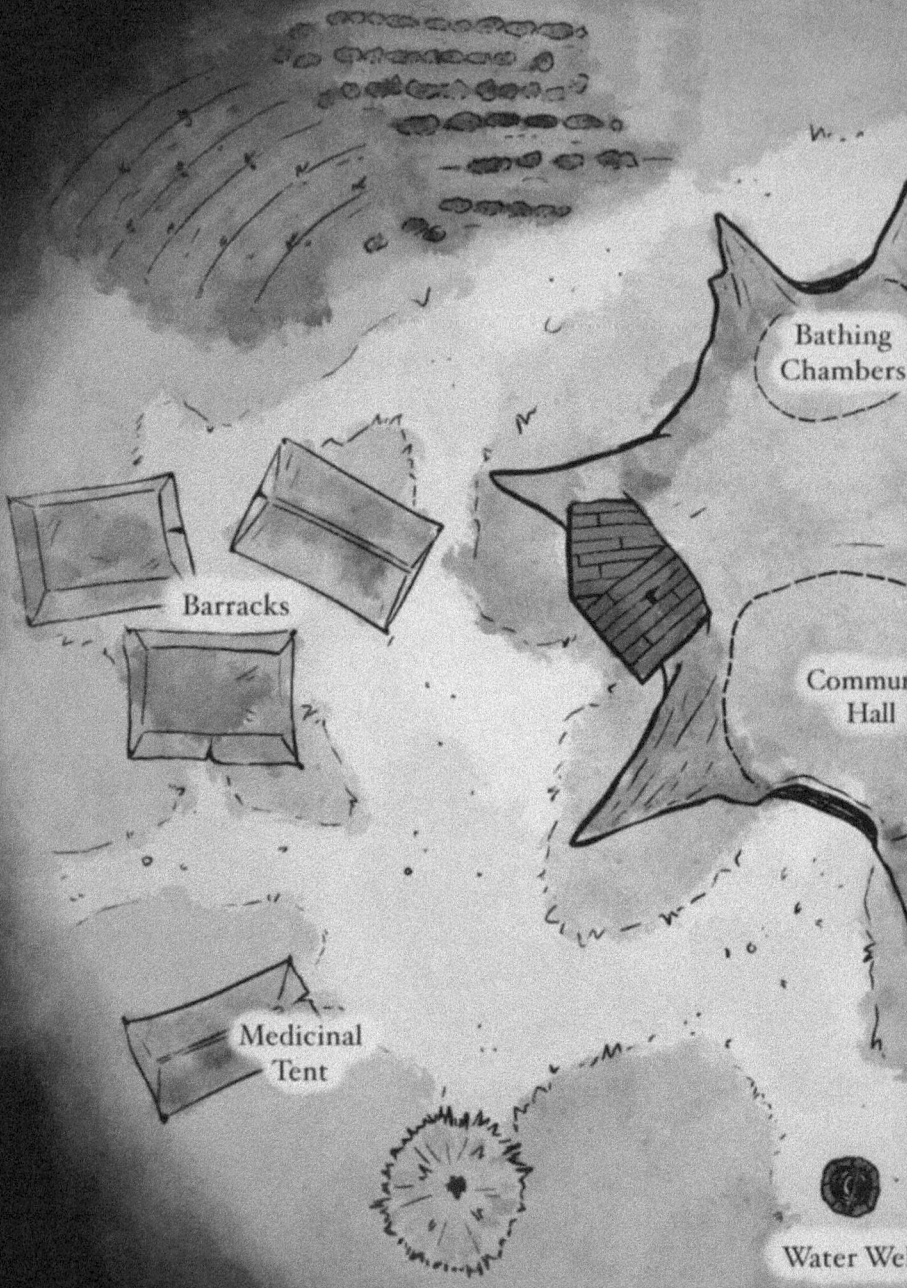

Bathing
Chambers

Barracks

Commun
Hall

Medicinal
Tent

Water Wel

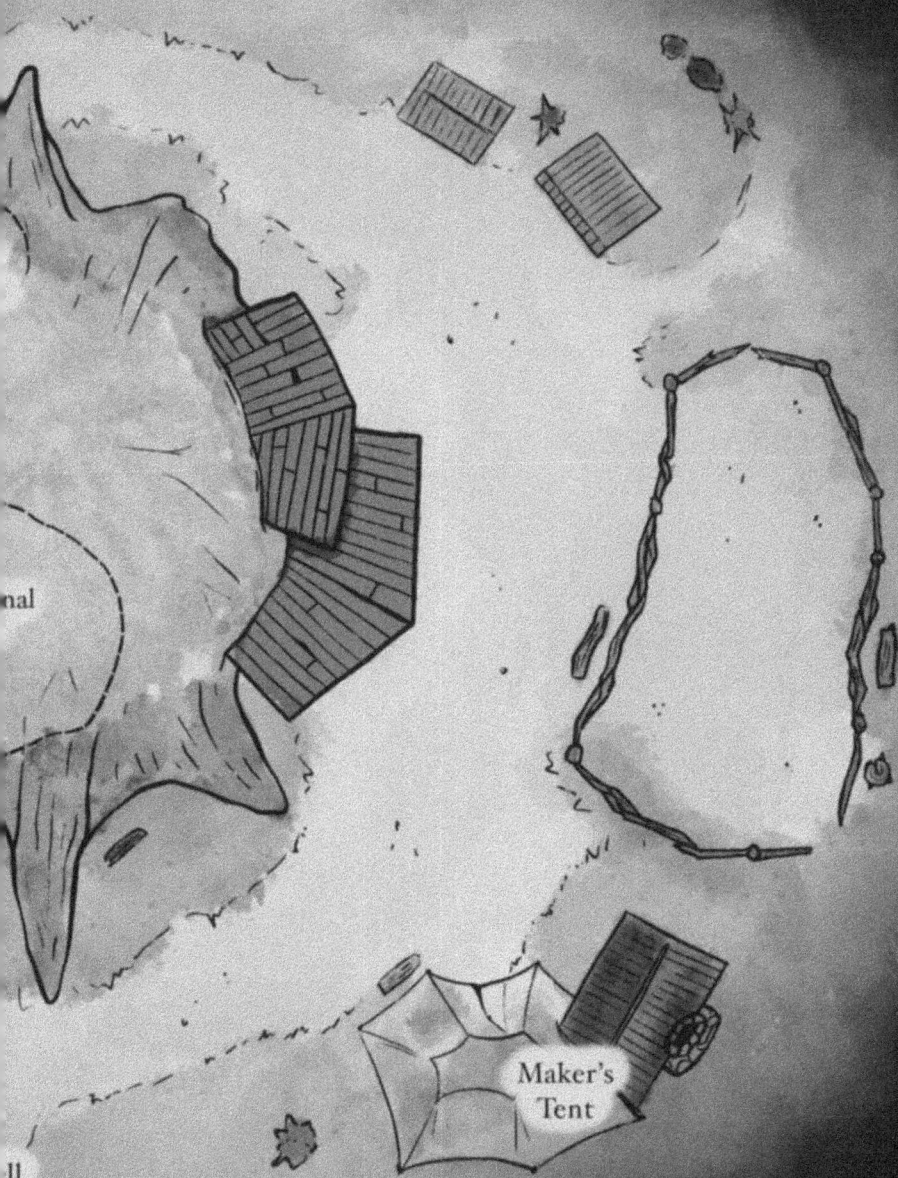

nal

ll

Maker's
Tent

CHAPTER ONE

Rune

It was the crack of wood splitting that startled me awake. Tooth-tipped arrows shot through the slit of my tent and into the tree trunk that held the thread-bare tarps together. The crunch of snow under boots grew louder as several attackers approached. Not wasting any precious time, I darted under the back of the tent and into the woods surrounding. I was too groggy for a fair fight. Let them have the tent—and cot, which took me weeks to find. I did manage to leave with my supply bag and the two hunting knives that were attached to my thighs even in sleep.

Leaving the illusion of safety the small camp presented, I continued deeper into the forest. The terrain took a sharp slope downward and my ankles shook with each step forward. I didn't need to look over my shoulder to know they were still on my tail. Snapping twigs and sloshing snow echoed behind me, along with the occasional boorish grunt. The blurred backdrop of barren shrubs and snow striped trees rushed past as the bandits chased me down through the icy woodscape. I hoped running alone would tire them out. Their greed apparently wasn't satiated by the resources I left behind.

It didn't escape the back of my mind that the loud rustling we made would likely alert any nearby creature, which kept me glancing around as I wove through the thicket. Even in the first circle of hell, the animal mind was relentless in its hunger for entertainment. It was, however twisted, a bleak and motivating comfort that animals didn't narrate the dissection of their prey like a human was prone to do. So I kept running.

An arrow grazed the side of my head, snagging my hood and throwing me off balance as I reached the bottom of the hill. I spat out dirt that forced its way behind my teeth and hauled myself up, taking a moment to look behind me. Descending were two men that I could see. One messing with the string on his bow and the other quickly gaining distance, sick grins flashing under eyes narrowed with obvious intentions.

I was certain they weren't close enough to get a good look at my face, but I wrapped my scarf up over my nose just in case. My head on a spike was worth more than a couple of strips of canvas and whatever they had planned for me. Not that I intended to find out.

The brush started to get thicker; the trees were spaced so close together that I slowed my pace down to keep from smacking my shoulder into rough bark and thorny branches. I just had to outrun them long enough.

Long enough came quicker than I anticipated, credit due to the loud screeching that pierced through the frigid air and halted me in my tracks.

Either the men didn't hear the high-frequency humming, or they didn't know enough to care about where it came from as they kept pursuing. Their long strides closed the distance between us, but I kept as still as I could despite the heaving of my chest and the shaking of my fists around my blades. An arm's length away, the man closest to me opened his mouth wider to say something.

His words were cut short as two long, thin talons hooked the side of his cheek and tore the muscle free from his face. Blood splattered the side of my cloak, but I dared not move.

The man reeled backward, hands lifted to cover his raw and exposed jaw. The creature returned with hawk-like speed, another set of talons braced to wrap around the man's wrist. I grimaced, but couldn't look away as the man was dragged sideways until sharp curved razors found the soft spot between the bones in his wrist and sliced them clean apart.

The man's cries of pain were again interrupted by another pair of talons, shorter and much thicker than the first, hooking into his back and hauling him up, carrying his writhing body skywards until meat tore from bone and the man's weight indented the frozen dirt below.

Aherrons hunted in teams. A joint effort of a mating pair to collect digestible-sized pieces of food for their shared young. An almost honorable task, if you weren't the object of their hunt. It was difficult to know exactly what they looked like, as they moved so quickly that the only time they were visible to the human eye was when they slowed down just before making contact. By then, it was often too late to do anything about it. But they moved so quickly that only moving creatures aroused any interest in them. It was possible to escape the encounter, I just needed to stay invisible.

I could make out the wings of the Aherrons as they continued to dive for more pieces of their meal—soft dust grey feathers tipped with white. Wings like a moth. If it weren't for their shrieks or hums of excitement, you would never hear them coming.

On the other side of the massacre, the other bandit stood shaking with his mouth open in horror. He had enough sense about him to stop still as his friend received the privilege of being the main target. Only when each muscle was plucked from their attached tendons did the Aherrons retreat from his skeleton to disappear back into the sky with a screech.

I locked eyes with my other pursuer, between us a trail of dark red blood and a man reduced to nothing but a pile of carrion.

Fearful, watery eyes met mine as the two of us stood frozen, the scent of metallic blood mixing with the earthy smells of the woods around us.

"Are they gone?" He whispered.

"Yes."

I didn't feel guilt for lying, not even as the second man's neck was exposed by the ripping of his head from his shoulders with deep, intentional cuts. It was either the creatures of the forest or me. It was less personal this way. Simply a beast and its prey. A nerve pinched in my chest. I couldn't place where it came from—fear, anger, from the tension in my body—I didn't care.

I stood solid as the trees, only allowing myself to shift my weight from time to time as long as the nearby branches were swaying beside me in the chilling wind. After what felt like an entire hour, I shuffled my feet where I stood. Nothing stirred.

The day the Aherrons learned to control their excitement when hunting would be the day The Colds would belong to them. In the meantime, the current lack of screeching gave me enough relief to make the truck back to my tent to see what was left of it. If it hadn't been taken by someone else instead.

Hells. In the time that had passed since I was rudely and abruptly awoken, the thin dusting of snow was enough to cover the tracks I made down the hill. The densely populated bushes kept me from fleeing in a straight line, so picking a direction and walking in it wouldn't help. I could eventually track my cot down, but it could take a while.

The growing ache in my stomach made me wince. After a few days without eating the weariness was catching up to me. I'd have to find something soon. I wasn't above resorting to cannibalism to fill my belly, but the Aherrons left only bone to rot away on the forest floor.

I walked at a leisurely pace, my only direction being any signs of edible vegetation. I was too far from any stream to fish, but I hoped a simple trap would bring me something warm to hold me over until tomorrow. That's all anyone could ever really wish for out here.

Survival. The driving force that whipped my back and wore down the calluses on my heels had always been survival. If I was an honest person I might admit that I wasn't really sure why I fought so hard to scrape by with my skin and bones as the only accolades. The lies were comfortable enough, I suppose. A warm broth of poisonous leaves steeping in my mouth, the unlikelihood of one day being my last day in hell was a strong enough lie to believe in. Maybe I was just trying to prove something.

Patches of dried grass poked out of dark earth in the distance, the best place for a trap out of seemingly worse options. I would need sticks and bark to form a crude cover for the trap so I looked around for dead, low-hanging branches. As I broke off the wood that I needed, I noticed intentional etchings in the side of one of the sparse cedar trunks.

There were no roads or pathways in The Colds, thereby making it easier to wander into starvation. But for those of us who survived out here for long enough, we made do with Marks. The carved notches in the wood didn't relay much. They weren't placed on routes of any sort, but they gave bits of vital information to passersby about the terrain—whose territory it was, how often raids occurred in the area, known monsters, and the like.

The tree that stood before me bore the Marks from two different communes, although it was difficult to tell if it was a border marker or a dedication of conjoining, where two might have merged into one commune. No major warnings were carved, so I decided to remain near what I guessed could be the borderline and walked the outskirts of the territory. Keeping to claimed land carried risks, but it was still far safer than walking the darker parts of the forest where more monsters dwelled. If enough people settled in the area, chances were good that they had chosen a safe location or had enough manpower to eradicate the deadlier creatures that lived there.

It only took a few minutes to set up a decent trap, camouflaged with what dead brush I could find available. Then, when I was far enough away that my scent wouldn't linger, I once again found myself stuck in place, waiting.

The forest was silent. The rocks sticking out from under the dark earth were silent. The snow clinging to the texture of tree bark was silent. Everything around me was frozen in time, always dying but never decaying. Everything, except the twitch of a whisker and a brush of fur.

The shoddy trap worked well enough to ensnare the poor unassuming rabbit under a flat rock, but before I could bolt out from behind my hiding spot, the sound of mumbled speaking broke the stillness in the air.

"Yes!"

A young lad no older than fourteen years popped out from behind a distant tree trunk. I remained crouched and unseen as he drew his bow and fired it at the neck of the struggling hare. It would have been a much more impressive shot if he hadn't stolen the profits of my preparation.

I turned my blade over in my hands with every intention of retrieving my rightful kill, but as the boy bent over the rabbit's corpse, I caught sight of what he was holding in his hand. Through squinted eyes I saw his bow was expertly crafted, made of fine wood and sturdy drawstring. My eyes roved over his attire. He wore a lush coat, the white and grey fur blending him into the surroundings.

He adjusted a quiver on his hip and revealed some sort of coin purse. Most likely used for storing small things, possibly extra arrowheads, but it was also finely made. I could just make out the elaborate stitching pattern on the side. This had to be from a well established commune, or maybe one merely lucky enough to have skilled craftsmen. Either way, I decided it was worth a trip to see their base. Perhaps I could rustle up another tent out of the adventure.

Although a clean shot when the target was stuck in place, the lad was a green hunter—cautiously looking about in all the wrong places. Following him was easier than I thought it would be with all the trees packed so closely together, but I also knew there would be safeguards near the base of the camp. There were rumors that some communes took advantage of the monsters in the area—*trained them*, even—to scare away trespassers, but I wasn't sure I believed that.

There was no visible smoke stack above the tall tree branches, but the faint smell of burning wood greeted me—probably the only warm welcome I would receive. I slowed my pace. We were still what seemed like a long way off from a base camp—ahead of us only more forest, but the boy also slowed down. He approached a pair of trees—trees that bore similar Marks to the two near the edge of the territory. He whispered something to one of the trunks, as if he were telling a friend a precious secret. Then he turned to the other and did the same. A loud groaning sound erupted from the large pines as their trunks started to grow wider. Wider and wider, until they collided with each other. Suddenly, the lad was no longer standing before two trees but a magnificent wooden door.

Shit. Magic. The Colds were a land of lawlessness so I shouldn't have expected any better, but this seemed a bit overkill. I sighed and sank to my knees as he reached into the coin purse and took something from it—some kind of grainy material—enchanted dirt, perhaps, and blew it into the door. Accepting his offering, the door creaked open and the boy disappeared through it.

The trees would probably shift back soon, but they gave me enough time to complain to myself and the shitty powerless gods I belonged to. I should have just taken his things and left with that. The rabbit was really the only thing that I needed. The bow would just be added weight and the coin purse was a beacon to other bandits... The coat would have been helpful. I removed a well-worn leather glove and blew warm air onto my numbing fingers.

My could-be tent and next meal beckoned to me from the other side of the ridiculous wooden door. Gods strike me. I really hated using magic.

I didn't hear what the boy whispered, but luckily (at least in this moment) I had a convenient—albeit slightly less delicate way of making enchantments work. I took my hunting knife and sliced through the skin of my palm, biting the scarf around my mouth at the sting. I pressed my hand up to the door, which made a small click sound, like the undoing of a latch. I gripped my knife in my good hand and slowly opened the door to a camp that was no longer invisible.

Thank the shitty powerless gods that it was a back-entrance of sorts and wasn't a grand entryway to a main road. The door was facing an empty alleyway between two barn-like wooden structures. The scent of livestock and dry grass hit my nostrils immediately and brought me back to a time when crashing in manure-filled paddocks was the closest thing I had to a bed and breakfast.

The commune was even larger than I had imagined, and indeed was settled nicely in the middle of the forest, unbeknownst to anyone walking near.

I could tell from the brightening sky that the sun was rising, but thanks to the never-ending fog that hovered over the forest I could sneak about shadowless even in day time. Sounds of townsfolk bustling about carried over the roof of the barns and bounced off the alley walls. Behind me was the forest where I came, and the lone wooden door. I wondered for a moment if anyone could see me approaching, or if the invisible wall worked both ways. Magic tended to work like that. There's always a catch. Hide yourself from your enemies but risk hiding your enemies from you.

I snuck along the back of the barn, aiming to stick to the edge of the camp and far away from its folk. As much as I would've liked to explore the invisible town in the middle of The Colds, I needed to get in, get what I needed, and get out.

The next building had windows with actual panes of glass in them. *How intriguing. This place is like a city.* I wondered what kind of people made up the commune. The majority of people in The Colds were banished here as punishment, either from the Kingdom of Skevsurvia to the north or the Kingdom of Aristus to the south. It was a death sentence for most. Those with hearty survival skills eventually allied together, formed communes, and claimed territory. People had a better chance if they combined their skills and possessions, but I had never seen anything quite like this.

Peaking in the window I saw a small cot. No, not a cot—a *bed*. A sturdy wooden bed with blankets and even a pillow.

I forbade my heart from sinking into jealousy. I've tried my hand at banding together with rogues and outcasts in attempts to join communes like this, but as it turned out my hand held shitty cards. I had many skills that were adequate enough to get me by in a wasteland, but I'm far more valuable dead.

His illustrious magnificence the Royal King of Aristus certainly thought a banishment to The Colds was an inevitable death for me, or else upon rumor of my still being alive, he wouldn't have placed a very large sum on my head. Large enough to purchase your way out of The Colds and into civilized society. A tempting mark for anyone who misses the warmth of sunshine. Thankfully, although word has spread of the bounty on my head, rumors have twisted the description of what I look like. A woman with pale skin and brown hair was vague enough. My only damning identifier was the large scar on the right side of my mouth, which was usually covered.

I lifted my scarf up higher onto my face to cover my nose. No one was inside, but aside from the lavish bed and a few other wooden pieces, there wasn't much for me. Sneaking to the back of the next building, I heard the murmuring of people inside. A woman and what sounded like a child. It was no small feat to keep a child alive, or to survive a pregnancy in the harsh conditions, but with the comfort and support of a town like this, it was probably a little more manageable.

I quickly ducked under the windows and walked through a tight alley that had collected lots of snow. I crept slowly, so as to keep the crunching sound from my boots low. Daring a peek into another building, I leaned against the wall. Another empty room, but the scraps of what looked to be a roasted bird were left on a table on the opposite wall. *This commune is certainly doing very well for itself, wasting food like that.* Just as I was able to pull the window open, a crash came from a few houses down. A few people started yelling angrily at a mystery disturbance, so I took my opening.

I crouched down, trying not to be too visible to anyone walking by the front window. The house was just one large room, with a bed in the back corner, and a table and chest of drawers near the front. I reached up to the table and sucked the tiny bones free of their tendons and skin. It was cold, which reminded me to hurry. From my crouched position I looked around and targeted the chest of drawers. My cut hand frantically searched through linens—too thin to be of any use to me—while my good hand remained rested on one of my hunting knives.

Suddenly the yelling from the townsfolk grew louder, and I realized they were headed this way. I leapt out the window and ran for the back of the house, not caring if my footsteps were heard. There were more footsteps behind me, pounding into the main street in front of the house I just left. Townsfolk running and shouting after something. Keeping clear of the windows, I kept a quick pace as I headed back towards the wooden door that I hoped was still there. I came to the barns and... there. In a stall opening I could see a tarp, draped over a fence. *Perfect.*

Content that a large portion of the town was occupied with something I had no interest in learning about, I found my way into the barn. I was greeted by a startled snort from a mule. *They have work mules? What is this place?* They had better living conditions than where I grew up in Aristus. I glanced around and started folding and rolling up the tarp. I took a nearby lead and fashioned it into a handle around the roll, slinging it over my shoulder.

As I was about to leave the way I came in, the mule in the stall next to me perked up. I too heard the footsteps, swift and growing louder and louder, and then for a moment, a pause. I was just about to swing my leg over the open window when—CRASH! The front doors to the barn burst open and through them tumbled the figure of a person, somersaulting over dirt and hay until landing right in front of me. They shook their shaggy black hair out of their face as they looked up, and as their eyes met mine, a gap-toothed grin spread across their face.

"Rune!" They exclaimed—and then shut their mouth with their hand.

I opened my mouth to respond, but as the hay-covered bandit jumped up to their feet and hopped over the window ledge, their small hand took mine and pulled me with them.

"C'mon! Gods I hope this stuff works."

Confusion overtook my senses as I heard them speak. They were still dragging me with them while digging with their other hand into their pocket and pulling out a coin purse similar to the one I saw earlier. We made it to the door just as a group of angry members of the commune saw us, some even grabbing arrows to fire.

"Please work!"

Letting go of my arm, the bandit next to me reached into the purse, pulled out a fistful of the sand-like substance, and threw it against the magical door. As the grains sizzled across the wooden surface, a clicking sound came from the door and it opened. A heartbeat later, they grabbed my arm again and yanked me through.

CHAPTER TWO

Rune

"Run!" The person pulling me along yelled over their shoulder at me, although I swore I detected a triumphant laugh at the end of their outcry. We kept racing away from the invisible town, knowing that a small group of angry townsfolk had charged through the door after us. We were in a full sprint for a while until they gave up chasing us; perhaps we were far enough out of their territory for them to care. We slowed down and stopped next to a small creek, both of us panting and looking for a dry place to sit. After I was able to catch most of my breath, I took a good look at my impromptu escort.

A wide smile I had not seen in years grinned up at me.

"*Sanders?*" My voice was raspier than usual after not speaking to anyone but myself for what was probably weeks. Or months. Confusion forced question after question out of my mouth. "What the hell was that? What were you doing in that commune—What are you doing *here?*"

"It's lovely to see you *too* Rune, glad to see you're alive and well, although I knew that already from your wanted posters. *Fifty-thousand in coin* plus *royal favors!* That must feel quite complimentary, but then again, you know I think you're worth twice as much—"

"*Sanders!*"

They put their hands up in a shrug.

"Alright!" Sanders started picking the hay out of their messy chin-length hair. "I wasn't *banished*, if that's what you're thinking. Not exactly, anyway. I was living back in Flatkeep—as you know already—with a few of the other rebellion supporters. We were keeping things quiet for some time when all of a sudden there was another huge raid. Town-wide. Aristus soldiers. Looking for wickeds, amongst other people."

A bubble formed in my throat. It was uncomfortably tight as I asked, "They were specifically looking for people? Human wickeds?"

Sanders nodded but didn't meet my eye. "They're not interested in animals anymore. Soldiers are pulling human wickeds from anywhere they can find them, any age..." Their voice trailed off at the last two words. I pretended not to notice.

I stooped down to collect water for my empty pouch. "What happened during the raid?" I asked.

The majority of the raids I had endured at the hands of Aristus soldiers were brutal, but nothing more than tactical intimidation. They didn't *take* anyone from shitholes, although they constantly added numbers to the already struggling lower city.

"Well, they found some of our letters to other rebels, and round up almost all of us—the ones living in that part of Flatkeep anyway. I managed to escape, but after I learned that most of them had been banished, I realized there was really no one left for me back home... I went with them."

"Willingly? *The Colds* Sanders? How long have you been out here?" I shook my head at my friend who I truly did miss, but was now gravely concerned about. They always had a penchant for making hasty decisions, but I was still getting over the shock of finding them here.

"We knew that traveling in a pack was the best chance at survival, and... I don't know, I didn't have anyone else at the time. I thought it would be better than the conditions we were living in, and in some ways it is. It was only a few moons ago."

"Where are they now?" I asked before I could think better of it. I already knew the answer. Sanders shrugged again and gave a halfhearted grin laced with bitterness.

"The rumors didn't exaggerate the monsters living out here, huh. Don't ask me how I escaped, I barely know how. I wish..." Their onyx eyes glossed over as their expression fell.

After a pause, I walked over to them and squeezed their shoulder to try to disturb whatever memories were surfacing.

"You've always had a knack for getting yourself out of trouble. Don't feel guilty, S. Everyone does what they can out here." Most of the time it wasn't enough. "Some are just luckier than others. I'm thankful you're alive. Even from out here I worried about you. I hope you know—"

Sanders immediately wrapped their arms around me. They had always been smaller than me—I wasn't tall by any standards and their head only came up to my nose. They lingered for a moment and it struck me that the sensation of arms around me felt a little foreign.

Taking a step back, Sanders held me by my shoulders and brushed dirt off of my cloak. "Well then," they said chirpily, "I guess that means we're allied traveling companions now."

"Hm. Are you certain?" I tried to give them an empathetic look. My facial muscles felt frozen stiff. "I have a bounty out for me, remember?" That was not a target I wanted to share with them.

They patted me on the back and picked up their small satchel of things. "All the more reason to stick together!

Maybe we'll even start a commune!" I started following the direction they were walking in, not having a better plan myself.

"I don't know about that S... People out here are crafty and desperate. In the few years I've been out here I've been stabbed in the back by more than one 'ally'. Besides, fewer people means fewer mouths to share food with."

Sanders shook their head. "I can't believe we ran into each other just like that. I knew I'd find you eventually." While they were obviously ignoring my remarks, the sentiment was touching.

We kept walking through the woods; every once and a while I could hear their teeth chattering. My mind also felt like it was chattering—thoughts were violently flying about in my head, the reverberation of thoughts threatening to turn into a migraine. *Collecting wickeds?* The King and his ruling nobles already had so much blood on their hands, but they've never been that *bold* about it. Gathering wickeds couldn't mean anything other than more unnecessary bloodshed.

I squeezed the wrap around my sliced palm. *Wicked.* Magic was a skill, mastered through years of study by witches and mages who learned to harness energy and power from other sources. It was usually reserved for higher-born houses, who could afford to be a part of witches' guilds and academies. Different forms of magic were widely used by the entire Kingdom; folk looked to witches to craft spells or potions for ailments, enhancements, luck... But it was still considered a dangerous resource by many—feared, even. Every now and then, a wicked was born and stirred up old hatred and new fear. The tightness in my throat remained.

As we kept walking, I realized I didn't know where we were headed.

As if reading my mind, Sanders chimed: "I'm taking us to a small cave that I found before MistView—don't worry, it's not very deep so I don't think monsters find it suitable for nesting."

"MistView?"

"The town we just came from."

I nodded. "Ah. You never told me what you were doing there."

Sanders turned to give me a wide grin, their pink tongue squished against the gap in their teeth. "Same as you I suppose. Looking for something worthwhile. I had heard rumors about a flourishing town in the middle of The Colds, and almost didn't believe it. No one I'd talked to had ever seen it. Because they couldn't! Man, they have a good thing going. Look at this!"

They whipped out the coin purse from their pant pocket. "It's some kind of magic dust—does the same thing you can do with, you know, your, erm—It's how they can get in and out of the town!"

I looked at the open bag filled halfway with thousands of tiny dull purple grains. Sanders put it back into their pocket and patted it reassuringly. I couldn't help but give a breathy chuckle.

"What do you intend on using that for out here?" I asked, amused by their admiration of special trinkets.

Sanders bit their lip. "I don't know. Maybe I'll go back to MistView and actually get something useful to keep me from suffering this cold. But I'm sure it'll come in handy."

As we approached what was indeed a small cave settled into the side of a small cliff, I paused. "You've been here before you said?" I checked out the stone slab wall and the terrain above us. A thick fog settled right overtop the edge of the cliff, keeping the forest above it barely visible.

"Stayed a few weeks, at least. One tussle with another bandit that surely wanted the shelter for himself but other than that it's as safe as any other part of the forest."

"So... not safe." I raised my eyebrow at them. Although a dry space to sleep would be a luxury, not knowing what was above us had me unsettled. Anything in front of us already had us cornered. We would just take turns keeping watch, I told myself. I might even get some sleep.

The sky darkened above us as we set up camp. I placed branches over the tarp to further blend in with the surrounding forest, but since they were so bare they didn't lend much camouflage. With a small fire struggling against the moist air around it, we warmed and dried our clothes as best we could. I retied the string of beads that held together the ends of my long side bangs. When I was done the beads rested lightly on my sternum; the two sections of hair framing my face warmed my cheeks.

The rest of my hair was surprisingly still in its usual long braid. I felt the tip of my mouth curve upward as I spotted a lone piece of hay sticking out of Sanders' shaggy hair. The smile faded as I looked down. Cuts and bruises covered the visible parts of their tan skin. Not that I wasn't also covered head to toe with scars and marks from living out here, but it pained me to think of what they had been through while I've been gone. What everyone back home had been through.

"Fuck—" I winced as I carelessly and unconsciously put weight on my inflicted palm. I gingerly peeled off the leather glove to check on it. Still open, but the bleeding had mostly stopped from the pressure of the leather around it. I shook my head at Sanders, who was about to hand me a corner of their cloak in aid. Sweet Sanders, who never cared about who I was. What I was. An ominous aberration of nature.

Wickeds. Living beings born with magical properties running through their blood. The blood can be used to bypass spells, or to enhance the power of one. Animals born with this were often used as sacrifices and sold at high prices at markets or given as gifts. Humans were usually looked down upon for possessing such an ability, unless of course you were of noble or high-birth, but there hasn't been a high-born wicked in ages. Lower-class wickeds, once discovered, were sold as servants to witches that used their blood for their craft.

It's not always a terrible fate, some guilds are known to treat their servants well by only taking the blood they need and providing comfortable conditions. Most... take too much for a person to survive. Then of course there are back-alley traders. Self-taught magicians that try to find and use wickeds to make up for the lack of skill they possess with the magic arts. There have been many horrible accidents caused by the misuse of wickeds, animal and human. Buildings destroyed, grave illnesses spread, the ruining of minds... but once you're used and can no longer speak, you're so much easier to blame.

A deep crimson had seeped into the stone that my palm rested on and I quickly covered the stain with my gloves. I glanced to Sanders and questioned to myself whether I had grown too soft or too heartless over the years. A younger, stronger me would have immediately marched Sanders through the woods to get them out of The Colds and somewhere safe. For the moment, I was content staying by their side through the night. They might be right about not having a home to go to. A part of me wondered if they were even real—that the friend in front of me wasn't just some mad trick of my own imagination.

A low groaning noise rose up between the crackling of the fire. Ignoring the growling hunger that rippled through both of our stomachs, I nodded my head towards the cave.

"Get some rest S. I'll take the first watch."

— 🔥 —

Snap.

Instantly I was on my feet with one of my knives in hand. I looked back at the tarp that enclosed the sleeping Sanders in their cave. No, the noise came from higher. I pressed my lips together and tugged at the beads on my chest. If a creature spotted us here, we would be trapped. After minutes of just standing and listening for any movement, I took a long inhale and stepped away from the cliff wall, turning my head to view the top. It was still shrouded in heavy fog. A portion of the cliff side looked scalable so I quietly made my way towards it and started to ascend. The fog made the rock slick, but luckily there was also enough dirt and dead roots to hoist myself up.

I climbed up onto the edge, repositioning myself into a defensive stance. Nothing. There was nothing but deep, dark clouds. The fire below had already gone out, and my eyes could see nothing but night. The ground in front of me was mostly flat dirt so I had an easier time navigating my steps. I kept creeping forward until it hit me that if the need should arise, I couldn't just run back without falling a distance of about thrice my height. *Hells.* I glanced behind my shoulder to see... nothing but more dark clouds.

Snap. On my left. My eyes were straining to see a glimpse of anything, any clue as to make out what it was. *Snap. Snap.* On my right. More twigs breaking underneath the weight of—I took two steps to my left and realized there were no low-laying bushes or roots near me.

Snap snap-snap-snap. No, not snapping twigs. Clicking? Popping? It was a familiar sound. *Snap-snap-snap-snap.* It started clicking faster and from all directions. *Snapsnap-snapsnap*—My stomach twisted just as I recalled that the clicking sounded identical to the snapping of bones in a dead animal. *Snapsnapsnapsnapsnap*—

I couldn't see it until it was right overtop of me, its reptilian head sliding from out of the mist. At about two arms-lengths out, I calculated that any move I made led to half of my body inside an over-sized snake. *Snap-snap-snapsnapsnapsnap.* It started to move the rest of its long, scaly form back and forth, writhing and lashing its tail. In doing so, the thick clouds dissipated to reveal the rest of it. For a moment I wished my eyes had not adjusted to the dark.

This wasn't a monster I had encountered before. My stomach twisted further into a knot, and my hands gripped my blade tight enough to hurt. Its legless body twisted around and around, enclosing me at every angle. It opened its long mouth to hiss softly, showing gums with no teeth in them. But the clicking noise... *Snap. Snap. Snap.* The monster's body twitched and contorted, small bulges sticking out and poking back in under its skin. As if it were breaking the bones of itself—or of prey it had already swallowed whole—from the inside.

HHIIISSS! It lunged, and I leapt just fast enough to avoid its toothless jaws. Its lower body wrapped closer to me, slamming into my stomach. I stuck my blade into the monster's scaly belly for stability. Using the sunken knife as an anchor I hoisted myself across the snake and started running. Its high-pitched hissing tone shocked my ears and my breath was knocked out of me as the reptile slammed its tail into my midsection. The momentum twisted my body around and my face hit the dirt first, keeping me down for precious seconds. The reptile opened its mouth to strike again just as a palm-sized rock was thrown into it.

Hhgh- With bulging yellow eyes, it reared its head back. It took several forceful head shakes to dislodge the rock from its throat which gave me enough time to be hoisted up, holding tight my stomach still stinging from the blow.

"He's pissed now!" Sanders yelled as we ran.

I silently prayed to the shitty powerless gods that we weren't running straight for the edge of the cliff. It didn't matter. We only got a few horse-lengths before we skid to a halt. The creature writhed its way out of the darkness, enclosing both of us in its coils. Once again, it reared its large slender head to strike, its gummy grin spreading wide.

The scent of bitter herbs dug deep into my nostrils and stung my eyes. I felt the grip of the coils loosen, but I could barely keep my eyes open to see what was happening. Clouds were creeping back in... no, not clouds... gas. Poison gas. I tried to hold my breath, but it was too late. My body went numb just before I hit the ground, and the night crept in.

CHAPTER THREE

Kaineres

I organized my dried herbs and wood chips into glass jars as quietly as possible, so as not to wake her. After corking the tops I placed them in their dedicated spots along the wooden shelves that lined the medicinal tent. There were rows of vials of varying sizes holding ingredients and ready-made potions, along with a few self-made scrolls containing remedies for illnesses and wounds. The tent always felt so much smaller with another person in it. My desk faced one side wall of the tent and behind me was a long workbench with absorbent cloths underneath, as clean as I could get them. Towards the back was a cot, where the woman still lay sleeping.

I was worried they used too much sleeping gas on her when they carried her in completely unconscious. Her smaller companion, however, was up on their feet much quicker, so I conjectured that the woman probably just needed her rest.

I ran my hand across my short beard, the scent of cedar wood still on my fingers. The glass jars clinked together as I reached to put another set back up on the shelf above me. I could hear her breathing lose its slow and steady rhythm. I sat back down into my chair and grabbed a quill to finish logging the day's events into my record book.

I didn't have to look back to know she was awake and looking around, taking in her surroundings. Her knuckles must have scraped the floor slightly when she was reaching under the cot; there was a small scuff sound and then a near-silent inhale.

"If you're searching for your weapons," I said without turning around, "They're not here. I find it wisest to not leave cumbersome sharp objects laying haphazardly around a medicinal tent."

More silence followed, and I continued writing as she surveyed me. I could almost feel her stare linger on my tattooed forearms—a thick red band wrapped around each arm with a line that trailed down to connect to another smaller band around my middle fingers.

Her voice was deeper than I was expecting—and raspy—but had a pleasant tone to it.

"You're... a witch." Her statement felt slightly accusatory.

"...Ex-witch." There was more bite to my reply than intended.

"Ex-witch." She said softly, more to herself than me. "Where is—"

"Your companion? At the moment, they are being given a tour of the rest of the camp. Woke up hours before you. They're doing just fine." At this point, I turned to look at her. "How do you feel?"

She was sitting up, her boots firmly on the ground. She was obviously still disoriented, but gaining consciousness quickly due to sheer will. The rigid cliff of her defined jaw above her slender neck gave away how tightly she clenched her teeth together. She looked at me for a few moments—scrutiny flashed across her face as she met my eyes. "Not dead."

"I would argue that 'not dead' is more a state of being, but I'll settle for your response."

I jotted down the status of the surprise visiting party into the record book before rising to my feet. She also stood, only to fall right back down again.

"Easy. You were affected by sleeping gas. Quite a bit of it. Enough to fell that creature you were getting so familiar with, as our scouts relayed. You can leave, but I advise you do so slowly and carefully, lest you fall backward onto your blade."

Her eyes widened. "Where—"

"Outside the tent. You are free to stay here a while if you feel unsteady—"

She stood up again, a little slower this time and with intention. " I would prefer to get back to my companion."

I opened the flap door of the tent and stretched my arm out, inviting her to exit. She narrowed her eyes at me and paused a moment before walking out, her effort to keep her balance showing with each precisely placed step. As we walked out, my heart shuddered at the sudden temperature change. The tent, heated ever-so-slightly with a magic enchantment, kept the chill of the air at bay to best encourage recovery.

The woman quickly picked up her two small blades and the leather straps that held them and quickly fashioned the set to her person, a knife on each thigh. How she kept from freezing completely solid was a mystery to me. Leather boots and pants, a thick long-sleeved shirt that must have once been white, a tattered scarf, and a thinning cloak. Suitable for city living, but egregiously insufficient for weather out here.

From the middle of the camp, her companion ran towards us along with my niece. They were both sporting grins from ear to ear, usually a tell-tale sign that Sora was up to nothing but mischief.

"Rune!"

The two guests were now in an embrace that made the woman take a few steps back to not fall over. "We got lucky, huh? Scouts from this commune saved our asses and took us back here to make sure we were okay. You've already met Kaineres, he's their healer. And this is Sora, she's lived here her *whole* life, can you believe that?"

"Almost seventeen years," Sora stated. "But I grew up here, so I suppose it's not that impressive."

Her newfound friend looked amazed nonetheless. "Sure it is! I've only been here through a few moon cycles and I've almost died countless times! Rune, you have to let Sora give you a tour of the camp, it's incredible! They've built structures around *and inside* a giant tree!"

Indeed true, behind them was a magnificent tree that was now the base of the camp. Buildings were built into the side and carved into parts of it. Due to its height, ladders and stairs had to be made to reach some of the structures built on its wide, lower branches. Of course, there were other buildings and tents near the outer parts of the campsite, but the majority of people dwelled near or in the trunk of the tree. The entire camp sat surrounded by a dense fog—fog nearly impossible to see through even in the middle of the day. This had kept the commune safe from human threats for years.

The woman—*Rune*—took in the campsite in front of her. "I've never seen the fog so low to the ground in The Colds." She marveled to herself.

A friendly voice chimed in. "That's because most of the fog lies near the Northern border."

Over walked Manden, my sister. Half-sister. Born to my father years before I was. I never met her until we discovered each other in the midst of an ancient magical forest of all places. We shared the same greying-black hair and sturdy frame. Even the differences in our lightly tanned skin were minimal—Manden had quite a few freckles scattered across her face and body that gave her a youthful appearance despite her age. She surveyed the two visitors with arms crossed.

"We're close enough to make use of the perfect hiding conditions, but not too close to be bothered. It's easy enough to get lost out here as it is. With the fog, unless you really know the land under your feet—you'll be wandering forever." Manden explained.

Rune's eyebrows narrowed in thought. She then turned to me and bowed her head slightly. "Thank you and your scouts for your aid. Sanders and I won't be taking any more of your time or resources as we make our way out. Your commune shall remain unknown."

I raised my eyebrows and couldn't stop an amused smile from spreading. She in turn cocked her head, obviously agitated by my response. Before I could say anything, Sanders took her by the hand.

"Sora said we could stay for dinner! *Dinner!*" They exclaimed.

"And it's almost nightfall," Manden added. "You slept for most of the day. Only a fool would wander out at this time. You are free to stay with us tonight. Have a meal, regain your strength—you look like you need it."

Rune took a long look at her friend's pleading eyes before sighing. "We'll stay the night, then." She bowed her head hesitantly to Manden in polite appreciation.

Her agreement was met with excitement from Sanders and Sora, who were now leading Rune to the giant tree.

I surveyed the visitors from behind. Death by Reptiscis was not a favored end, but the pair had not been spared out of the kindness of anyone's heart. Unbeknownst to them, their fortune was the result of Manden's first "recruitment".

My half-sister walked closer to me and lowered her voice.

"What do you think? They could be a useful pair?"

I ran my fingers through my hair. "Perhaps. They might bring more trouble than they're worth."

"Did you see her scar?" She asked, even quieter.

"I did. I also noticed that she's the type of person who makes a list of everyone who sees her scar." I replied, making my way back towards the warmth of my tent. My arms were freezing cold. Almost as cold as the distrusting stare Rune gave everything around her.

"She has to be the one they're looking for, right? The woman from the rumors. She's wanted by the King." Manden pressed.

"*I'm* wanted by the King." I gave her a look.

"No, you're the furthest thing from wanted. You're *un*-wanted. *She* has a price on her head." Manden had that tinkering, calculating look in her eye. It was clear that she considered the outlaw a snakeskin-wrapped tool for her arsenal. I wasn't convinced. The woman was certainly intriguing, but every new face had a tendency to leave such an effect.

"Which is why I think she's just an added risk."

"She could *help us*, Kaineres. Think about it."

I opened the door to the tent and walked through, but before the flap closed my eyes met hers. It was pointless arguing with her, as she was apt to twist my arm into it eventually.

"Whatever you wish."

— (··) —

Rune

The dining hall existed in the center of the giant tree—a room carved out of a portion of the trunk large enough to fit multiple tables. Intricate designs followed along the length of the wall and around the double-door entrance. I had never seen anything like it. I was curious if this had been done by hand or magic, but I didn't ask.

Sanders and Sora had given me a very hasty tour of the campsite, both eager to join the rest of the commune for dinner. Made up of forty or so people, it was obvious that most of them were very closely knit. Being close to the Northern border, some of those in banishment were from the Kingdom of Skevsurvia. I didn't realize that I was so close to the borderline. Nothing in the Marks people had left gave any indication. For probably months, I've only been a few days' journey away.

I glanced over at Sanders, telling wild and likely-embellished stories to Sora, who stared at them with big brown eyes. She had Manden's black hair, but much longer and curlier. She had it tied up in a large knot on the top of her head, with flyaway coils framing her face. She slammed the table with her hands. "You didn't!" She shouted.

Sanders leaned forward onto the table and shouted back. "Did too! Rune was there—tell her Rune!"

I obliged. "It's true. Most of Sander's tales are a bit lacking in evidence, but they did swap out pigeon eggs for chicken eggs."

"How did no one notice?" Sora asked.

Sanders crossed their arms, visibly proud of their past craftiness. "The masters never *saw* the eggs, they just ate them cooked. Other servants thought it was hilarious—for a whole year the entire family just thought they had *really* unhealthy chickens!"

Their laughter echoed in the large wood dining hall, and for a moment I was just a little girl, hiding in the hay stacks of Sanders' lord's barn. We had spent our childhoods together in Flatkeep, both born to servants, both desperate to do anything other than work. Although a few years younger, they had always been a little more courageous than me. Never took no for an answer and never stopped to think about the consequences. It got them thus far, but still I couldn't help but worry.

I could make it through dinner, and I could wait the night, but pulling Sanders away from their new-found friends was going to be difficult. I knew they were enjoying the company. Hell knows I wasn't much of a conversationalist. But I felt uneasy here. I couldn't wrap my mind around why someone would save us from certain death. Surely it was a waste of resources to aid two strangers—and had they not stepped in, wouldn't they have benefited from us satiating the monster's appetite? No, something didn't feel right. I just needed a way to explain it to the bard in front of me.

I had smelled the drinks in front of us for the common poisons, and confident that they were just foul-smelling fermented juices, I didn't bother to keep an eye on how many Sanders had guzzled down. They were leaning their full weight on the wooden table and singing an upbeat folk song that had apparently become popular in the city. Sora was clapping along and invited a few of her friends to join us. A few near her age, most of them closer to mine, having anywhere from twenty to thirty years under their belts. At that moment it occurred to me I wasn't quite sure how old I was.

The food arrived not long after, and I watched as a few members carried trays of food to the round tables and placed them in the center. The usual game found here—hare and small birds, along with an assortment of herbs. The bounty of it was equivalent to a feast.

"I hope you don't mind if I make myself comfortable." From behind me, Kaineres walked over and sat down in the empty seat next to me. Sora smiled at him.

"You missed the performance uncle!" She said, grabbing wooden plates and bowls and passing them along. The only thing missing from Kaineres' wide returning grin was sincerity.

"Oh not to worry, I didn't miss it at all—heard it all the way from the tent."

The food was plated and placed before me, bribing all my senses. I tried not to be obvious as I glanced around, making sure everyone was eating and it wasn't a cruel trick. Not inconspicuous enough—an audible groan came from my left as Kaineres hauled a thigh of his roasted bird off of his plate and onto mine. Making deliberate eye contact, he took his fork, carved off a piece of the meat and ate it. After swallowing he pushed the plate back over to me.

"It's not poisoned, see?" He said, then added gently: "You're recovering. Eat."

Sora looked mortified. "Kaineres!" She glared. "Leave her alone—it's been a long day for her."

Kaineres huffed back at her with a smirk on his face. "A long day? She's been sleeping for most of it."

Before I could reply with something just as snarky, Sanders offered me a bite from their plate. "Here, you can have some of mine if you want." They said softly.

"That's sweet of you S, but it's fine—" I trailed off and took the offered bite to dissolve the tension the witch had stirred up.

When the meat hit my tongue I would have sworn upon my life that it was seasoned. Someone in the commune must belong to the gods of harvest; it was the best-tasting meal I had ever eaten. I allowed myself to slowly finish off half my plate and gave the rest to Sanders. Enough to keep my stomach from growling but not too much that I would be riddled with nerves all night. Kaineres finished his plate rather quickly and excused himself. Sora introduced us to everyone at the table. Names I would need to be reminded of later, but faces I was at least able to familiarize with.

Manden had sleeping arrangements made for us while we ate. After the meal she led us to a room built on a low-hanging branch of the tree, almost touching the ground but still requiring a small ladder to get in and out of. *At least pests won't be much of an issue.* Three cots lay inside, tucked tightly next to each other. *How often do visitors waltz through?* She left us with a blanket each, which— trustworthy or not—I was grateful for. Sanders curled up and drifted off almost immediately, before I could ask them to take watch shifts.

I sat back in my cot and leaned against the wall, hoping to keep myself from falling asleep. Events of the day turned over in my mind. Kaineres was right—I *had* spent most of the day sleeping. It was the most satisfying sleep I had experienced in... years probably.

Ex-witch.

His response circulated in my thoughts. For an ex-witch, it looked like he still held to a lot of the practices and customs of a guild. Under his cloak I spotted his faded red tunic, bound to his waist with a braided leather rope. Other tells were the long silver earrings, tattoos adorning each arm, and an unnecessary commitment to document everything.

Medicinal Healer or not, any witch raised the hair on the back of my neck. Respect for the sanctity of life was not a value magicians possessed. There was not a single witch alive that was not drawn to power or easily corruptible. This man would be no different.

It was hard not to stare into his eyes though. Most intriguing. Deep, russet brown irises, surrounding not one—but *two* pupils in each eye, with the slightest hint of emerald green stemming out from the bottom corners. As if he had somehow captured the first growth of Spring sprouting from ancient woods and trapped it inside. I had never seen such eyes. It made his gaze feel twice as intense. Nevertheless, it was not the mystery for me to uncover. I needed to keep my focus on making it to the border. And I needed something to persuade Sanders to come with me. *That* would be the challenge.

Chapter Four

Rune

Shit. I woke to the sounds of the commune going about their morning—which meant that I had fallen asleep. Sanders was still snoring in their cot, curled up into a ball to preserve body heat. I had layered my blanket over theirs sometime during the night to keep their shivering at bay. I was cold, but the unnatural blood in my veins somehow kept me a little warmer than most.

Well, we were alive. I regretted not taking my boots off, and shook my legs around to try to get the tingling sensation out. After the numbness subsided, I straightened myself out the best I could given the limited floor space and peeked out the small window near the door. In the heavily fog-filtered daylight I could see the camp much clearer. Below me, people started their day: fetching water from the well, sweeping out last night's footprints from their small wooden homes, organizing supplies into their canvas drawstring bags—*Shit. Supplies.*

The rest of mine were sitting in a shallow cave who knows how many miles away. If they hadn't been snatched up already. I didn't have the stomach to steal anything from these people—at least not until I knew for certain what they wanted from us. If they wanted us dead, they needn't have saved us at all. If they had heard of the bounty...

The floor of the tree-house shook as Sanders plopped their feet onto the ground. Their clothes were all ruffled, but somehow their hair was no messier than usual. They stretched out their limbs and yawned.

"Wait! Don't head out without me," They said sleepily, slowly putting on their boots.

"I actually wanted to talk to you about that..." I leaned my back against the wall. "I know this place is well established, but I don't think it's a good idea for us to stay." I started, noting the slight frown start to form. "S, no one gives away anything for free out here. Why would they save our hide? Why would they feed us?"

"Hm, I don't know, perhaps because they're good people!" Sanders replied, visibly annoyed that I would ever mention such a thing.

I took a breath to keep myself from feeling equally as agitated. "You don't *know* that." I pressed. "We've spent one day here. That's not enough to make an assessment of character."

They crossed their arms and refused to make eye contact. I hoped they were thinking and not just pouting. I sighed and sat down next to them.

"Listen," I continued, "I didn't realize we were so close to Skevsurvia. That's where we'll go. A new Kingdom—a new city. A fresh start. We'll be free of this monster-ridden forest and its gods-dammed cold. It will be an easier life than scraping by out here. We just found each other again—I don't want to lose you to a well prepared trap."

A few moments passed before I concluded that they were in fact, thinking.

Sanders looked up. "I do hate freezing my ass cheeks off." They gave a half-smile. I hadn't won them over completely, but maybe they could see my point.

Someone knocked on the door. With my hand resting on the tip of my knife handle, I cracked it open only for it to be pulled wide open by Sanders.

"A pleasant morning to you Sora!" They exclaimed, their smile carrying no residue of the demoralizing conversation.

Sora beamed right back, the coils of her hair now tucked away into a long braid running down her back. There wasn't much space for her to stand outside the door—just a plank of wood. She held Sanders briefly by the arm as she invited us to join her and her friends in the dining hall, and then she descended the small ladder. Sanders gave me a quick shrug and trailed after her. Once again not having a better plan, I followed them.

Manden was waiting outside the double doors of the communal dining room, nodding to Sora as she and Sanders went inside with a few others already giggling about last night's impromptu performance. Manden stepped towards me, and with her extended hand invited me to join her on a walk. I bowed my head slightly and matched her leisurely pace as we walked along the dirt pathway that circled the giant tree.

"You mentioned last night you intended to make your way through the fog and back into the first layer of hell." Manden spoke to me, but her eyes were checking out the camp, nodding her greetings to people going about their business. When she didn't say anything else, I responded.

"I am aware resources are precious, even in an established commune. I wouldn't want to take advantage—"

Manden laughed. "No one will let you take advantage of them here, I can assure you of that." Her laughter faded as she rolled her eyes. "Maybe my Sora, but her naivete shows her age."

"Your daughter is quite spirited for living in The Colds her entire life." Other than Sanders, everyone I've known or encountered in the winter wastes had grown as cold as the world around them. The killing and stealing and hiding—selfishness is a survival tactic that changes a person. I could feel myself slipping from time to time. I couldn't remember the last time I genuinely laughed.

"Sora has not experienced The Colds as most people have." Manden said, gesturing to the camp around us. "She was born here—in this sanctuary. All she's ever known is this community. The gods have bestowed upon us a refuge by means of this land. We do what we can to keep us safe, and I do what I need to do to keep my daughter from a miserable life."

We continued walking along the dirt path, and I tried to remember the information Manden was willingly giving me about each part of the campsite. The kitchen, a structure called the Maker's tent, a fenced training ring, a field of sorts used for growing food, and a few more wooden rooms built into the center tree. At last we made it back around to the doors of the communal hall, with the medicinal tent (along with a few other tents) lined up to our right. Manden lowered her voice.

"I will not prevent you from leaving. I don't have the manpower to spare, and I don't know you well enough to care whether you live or die. But that is precisely the reason I suggest that you stay awhile and re-think your options. My scouts were able to rescue you from the Reptiscis, but they will not be guiding you out. You will need to find your own way through the fog—which is much more difficult than it seems. As I'm sure you know, there are more deadly creatures than the one you encountered, and the unforeseeable terrain is dangerous even when you know the layout of the land."

"Why did your scouts save us to begin with?" I asked, not expecting a fully true answer, but curious nonetheless.

"They were on a mission to hunt the serpent, but I had given them orders to capture any passersby." Her eyes lingered on the dining hall with Sora undoubtedly in mind. It was a few long moments before Manden replied, her voice still low.

"I'm losing scouts." There was a pang of sadness in her voice that she cleared away with a cough. "Monsters seem to be multiplying quicker than before—and while this camp is a safe-haven from humans, it is still susceptible to creatures. Our scouts hunt and kill them, but the monsters are getting bigger—stronger. We've lost ten of our best hunters *in the past three moon cycles...*"

She wiped something out of her eye and ran her fingers through her short black and grey hair. "I can no longer pull from other members of the commune—everyone has their own responsibilities to keep it running. I need more people. Capable people. People that already know what surviving The Colds requires." She looked at me again. "As you said, this commune is established. We have stable shelters, viable crops, cooks and craftsmen—hells—my brother is a healer. Other than the shitty weather and unusually sized vermin, this place is as well-off as any town. I'm offering you a place here in exchange for your services. My scouts will train you, you will be well equipped to handle any creature you encounter, and won't face anything alone. Think it over."

I weighed her words over in my mind, trying my best to decipher the truthfulness in her calm but serious tone.

"Sanders..." I didn't mean to say out loud.

"Your friend is also welcome to stay, providing they pitch in. As a hunter, stealth is an... important skill... I'm sure I'll find a fit for them somewhere." Her face suggested that

Sanders did *not* possess such a skill, and I wasn't sure if I disagreed. They were handy and hard-working when they needed to be. Quiet?

As someone opened the doors to the dining hall, Manden and I both turned toward the sound of echoing laughter.

—❀—

Kaineres

"That should be enough for a few hours. I wouldn't count on it lasting through nightfall." I finished smearing the enchanted clay on the bottom of the scout's boots. A softening spell to help keep footsteps light and undetectable. He rose to his feet and adjusted his worn leather arm guards.

"We're only hunting for game today, so the stakes aren't as high. Hopefully." He said, a thin grin on his freckled face.

I escorted him out of the tent and found Manden waiting outside. She patted the scout on the back. She wished him good speed and good hunting, and watched him and two other scouts—whose boots were also caked in enchanted clay—disappear into the fog. I held the tarp door open for her to come inside. She made her way to the workbench and hopped up to sit on it.

"What would we do without you, oh gallant healer?" She cooed facetiously , stretching her arms out to thaw in the warmth of the tent. I leaned against the desk facing her and shook my head.

"As I recall, you managed just fine before me," I replied.

It was true. Manden had already established this campsite and had enough people to call a commune. Sora was already seven years of age when I discovered them. I was lost in The Colds and had used a finding spell of sorts to lead me to a person—anyone—to make sense of where I was. By work of the gods, it led me to my half-sister, who I didn't even know existed. I will always think of my father warmly, but knowing he knew of, but never mentioned Manden does cast a shadow over my memory of him.

Manden—eight years older than I—was born to a woman of prestige who did not want the world to discover her affair with a mage's scribe. But eventually, the truth somehow found its way to the surface and her mother was forced to choose between her illegitimate child, and her status.

My sister looked at me with tired eyes. "There weren't near as many monsters then. I don't understand where they're all coming from. We've found no nests nearby, and most creatures are viciously territorial; there's no explanation for why there are so many different species this close to each other." She grabbed her chin and looked down, as if the solution to all her problems would be on the floor in front of her.

I kept silent to allow her to think. After minutes of us each staring at the ground and receiving no solutions, Manden looked around the tent and asked, "How are your supplies? I know you've been busy attending to the scouts."

"I'm running low on some ingredients, but most of them can be found relatively close by. I could easily make the—"

"No. Take someone with you." She interjected, then added softly—"if only to ease my worries. I won't make you take an entire squad, just one scout. Take... hmm... Take that Rune girl."

I didn't realize how much air was in my chest until it all came out in a huff. "You're not serious. Does she even want to stay?" I remembered the voracious gleam in her eyes when she found out how close to Skevsurvia she was.

"I spoke with her today and laid out my proposition. She hasn't decided yet, but she didn't say no."

"And you're offering that it's better for me to take a stranger—who is unfamiliar with the land and most likely a dirty rotten bandit—than for me to make this brief venture by myself." I raised my eyebrows in bewilderment.

"Think of it as a test. To see if she can, in fact, handle herself out there. She has to have some useful prowess for getting by this long—she's been out here for years."

"According to *rumor*. And that's partially why I'm so skeptical. Don't you see that as an added complication?"

She swatted her hand towards me like she was shooing away a gnat. "I see that as a testament to her ability to travel unnoticed. Once she is a little more at ease here, I doubt she'll cause you trouble. Not as much trouble as Arrowette already causes you."

I jerked my head in the direction of the scouts' tents that were adjacent to mine. "People like Arrowette are precisely why I'm concerned! What happens when Arrowette discovers that this woman is her ticket back to Aristus? As much as this feels like a home to you, there are still others that would do anything to see the sun again."

Manden stopped pacing. "So you're concerned *for* her..." She said, drawling out each word. "I noticed your expression perk up when we first brought her in."

I refused to acknowledge her obvious pestering "I'm *concerned* for the mess that will be made if you end up *losing* scouts in this endeavor. No one wins a price tag on their head of that magnitude for petty theft. How insouciant you're being by sending her out with me is a tad concerning but will be ignored. I just don't want to waste our time and efforts on a poor gamble for the sake of raising numbers."

Manden thought for a moment, then hopped off the table. "Then it's settled. You take the outlaw on your scavenger trip, and decide if she's worth our *time* and *efforts*. Consider yourself an investor." Smiling at what was a victory in her mind, she walked out of the tent, the frigid air hitting me like a blow to the face.

— 🔥 —

Rune

"I'm doing what?" I pressed my fingertips into the inner corners of my eyes. Sanders and I were sitting at a table in the dining hall. People walked in and out, tending to various tasks or chatting amongst themselves.

Sanders was carving a figure out of a chunk of wood from I didn't know where using a knife given to them by I didn't know who.

"Sora told me that you've been given a test to earn us a spot here—isn't that great? They want us to join them. I already have my eyes set on a room in the trunk of the tree—or maybe they'll have us build our own?"

"Slow down, S. What exactly did Sora say?" My fingers moved up to my eyebrows to massage the headache that was building. My ears weren't accustomed to hearing constant conversation and I wasn't sure if they would ever get used to it.

"She said that Manden is keen on letting us stay here if we help out around the camp—easy right? And she wants *you*, my dearest friend, to be one of her scouts."

"Yes, that I heard. What about the 'test'?"

"I guess you're going to help the healer collect ingredients. Sora said he's never gone long when he's out, so it won't be that difficult. Not for you anyway. You know I have unlimited faith in you." They pressed their tongue to the gap in their teeth in concentration as their knife carved away a delicate wooden curl.

"...and I agreed to this, when?" I asked, pointedly.

Sanders finished another stroke of the knife before turning to look at me. "Please, Rune. I know you don't trust these people, but what if it all works out? I'm tired of wandering around the forest, running from anything that moves. And who's to say that the Skevsurvians will even let us in? We're better off here than we are in any other part of The Colds." Their big dark eyes pleaded with me, and for a moment I wondered where I would be if I had just taken the rabbit from the boy in the woods and left.

I *had* been thinking it over—what Manden had proposed. The arrangement would at least give Sanders promising living conditions. They didn't have a bounty on their head, so I couldn't think of any reason they would be in danger here. I've survived worse. I slumped back into my chair and sighed.

"I'm only doing this for you—"

Sanders dropped their project onto the table and threw their arms around me. "Thank you-thank you-thank you!" they shouted. Then before I could blink they were up from their chair and out the door.

CHAPTER FIVE

Rune

"We should get going before nightfall." The healer was curt, seemingly as thrilled about the trip as I was.

He tossed a small leather pouch to me, filled with a few tools for scraping and digging. I fashioned it to my person and double-checked the two hunting knives on my hips. Kaineres had donned a black leather vest and a large grey hooded cloak, as well as a thick belt that had compartments for vials and pouches. Most were empty, but some were already filled with ready-made potions. He swung a leather bag over his shoulder and gestured toward the direction we were going.

"Do you find those little utensils particularly useful in a fight?" He asked as we headed in the direction of the fog.

"What, my knives? No, I prefer to carry useless weight on long journeys." I retorted. Kaineres placed a hand on his chest, feigning emotional injury.

"I was *only* going to suggest you take a look at our maker's armory. Thought you could utilize a wide variety of tools—but I do apologize, my lady, for accusing your choice of weaponry of being anything other than the most advantageous of instruments."

Exiled or not, he was most certainly a witch. What other kind of human could find so much enjoyment in being a patronizing novelty—walking about the world as a gift to man, knowing they are the power behind someone's purchased societal gain. I suppose I should've felt pity for him. He too, was once someone's most *advantageous instrument*. But I didn't.

After about twenty paces into the forest, the camp faded from view completely, and all I could see in any direction was the cloudy blanket that formed around us. I followed behind the witch, trying my best to memorize the ground beneath me. His pace was steady and he didn't look back once. After a few minutes, we walked into a denser part of the forest. Trees started to appear closer together, and the ground underneath us started showing more vegetation. I could have sworn that one of the trees had Marks carved into the lower trunk near its roots, but we were walking too quickly for me to examine.

Kaineres halted. I looked up from the ground just in time before hitting my face on his outstretched arm. I bit my tongue and looked around. There were stones at our feet—smooth—like stones from a riverbed. Kaineres turned his head towards me as if he was waiting for me to do something. I rested my palm on the end of my knife handle and continued looking around. There were no sounds of running water—we weren't near a river. These stones must have been placed here. They varied in size, but were laid out in a line. Was it a border?

I took a tentative step closer, and Kaineres followed suit, keeping his arm stretched out in front of me. Noticing no panic in his eyes, I kept inching forward and stepped over the stones. I squinted my eyes into the fog and—there. A few paces ahead of us, the ground had vanished.

I nodded my acknowledgment of the sudden drop, and the witch continued his lead, rummaging through his satchel to retrieve two hand-sized picks. He handed one to me and then began his descent.

"It's not a far distance down, but it's enough to break a limb if you fall." He said just loud enough for me to hear.

I followed him down, using the pick and roots I found along the cliff side to aid my down climb. The pick was admittedly much more manageable than my blades, it curved like a fishing hook and dug into the hard earth easily. At the bottom of the cliff, he brushed off the picks on a nearby branch and stowed them back in the bag. We walked until the fog grew less and less dense. I could see several horse-lengths out now, and it seemed to be the spot the witch was looking for.

He knelt down and pulled back the lower branches of a bush. He then picked through some smaller vegetation underneath and brought his hands up to me.

"This is what we're looking for." In his palms were tiny sprigs of a sweet-smelling herb with short, stiff leaves. He opened a cloth and laid his findings inside. He handed me another piece and pointed to another bush. "There should be more under those bushes, you may need to pull them back to get a good angle."

I draped the cloth over my arm and made my way over to the bush. I could smell the herb before I could see it. I collected as much as I could find and wrapped it up the same way the witch did. I was about to rise to my feet when I noticed a clump of mushrooms growing at the base of the bush. It was grey and white in color—almost camouflaged in with the bark it covered. I recognized it as a popular ingredient in potions and took some with me. Even if the witch didn't know what to do with it, it was still edible.

Kaineres had already moved on to scraping small pieces of wood off of a nearby tree when I approached him. He opened his satchel for me to put the cloth in. I asked him for another to wrap up the mushrooms.

"Mushrooms?" His brow wrinkled.

I showed him the flat grey fungi in my other hand.

"Turkey Tail... clever." In exchange for the mushrooms, he handed me a few cloth strips and glass vials. "Collect anything useful," he instructed. "If I need something in particular, I'll ask."

We spent another two hours foraging through the nearby brush, gathering herbs, flowers, and fungi from the area. The space was quite abundant, and we had filled up almost all the jars the witch had brought. After both of our satchels were nearly filled, Kaineres decided it was enough and we started the trip back.

"A small benefit to the increasing monster population," Kaineres said without looking back. "More monsters, less game, more plant growth. Any vegetation that can survive the frost, that is."

"What do they do with the monsters they kill? The scouts?" I asked.

"For a period of time, we just studied them. We're not sure how they repopulate so quickly. We've tried using them for meat, but..." Kaineres shook his head.

A memory from my first encounter with a small monster flashed in my mind. "They don't cook. They—"

"Melt, precisely. I see you've tried."

I remembered the adrenaline pumping through my veins as I carried the headless hell-hound over to my fire. I remembered the excitement and hunger stirring in my core as I started to roast my first big meal in The Colds. I remembered the stench that assaulted my senses as the beast started to ooze from the inside out—the thick black sludge dripping out and smothering the fire. By the grimace on his face, Kaineres must have had a similar memory in his mind. He shook it off with a shrug of his broad shoulders.

"Now that there are fewer scouts, the ones that are successful in defeating the beasts are usually too weak to return with them. They have their hands full with making sure the injured return to camp safely."

"You're quite the salesman."

"If you want the spot, you should know what you're agreeing to. That said, hunting with a team is surely an improvement from hunting alone. You can't take down a Reptiscis with one person."

It wasn't worth telling him that the monsters weren't the only danger I had to consider.

We had only walked for a few minutes before we heard rustling in the woods behind us. *Crack*. The echo of a whip pierced through the thickening fog. We whipped around, and my eyes could barely make out a large group of people in the distance—on horseback and headed our way. *Crack*. The sound of screaming was cut short with another shout. *"Get down and stay down!"*

Aristian mount-soldiers. A small troop of them, riding towards us with a cage full of people pulled behind them. On horseback, they would be on us in a matter of seconds. My hands found my knives, but before I could get into a defensive stance I was pushed up against the trunk of a large tree. The witch clasped his hands over my mouth to muffle my surprise. With his free hand, he reached into his cloak and pulled out a vial filled with ash. He uncorked it with his teeth, and dusted it over the top of me, moving his hand out of the way. As it fell onto my face, I could feel my skin start to burn slightly. I tried to move, but he gestured curtly to keep still.

He leaned close to my ear just as I could hear the soldiers approaching. His voice was a harsh whisper as his bearded jawline tickled my cheek. "Don't move. Don't speak, they can't see you but they can still hear you."

Kaineres backed away from the tree just as the horses surrounded him and the soldiers raised their spears. He froze, his arms raised in innocence. Each soldier wore thick metal armor bearing the crest of Aristus on the chest plate. Tufts of fur stuck out around their necks that gave them almost bird-like appearances. Behind them a few of their horses pulled a wheeled metal cage full of people they must have found in The Colds—each thin, shivering, and covered in scars. They all had a fresh cut across their arm.

"You there." A soldier with thin eyebrows and a deep voice addressed Kaineres. "State your name and your business here."

Kaineres' response was slow and calm. "My name is Bandin, I was banished from the Kingdom of Skevsurvia."

Bandin was a common name of Skevsurvian-born people. The witch's eyes flickered between the head soldier in front of him and the cart of captured people behind him. The head soldier jerked his head towards Kaineres.

"Check him." He commanded.

I could only watch as another man dropped from his horse and walked over to Kaineres, stripping him of his cloak and satchel, tossing the vials onto the ground. The soldier then grabbed hold of Kaineres' arm and took out a short knife. Kaineres must have known I was about to move, because he shot me a warning glance to stay where I was. His gaze was stern, but earnest. The soldier sliced through the witch's arm, not bothering to pull up his sleeve before digging in his blade. He held the cut arm over a small bowl of powder, and let the blood drip into it. After a few seconds, the man withdrew, shaking his head at the other soldiers.

"Pure." He said gruffly as he mounted his horse.

The head soldier gave Kaineres a final assessment, looking him up and down. "His Grand Majesty, King Amos of Aristus asserts his claim over wicked-borns, and commands that every wicked turns themselves in for His Majesty's will. If you come across those with unholy blood, Aristian or not, it would be in your best interest to surrender them to face their due judgment. Let it be known the hand of King Amos knows no boundary, and shall purge the lands of their wickedness. Long Live his Grandness." With a flick of his hand, the soldiers surrounding Kaineres circled him and then formed a line alongside the head soldier, their spears still in hand, aimed at the sky.

The man squinted his thin eyebrows. "How long ago did you say you were banished?"

"Err, a mere week ago," Kaineres replied, gripping his forearm tight.

A few of the soldiers laughed. The head soldier gave a quick whistle and the party started to walk on. "Far be it from me to bestow a quick death on lawless criminals." He called back. To his men, he chuckled "Let the winter starve out the Skevsurvian scum." The troop rode into the grey clouds; both Kaineres and I refused to move until the sounds of the horse's footsteps had faded completely.

When I was certain they were gone, I slowly walked over to Kaineres, who was still looking in the direction they went. I came up beside him to tap him on the arm.

"*I said—I said you could still be heard!*" He exclaimed, flinching. "*A simple 'I'm next to you' would have sufficed!*" He brushed off his arms and picked up his cloak. "Gods be, don't startle me like that."

"Sorry! I thought you would know it was me!" I said, handing him a cloth from his satchel to wrap around his arm. The double pupils in his eyes narrowed as he took it gingerly. It *was* a little strange—even I couldn't see my own arm in front of me. In fact, the only part of me that was visible was a small portion of my boots, which must have not been covered by the enchanted dust.

"Are you alright?" I asked softly.

He put his cloak back on and straightened himself out. "The cut isn't deep. Our focus should be on making it back to camp."

As we made the journey back to the campsite, the rest of my body started to reappear and the tingling sensation died. Luckily, the invisibility charm completely wore off before the climb back up the cliff, when I needed to see my hands and feet the most. We were silent for the entire trip back. My eyes studied the ground in front of me, desperately trying to think about anything other than the faces I saw in the metal cage. *I should have done something.* Not that anything would have helped. Twelve armed soldiers against two tired wanderers were bad odds. Still, images of bloodshot eyes and quivering lips flashed across my mind until I felt sick to my stomach.

Sanders was right. They really were rounding us up. Like cattle. My hand tugged at the beads on my chest. '*Asserts his claim...*' The filthy snake. I looked at my glove where the scab on my hand was. *Now not even The Colds are safe...* Not that they were ever 'safe', but running from bandits and creatures was a more welcomed challenge than running from bands of highly trained soldiers. All at once the sounds of the commune grew louder as we approached the campsite, and I could feel my chest weigh heavier as I realized just how tired I was.

We approached the back of the medicinal tent. There was no one outside aside from a few scouts patrolling the perimeter. *Everyone must be at dinner.* I followed Kaineres into the tent and rested the satchel of things on the desk.

He removed his cloak and hung it up on a peg near the entrance.

"You're free to join the rest of the commune for the meal, I imagine they've just sat down." He said as he exposed the cut on his arm. He began dabbing the wound in some kind of ointment. I turned to walk out, but my curiosity stopped me from leaving.

"Why did you only use your invisibility charm on me?" I asked.

The witch didn't look up from his task as he answered. "Because it was only powerful enough for one person. It is one of the most difficult enchantments to make, so it is used as sparingly as possible."

"Aren't you the only healer here? Why would you take a risk like that? They could have done far worse than cut your arm." It didn't make any sense to me why he would expose himself over a stranger, especially considering his role for the commune.

He huffed, but didn't look at me, instead reaching for a bandage. "Out of the two of us, you were the one they were looking for."

I opened my mouth to say something, but nothing came out.

"I had heard from a few of our scouts who Aristian Soldiers had been capturing. I wasn't being noble, I was being practical." Kaineres continued, grunting as he tightened the strip of cloth around his arm. "Has anyone ever mentioned that your gratitude is quite overwhelming?"

My mind circled itself for a moment. "How did you know..."

"—You're a Within?" His russet and green eyes met mine, his face mostly stoic but I could detect a smugness behind his voice. "My dear, I have trained and studied extensively under one of Aristus' finest mages in one of the world's most distinguished guilds. I will admit it has been a few years since then, but I know a Within when I see one." He gave a flirtatious wink, and immediately got to work unpacking the items we collected.

I stood awkwardly in front of the door, my head slightly cocked to the side.

"What did you say?"

He sighed and repeated himself, enunciating each word "I know a Within when I see one." He smirked until he glanced over and saw my confused expression. "A Within? A person born with magical energy? What you are? A *wicked* if you prefer the derogatory. Knew it as soon as they brought you in. Might I add—your hand? A terrible place for a cut. Extremely impractical. What's the point of having two knives when you can only wield one at a time?" He paused and then gestured to the other bag, offering something for me to do while I interrogated him. I started taking out the bundles of cloth and unwrapping them, my mind still repeating the word he said, feeling it out.

Wi-then.

"But if you knew I was... one... why didn't you make the invisibility charm strong enough for both of us? You could have used me to enhance it." I asked. It would have been too easy. Some additional quick thinking would have prevented the soldiers from ever noticing either one of us.

He let out a short ingenuine laugh. "Well, we were a little sparse on time for me to properly explain what I was doing."

"I would've understood from context!" I countered. "You had access to my blade and—"

"*Your blade?* What and gash you open right there? Gods, I don't see how that could have ended poorly. We already trust each other so much!"

"*I would have known what you were doing!*" I insisted. He crossed his arms and faced me directly, his exasperated smile a sign of his failing patience.

"I'm not going to *drain you* like a tree for sap! If you'd like to aid in the potions I make in the future we can revisit that in another discussion. I'm not going to apologize for the way I handled the situation. We are both alive, we have both returned—that was the goal." Kaineres took the cloth of mushrooms from my hands and nodded to the door. "Go and eat something. I'm sure your friend will want to know you're back. I'll brief Manden on what happened."

I stared at him a moment and gave a quick bow of my head before exiting the tent. Before I thought better of it, I leaned back inside.

"Kaineres?"

"Hmm?" He leaned up against the desk, his arms once again crossed.

"I... suppose I should thank you."

As he looked at me through tufts of dark hair that had fallen over his brow I hated to admit how handsome he was. His eyes softened for a few beats. "Far be it from me to impose the laws of shoulds and shouldn'ts out here." He jerked his head at the door. "You're letting the cold in."

I shut the flap and slowly headed for the giant tree with my head still circling. My nose tethered me to the present—catching the scents that floated around me. Roasted bird, burnt potatoes, crackling fire, chilled night air, and... from the skin under my nose, the slightest hint of cedarwood.

Chapter Six

Rune

"Listen! Aye, *Listen!*" Manden snapped her fingers three times.

She was standing with one leg resting on a stool, addressing a table of her scouts. Most of us were seated at the round wooden table, while a few others sat on stools or leaned up against wooden posts around the edge of the scout's tent. It was one of three large tents. Two tents served as barracks, with wooden beds stacked on top of each other, whereas this one was mostly for planning. A large map of the commune and the surrounding area was posted on one wall. I did my best to memorize the figures drawn on it, rock formations, trees, and other land markers.

Manden snapped her fingers again, but it still took a few moments for the bickering to settle down.

"We've been over this. We do not engage. We'll take precautions to keep them from wandering too close to the camp, but *no* confrontations." Her words were met by angry grumbles of protest. She shot a piercing glance at Twig—a tall, nimble fellow with shoulder-length brown hair and a face full of freckles. Although he was near forty years of age, he had an unkempt boyish appearance. He shook his head slowly as he played with the knife in his hand.

"I'm serious." Manden pressed. "Our numbers are drop-ping as it is. I'm not losing scouts to Aristus soldiers."

"Something big is churning!" Twig shot back, his voice higher-pitched than I expected. His outburst collected the rumbles of agreement from several other scouts. "The troop was spotted this far North? That's a two-weeks jour-ney from Aristus—if—you don't get lost, and even troops can get lost out here. His Heinous is up to something that we should be aware of."

"In that regard, The Colds work as a barrier for us. It is highly doubtful that any Aristus business will carry here." Manden took the knife from Twig's hands, who crossed his arms forcefully.

"It's *already* here—if they're marching troops through The Colds, Amos must think he can go wherever he pleas-es," Twig said to the group as much as Manden. "The Colds are ruled by no one. That is, until Aristus decides to take it."

"And what would you do, hm? With a handful of un-derfed, under-geared people? Risk your life and the lives of your crew to get as far as the borderline? You have a commune to protect, Twig. You all do." Manden stuck the knife into the table and put her hands behind her neck. Twig bit his top lip, but kept silent.

A minute passed before Manden slid her hands down to rest on her hips.

"I'm sorry to douse your fire, Twig. It's not our fight, and we don't have the numbers to spare." She waited for a moment, and after no words of backlash, she shifted her tone.

"Speaking of numbers... I trust you all have met Rune by now, or have at least heard the news. She will be joining this commune as a scout. She's lived in The Colds for quite some time and should only need help getting a lay of the land. Twig, Bandin—see to it that she's well prepared."

Twig nodded, along with another middle-aged man to his left. The man—Bandin—had a large frame and a thick white beard that was a stark contrast against his dark skin. He rubbed his neck, which was covered in tattoos that trailed down under his collar. He bowed his head towards me in a manner of greeting.

"When will Sora be joining us?" The voice to my left had a singsong quality to it. I recognized the girl from my first night at dinner. A friend of Sora's, and closer to her in age than anyone else I had met here. The entire meeting, she had been putting her silky light brown hair up into an intricate braid, and was now examining her dirt-free fingernails.

"Soon, Arrowette. I need to be confident she's ready to handle the work." Manden's tone conveyed that this was not the first time she had answered the question. Arrowette didn't look up from her nails, and made no response or acknowledgment that she had heard.

Manden sighed and excused herself from the tent to go find Kaineres. Small conversations broke out amongst the scouts in her absence. Across from me, Twig and Bandin leaned forward onto their elbows.

"So," Twig started, "what were those Aristus shit-clouts doing all the way out here exactly?"

"—They're collecting wickeds" Arrowette answered, her eyes still on her hands. "I heard Kaineres talking to Manden earlier. The soldiers had a whole carriage full of people already."

Twig and Bandin looked at me, and I nodded in confirmation. Twig rested his chin on his hands. "Then they really must be up to something... hmm." He and Bandin exchanged glances before looking back at me.

"So," Twig continued, "You've been scraping by out here for years. What kicked you to The Colds? Banishment of some kind I presume."

I nodded again. "...Yes. I—er—got caught aiding the rebellion."

Twig's eyes lit up. "You're a member of the rebellion! So are we!" Twig gestured to himself and his friend. "Well, Bandin's from Skevsurvia, but he's definitely on our side, and when the time comes—you'll find him sticking it to those noble fuck-alls. Oh and over there is Gwenna—she was a servant to one of the noble houses. She's also a rebel—a woman on the inside, if you will..."

Gwenna looked up from the other side of the tent at the mention of her name. She squinted and got up to move closer. Her curly ginger hair was untied, and it bounced up and down as she walked over. She had to be even shorter than Sanders.

"She can't see very well at a distance," Twig whispered across the table. "Practically have to be an inch away from her face for her to get a good look at you."

Gwenna twisted her lips. "I can hear just fine. Hello, I'm Gwenna." She smiled in my direction.

"You served the nobles?" I wasn't sure I wanted to imagine what that was like.

Gwenna sat down on the stool Manden had left open.

"That's right. I suppose it wouldn't shock you to hear most of them were selfish bastards. Dismissive or downright terrible to anyone not of good standing. I'm surprised my hearing didn't leave me as well with all the screaming. Nothing could ever be done quick enough or well enough. Although the young ones could be really sweet..." She wiped her hands on her pant legs, looking for something to do to clear her memories.

It was hardly a surprise that the majority of folks who banded together were once members of the rebellion. The cause itself was born out of resistance to the cruelty the servant class faced from Amos and his noble Houses. Lower-born class members and wickeds alike were treated like stock animals. Banishment was a lazy but effective way of dealing with the unruly unwanteds. Punishment by death was frowned upon by the other Realms, but there was a lack of social commentary around banishment bringing about the same outcome. According to the King, any rebel was considered a threat to the peace of the Realm. The way some of the rebels operated, it seemed a harsh truth at times.

Growing up in the dank and penniless hole that was Flatkeep, I heard about dreams and hopes for an uprising when I was a child. Restless visionaries stirred all around me wanting to overthrow the Aristus rulers and end decades of oppression. I listened to dreams become plans and hopes become strategies. That was before tragedy struck and everything fell apart. I once believed it a worthy fight, maybe one even possible to win. I wasn't sure I believed that now. And maybe it was the cold or maybe just the knowledge of the King's sudden quest for magical blood, but my resolve didn't feel as solid as it used to be.

Arrowette scoffed. "I'm so glad your little party of sympathizers is growing." She said coldly. Twig made a face at her.

"Are you jealous you don't have any friends of your own?" He poked back.

"Please. I have found a way to make friends that doesn't require the shared pity of miserable life choices." She rolled her eyes. Twig dismissed her with a wave of his hand.

"Don't mind her. She's just vexed because she was punished for the only act of kindness she's ever committed."

Arrowette slammed her manicured hands onto the table. "I *did* not *help them!*" She shouted. "I don't want to explain this again—I was *framed!* I would never aid Skevsurvian scu—" Bandin shot her a look. She swallowed and adjusted her leather jacket. "Well—in my post—I would never help them."

Twig explained that Arrowette was an archer for the Aristian army—a high-ranking archer at that—and was accused of treason when several Skevsurvian spies somehow escaped containment under her watch. He laughed as he antagonized her further.

"What will it be then, hmm? You were either terrible at your position... or—*gasp*—You did something nice for once. Although I will say, the last one does seem unlikely..." He laughed as Arrowette shot up from the table and went over to the other side of the tent.

Just then, Manden reentered the tent with Kaineres.

She held up a hand to Gwenna. "No Gwen, stay where you are—this won't take long."

Kaineres was back in his faded red tunic, with just a cloak thrown over for warmth. Both the medicinal tent and the scout's tents were slightly heated, so there wasn't much need for thick layers inside. The witch cleared his throat to gain everyone's attention.

"To combat the lack of scouts in the ranks as of late, I will be working on enhancing my current supply of enchantments and potions. I'm hoping to gain progress on this in the next couple of weeks, so at some point I would encourage each of you to stop by the medicinal tent along with your weapons and armor to see what improvements I can make." His eyes met mine for a second before continuing on about what kind of enchantments go on what piece of equipment, how often they would need to reset, what potions the scouts could take with them, etcetera.

I had agreed earlier that day to aid the witch in procuring stronger spells and enchantments. I was tip-toeing a thin line in my mind, torn between my hatred for feeling used and my inclination to be helpful. I told myself it was mostly selfishness—I would accept any extra defenses against the dangers of The Colds. If I was the key to making the defenses stronger, then so be it. This was Sanders' refuge now,

I had asked Kaineres to keep my 'ability' a secret, and he was keeping his word as he dodged questions about the sudden capability for improvements. I wasn't ready for everyone in the commune to know. At least for now. I knew I couldn't count on Sanders to be as reserved as the witch, so I would have to make amends with the secret spreading soon.

After Kaineres was through, Manden scanned the room as she dismissed the meeting with a final instruction.

"There were hell-hound prints sighted south of the camp. Twig, Bandin—take a few scouts and do what you do. Take Rune with you—this will be a good introduction to our way of monster hunting. And Twig—I mean it. You're hunting creatures only." She waited for Twig to give a reluctant nod before following Kaineres outside of the tent.

Twig drummed his long fingers on the table. "Alright, who wants their blood pumping tonight? Ack—Grow up, Ivon." A young man sitting on the other side of Twig chuckled and nudged him with an elbow. His bright golden eyes squinted in laughter.

Twig in turn slapped him on the back. "Actually, you've just volunteered yourself my good lad. Anyone else? Let's see, two more should do, aside from Rune. Make it an even six."

Gwenna's hand poked above the table. "I'll come."

Twig gave her a charismatic smile and counted with his finger. "Great, we have Gwenna, Bandin, myself, Ivon, and... *Arrowette*, thanks for joining!"

She huffed from across the tent. "If you *need* me, you can just say that."

Twig stood up from the table and headed towards the door. "Oh, I *do* need you. If this mess gets turned around and the monster hunts *us—*" Twig winked at her on his way out the door, his voice trailing behind him, "—I'll need someone to trip!"

— ◉ —

"This one's all yours." Twig knocked his knuckles against the double-stacked bed. It was of solid wood construction, and had mattresses made of cloth sacks filled with dried grass. After the meeting, Twig offered to show me the sleeping arrangements and anything else useful to a scout member. I had brought over the blanket that Manden gave me the first night, per Twig's suggestion.

"You can take the top or the bottom—both are available." Twig gestured to the bed frame and then to the chest of drawers against the wall. "You can also have one of those drawers for storing your things, not that you have much, and not that there's much to have out here. Still there if you need it." The piece was large, and almost reached the top of the tent. It had discolored planks of wood as if made from different types of trees. The drawers, twelve in total, were stacked in rows of four and had no handles. I pulled one open gingerly by the sides.

"Ivon collects rocks," Twig said. "I made him take the bottom drawer though, so no chances of it tipping over." He pulled out the bottom drawer, and sure enough, there was a neat assortment of rocks, all different shapes and colors. Some even had crystal pieces. I looked back at the empty drawer in front of me. My finger swiped the wood inside and picked up a light layer of dust. Even if I didn't have anything to put in it, I never had a storage space like this all to myself. My throat gulped down what felt like a strange mixture of humility and pride.

After I had placed my blanket on the top bunk—which seemed the safest option—I followed Twig out of the barracks and down the dirt path to the maker's tent. It was called a tent, but a large part of it was made out of wood and stone—thick canvas tarps only covered half of it. The sound of constant scraping grew louder as we got closer—like dragging a blade against stone. Twig knocked his knuckles against a beam of wood before flipping open the tent flap.

"Good day Celeste!" Twig said brightly to a woman sitting at a grindstone—sharpening a longsword. She paused, rested the sword on a table near her and stood to greet us. Her brown skin was covered in a light dusting of shiny metal, where the grindstone had scattered what it took off the edge of the blade. She wiped her hands off on her apron and gestured for us to sit.

"Oh, I'm just giving Rune a tour. Wanted to show her where the *real* magic is made. Don't tell Kaineres I said that." Twig winked.

Celeste smiled back. "Kaineres has often made that remark himself! Is there anything in particular that you wish to see?" Her voice was quiet but cheery, and her hands danced along to what she was saying.

"I just wanted her to get a good idea of where everything is," Twig said. "Rune, if you need anything fixed, made, or invented—Celeste is who to see. Kaineres said you might need a new holster for your left knife, is that right?"

"I—" I looked to my left thigh. I had noticed the tear in the stitching weeks ago and had been meaning to patch it up if ever I came across the tools. I had not mentioned it to the witch. "It's just a small tear, I'm sure there are more pressing—"

"Nonsensical!" Twig held out his hand. "Can't have you losing blades out on routes—leather is a little easier to come by than metal in these parts anyway."

Celeste nodded her head, a strand of her long black braids falling over her shoulder. "I could even repair your blades if they need attention. I—" Her head tilted ever-so-slightly as she looked at the knives. Her eyebrows drew together slowly as she asked "May I take a closer look at those?" Her hands continued to talk alongside her as they pointed at the knives.

I pulled them out from their holster loops and handed one to her.

An expression of warmth spread across her face. "Incredible." She whispered. A brightness twinkled in her eyes."These knives... These were made by my father. He was a skilled blacksmith—trained me under his wing. I can tell his workmanship anywhere." She smiled as she traced the wooden handle with her finger. It was indeed a fine weapon. Weight distributed perfectly, the grip of the once-polished wooden handle fit perfectly in my hand, and the steel was high-quality.

"I, er, wish I could say I came about them more honorably." I kneaded my hands together. "I swiped them from another bandit my first year out here." I gave a sheepish grin. Celeste and Twig laughed.

"Honor favors no one in The Colds." Twig declared. Celeste shrugged her agreement.

"It will be a privilege to restore them to their original beauty." She said as I handed her the other.

"You can keep them," I said. "I suppose they belong to you."

"Oh no, I couldn't possibly. Not without a fair trade." She winked, her black eyes glistening. "It's better that they are put to good use. The real shame would be letting them sit idle and rust."

Twig nudged me in the arm. "'Good use' being slicing open a hell-hound or two. Can you have them done by tonight Cel?"

The maker gave a nod of affirmation. I handed over the holster to be stitched, and bowed my head. "Thank you."

Celeste weighed them over in her hands. "It will be my pleasure to work on these. You have quite the eye for weaponry!"

As I followed Twig out of the maker's tent, I turned back remembering what the witch had said about my knives. "Do tell Kaineres that."

CHAPTER SEVEN

Kaineres

I gave the stem a final twist and snapped it off the rest of the branch. My fingers fanned out the tiny leaves, admiring their shape and color as I placed the segment in a cloth bag. The commune had been successfully growing a few crops over the years and recently added a few berry bushes. Small clusters of tiny purple orbs were tucked away on the inner branches of the bush. Drumberries. One of the only fruits that could grow without sunlight. The berry wasn't ripe enough to eat yet, but the leaves were edible and when added to hot water it was flavorful enough to convince yourself it was tea. Without thinking, I plucked off one of the berries and popped it into my mouth. Immediately my face puckered as the bitter innards of the fruit gushed onto my taste buds. Definitely not ripe enough.

Despite knowing better, something in me wanted to try it anyway. That had been happening more often. Acting upon whims I didn't know I had. Compulsions of nonsense. I shook my head and shifted my tongue around my mouth to get rid of the flavor.

Content with the leaves I had in my bag, I walked down the dirt pathway that circled the giant tree back in the direction of my house. The circular structure was right next to the medicinal tent and offered more privacy. I had made it by hand when I first arrived. By hand, and a small amount of magic. Unlike most of the other wooden structures in the commune, it was made of brick. Roughly made bricks, to be sure, but it had held up well the past ten years. The only occasional repairs I needed to make were on the thatch roof.

I closed the wooden door behind me and sat at a small table facing the only window. I cursed under my breath as I realized I had left the shutters open. It was just as frigid indoors as it was outside. I picked the leaves off of their stems and laid them out on the table. Then, taking a large wooden rolling pin, I pressed them flat and left them to air dry.

As I pulled the shutters closed, I caught a glimpse of the scouts convening outside their tents, prepping for their hunt. Night was falling, and they would be leaving any minute now. Earlier, I requested Twig to bring back some of the hell-hound's teeth. Their teeth and bones didn't melt like the rest of the body when burned and could be made into charms.

I stood up from the table and went over the small brick fireplace I had built into the wall. No one slept here but me, so it seemed unreasonable to keep the place heated with enchantments; during the day I was usually in the medicinal tent anyway. Fire was magical in its own right. After I had a tiny flame growing, I sat on the floor in front of it, leaned back against my bed frame, and sank into the rising warmth.

Tiny fingers of light reached up to grab onto any scrap of tinder they could touch. I watched as specks of heat fell away from the heart of the fire—burning, and then fading, and then dying as they hit the cold, hard ground.

I gently rubbed the cut on my arm. The bleeding had stopped and it was starting to scab over. I would let this one heal naturally—save the healing potions for wounds more severe. Under my breath, I let out a silent prayer to my gods and the gods of the caged Withins. My gut had been in a knot ever since the encounter with the soldiers yesterday evening.

I heard the rumors of Aristian soldiers marching through the woods, but I didn't expect to run into them so close to the camp. I certainly wasn't expecting their presence to affect me the way it had. Sleep last night was elusive, and when it did come, all I could hear and see in my dreams were voices of people I didn't know and places I'd never been. As a witch, visions of this manner would normally mean something of importance, but I'd been having these kinds of dreams for years and could still make nothing of it.

The fire crackled on, the logs shifting weight under its appetite. The crest of Aristus on the soldiers' breastplates tugged at something deep in me. An aching, almost. I sighed and thought back to my guild. It had been a while since I felt this homesick. I had, for the most part, made peace with my life here in the commune. Finding Manden and Sora was a true miracle, or perhaps my gods were able to pull some strings for me after my banishment.

Lately it had been difficult to not let my mind hopelessly wander about illusive and taunting possibilities. To think of what could be. Going back home, accepted back into the guild, bringing my sister and niece with me and out of this desolate winter. How I would do anything, give anything, to find a way for Sora to see the Sun.

It was cruel—the alignment of her birth. Cruel, that anyone born in The Colds, no matter the season or day of the year, belonged to the gods of the sun. It was declared by the ancients long ago—some say along with the creation of the forest itself—as a kind of curse to those who wandered the woods. A curse that extended to their children. Children who would never see their gods, and whose gods would never know them.

I didn't feel my eyes water until the tear slipped down my cheek.

When I had first arrived at the commune, I was much more expeditious to return to Aristus. Zealous for the art of magic, grief-stricken from being torn away from my home, earnest to undo any wrongdoings...

But time passed, as it does, and my excitement faded along with the possibility. The reality of the situation set in deeper and deeper as the days came and went. While it seemed selfish to give up on a better life out of fear, it also felt selfish to ignore the new one I was given.

I wished I had the same contentment as Manden, truly making the most out of what little was found. Making space for everyone and making use of every skill. Everyone in the commune was once a passerby, and I had seen scouts come and go without getting to know them well, but there was something about the newest visitors that intrigued me. The woman—the Within—pulled at something in me that I was hesitant to investigate. Mainly because she would make it incredibly difficult to do so, but also because I was afraid of what I might find.

Although guarded, pieces of her personality slipped past her steely demeanor. A ruthless wit. Necessary independence. I could see by the way she rotated the weapons in her palm that the Colds had turned her into a formidable competitor. And by the power of her gods, she was as beautiful as she was stubborn.

I rubbed the thoughts away from my brow.

There were certain intimacies I was not allowed as an expelled witch if I ever hoped to regain the title. Although my hope was nothing more than an ember now, the only tinder keeping it from dying out completely was either my obstinance or guilt. It might be a pleasant change to trade those feelings for something a little warmer. Perhaps with someone whose stubbornness rivaled my own.

The tears abruptly stopped welling in my eyes as if my mind was warning me I was becoming too candid with my thoughts. I laughed to myself and wiped the wetness from my cheeks with the sleeve of my tunic. After stretching my arms out, I stood and took stock of the room and what I could bring back to the medicinal tent. I had prepped a few potions and herb bundles earlier in the day, but I wanted to double-check the supply. I had a feeling it was going to be a long night.

— 🔥 —

Rune

A branch smacked me across my face, its leafless limbs scraping the skin of my cheek.

"Ow!" I muttered under my breath as I bent the branch back and walked around it.

"Oops, I didn't realize you were that close behind me," Arrowette hummed, her voice lacking any emotion. Twig, who was a few yards ahead, snapped his fingers at her.

"Quiet!" He whispered. "*Rune, follow behind Ivon instead. Arrowette will lead you straight off a cliff.*" He shot an irritated look at Arrowette before continuing on, his footsteps almost silent. I didn't say anything, but could have sworn Arrowette stepped in front of me just as we were passing the tall shrub just to land the blow. How she had befriended Sora was anyone's guess.

I paused for a moment to let Ivon pass me and followed him through the thick fog. His back was covered in a cloak made from a fur pelt. It was adorned with small spiky crystals on each shoulder, making his broad upper body appear even wider. Every few minutes, he would glance back at me to make sure I was keeping up. I was again trying to take in what I could see of the ground, hoping I could find my way back if I needed to.

We walked on for what felt like a half hour, the fog thinning slowly. I could see the entire group clearly now—Twig in the lead, then Gwenna with Bandin at her side— touching her arm if she needed to step over something—followed by Arrowette, and finally Ivon and me in the rear. Before we left for the hunt, Twig had mentioned that we were most likely going to split up as we got closer to where the hound was last sighted. We would have better luck if we could surround it from all—

"Aye, shit!" Twig stuck his leg out in front of him. While looking back to check on the group, he had somehow managed to step right into a pile of... not shit. Sludge. The dark remains of a monster that had been melted by fire. There were small piles of it everywhere, as if someone had carried a carcass over the ground and let it drip. Perhaps a lone bandit had tracked it down first?

We moved closer and a sudden gust of wind blew away some of the clouds in front of us. Not a lone bandit. Three of them. Their bodies lay on the dirt, some of their limbs missing or dislodged, still loosely holding their weapons. *It didn't even eat them...*

Twig made eye contact with each of us, instructing us to split up. Twig and Arrowette veered off to the the right, Gwenna and Bandin to the left, which left Ivon and

I heading straight through the carnage in front of us. I unsheathed my hunting knives and turned them over a few times in my hand.

They really were expertly made. Celeste not only sharpened them, but polished them and oiled the handles. They felt brand new, and I couldn't help but feel guilty taking them back from her. I would hold up my end of the bargain as best as I could.

Ivon retied the knot that held his long black locs out of his face, and then reached back for his shortbow. We crept forward, silently stepping over the piles of blood and black goop. The stench finally attacked my nose, and the rotten mix of dead flesh and monster innards almost made me puke. I nudged my scarf over my nose, but it was little help. There was also the faint trace of smoke—as if one of the bandits had attempted to kill it with fire. That probably just pissed it off.

Fortunately, I knew what I was up against. Hellhounds were the most common species of monster in the forest, and I had come across a few already. They shared a close resemblance with a wolf, but much, much larger. They tended to be quite bony—food scarcity resulted in a gaunt predator that was usually desperate for a meal. Except for this one, who left its dinner scattered across the forest floor.

Even with the covering on my nose, I could still see the little puffs of steam rise up from the heat of my breath. It was just me and Ivon now, with nothing around us but forest and fog. I could hear nothing but the soft squishing of dirt under each step and the squeaky shifting of our leather gloves as we tightened our grip around our weapons. I kept kneading my fingers, trying to keep them from going completely numb. The scab on my palm threatened to re-open with all the friction.

Ivon stopped walking.

I paused with him and squinted in the direction he was staring to get a glimpse of what he saw. I could only see more grey clouds, with maybe a shadow or two from the trees—no, not shadows.

Ivon drew his bow and aimed it at a dark cloud that was several horse-lengths beyond us. A dark cloud that moved slightly quicker than the fog around it.

"THERE'S TWO OF THEM!"

Twig's shout reverberated off the trunks of the trees. Ivon released his arrow just as another larger shadow came billowing up behind us. I leapt next to him, our backs against each other, each of us facing a long muzzle full of teeth. The canine stood two yards taller than me, its body dripping sludge from where its front right leg should have been. It curled its lips into a menacing smile, blood still in its gum line. From the size of their shadows, I guessed Ivon's beast was a bit smaller.

"Want to trade?" I asked nervously.

"Heh, yeah—careful what you wish for—" I could hear him gulp down a lump in his throat. "This one's got two heads."

I didn't dare look back, not while the hound in front of me was sizing up the best place to sink its oversized teeth into. I could feel Ivon shaking against my back, his arm moving slightly. His quiver pressed into my back. I realized he was no longer armed. With my injured hand, I slowly brought my arm back, until I could feel his callused fingers. I placed the handle of my knife into his palm and felt him take it. We would have to strike soon. *Gods damn it all.*

As if the hounds felt our energy shift, they both lunged with teeth bared. I was able to get my face out of the way, but its long fangs caught hold of my shoulder, the leather padding a weak defense. I was sharply turned around and saw Ivon, also in the mouth of the smaller hell-hound. His arrow was stuck firmly in its neck... *One of* its necks. While Ivon had managed to stab one of the hound's eye sockets, the other head was able to take hold of his cloak.

I struggled against the jaw that was tearing into my shoulder, trying to land a blow with my other arm. Each movement brought searing pain. After too many futile strokes, I was able to slice my blade across its nose, causing it to let go briefly with a yelp. I slammed onto the dirt, foul-smelling sludge dripping onto my legs. The beast whined in pain, licking its nose now gushing deep red blood. It snarled, opening its jaw again to finish what it started.

Zip. An arrow shot directly into its neck. Then another. Then another.

"*Hang on!*" Twig's high-pitched voice once again rang out, and I was hauled off a few yards away from the injured hell-hound.

Arrows kept flying through the chaos, shot after shot meeting its mark in the hound. Ivon was also pulled over to the side as Gwenna and Bandin took over his fight, Gwenna wielding a wooden club almost as big as she was.

In front of me, Twig swung his ax at the monster's good leg as its face was pelted with thin wooden arrows. As Twig raised his hands up in a back-swing, the hound swiped at his midsection, knocking him backward. The hound placed its paw on Twig's chest and leaned forward, its weight crushing him.

Arrowette called out from behind me "*I'm out of arrows!*"

I couldn't move my right arm. Nothing but agonizing pain erupted through my shoulder, but I was able to push myself up with my left arm. My legs still worked, so with my teeth clamped down on my cheeks from the pain, I ran to the beast with its back now turned away from me.

With my knife blade-side up, I slid under the hound's belly, stabbing the tender flesh near the end of its ribcage and slicing it through to its lower abdomen. Its shrill cry was drowned out by the warm dark blood that gushed out around me. Blinded by the blood and sludge, I staggered forward to avoid being crushed by the falling monster. Once again, hands gripped my good arm and dragged me out of the way. I felt the thud on the forest floor, and the silence that followed assured me that the other hound had met the same end.

I wiped my sleeve across my face. The fabric was just as filthy and left streaks of dirt, but at least I could open my eyes. We were all quiet for a while, all still catching our breath. Arrowette was going around yanking her arrows out of the canine's body, wiping them on clean earth before putting them back in her quiver. Ivon had removed his pelt, which must have taken the brunt of the bite. His shoulder was wounded, but not as deeply as—

"Aagh" I twisted my head too quickly and felt it in my shoulder—the pounding sensation growing as my adrenaline was wearing off.

Twig gingerly rose to his feet, checking his sternum for any breaks. "Bandin!" He jerked his head at me, and Bandin came running over, pulling out a potion from a small satchel attached to his waistband.

He gently pulled back the strips of my shirt that had been shredded, and exposed as much of the bite wound as he could. I bit down on my cheek again as he poured the potion on, the oily substance spreading over the broken flesh. It stung, but only for a moment before the pain started to numb.

"It's not going heal it," Twig said, grunting as he picked up his ax and handed it to Bandin's outstretched hand, "But it will ease the pain and slow the bleeding until we can get back to camp. Take a few more minutes scouts—catch your breath—but let's try to get moving soon."

"You really are a good shot." I wasn't sure why I felt the need to compliment Arrowette, perhaps it was my way of thanking her. She shrugged as she counted her arrows.

"I know." She quipped. Somehow she had managed to stay relatively clean. Only her boots were splattered with blood and sludge. I walked over to look at the head of the lifeless beast. Its eyes were still open. The pale, glassy orbs were not as dark as the other hounds I'd encountered. These had an unpleasant surrealness to them, something not entirely creature-like.

Twig stretched his arms and yawned as if he had just woken up from a nap and hadn't barely escaped the jaws of death. He gave a quick whistle, and the scouts slowly started their way back to camp. I looked back down at the hound, its teeth bared forever in a permanent snarl. I *wonder if...*

"Rune?" Ivon called. I nodded at him and collected my things together as best I could with one hand. I caught up to him; his shirt was caked in blood from his arm. He handed me the hunting knife.

"Hey—thanks," he said, a half smile across his tired face.

"I didn't want to die a selfish bastard," I said jokingly, wincing through each word.

He almost nudged me with his elbow, but thought better of it and laughed nervously. "I'll show you one of these days that I'm not all that bad with a bow, I promise."

He tapped the shoulder strap of his quiver and then strode a few paces ahead of me to talk with Arrowette about the fight. I took the biggest breath I could without feeling like I was breaking my chest open and followed them back to the safety of the camp.

Chapter Eight

Rune

I had almost made it back to the campsite before the effects of the potion wore off. The pain came back first, making every step near impossible to take without sending ripples of agony throughout my body. Then came the bleeding, and my tattered shirt was doing nothing to help it clot. Bandin was leading me by my left hand, making sure I didn't stumble over a rock in my exhausted state. He had given the only other potion to Ivon who was also clutching his upper arm.

Tiny hazy dots of light twinkled through the fog. I squinted my eyes. Lamps, lit and shining from the inside of the camp. Twig gave a whistle that rang in my ears as everything around me went in and out of focus. My body gave out underneath me. The last thing I could feel was Bandin's grip tightening around my arm as he tried to keep me from collapsing.

— 🔥 —

"*Rune! Rune!?*"

Sanders' voice was distant, muffled—I couldn't pinpoint the direction it was coming from.

"*Get them out of here now—everyone out but Bandin!*"

"*Rune!*" Sanders' distressed cry was pulled away from earshot. My vision was blurred, and my arm—

"AAUGH!" I screamed at the force on my shoulder that made every nerve in my body burn.

"No-not that one—we need to stop the bleeding first. The yellow powder—grab the yellow potion too. Hurry. *Never mind that they're not finished—I said hurry, Bandin!*"

The high-pitched clinking of glass above me sent more ripples of pain down my nerves. The layers of cloth pressing into the wound aggravated the excruciating sting and I tried to move, but the hands that held them there were solid and unyielding. My brain was spinning inside my head—no thought complete and every sensation over-whelmed by another. It felt like fire—white fire—seeping into my skin and leaking out of my eyes. Visions blurry and jarring slithered through each shock in my system. Blood-stained cobblestone... shattered windows... arms pulling me back as I screamed...

"Make her drink it—*all of it*."

Fingers opened my mouth, and I couldn't resist as liquid was poured down my throat. Herbs, salt, and blood coated my tongue. I kept my eyes shut tight, as if I could force myself to black everything out.

The pressure on my shoulder lessened, and for a mo-ment, all I could feel was a deep aching stemming from the right side of my body. *Pop.* Another jar uncorked and a tingling sensation came over my arm all the way to my chest. Hands wrapped a cloth around my wound again and pressed down firmly as I winced.

"Was she bit anywhere else? Take these to Ivon and make sure his bleeding has fully stopped. I'll come to check on him momentarily."

Shivers ran down my spine as cold air hit my wet, blood-covered skin. The sound of footsteps faded away until all I could hear was my own shallow breathing and the ringing in my ears. I laid there on the table, almost senseless, my body still aching but slowly starting to numb.

My sense of time was warped. After what might have been five minutes or five hours, the cloths were taken off my wound and replaced with fresh ones. They were tightened in place, and my arm was left to rest on the table. Water sloshed around on the other side of the tent. Droplets trickled onto the floor.

My face twitched at the warm compress that gently touched my forehead. With a slow pulling motion against my skin, it wiped some of the grime away. Soft, intentional strokes were drawn across my cheeks, my nose, my lips. His hands gently massaged through the caked-on blood, until my face felt fairly clean. The foul stench of monster innards was driven away with a minty smell—rosemary I think it was called.

"Try to slow your breathing down. You lost a substantial amount of blood." His voice was quiet.

I blinked open my eyes to the ceiling of the medicinal tent, straining at the lights from the lanterns. Kaineres was piling up the red-stained rags into a basket, his tunic darkened with stains across the front. I wondered for a moment if that was the reason healing witches wore red.

His face was difficult to read, but there was exhaustion in his eyes. He walked over and took a blanket from the cot in the back.

"I need to check on Ivon." He said as he pulled the blanket over me, careful to avoid my injured arm. "*Don't move. Just* focus on steadying your breathing. I'll be back." He took the basket, a few fresh scraps of fabric, and ointments and left, carefully parting the tent flap on his way out to prevent the cold from rushing in.

Everything was sore, even through the numbing. I could feel my heart pounding in my chest, beating up against my sternum. I stared up at the ceiling for a few minutes, trying to settle my mind.

I ran through my memory, trying to piece everything together. The walk out of the camp—the carnage of the bandits left to decay—the weight of the knife in my hand—the crunching sound my shoulder made as the hell-hound bit into it—the temperature of its blood as it splattered against my face—the pain that pulsated through me with each step back—the bitter taste of herbs trailing down my throat—the gentle touch of his fingers running across my cheek...

The excruciating pressure he placed on my shoulder while clotting the wound, the sting from the treatment, the bitter herbs, all the pain of it I anticipated. What I didn't expect was how gentle the healer could be. The witch even wasted material to remove the caked-on grime from my face. I was surprised I received treatment at all.

I shut my eyes tight again, hoping everything would be clearer in the morning. Or maybe I'd be lucky enough to forget everything. *Breathing. Focus on breathing.* I inhaled and exhaled as deeply and as slowly as I could and let myself sink into the numbness around me.

—◖◗—

I kept blinking, trying to get my vision adjusted to the light. I was still in the medicinal tent, but somehow had been moved to the sleeping cot. I had no idea how long I was out for, but the small streaks of sunlight that fell through a small tear in the fabric of the wall meant the night had passed.

Gods I smelled awful. The exposed skin on my arms and hands had been wiped clean, but my clothes were in rough shape. No one else was in the room, but there was mumbling coming from out front.

"When can I see her?"

"Soon. She's still resting."

"When will she wake up? Is she okay?"

"She's... stable. She lost quite a bit of blood—"

"*I'm fine.*" I called out, my vocal chords straining against my throat. Most of the pain had subsided and left a low aching in its place.

The tent flap flew open and Sanders pushed past the witch to get inside. They knelt next to the cot, but I swatted them away as I tried to sit up. They grabbed my left arm and helped steady me upright.

"I'm so glad you're alive! When the scouts brought you in you were unconscious and covered in blood and I was so worried—*ugh*—you smell like death." They covered their small button nose with their sweater.

Air rushed out of my stuffy nostrils. "We brushed elbows."

Kaineres walked in, carrying a pile of clothing. His face was weary—he must have stayed up all night tending to the returning scouts. He put the clothes on the desk, the table still showing visible stains that needed a deep cleaning. He motioned to the clothes.

"These are for you—I was able to dig up some clothing for you. Some extra items we had lying around. We're running a little too low on fabric to make you new ones so these won't fit perfectly, but they're clean. Sanders can show you to the bathing chambers. Try to clean the wound as best you can."

Sanders stood up. "Oh! Manden said one of the makers was finishing up fresh soaps—I'll go get some—I'll be quick!" They lowered their chin in what could have been a hasty bow and ran out of the tent. I took a deep breath and stretched my legs out in front of me.

"Rune." Kaineres sat at the desk, turning the chair to face me. There was a hint of concern on his tired face. "You are probably aware of this, but you're going to heal quicker than others. And a few people here have had injuries like this before, so they're going to notice. You can't keep it hidden for long. Bandin, I'm sure, has figured it out after last night. He's quiet enough but you should be prepared for the knowledge to spread."

I sighed again in fatigued acceptance. Kaineres' eyebrows furrowed together.

"If I may... offer some consolation..." he started, "this commune is still the safest place you could be right now—with soldiers rounding up people this deep into the forest... I know you've only been here a few days, but consider your merit proven. Manden already values you as a scout—and no one crosses Manden." His lips twitched upwards into a half smile. "You are not the only outsider here. If you choose to stay, Manden will ensure your safety as much as she is able. So will I." He looked like he hesitated to add the last remark.

I suddenly remembered the weight in my pocket. "Oh, er..." I reached my hand down to the small pocket of my pant leg. "I suppose this could be a repayment of sorts, for last night."

I opened my hand to him to show the large canine tooth I had pulled from the hell-hound's mouth. It was just longer than my palm, and still blood-stained. Kaineres took it from me slowly, his expression once again unreadable.

"I thought Twig forgot?" The way he said it sounded like a question.

"Twig forgot about what?" I asked. Kaineres shook his head and smiled softly.

"Nothing." He said. "Thank you. You have more than just common knowledge about magical ingredients."

I shrugged with one shoulder. "I've seen few back-alley practitioners buy and sell this kind of thing. I'm not sure what you use it for. The tooth was loose anyway—thought I might as well take it with me."

He turned it over a few times in his hands.

"At the risk of sounding crass..." He gave a nervous laugh through his nose. "Is this yours?" He held up the blood-stained tooth.

I forced a light chuckle in response. I did have every intention to clean it, but after all the chaos, I'm surprised I remembered it at all. "The blood? Consider it an added enchantment."

There was a steady crunching of old leaves and dirt as someone approached the tent. I rose to my feet, Kaineres gently guiding my arm up to steady me. I grabbed the pile of clothes as he walked me to the door.

"Oh, and Rune..." The witch lowered his voice. "You never need to repay me. My aid is yours, should you ever need it."

I met his gaze, his double pupils dancing back and forth between my eyes. I suddenly felt embarrassed at the condition I was in—covered in filth and blood, reeking of dead animal. Still, there was no sign of disgust in his gaze, just a gentle curiosity and calm reassurance.

The muscles in his face twitched. He made a curt bow with his head and smirked. "Can you imagine if I charged for my services? It would be quite the lucrative business with this lot." He opened the tent flap and I joined Sanders outside. When I looked back, the door to the medicinal tent was closed with Kaineres on the other side. I exhaled a long breath of air and turned to face my friend.

They were carrying a small woven basket of soaps. They looked me up and down, as if making sure I was fit to walk, and then stepped around to my left side.

"You can hold on to me if you need—"

"I'm *fine* S." I nudged them on the side playfully. They hummed their disapproval but started leading me in the direction of the bathing chamber.

The chamber was on the other side of the giant tree from the communal hall. It was also carved right into the trunk, albeit much smaller. It was dimly lit, but I could still see the giant stone basin that took up the majority of the space. It was already filled with water.

"I saw this when I first toured the camp. Isn't it neat?" Sanders wrapped their arms around themselves. "I could stay in here all day it's so warm. The water is kept heated with magic I think—feel it!"

I dipped my fingers in, the warmth gently kissing my skin. Sanders helped peel my disgusting clothes off with no shortage of remarks on their foul condition and guided me into the stone basin. They rested a bar of soap on the edge for me to use. After I convinced them I was fit to wash myself, they excused themselves. While Sanders assured me they would be back later to help me out, they were seemingly excited about going somewhere—mentioning something about desperately needing to see a game of toss-ball.

The basin had a ledge built in to sit on so I sank myself down to rest on it, water rising to my collarbone. I winced slightly at the sting of my wound as it submerged under the surface.

A bath. I couldn't remember the last time I had taken a bath. I thought myself fairly clever once at the invention of a shower using a canteen, snow, and fire. Soap, I discovered, was difficult to produce out of nothing. The small bar in my hand smelled faintly of herbs and a pleasant scent that I couldn't quite make out.

I undid my messy braid and untied the string of beads that was barely holding onto my long side bangs. Dunking my head under the water, I let liquid fingers of warmth comb through the strands of my hair. It wasn't until my lungs started to contract that I broke the surface again and started to wash the rest of my body. The new wound made all the other scars on my body appear faded. I did heal quicker than most people, but seemed to scar just as much.

After I had scrubbed every inch of my skin to the best of my limited ability, I sank back into the warmth of the bath. The water was no longer crystal clear, but the heat eased the aching in my muscles and begged me to stay.

After a while, my eyes adjusted to the lack of light. The wood walls were covered in intricate carvings. Some were similar to the designs in the dining hall—flourishes and trees and decorative images. Most of the carvings here were images of deities, one after another, wrapping around the room in order of their seasons. On the ceiling were gods that didn't align with a specific season—a woman, faceless but beautiful, held up the moon near the center of the ceiling. Next to her, many hands making up one hand held the sun.

I looked around at the depictions of the gods alongside their duties and creations, most of them represented on the walls of the bathing chamber. Not all of them though. *Just the ones that actually do something.*

I sat for a few more minutes until the skin on the tips of my fingers started to prune. There was no sign of Sanders, but I could manage getting out of a tub. I hoisted myself up and by the gods was it freezing. The cold air latched onto my skin and sucked all the warmth out of it. Shivering, I shook as much of the water off as I could and wrung out my hair. I started putting on the lower half of my new wardrobe first, which was accomplished without too much straining. Thank goodness someone had cleaned my belt at some point during the night—the pants were huge. I grabbed the accompanying black shirt—

The door to the chamber swung open to Arrowette, holding a set of her own clothes. As usual, all emotion and any sign of humanity was missing from her face. She stared an uncomfortably long time at my current state—dripping wet half naked, baggy pants holding on by the grace of a thin leather belt, and my arms clutching a shirt over my torso. Her eyebrow twitched upwards as she pointedly glanced from my chest to my eyes, my freezing nipples undoubtedly showing through the shirt.

"I'll come back later then." She gave me a final look up and down, a smirk growing across her face as she turned to leave. "I do hope they find you warmer clothes. The cold out here can be so wicked at times."

The door slammed shut. *Fuck me.* I put the shirt on in a hurry, not caring about the searing pain that came with shoving my right arm through the sleeve. I cursed my gods under my breath. *This is why you'll find no carvings of you in a bath house.*

Chapter Nine

Rune

I stayed close to Sanders for days following the injury. They didn't seem to mind my intermittent napping on their shoulders whenever we were seated. Sleep had turned into a pestering old merchant, begging me day and night for attention, waving her wares under my nose with empty promises of contentment and rejuvenation. Although tempting, my unease refused to let me give in. My shoulder kept me from climbing painlessly to the top bunk, and I felt much too exposed lying in the middle of all the other scouts. Arrowette had unnerved me more than I cared to admit, and my only consoling thought was knowing that most of the other scouts seemed to find her just as irritating.

The scouts' tents were split mostly by age. In my tent was everyone thirty or so years and younger. This included Ivon, Arrowette, and a few others. I recalled someone mentioning it was due to the noise difference. At first, I thought they meant the late-night chats that would sometimes break out in the younger tent—scouts whispering about their findings of the day or the crush they had on a kitchen crew member. On a particularly restless night, I realized as I was strolling about the commune that the noise that was mentioned was in fact the monstrous growling that came from the other tent. An unholy chorus of snoring from the older scouts, breaching the eerie peacefulness of the night.

"Psst—hey, Rune." My head bobbled up and down as Sanders shook their shoulder. I sat up, wiping the saliva dripping out of the corner of my mouth where my scar was. We were outside the maker's tent. Sanders had been tasked with assisting Celeste wherever she needed help, which mostly consisted of running materials back and forth between members of the commune. When Celeste didn't have a job for them, she let Sanders watch her work or gave them items to work on themselves. Sanders put down the wooden figure they were carving and joined Celeste in the maker's tent.

I yawned and stretched my good arm. The palm of my hand had healed back to normal, only minimal scaring that would probably fade just fine. I would rejoin the other scouts tonight in a perimeter check. Manden gave me a few days to recover, but with one usable arm I wasn't completely out of commission. I didn't mind though; it gave me something to do, and as I was bound to pace back and forth all night anyway, it was better to make the insomnia worthwhile. I had heard her mention to Kaineres that he could recruit me to gather more supplies for him, but he had yet to approach me about it. He had yet to bring up working together on creating enchantments and potions too.

"Bum bra bum!" Sanders peaked out from the tent making a noise that could only be described as a poor imitation of trumpets' fanfare. They held out a bundle of folded clothing in front of my face. I took the fabrics from them as they explained that the weavers were able to rustle up enough fabric to repair my old attire. The last few days were spent with my hands around my belt to keep the oversized trousers from sliding down, so I gave Sanders a big squeeze on the arm in thanks.

"You already have enough leverage here to pull a few strings for me?" I teased.

"No—but I do. And I did."

Hearing his voice behind me I turned to face Kaineres, who was strolling up to the maker's tent with his hands in the pockets of his long red tunic. He read the annoyance on my face. "Oh, not for you, though." His russet and green eyes trailed down my body, glimmering in amusement as he paused at the hands bunched around my belt line. "I want my pants back."

"These are *your* pants? I thought you said they were extra—just laying around!" I'm not sure why I suddenly felt embarrassed for wearing them—strips of scratchy fabric for fuck's sake. Sanders, however, thought it was hilarious and let giggles slip freely from their mouth. The witch just stood there smiling smugly, gods damn him.

"That's right. They are my *extra* pair of pants, and when I found them, they were indeed *laying* on the ground." His subtle head tilt turned any embarrassment I had into anger.

I scoffed. "They weren't even clean?"

He clicked his tongue. "No-no, they were clean. Or, at least, cleaner than you were at the time."

Before I could retort, he took the clothes from Sanders and pushed the repaired set into my arms. "Hurry back now—I want to wear my cloak this evening and it's imperative I get those back to complete the ensemble." He gave me a wink and bowed his head to Sanders before walking past us into the tent. Sanders giggled again.

"I like him." They raised their eyebrows at me.

"You like everyone, S." I nodded my head towards the direction I was headed in a silent request for their company.

"I'm surprised you don't." They said, keeping pace next to me.

"Like *everyone*?"

"No—Kaineres. You two are of the same stuff."

"What, we're both sarcastic and difficult to get along with?"

Sanders' right eyebrow twitched upwards. "Well, yes, actually. I'm sure you'd have even more in common if you got to know him."

"I don't dislike him, I just... I'm not as open as you are. And we haven't been here that long, there hasn't been enough time to get to know *anyone*."

They shrugged and held the door flap open to the scouts' tent to let me inside. I changed into my regular clothes that were no longer covered in holes and folded the set Kaineres had loaned me. As I braided my hair back and separated my bangs, Sanders ran the *extra* pair of clothing to the medicinal tent to return to Kaineres. I wasn't sure if they needed to be washed or not, but I'm sure the witch had some sort of magic cheat for cleaning fabric. I had just finished tying the last bead into my hair when Sanders popped their head into the tent.

"C'mon, I told Sora I'd meet her at the training ring." They said, waving me up.

"Are you... training Sora? Or are you receiving training?" I inquired. I couldn't imagine Sora gaining any knowledge from either one of us after living in the wasteland her entire life. Surely she'd be fully prepared under Manden's encouragement. Sanders scoffed.

"Um, would you be that surprised to know I have a few tricks to pass on? I may not be a *scout* like you my dear Rune but I know how to scramble when the need arises."

"That's not what I meant. And—the only reason you're *not* a scout is your mouth, which often leads you *into* scrambles."

Their hair swished around their face as they shot me a look over their shoulder but I could detect a sparkle of humor in their eyes. "She's training with Manden—she just invited us to watch."

We walked the path around the giant tree to the training ring, located just past the maker's 'tent'. It was a circular lot that had been cleared free of any vegetation. Thick wooden branches twisted and locked together formed a crude fence around the ring, with an entrance opening towards the pathway. There were wooden stumps and logs placed around the perimeter for spectators to sit and watch those in the ring.

As we walked closer the sounds of dirt shuffling underfoot and heavy breathing grew louder.

"Good. Nice light feet Sora." Manden stood near the edge of the ring, arms crossed and eyes focused on the two sparring in front of her: a scout wielding a wooden baton, and Sora, with her hands tied behind her back. They were both wearing blindfolds. Sanders and I leaned against the makeshift railing to watch. Sora wasn't as quick as I assumed she'd be for her frame, but her movements were light—airy. She looked almost weightless as she directed her body away from the swinging baton in front of her with ease and control.

"The blindfolds aren't completely solid—you can still see through them," Sanders whispered next to me. That would explain why the scout didn't seem phased by it. Neither did Sora. "Manden uses them to mimic the fog," Sanders continued, "They just make everything blurry."

Manden thinks of everything. Another scout approached Manden from the side of the ring and the two exchanged a few words before the scout moved into position. He slowly crept up behind Sora while her attention was honed on avoiding her match partner. Her long black braid swung side to side as she did, knees bent and feet soft on the dirt. The scout with the baton swung to her left and right, keeping her trapped in the same place until the man behind her was only a few paces away. Sanders gripped the railing, and I shot them a look to not interfere with a warning call. We weren't the only ones watching the training—other scouts, and a few of the makers as well, were scattered around the outside of the ring. Out of the corner of my eye, I spied the witch far to our right, his eyes focused on his niece.

Almost arms-length from the scout sneaking up behind her, Sora started taunting the man wildly wielding the baton.

"Are your arms tired already? I don't know if they can make a weapon any lighter for you since that's basically just a big stick." She gave a cheeky grin.

"Sora, concentrate." Manden's mouth was a thin line.

Sora tossed her head back to keep a loose curl out of her face. "I'm just saying! It's not much practice with the bloke just swinging it about like that. Oh—I bet you're just not used to the length of it—should Celeste make you one more your size?" Sora was bribing the scout to anger now. Stifled laughs echoed around the ring, and directly across from me I saw Ivon's eyes were wide with delight. His humor had rubbed off on her, no doubt.

"Although you wouldn't really be able to swing it, would you? You'd have to throw it to do any dama—" Sora's teasing was cut off by her opponent's roar as he swung the bat with full force toward where she stood. Sora's next movements were lightning-quick and cunningly calculated. She leapt to the ground towards her attacker's right, rolled over her shoulder, and kicked out her legs to make contact with the scout's back, pushing him off his balance. With the swing of the baton already pulling him forward, the scout flew into the second surprised opponent, who saw the whole thing unravel a few seconds too late to do anything about it.

The viewers around the training ring broke into a cheer as Sora stood up to brush herself off triumphantly. Manden's face was scrunched together in obvious internal conflict. Ivon and Arrowette had jumped the fence and congratulated Sora on her presumed win.

"Do people normally get this excited over training matches?" I remarked to Sanders, who had also jumped the fence and was walking over to the group in the middle of the ring.

"That was amazing!" I could hear them say. The group took turns patting Sora on the back and talking about the match. Manden said a few stern words to the scouts involved in the training, no doubt about the loss of composure they displayed, and then walked over to the bubbling mass surrounding Sora.

"Ahem." She cleared her throat and the noise in front of her dissipated.

"So?" Ivon's voice rang out about the small crowd. "She beat them, right?"

Arrowette stood behind Sora with her arm around her shoulder. "Yeah, did she? Advance, or however you want to put it?"

Manden clicked her tongue as she surveyed the young scouts. "Although her methods were *unorthodox* and in my opinion, potentially *dangerous*..." The stare she gave her daughter implied this was not the first time Sora had used coy teasing to her advantage, "she passed."

More cheers erupted from the center of the ring and Manden shut her eyes at the noise. She then exhaled, held out her hand, and as Sora took it in hers Manden returned the beaming smile on her daughter's face. She was about to say something else when everyone gathered in the middle started talking amongst themselves about the long-awaited scouting member.

"I'm going to have to strengthen that sound barrier."

I jolted upright at hearing the witch's voice next to me. Kaineres was looking up at the clouds—as if there was a giant invisible bubble surrounding the camp. I realized in that moment that there might have been. I wasn't entirely sure what he was or wasn't capable of. It seemed like complicated magic to create an ongoing enchantment that size, but I had also recently passed through an invisible town so my understanding of magic felt quite limited.

He gave me a half-smile. "That might be something I could use your assistance with, if you're comfortable."

I nodded slowly. I had been eating well the past couple of days, but I wasn't sure I had the physique for something that draining. Maybe in small increments. Did blood keep well?

"Do you have any interest in learning magic?" Kaineres was looking at the crowd now, returning a wave to Sora who was being boosted onto other people's shoulders.

"I never gave it much thought." That wasn't a complete lie. I never really let myself think about it. I had no use for it and didn't believe it was worth the cost. The witch pulled his eyes away from the ring and met mine.

"Would you like to—think about it?" Another half-smile. I had a feeling as he aged he would grow wrinkles only on one side of his face. "I'm not a credited witch anymore," he continued, "but I have the suspicion you're not a credited anything anymore either, so perhaps we can help each other out. *Trade* trade secrets, if you will."

"I'm not sure street sweepers lose their credibility if they never had any to begin with, but if you were that well-off to never have held a broom I'm sure I can show you some pointers."

The half-smile dropped. His eyebrows twisted into an expression that verged on pity causing my gut to lurch. I could see the well-meaning words take form. "Rune, I didn't mean to imply—"

"No-that—" I waved him off, "came off more bitter than it should have. I'll think about it. The magic." I nodded my parting and turned for the pathway back to the scout's quarters. After a few paces, I heard footsteps beside me. I concluded that the camp was much smaller than it first appeared. Kaineres walked with his hands in his pockets, his cloak whipping chaotically behind him.

"I gather your unease around magic differs from most people's." The softness in his voice carried no trace of pity, but I still couldn't look at his face. "Where in Aristus are you from?"

I slowed my pace a little, giving myself a moment to phrase my response carefully. "What makes you think I'm from Aristus?" I don't remember telling him. Or anyone. Although there was a good chance Sanders did at some point.

"Well, you looked surprised to know how close we were to Skevsurvia when you first arrived. And it's near impossible to reach the other Kingdoms on this side of The Periven Pass on foot."

Early on in my banishment, I *had* spent futile months attempting the climb up the mountain range that divided the continent. The Periven Pass led to the Kingdom of Elynchester, but there was little chance of making it there alive without proper equipment and a guide who knew what they were doing. I had neither.

"Perceptive," I admitted, hoping that any rumors about the bounty didn't seem worth the risk all the way out here.

Kaineres nodded. "I assume you've made the same judgments."

I had. Or, at least, put together a rough idea of where he came from based on all the information I knew about Aristian witches.

"Your markings—do only Aristian witches have those, or is that practice shared by all the Kingdoms?" I asked. I was genuinely curious—it occurred to me that I had never seen a witch or mage from any of the neighboring Kingdoms.

Kaineres held out his hands as though looking at his tattoos through his thick leather gloves. "All appointed witches belonging to a guild share markings, usually on the lower arm or neck, where they can be seen. This practice is used by each of the Six Kingdoms, although I think the designs change based on the guild. The earrings—" He pointed to the long silver earrings that hung from his ear lobes. They danced around his jaw and neck as he walked. "—are also worn throughout the continent, but they vary in color. Witches and mages of Aristus wear silver."

"And the others?" I asked just in case I ever came across another magician.

Kaineres let out a small laugh and clicked his tongue. "Let's see if I can remember. It's been a while. Aristus-silver. Skevsurvia... white. I'm fairly certain they use polished stone in place of a metal. Queendom of Elynchester—gold, of course. They find a way to put gold everywhere. Periv, ah—copper?" He rubbed his chin with his gloved hand. "Mistum to no surprise wears some kind of black metal or stone, and Whelms, well, is Whelms."

"It felt like Aristus was going to follow suit any day."

"What, and outlaw magic outright? The city was too reliant on it, and still is, no doubt."

Kaineres wore all the attire and pieces of a well-taught magician, from a credited guild probably somewhere in high city. "What guild were you in?" I asked.

"Ah-ah. I asked you first. I was thinking about asking Sanders, but I'd like for us to get to know one another if we're going to be working together, hm?" Kaineres stopped walking once we reached his circular hut. I turned to face him.

"Very well." It certainly wasn't information he could use against me anyway. "Flatkeep. It's where Sanders and I met as kids."

"I'm ashamed to say I don't know it."

I let loose a huff of air from my nostrils. "Most people would be more ashamed to know it," I said. Kaineres cocked his head to the side in questioning.

"It's not near high city. In fact it's very far from it. Outskirts of the city limits, nearing the border wall, but not quite in the farmland. Proper people don't go there unless they find themselves craving improper things."

"Now I can't tell if you were born there, or if you're just the kind of person that craves improper things." His smirk was back again, now on both sides of his face. I rolled my eyes in return, but I appreciated the banter.

"Both, I guess."

"I thought as much. You handle yourself better than haughty noblemen, and are far more interesting."

I wasn't sure what to do with that sentiment and was about to turn for the barracks to prepare for the perimeter check when Kaineres spoke again.

"Rune." His gaze was earnest. "Do think about it. With the knowledge you already have about magic, I think you could be quite adept at the practice."

I dipped my head in acknowledgment but didn't respond as I started back along the pathway to the tent. But I would, for the first meaningful time, think about it.

Chapter Ten

Kaineres

"Kaineres!" Manden's voice brought me out of whatever cloud of thought I was in. My head snapped to the entrance of the medicinal tent, where my sister stood with a basket. I rushed out of my seat at the desk to take it from her, but she jerked it back from my reach.

"I said I'm *taking* these vials to clean them. They're empty but they could use a good scrub. You're doing that thing again." She gave me that concerned mother-look I tried to avoid.

"Sorry, I was just lo—"

"Lost in thought, yes, so you've said every other time your eyes glaze over. So much to be thinking about I suppose. Like how you're going to catch up on filling these vials back up when they return? I thought you were working with Rune to make more potions."

"I am. I *will*. I don't want to rush her."

Manden rested the basket on the work table. "Well I don't mind rushing either of you. Supplies are running low, but you insist on getting them yourself, potions are almost out and you and Rune haven't even started making any enhancements. She likes to work. Or at least, is someone who likes to be useful."

"Magic is complicated Manden."

"Not when *you* already know what you're doing." She massaged her temple with her free hand. "I won't lie to you, I want those enhanced potions and enchantments ready for Sora. Call it selfish, call it what you want, but I want her to have every chance of success when she's out there." My sister's face was stern, but her eyebrows were furrowed. I knew she was nervous about Sora leaving the camp.

"I understand, M, I do. She's just doing perimeter checks for now anyway. There's time. *And—*" I kept talking over her attempt to cut me off. "I've already been making something just for her. I'll make sure she has everything she needs, I promise."

Before she could press any more on the matter, I pushed the basket into her hands and walked her out of the tent. I sat back down with a sigh and looked around. I *was* running low on a lot of supplies. Each hunt meant more preventative charms and more healing potions to go through, and the once short journeys out to scavenge were getting longer and more dangerous.

My head started to pound. My pulse echoed in my ears and I shut my eyes at the pain. The headaches were a daily occurrence, most likely from the lack of sleep. After a few seconds of wishing the pain away, I got up and searched through the remnants of the herbs and other ingredients to find nothing useful. Not that it mattered. Nothing had helped before. *Some healer.* At times I wondered if my guild had put a curse on me when I was banished. A Punishment, of sorts, that prevented me from healing my own ailments.

I settled for an herbal ointment that I smeared across my temples and the top of my forehead. The coolness helped a small fraction, but I decided to put myself to work to distract from the pain. I opened my logbook of ingredients to make a list of what I needed. I had gone out last night to gather what I could around the camp, but with the fog so thick there wasn't much to find. Maybe I would enlist Rune to help gather more supplies. She proved to have a good eye for valuable things, unlike some of the other scouts. I had lost count of how many times Twig brought me something poisonous.

I knew Rune wouldn't protest if I asked, even if she did seem cold at times. I still found myself hesitant to request her help—with all the soldiers still preying close to camp. I lightly traced the cut in my arm. The faces of the Withins caught and caged burned in my mind. Maybe the news of Rune's magical nature spreading throughout camp would benefit her. Surely some of the other scouts would keep that in mind when out patrolling. Although some would also use that to their advantage if the opportunity arose.

I groaned as another wave of throbbing rushed through my head and seemed to reverberate off the inside of my skull. Sleep. I needed sleep. I pushed the logbooks aside and folded my arms into a cradle for my aching head. I shut my eyes tight and let racing thoughts and pain fight each other for the landscape of my mind until I passed out.

I don't know how long I was able to sleep before I was stirred awake by the sound of footsteps and muffled voices.

"Go!"

"I'm going."

"I'll meet you at the dining hall afterward!"

I straightened up as best I could before the tent flap opened and Rune poked her head inside. I must have still appeared ruffled because she eyed me up and down and bowed her head in exit.

"Sorry, I'll come back later." She started backing away when I put up a hand in protest.

"No! I mean, good timing, I was just getting up anyway." I stood up and brushed the wrinkles out of my tunic. I probably looked a right mess.

Rune paused, but stepped back into the tent. The chill from outside woke senses that were still dosing back to life.

"Oh." She said. "Manden said you wanted to see me."

"Did she now?" I rubbed my head, only to discover the ointment still slathered on my face and pushed into my hair. I quickly searched for a towel, and could have sworn I saw a slow smile creep into the corners of Rune's lips. I found a piece of fabric that looked clean and wiped my forehead dry, leaving a formidable cowlick in my hair.

"I can come back later." Rune was definitely grinning now. Her smile was mostly aligned aside from the adorable way her two front teeth turned slightly in towards each other. I was too busy trying to decide what to do with her that I almost didn't have time to remark to myself that her expression was quite endearing. Almost.

"Er, I just wanted to know if you had a chance to think about learning magic."

"I wasn't aware there was a deadline." She lifted an eyebrow. "You asked me yesterday."

"I did. Regardless—"

"Regardless, Manden wants my lessons to start sooner than later?"

Good. At least she knew Manden was the pushy one.

"Something like that," I confirmed. "She wants us to get started refilling potions and charms. She doesn't know about the lessons." She would probably see that as a waste of time. Rune processed for a moment, and by her expression seemed to come to the same conclusion.

"Why offer them then?" She asked.

"Because I think it's important for you to learn what you're doing. You'll have an even greater effect over the creation of say, a potion, if you're the one crafting it instead of just volunteering energy."

"You put it so eloquently" She hummed, repeating the words *volunteering energy.*

"Well, the practice of magic is an art." *Or at least it used to be.* "So is the practice of being eloquent, although as I can see you clearly have no interest in learning that particular skill, I won't make you suffer through any lessons." I gave her a wink and grabbed my coat. I didn't give her time for a snarky remark before I said: "I'll be out near the crop fields honing my own skills in the magic arts, you are more than welcome to come along and join me."

"I didn't give you my answer." She crossed her arms as I slid past her to the door.

"I'll have my answer whether I see you in the fields or not." I flipped my hood over my head and bundled the sides around my chest as I made for the fields on the north side of the camp. I felt the crunching of dirt and ice under my boots as I walked down the path. The field was near the perimeter of the camp; a light fog drifted lazily over parts of it, making it the perfect place to practice without much of an audience. No one was tending to it today, and with the addition of some of the berry bushes acting as a hedge it felt very private indeed.

As expected, there were no footsteps behind me, so I made myself as comfortable as I could in a patch of dirt on the ground. I took off my gloves and let my fingers feel the cold earth. Eyes closed, I inhaled as much of the crisp air around me as I could, let it pierce my nose and fill my lungs, and held it until the air I breathed out was of my warmth. Steam billowed out of my mouth and rose up into the sky to meet with the fog hovering overhead. I sat for a few minutes, just listening to the sounds around me and breathing. I let my mind drift backward in time, until I was just a boy, sitting on the courtyard steps in winter, tasked with breathing even breaths into the dusk air.

"Is making clouds the first lesson?"

I opened my eyes to Rune leaning against a wooden post at the end of the row of bushes. She mockingly let out a puff of her own breath, sending up a small cloud of steam.

"Nice attempt, dare I say your form is disastrously archaic. That kind of magic might be too advanced for you on your first day." I grinned. She rolled her eyes and came to sit down in front of me a few paces away.

"Were you a teacher?" She asked, staring at my glove-less hands with apprehension, as if dreading I was going to ask her to remove hers in this weather.

"Not officially. I helped some of the younger kids in their studies as a witch, but I was never able to become a mage. But that's not important. I know enough to teach you the basics."

"You mentioned a sound barrier—can you really do that? Or were you joking?"

"Well, I did mention it in humor, but yes, I can. Not quite to the extent I would like to be able to. It does get damaged and weaker over time, but it's there."

Rune looked up at the sky for a moment, then back to me with a nod. "Okay. I'm ready. What did you have in mind for the first lesson?" Her grey eyes were focused—impervious—so at odds with the fog that settled over us, drifting about aimlessly.

"The first lesson is locating where you feel the most connected to magic," I said, and watched as her concentration turned into confusion. "You've, as some would say, used magic before, correct?"

"You wouldn't like how." She grimaced. No, *probably not*. Double-checking with myself that I didn't say that thought out loud, I gestured for her to continue. She shrugged with her good shoulder. "I feel like I've—*cheated* at magic. I don't know any spells or enchantments, but I know how to bypass a lot of those 'proper' things."

"I'm not sure if 'cheating' is the word I would use. How do you bypass a spell?"

"Well, if it's written out somewhere or ingredients with certain properties are already put together, I can 'activate' them by you know, *adding* a magic ingredient."

"So... you use your own blood. For everything?"

"...Yes?" She met my tentative expression with her own. Finally she huffed out: "What, your guild didn't have wick—Withins at your disposal? Don't tell me you're surprised to hear—"

"I'm not surprised to know Withins are mistreated—I know our history and Aristus' twisted perception of magic. I'm just a little surprised to hear you would mistreat yourself in such a way."

"Mistreat *myself*? Come off it! It's why I avoid magic until I *have* to use it. It's not like I enjoy it."

Flatkeep. She told me she was from Flatkeep. I reminded myself that her experience with magic thus far was very different than mine. Lesson. Focus on the lesson.

"The art of magic, is in truth the art of *energy*," I said calmly. I tried to think back to my first lessons as a child. The mages gathering us into a circle and giving us each a small piece of paper. I looked around and picked up two leaves that had fallen from one of the bushes. I scooted closer to Rune and held one out to her.

"Here."

She took it from my hand and I demonstrated how to hold it, laying it flat in the palm of my hand.

"The wind can carry this leaf with its current, making it move from where it was. It's a force of energy that affects the things around it. Magic mimics this—using the flow of energy to affect the things around it. I can, with the energy of my being, force this leaf to move by blowing on it." Rune watched as I did so, blowing the leaf off of my hand and onto the ground. "However, nature will always have an energy of its own, which will often conflict with what a magician wants to do. For example—" I took the leaf and stood up, searching for a small breeze in the air. I gestured to Rune to follow as I held out the leaf in front of me. "I can blow this leaf forward only so far before the wind blows it right back. My energy source is limited in comparison, so the effect I have on this object will not hold forever."

I blew on the leaf, and it danced in the air away from me for a second before riding on the wind in the opposite direction past my face. Rune nodded slowly.

"Okay," she said, "So magic is just manipulated energy?"

"It depends on who you ask and what school of thought you train under." I replied, and seeing as that wasn't answer enough for her, added, "I believe that magic *is* energy. All of it, even the natural forces like wind or rain. But the skill is learning how to draw from it yourself and use it to your advantage."

"So... manipulated energy." Rune said, squinting her eyes. I ran my hand through my oiled hair.

"Sure. Whatever helps you process I guess." I sat back down to get out of the wind chill. I pat the ground next to me inviting her to do the same. She slowly dropped to her knees and tilted her head in question.

"What did your guild do with wickeds? How did you get them?" She asked softly. As soon as she said it I knew the concern had been plaguing her mind for a while.

"To be honest, I'm not sure where a lot of them came from. They were mostly animals. Working with people was... always complicated, but not for the reasons you're thinking of. I know of a few animal breeders who tried to raise Withins to sell at market. Birds, cats, even cattle. Of course that never works out, it's not the nature of things to just regurgitate fantastical properties like that." Her expression was unreadable as I added, "My Within found me."

"What do you mean?"

I leaned back against a wooden post stuck in the ground behind me. "My guild was settled near the castle walls, on the upper side of the city. The dwelling was a series of flat buildings connected by one long red-tiled roof surrounding an open courtyard. It had the most magnificent garden in the middle of it with a stone fountain, where all these birds would congregate to drink or bathe, or whatever it is birds do. I tried to feed them crumbs from my lunches, but I was always scolded away by the mages.

"So, late at night, I would leave crumbs out on my window sill, and every evening I was visited by the most beautiful black dove. It was our little secret for weeks, until one day she dropped a few feathers on the sill—a gift of sorts—and I decided to make a quill with them. Some of the mages saw my written work now infused with subtle magic, and when I explained the companion I had made, they informed me that the dove was a Within. I'm not sure if they would have let me keep her if she wasn't, but during the evening hours I walked everywhere with her perched on my shoulder."

"What did you use her for? How were her feathers magic?" Rune pressed.

"She was magic. Her entire being. Her blood, sure—but her feathers, her coos, her tears—even her droppings!" I chuckled. "You should have seen the glue I made. One misplaced drop and your fingers would be stuck together for a week."

"But how?"

"We had an understanding of sorts. As much of an understanding as a person can have with an animal, at least. I cared for her in every way I could think of. Food, shelter, affection, and in return, she gave her energy when she felt up for it. It was usually in the form of her cooing. She could add a kind of beautification or softness to any charm or spell just by singing into it. I was able to craft healing spells and potions for children because that effect made the potions more appealing to take."

I saw the wheels of thought turning behind Rune's eyes. Even the thin branches around us stopped swaying as if they were too scared to disturb her.

"Blood isn't the only magical thing about a wicked—er, a Within?" She asked.

"Withins are people—or animals—that have magical energy *within* their entire being. They don't need a secondary source. That's where the name comes from. Blood is merely the easiest to take by force, but it's not without consequences, which I'm sure you're aware of."

She turned her face away abruptly and clenched her jaw. "A lot of spells go wrong..." She said mostly to herself.

"It's a skill of give and take and should be treated as such. Killing and abusing magical creatures by force is a threat against nature, and will always result in catastrophe. Or, at the minimum, a very shitty spell."

Thoughts crinkled her forehead and cycled through her mind as she focused on the ground in front of her. The breeze reached out and teased her hair into soft coils that brushed against her neck. For a moment I forgot where I was and lost myself in the colors of her winter-kissed face. The thin skin under her eyes was faintly purple—a deep lavender that faded into the bright pink of her cheeks. Her scarred lips were a deep, almost burning red.

Rune shot up to her feet. "That's probably all I can take for today. Thank you for the lesson." I watched her as she hurried out of the field and headed towards the rest of the camp, leaving me still sitting in the dirt. I exhaled a long, pent-up breath and watched the vapor dissipate. The branches rustled quietly around me and from the distant contents of my mind, soft melodic chirping stirred out of almost forgotten memories.

— 🔥 —

Rune

A few weeks had passed, and life was starting to settle into a routine. It was easy to see why members of the commune took remembrances and celebrations so seriously. There wasn't that much to do. After mealtime in the dining hall, Sanders followed me back to the scouts' tent, where Arrowette and Ivon were talking with Sora, whose birth celebration was the next day. I'm not sure how they knew, but someone had been keeping time. It wouldn't surprise me if I was told Sora had been keeping track of every day.

"Of course, you can share a bed with me, although I'm going to make you take the top!" Arrowette sat on her bed, threading Sora's hair into a delicate braid matching her own. "Oh it's going to be so great to have another girl here I can talk to." I didn't miss the look she gave me from the corner of her eyes. I made for my bunk when Ivon patted the empty spot on the bed next to him.

"C'mon. You and Sanders both. Hang out for a while!"

"Yeah! I want to hear all about what The Colds is like from someone who lived in the thick of it!" Sora grinned up at me as I took a seat next to Ivon in the bed across from her.

"She probably only survived because she's not a normal person." Arrowette said coldly.

Sora whipped around, her hair flinging out of Arrowette hands. "Arrow!"

"What! It's not a secret, is it?" She asked me directly. "News spreads fast here, it's not my fault I don't want to dance around it like everyone else."

For the first time since I've known them, Sanders was awkwardly quiet, whipping their eyes between me and Arrowette at a loss for what to say. Ivon was the one to break the tension.

"Ignore her, she's cranky because Manden says Sora can't stay here tonight." He stretched out his arms in front of him and started massaging his healing shoulder.

"Why?" I asked.

"My mom says she wants to wait until I officially turn seventeen, as a 'passing of threshold' of sorts. I know she's just having cold feet about me becoming a scout."

Arrowette groaned. "Ugh, when is she going to give it up? You passed every test she's put up for you, and you already know the perimeter of the camp better than the newer scouts!" Her fingers furiously finished braiding the last strands of Sora's hair. "Our mothers couldn't be more different."

"That's not too hard to piece together."

If I was drinking something it would have spewed out of my mouth at the dig Sanders muttered under their breath. Arrowette glared up at them but said nothing. Ivon chuckled to himself before giving an apologetic look towards Arrowette.

Sora sighed. "Actually, while on the subject, I should head back before Manden prepares a monologue. But bring your best tomorrow, okay? No going easy on me or I'll make you regret it." She pointed at Ivon, who put his hands up in innocence. I wasn't sure what she was talking about, but Sanders seemed to as they laughed and said their goodbyes.

Minutes after Sora left, the tent opened to Gwenna and Twig, holding an opaque bottle of mystery liquid.

"Tonic's ready!" Twig cheered as he tossed the bottle to Ivon. As soon as Ivon popped off the lid the potent smell of bitter leaves stung my nostrils. Ivon bravely took a sniff straight out of the bottle and recoiled.

"N*ngh*—What in any realm of hell is this?" His words were separated by coughing as he handed the bottle to Arrowette. Twig leaned against Ivon's bunk as he proudly waved his arms out in presentation.

"*This*, is a potion of my own making. Finally ready. Or, ready enough to be called ready. Go ahead, take a swig. It's not poison."

Arrowette made a face. "That's literally what this is." She took a sip anyway. Every muscle in her face contorted as she forced it down with an audible gulp. She shuddered and quickly handed the bottle back to Ivon. "That's vile." She managed to get out.

As Ivon took a sip I learned that Arrowette's reaction was quite composed. I thought briefly of the sound barrier as Ivon shouted various curses into the rising laughter of everyone in the tent. Wiping the tears from his eyes, he shoved the bottle into my hands.

"Consider this an initiation of sorts," Twig said to me, his freckled cheeks pressing wrinkles into the corners of his eyes.

"Fuck it." I drank it back and shut my eyes at the sting that ripped apart my throat from the inside. I held out the bottle to the last victim as tears filled my eyes.

Sanders took it gingerly and gave me a nervous glance before drinking their share. The group silently waited for an intense reaction that never came. Sanders simply licked their lips and handed the bottle back to Twig, who was wearing a bewildered smile.

"S, did you drink it?" I asked. There was no way that taste would leave my mouth any time soon.

They shrugged. "One of my master's chambermaids used to make strange concoctions like that all the time. Said it would stop bad breath."

"Stop breathing, you mean." Arrowette scrunched up her nose. "That stuff is awful!"

Twig let out a high-pitched laugh and swung back the bottle. He shook his head vigorously, then made himself comfortable on the floor next to Sanders. "Alright, if Manden asks, we were curing bad breath from the likes of you. Since most of you like to talk shit." He laughed again, mostly at his own joke. He looked up at me and asked: "So, Rune—how did potion-making go? I saw you and Kaineres head out to the field to gather supplies or something. If you don't mind, could I have you bend his ear for more trackless dust? He always says that's a waste of ingredients but as someone with large feet I beg to differ."

I wasn't sure what trackless dust was, or if the witch's ear could be bent by me, but I nodded anyway. "I'll ask him."

Arrowette huffed. "I wouldn't buddy up with the exiled witch if I were you."

Thank my worthless shitty gods she's not me.

"Don't start," Twig muttered into his hand.

Arrowette jerked her head towards him and raised her eyebrows. "I'm only saying, I wouldn't trust him."

"Why?" Between the two of them, it was Arrowette I didn't trust, but my curiosity asked anyway.

She paused for a moment and looked at the tent door, as if making sure Kaineres wasn't walking by. She lowered her voice, but the honeyed tone remained.

"You don't know?"

Sanders and I exchanged glances before I raised an eyebrow at Arrowette to continue. "He was exiled ten years ago—and back then, you actually had to do something of consequence to get run out, not like recent years where everyone gets slapped with a banishment. I know you've heard about it, the news shook the entire Kingdom." She paused again, this time only for dramatic effect. "Kaineres was the witch that murdered the King's eldest daughter. A cold-blooded kill."

"It was not *cold blooded*." Twig interjected. "It was an accident."

"So *he* says. So Manden says. Manden wasn't even there!"

"Wait—" I held up a hand before they could go at it. "The witch that killed the princess—that was *him*?" I didn't know him that well, but I still couldn't imagine the healer killing anyone, even on accident.

Twig shook his head. "Don't listen to the kid. I mean—yes, he did kill her, but it wasn't on purpose. He doesn't even know how it happened."

"It's always the ones you least expect," Arrowette said in a sing-song manner.

"And what about the ones you *most* expect? Are you going to tell me you've never killed anyone?" Twig stood up and brushed himself off, his eyes darting to the dark stain on his cloak from the mystery tonic.

"Hm, I was a soldier, so does that answer your question?" Arrowette replied smugly.

"Neither of you should be speaking so lightly on the matter." It was Gwenna who spoke, her voice solemn and stern. "That night was the night a terrible chain of events was started, and the result was the loss of more than one innocent life." Suddenly her fingers found both Arrowette's and Twig's ears, and they both yelped as they were twisted around. "I'll not have you picking worthless fights at each other about what Kaineres did. The man feels enough guilt about it as it is. This commune only thrives if we play our roles. So stick to your roles and shut it."

She released her grip and returned her hands to rest on her belly. Twig muttered his apologies to her and Arrowette muttered curses under her breath. Everyone else was too smart to say anything after that, so as Twig and Gwenna departed with the tonic in hand, we each made our way back to our respective bunks. Sanders decided to stay the night and made themselves comfortable in the bed above me. As the rest of the scouts trickled in for the night, I was kept awake with each little scuff, whisper, and footstep.

I let my mind swim in and out of memories, thinking back to ten years ago when the news of the princess's death spread like wildfire through the Kingdom. Everyone in Flat-keep thought it *was* planned. The violent act that sparked the rebel movement—to dethrone the sitting King and the rest of the Nobles. But after years of uprising and planning a second attack, everything went wrong. The majority of the rebellion believed that peace had to be taken—it was surely never going to be given freely. To some extent, I believed that too, although after seeing dishonorable brutality from both sides... At some point, the only collateral damage in a fight of that magnitude is the lives of people who didn't deserve to be caught in the middle.

Maybe it was the exhaustion I felt after everything I had learned earlier that day, or maybe I was a coward running away from my own bloody memories, but I finally gave in to the heaviness hounding me and fell into sleep.

CHAPTER ELEVEN

Kaineres

There was always a different energy in the air on festival days. Uplifting. I washed my hands clean in the wide ceramic basin near the open window. The water was cold to the touch, so I let my fingers linger in the refreshing coolness before letting them dry in the warm sunlight pouring in from outside. The sounds of people going about their afternoon filtered through the thick green shrubs in front of me, separating the building from the street. I took a look over my shoulder at the cozy room behind me. Faded ivory-colored walls that held wooden shelving presenting rows of books and scrolls that I would leave behind for the next witch.

The intricately carved wooden door on the opposite wall creaked open, and through it reached a dark hand that knocked on the wall, followed by a friendly face.

"You all set? Headmage is pacing back and forth again." Marcus shook his head. "The courtyard is going to have drainage issues during rainy season if he continues to worry like this."

I smiled at him and tightened the leather braided rope around my crimson tunic. "He just wants everything to go as practiced, and you know how unpredictable some of the noble houses can be."

As I left the room Marcus grasped my arm firmly. "After seeing you today, every Nobleman will want to become *your* apprentice." He said with a squeeze of confidence.

"Or they'll just want to hire me." I returned.

"Yeah, well they think it works like that. When you have that kind of coin you want to buy everything. Even magic."

"Even magic," I repeated, my eyes adjusting to the bright sunlight peeking over the red-tiled rooftops and spilling into the courtyard.

The Headmage was indeed pacing in his usual spot near the garden. His wrinkled eyes met mine, and he clasped his hands together.

"Oh, my boy, I admire your patience but I really must press that this is not a day to dally about."

"Gustan, the ceremony doesn't start until after sunset," Marcus said.

The Headmage gave a weak smile from underneath a thick grey mustache. "As it does, lad. Nevertheless, it would be advantageous for Kain to make his presence known early, if not to get a feel for the energy in the royal courtyard then to familiarize himself with some of his future patrons."

"Gustan," I started, "My desire is to become—"

"A mage for the masses, yes, the good people of the lower cities. And that you shall be. It doesn't hurt to secure a favorable eye in the noble class, however, does it? After all, they too have a great impact on the lives of their people."

I dipped my chin to the Headmage as he covered his head with his rich red cloak and gestured for us to follow. Marcus gave me an uncertain look before falling in line behind me.

"Oh, yes! Marcus, I trusted you would be in Kain's shadow today." Gustan said over his shoulder. "I foresee you following his footsteps in the next coming years, no? You're a fine witch. Both of you are quite gifted indeed. A credit to the guild."

We exited through the wire gates at the entrance to the guild and turned to walk uphill towards the castle. The looming stone castle walls were only a few buildings down the main cobblestone street. The entrance was open and secured by some of the stationed guards, who bowed their heads in greeting as we passed. I returned a nod, and my eyes widened as I lifted my head back up.

Aristians certainly knew how to put on a celebration. Stepping behind the castle walls was like stepping into a different realm—on each side of the main street, colorful buildings separated by lush gardens hoisted brightly decorated banners and flags, most likely representing their house name or their gods. Musicians were scattered about the streets, each playing their own instrument but all in the same key. Walking down the street felt like listening to a different version of the same merry song. People in finely dressed clothing were dancing on their balconies or right in the middle of the street near the musicians.

As we made our way through the thickening crowd, the large stone castle grew nearer and nearer. We passed through another set of smaller stone walls covered with ivy that opened to a grand open courtyard. It appeared that no expense was spared—skilled artists painted the walls as onlookers drank wine poured from large, hollow glass sculptures. Merriment and cheering continued as people laughed and danced and mingled about. Servants ran around diligently picking up discarded glasses or forgotten food from the tables and chairs set up near the walls. Near the center of the royal courtyard, a stone dais was being hauled by two mules in preparation for the King's arrival.

Each year the top guilds in the Kingdom were given the opportunity to present their top witches—who would then advance to the status of a mage. Mages could then take on other apprentices or establish their own magic practice.

Many were adopted by noble houses or high-ranking officials in the King's order. I couldn't help but feel foolish, parading my talents around to people who would try to auction me off to each other. But a larger part of me felt grateful to be chosen by the Headmage, who was notoriously picky with the witches he allowed to advance.

I must have stopped walking in awe of all the splendor because Marcus tugged at my sleeve to pull me out of the way of the crowd. He pulled me aside and laughed.

"Incredible isn't it? I had the fortune of attending one of these festivals when Helna became a mage. It was winter, and they had giant torches along the entire inner wall."

"Ha! Did she show off her purple flame trick?" I asked.

"Of course. Always the entertainer." Marcus and I stood and watched the fun in front of us for a few minutes before I realized Gustan was no longer with us. I excused myself to find him, and after wading through the crowd I saw him near one of the entrances to the castle, pacing back and forth and talking to himself.

"Gustan?" I reached out to stir him from his muttering, and he snapped his head up.

"Oh, my boy, I apologize. It gets busier and busier each year. I suppose that alone is reason to celebrate. People seem more taken with the magic arts in recent days." He sighed contemplatively.

"Only if it benefits them. Or if it's wrapped in grandeur." I said quietly. "If I'm honest, I'm not sure what I have planned is the best presentation of magic."

The Headmage grabbed my arms tightly. "My apprentice, what you have to show is exactly what the people *need to see*. Not just any witch can perform the spell you've crafted for tonight. It shows not only your strength but your devotion to the practice. You deserve this honor."

"Thank you Headmage." I bowed in gratitude, and in part, shyness. The contrast between life behind the guild walls and these magnificent stone walls was stark. "Gustan, may I ask why you've been so nervous? Forgive me if it's not my place."

He rubbed his mustache, and let his gaze wander to the crowd. "I feel... most unsettled, but to tell you truthfully I have no reason for it. A sense of dread perhaps, on the account that there are so many variables at play here, in this bustling center of life and amusement. It could just be that curious-looking pastry I indulged in this morning. Nothing for you to concern your thoughts about. In fact, I encourage you to have your fun. Take in the space, the vibrancy, during your final hours as a witch." His smile didn't quite reach his eyes, but he patted me on the shoulders and waved me back toward the music.

I stepped back into the crowd to make my way towards Marcus when the sheen of raven-black hair caught my attention. I whirled around, only to find a group of very intoxicated gentlemen making a toast to each other out of half-empty glasses. My eyes darted from person to person with a growing nervousness.

Would she be here? There was already so much excitement building up I didn't even consider that I could run into her here. Did I want to? Gustan had mentioned earlier that I should notice every distraction as I would a grain of dust, and 'blow it away from my mind until a more appropriate time'. Was she a distraction? Wasn't this the perfect time? My grand performance of skill and craftsmanship, earning me an honored title as a mage in one of the finest guilds in the Kingdom—this could very well be one of my proudest achievements. Didn't I want her to see it?

Pull yourself together. I stopped myself from weaving in and out of people near the courtyard gate and looked out at the colorful buildings lining the main road. I didn't even know her name. She probably wasn't even nobility. I had only ever seen her outside the castle walls.

Brief interactions, usually near the forest by the edge of the city where I would go to practice my spell work. We would run into each other as I was coming and going—she was always in a hurry to get somewhere. But the most recent encounter was different. *She* was different. I had never seen her smile like that before. Maybe she had heard the news of my promotion and knew it was me.

Don't be ridiculous. A distraction, she was just a distraction. One I was having a very hard time blowing away like dust. I turned my search for the mystery girl into a search for Marcus, who I eventually found near the large gathering of musicians. He was almost a head taller than everyone else around him, and his bald head stuck out amongst the colorful hats and coverings everyone else wore.

I joined him in listening and dancing to the music, and let myself give in to the energy circling around me. It was only when the sun started to set that I stepped away from the joyful chaos and found a moment to center myself for the task in front of me. Gustan found me shortly after and brought me over to stand with the other witches ready to demonstrate what their years of training had taught them.

The lively music started to fade, but the drummers beat on, slowing their rhythm and keeping a loud, steady beat. As the crowd was ushered away from the center of the courtyard, a low horn was blown from the front of the dais, announcing the King's arrival as he stood atop the stone pedestal overlooking his nobility. He wore an ornate coat bearing the Aristian insignia of a long-furred rabbit resting with one open eye, and the phrase: "Peace for the People". He wore no crown on his head, but instead was adorned with a thick silver necklace that encased the length of his neck. His thick black hair was tied back away from his olive face, and his short beard was perfectly groomed and oiled.

His advisor sat in the chair to his right, her hands returning excited waves to the children fighting to get her attention. She was almost more popular with Aristians than His Majesty, if only for her involvement in many of the community practices. Although erected on the dais, the chair prepared to the King's left was empty.

King Amos raised his hands to settle the remainder of the spirited crowd, and once satisfied with their attention, nodded to the court mage near the right of the dais. The mage, not a woman I recognized, bowed low before scattering a bowlful of dust into the air. When the King spoke, his voice carried out through the crowd, the magic dust amplifying the sound.

"Good people of Aristus, today is a day of great importance. I commend the ever-exceptional House of Vapirus, for their diligence in making this a festival to remember. Your artisans and players are unrivaled in talent."

He nodded to a handsome man near the front of the crowd, who returned his nod as the audience gave a short round of applause. I recognized him as Lord Vapirus. I had seen him interacting with Gustan concerning potions and remedies for small ailments.

"Now then, to the main event, no?" King Amos waited as cheers erupted, echoing loudly throughout the courtyard. "Once a year, the Kingdom recognizes the addition of new mages in our midst, brought forth and selected by only the finest magical guilds. Here me now, good people, as I say this—these are no ordinary magicians. Here tonight performing before us are persons with a true gift and superior ability to wield and control such a dangerous force. We as a community must reward these fine witches, who practice magic with honor and respect for their King and their people.

"We hold this celebration to uplift the witches and mages who uplift us, *and* to see with our very eyes the wonders they can create, the possibilities that lie before us." The King paused for another round of cheering and lifted his arm to gesture to where the other witches and I stood, each beside our mentor.

"High on the hill, you will not find a person of consequence that does not know the name Gustan Cre-Twelle, Headmage—of the South Society Guild of Medicinal Magic. It is with great anticipation we welcome his apprentice. Headmage." King Amos smiled wide in greeting, wrinkles stretching out on his tan cheeks. I watched as Gustan bowed low in return, and subtly waved me forward with him.

From his pocket, he procured similar magic dust and scattered it through the air. His usually soft voice carried through the young night air. "Many thanks to you, our King Amos, as well as the folks gathered here tonight. It is my grand privilege and pride to introduce to you, our most talented witch, soon to be mage— Kain Cre-Twelle."

My chest swelled as he bestowed upon me his name, a tradition and a gift that mages passed on to their successors. Tonight would be the night I earned it. A whistle pierced the crowd, and I gave a wink to Marcus, beaming from the sidelines.

"My good people!" Gustan spoke with one arm raised, one grasping his chest. "You have surely seen feats of magic, procured before you from one source of energy to create another. The rushing surge of a river, the rising heat of a flame, the life of a magical creature, but I present before you, a witch that can draw tremendous amounts of energy from the very air around him. You see before you a man that can tether all the raw power invisible to you in this courtyard to his very soul, and hold it at will." He lowered his hands and made a brisk walk to the edge of the crowd, leaving all of their attention on me.

The drummers picked up their beating, hypnotizing people to the moment.

I bowed low, once to the crowd and once to the King, before closing my eyes and breathing slow and deep, guiding the air through my lungs and out my mouth. My next moves were controlled, calm, practiced, felt. I connected myself to the life and movement around me. The murmuring of whispers under breaths, the vibrations of sound from the large drum heads, the soft breeze gliding overhead, the solidness of the stone under my feet, the heart beating steady in my chest. I willed it, all at once, to join together as an extension of myself. I pulled where there was freedom and I gave where there was tension. My arms outstretched, I made wide circles in the air, drawing the energy around me like a current in the sea.

I remained focused as gasps grew louder across the courtyard, and only when I knew I had the power in my control did I slowly open my eyes. Billowing up in the air above me was a cloud-like mass of swirling energy. Although almost transparent, it gleamed like a rainbow over a trickling stream, its colorful light reflecting off of every surface. The astonished and intrigued expressions of the nobles were painted with shades of blues and pinks and greens. The drumming was no longer coming from the players but from the cloud above me. In fact, every noise came from the swirling glittering river of color. Whispers and gasps of aw, the tinkling of glasses, even the rustling of bushes and trees.

I slowed my breathing again as the amount of force I was containing put a strain on me. The release needed to be slow—directed—like a fork being carved into a stream.

The energy started to change its pattern of movement when suddenly I felt another pull. Another source of energy, almost begging me to take it.

A bead of sweat rolled down the side of my face. This was surely spectacle enough, but I had handled a greater amount of magic during my trial attempts in the woods, I could do this. On my next inhale, I gave space for the new energy presence. Tiny bolts of lightning crackled through the cloud, resulting in more enthusiasm from the onlookers. It grew, and my arm movements grew with it to keep it tethered to me. The lightning changed color—a deep and vibrant green I only saw in dreams.

Then it burst.

Her screams carried no sound, eyes wide in terror as they locked with mine. Raven-black hair whipped around her face through the smoke that had scattered itself across the courtyard now in chaos. I cried out for her as a second explosion erupted between us, and I felt the snapping of her bones in my soul when her body vanished into a pile of ash and smoke.

—()—

"*Ghu—*" I jolted awake from a nightmare I still felt but couldn't remember. Cold sweat dripped down my back and met the damp blankets that were wrinkled from my tossing and turning. It was dark. The fire had gone out and left little heat behind. My back ached and my fingers trembled from trying to untangle my memories unconsciously. I rubbed my eyes and pulled my feet off the bed and onto the floor.

Sleep was avoiding me, and I wasn't in the mood to chase it. I put on my warmest clothes and draped my cloak over my head. Manden would kill me for going out of camp without telling someone, but at the moment her lectures were preferable to the exhaustion plaguing my head. I picked up my satchel from its spot near the door of my hut and headed into The Colds.

I didn't carry a light with me, as it seemed pointless in the thickness of the air. It would only help me see the fog better, so I relied on finding markers with my feet. I wasn't going far, just far enough to put something else on my mind. I needed more ingredients anyway. I set my steps for a tree that often collected moss. It was right in front of a creek that ran near the east of the campsite. The movement in the water cleared up some of the fog usually making it easier to see, but the night was so dark it was a triumph I didn't twist my ankle.

A snapped branch across the river made me pause. I stared out into the direction of the creek, but I could only hear the sound of running water. I felt for the knife I forgot to pack in my hurry. I pondered for a moment if I deserved the lecture or not. Another snap. I sent up a prayer to my gods that the earth behind me wasn't covered in dry leaves or twigs. I took a silent step backward into soft dirt and cursed myself for not praying for something a little more substantial.

A child's giggle came from the other side of the creek.

"Shhhh!" It said, the voice vaguely young and feminine. A Birthless. Small but sinister creatures that someone once described to me as 'a deer trying to shape-shift as a human child'. I shuddered and backed away another step. I might be able to outrun it, but I didn't want to lead it straight to camp. Perhaps if I could alert the scouts when I got close—

"Shhh!" It laughed again, followed by splashing. It was crossing the creek. I turned on my heel ready to bolt when something flashed across my line of sight. The Birthless squealed an awful, shrill cry and in the darkness, I could see its thin figure sink into the water with another splash. Rune stepped out of the mist from behind me.

"Mother of gods those things unnerve the shit out of me." She said in passing as she walked over to grab her knife. She turned the monster over with her boot to ensure it was dead. She pulled it out of the water's reach and covered it up with a few fallen branches.

"I'm not hauling that back." She said wiping the dirt and blood on her pant legs.

"Th-Thank you," were the only words that surfaced from my throat.

"Don't. It's my job now, I suppose." I couldn't see her face, but accounting for the fact that it was usually un-readable it didn't matter.

"What are you doing out here?" I managed to ask. There was no sign of the other scouts, and the perimeter patrol didn't come out this far.

"I was going to ask you. I couldn't sleep so I was pacing about the campsite when I saw you head out mysterious-ly. Didn't want you to have all the fun in monster-infested woods by yourself."

"You..." I wasn't sure what I wanted to ask.

"Won't tell Manden, no. I'm good at keeping secrets." She said with a smile in her voice.

"Somehow I already knew that. Thank you, truly. Death by something with flat teeth sounds like a terribly slow end."

"I do apologize I couldn't rush to your rescue armed with something of respectable size." She flung the tip of her curved knife out before twirling it back into her holster.

I let out a defeated chuckle. "Forgive me for my poor knowledge of what constitutes fine weaponry. I admit my inexperience around such things." I grabbed a hunk of moss off the tree before following her back towards the commune.

"Did you always want to become a healer?" Rune asked.

"As far back as I can remember. Although to be honest, I can't remember much. I know my father worked as a scribe for a well-known mage, and the guild decided to take me in as an apprentice. They specialized in medicinal magic, and I remember being excited to learn since boyhood." I paused, and ran the question around in my mind a few times before asking: "What did you want to do?" A bold question.

"I…" Rune hummed low in thought. "I don't think I gave it much thought. There was no use in *wanting* to be anything. I wanted my mother and sister happy. I wanted to not live in fear all the time. I wanted some nice knives." She huffed a weak laugh and patted her thighs. "I got one thing I wanted."

Marks on the stones underfoot told me we were close to the camp. The fog wasn't as dense anymore and I could just make out Rune's features. Her long bangs delicately framed her face and her tired eyes were softer than when she was first dropped on my work table. She let out a long slow sigh and spoke words that buried their weight into my chest.

"I wish I had known that for every choice I didn't make, there would be someone who would make it for me."

I almost reached for her, but she dipped her chin and walked back along the pathway towards the barracks. I stood on the edge of the fog and the clear night air of the campsite and looked around as windows started to glow with firelight. It was still dark out, but morning would creep up soon.

Back in my hut, I tossed the satchel to the side of the room. I'd get the moss later. Without changing I flopped down onto the bed, ready to test my luck on a few hours of uninterrupted sleep. Seconds after I closed my eyes I drifted off.

I might have been unlucky, or my few hours were up, because I was awoken by the obnoxious pounding sound on my door. The wooden bed and my body groaned in unison as I pushed myself up and dragged myself to the door. I trusted Rune not to say anything to Manden, but maybe my sister found out about my midnight adventure from someone else. The knocking grew more impatient, and I flung open the door to find not Manden, but Sora.

"Now how, my dear, can I help you at this time of morning?" I asked, yawning.

She raised her eyebrow. "Morning? It's mid-day. Gods you look awful."

"Thank you."

"Did you drink that tonic Twig made?"

I winced at the mere thought. "No, and you shouldn't either, I told him that stuff will make people sick."

"So you're just sick then?" She questioned.

"No, I'm not sick."

"You look si—"

"What do you *need* Sora?" I crossed my arms and leaned on the door frame for support. My niece rocked on her heels and smiled.

"It's not what I need, but what *you* need, from the looks of it." She reached over and brushed dirt off of my wrinkled cloak. "You're going to want to freshen up or take another nap. You'll need some energy later today."

"And why is that?"

Her grin widened into a toothy smile. "Today is my birthday, and Manden says I can choose how to celebrate it."

"And how is that?" I asked coyly, already knowing the answer.

"With the most memorable game of toss-ball these criminals have ever played."

Chapter Twelve

Rune

"Toss-ball?" I asked as Sanders thrust my boots into my hands and pointed for me to put them on.

"Yeah, for Sora's birthday. The makers drew a court line in the training ring and everything." They finished buttoning up their dark green trousers and began trying to put their hair back. They were able to tie a small portion of hair out of their face, but most of it fell back down around their chin and neck.

"Are you playing?" I asked, tying up my boots as ordered.

"I hope so! You too!" They barely waited for me to finish tucking in my leftover laces before grabbing me by the arm.

My shoulder was mostly healed, and with proper stretching didn't bother me too much. I couldn't remember the last time I played a game of toss-ball. As a kid I usually just watched the others play in the streets or the middle of the paddocks when Sanders' master was away.

We made it to the training ring, where indeed a court was drawn out. A large circle, divided down the middle. On the court was a gathering of people, from scouts to makers to cooks. Sora was on a tree stump near the center of the circle. She waved her hands in the air and whistled for everyone's attention.

"Alright everyone! You know the rules—two teams, two courts, two balls—Gwenna's keeping time and when the sand runs out, whichever team has both balls on their side loses! No hogging balls, *Twig*," she said pointedly. "It's gotta keep moving. One ball on each side means the round is tied, and that's boring, so don't let it come to that."

She handed a small sandclock to Gwenna, and she picked up two leather-covered balls that were near her feet. "Okay, now to teams! Since it's my birthday, I get to be Queen of one team, aaand... Kaineres! Kaineres is King of the other."

The witch was still in the garb he wore in the woods, minus the long coat. His tight-fitting shirt and vest were both slightly wrinkled, but his eyes seemed less weary. The way he carried himself was alluring in a roguish sort of way.

I didn't push him for the reason he was wandering about the night before. It was probably the same reason I was. I still didn't know how I felt about the knowledge of his past, or if I truly believed it. His lips twitched into a genuine smile, and he bowed low at the waist towards Sora, extending his gloved hand in a regal manner.

"May Her Majesty the Queen of The Colds take the first pick for her army."

Without a second's thought, Sora pointed to her first pick. "Arrow!"

Arrowette gave a smug smile at the rest of the scouts next to her before joining Sora at her side. I didn't have time to process whether or not I wanted to be involved in the game when Kaineres surprisingly called out my name. Sanders nudged me forward. I awkwardly stepped in line beside the witch.

"Are you sure you made a wise choice?" I whispered as Sora picked out her next victim. Sanders bounded over to join her as Kaineres winked at me and spoke under his breath.

"I saw your aim firsthand last night. I have a suspicion it's wiser to have you with me than against me." He raised his head to the crowd again and called: "Manden!"

Manden pinched her daughter in the arm as she walked over to us, receiving an over-dramatized yelp. "Mum! Kaineres, you won't let me have Manden on my birthday?"

Kaineres laughed and again leaned over to me. "Someone else I'd rather have *with* me and not against me." He joked softly, easily. Like how a good friend might.

After a few minutes the teams were picked and Gwenna was ready on the sidelines filling the sandclock with a small pouch of sand. Neither team knew how long or short the rounds would be, all to make the passing of the balls a little more urgent. She brought the clock near to her face and turned it over.

"Ball on!" She shouted.

The balls were immediately in the air, bouncing from hand to knee to foot to hand. Dust rose up from the ground as feet shuffled around.

"*Twig!*" Arrowette shouted as he bounced one of the balls on top of his head repeatedly.

Twig rolled his eyes and with a jerk of his head, sent it flying towards her side. It was difficult at first to keep track of where both balls were at all times, but after a minute or so I got the rhythm of it. So much so, that I detected a pattern on where the balls were going to land based on who was tossing it over. Sora tried aiming the balls towards wherever the largest gap in players was, Sanders seemed to be passing it over to each person on my team sequentially (probably making sure everyone was involved), Ivon tried hitting it as far as it could go, and Arrowette kicked the ball as hard as she could at either Twig or me. I admitted to myself that I thoroughly enjoyed the latter because sending it back twice as hard and seeing her struggle to catch or block it made the game worth playing.

The round went on for a few minutes. Block—throw—catch—pass. Sweat started to form on the top of my lips and forehead when a rattle rang through the air.

"Still as you are! That's game!" Gwenna shook a long wooden gourd-shaped object that must have been filled with pebbles.

Out of breath, we surveyed the ring for the results. One ball on each court. A tie. Sora and Ivon made crude sounds with their lips. Kaineres stretched out his arms and took a few steps toward the middle of the court.

"Why don't we make things a little more provocative?" He reached into his pockets and pulled out tiny glass vials and a leather pouch. Manden's mouth twisted into a frown as everybody else grinned in excitement.

"Shouldn't those be used for something a little more practical?" Manden said skeptically.

"Oh yes, they should." The witch grinned wide and un-corked one of the vials. "But it's your daughter's birthday and neither team is going to win without some extra chal-lenges."

Twig tossed him a ball and we all watched as Kaineres smeared something over the leather and rubbed it in. He held it for a few moments and exhaled loudly before tossing it back to Twig, who stumbled back a few steps.

"Gods! Ha—Ivon and Rune better take care with your shoulders when you catch this." Twig lugged the ball to-wards Arrowette. She caught it with a grunt and sent a hand gesture back. Kaineres used a powder on the other ball, and this time inhaled loudly before giving it to Sora.

"It's so light!" She said as she bounced it into the air and watched it linger before falling gently back into her hands.

"Now we can have some fun!" Kaineres clapped his hands together, satisfied with his addendum to the game. Manden tried to hide her smile with a cough.

"Alright, the sand amount has been changed, and it's ready for round two!" Gwenna called out. "To your allotted sides, and... ball on!"

The game was off to a great start as Ivon launched the heavy ball into the air and it came crashing down in my direction. I made a poor attempt at catching it, loudly sending a few choice words directed at the witch. He laughed heartily, his eyes too crinkled to notice the second ball on course to smack him in the face. Manden was visibly having fun now, and she picked up the heavy ball I had dropped and gave it a swift kick straight for Sora.

"*Mum!*" She tossed the ball as high as she could and Arrowette took the opening to spike it with her fists.

Sympathetic moans grew from the side of the ring where onlookers peeked through their hands at Twig, slowly getting up with his hands around his stomach.

"You're on perimeter duty for a month!" He wheezed out.

The game continued on, Kaineres still smiling to himself at the additional complexity he created. It was all I could do to keep my attention on the heavy ball, never mind the lighter one that was floating around occasionally tripping someone. Ivon must have gotten them mixed up, because he drop-kicked what he thought was the heavy ball and sent the lighter one flying out of bounds, over the railings and into the fog.

"Shit. Whoops!" He made to run for it, but Sora was already sprinting after it.

"I'll get it!" She shouted over her shoulder.

Twig tilted his head, looking in the direction the ball flew. "Quick! Before it hits the creek!" He joked.

Everyone else was grateful for the break. Even Manden spent a few seconds with her hands on her knees, panting. After a minute had gone by, she shook her head.

"What is she doing?" She stood up and started walking in the direction Sora went. "It wouldn't really make it to the creek would it?" She asked no one in particular.

Twig shrugged. "It probably got stuck in brambles or something. She knows the Marks back, she'll be fine."

Manden only let a few more minutes pass before she shook her head again. "Twig, let's go."

Twig sighed, but walked with Manden into the fog, shortly joined by Arrowette after she threw her hands up at Ivon. Sanders looked like they too wanted to join, and gave me a nervous look.

"I'll go," I offered. "I'm sure she just lost sight of the ball." I twitched my lips up in a smile I hoped was a little convincing, and followed the group to find Sora.

We found the ball. It did indeed make it to the edge of the creek, easily spotted next to a log. Manden was frantically looking around, occasionally calling for Sora. I searched for footsteps thinking that perhaps Sora did get lost, although I knew she had been down to the creek before to gather water so my theory was not a strong one.

"Here!" Twig shouted and gestured to the ground in front of him, where Sora's boot-prints were made in the dirt, surrounded by other sets of footprints.

A knot formed in my stomach. A group of people had come by. The scratches and lines in the dirt showed a scuffle leading into parts of the forest where scattered leaves left no traces of prints to follow. Manden's jaw was clenched tight, her eyebrows furrowed as she scoured the surrounding forest, but all that started back were the clouds. I saw Arrowette narrow her eyes at a bare bush, and I traced her line of sight to a charm necklace that had been caught on a branch near the scuffle.

A white stone pendant swung on the end of the necklace, carved into the shape of an owl. A religious symbol I've only seen worn by the Kingdom to the North. Arrowette picked it up gingerly and rubbed her thumb over the owl in thought.

"Soldiers..." She murmured.

"Soldiers." Manden repeated, red anger flooding her face and eyes. In her hand was a metal helmet. The part of me that wasn't deeply concerned for Sora was impressed by the fight she must have put up. "Aristian soldiers." Manden spit on the ground. Arrowette and I exchanged a quick glance.

"Not Aristian—Skevsurvian" Arrowette said, holding up the necklace. "This is a Skevsurvian pendant."

Manden threw up her hands in frustration. "No." Her voice was firm, but frantic. "I know you don't like them, but I don't have time to cater to prejudices right now—"

I tried to interject. "Manden, I think she's—"

"I *said I don't have time*. You two are to go back and get the other scouts to send out a party after us. Twig and I will get a head start. We need to catch up with them *now*." She didn't wait for a response as she trudged along into the forest. Twig turned back to us and gave us a look that meant we better do as ordered. I looked at the helmet Manden had tossed to the side. It didn't match the ones the Aristian mounted soldiers wore.

Arrowette cursed under her breath and marched back to the camp. I caught up with her and heard her talking aloud to herself.

"Why would they even take her?"

I pondered this too. "The Aristians are looking for wickeds, but they check first."

"How would they do that?" She snapped.

"They have some sort of powder that tells them, I don't know exactly how it works. I saw them use it on Kaineres. They wouldn't have taken her, unless..." I didn't consider that she could be—

"She's not one of *you*," she cut. "And Manden knows that but she's too scared to stop and think straight. No one in the army wears those ridiculous charms if they don't want a beating."

I noticed the necklace string dangling out of her pocket but didn't dare say anything. We made it back to the camp, everyone still hanging around the training ring, watching us expectantly. Kaineres slowly walked up to me and looked over my shoulder, his eyes narrowing with worry.

Arrowette explained what happened, but before she finished, Ivon whistled and led a group of scouts in the direction of the creek. Bandin agreed to stay behind and defend the camp in case the soldiers returned. Kaineres was about to run to the medicinal tent when Arrowette stopped him.

"I think Manden's wrong about the soldiers." She dug into her pocket for the necklace, but Kaineres shook his head curtly.

"Arrowette, I know you don't see eye to eye—"

"*Listen* to me—Rune thinks the same thing!" She dug her hands through her hair that had fallen out of its normally perfect braid. The witch furrowed his brow further, but looked at me to confirm.

"I don't think they were Aristian—Manden found a helmet that didn't look like the ones we saw." I tried to explain calmly and quickly, knowing time was precious. "And they would have tested to see if she was a wicked."

"I found this." Arrowette held up the owl pendant. Kaineres clicked his tongue against his teeth.

"But why take her? What are they looking for?" He asked, still not convinced.

"I don't know," I said, "but if we are that close to the border, it's not implausible."

He aggressively ran his hand through his hair, then pointed at the charm.

"Can I have that?" It was more of a demand than a request, and Arrowette hesitantly let him take the necklace. His lips formed a thin line as he clenched his fist around it. He turned on his heels and made briskly for the medicinal tent.

"What can I do?" I jolted at the voice behind me. Sanders had a small pocket knife in their hand and they had put up the hood of their cloak, ready to join the fight for his friend's return. I surveyed the commune. People were running about, debating whether or not to send another search team. I reached out and held Sanders by the shoulders.

"S, I think you should stay here. See what Kaineres needs and help him." Their black eyes darted around my face.

"What are you going to do?" They asked nervously.

"I'm going to go find Sora. I'm heading north to the border."

"The soldiers are probably heading Sou—"

"Not those soldiers. There's not much time to get into it. Just keep a look out, and help the healer." I started for the scout tent to grab my cloak, but Sanders quickly untied theirs to give to me. I gave a weak smile and let my friend wrap their arms around me in a tight hug.

"You shouldn't be going alone Rune." They said.

"She won't be."

To my surprise, Arrowette was still behind me with her arms crossed tightly across her chest. "We're wasting time—we need to go *now*."

I cocked my head. I wasn't sure what the best way to phrase 'you are the last person I want to be lost in The Colds with' was, but her exasperated groan embodied the sentiment.

"I don't trust you not to make things worse. She's *my* friend. I'm getting her back even if everyone here is running around like mindless poultry."

With that, she marched for the Scouts' tent, retrieved her bow and quiver, and walked north past the crop fields. Sanders and I exchanged apprehensive looks with each other before I followed after her, my gut twisting in my stomach that this was a terrible mistake. I just couldn't shake the feeling that Manden in her fury and panic had truly led everyone in the opposite direction of her daughter, and Sora was somewhere minutes away, hauled towards the borderline of Skevsurvia.

Chapter Thirteen

Rune

Arrowette gave the impression that she knew where she was going, and considering that her time spent scouting the territory exceeded my own, I let her lead us north. We walked for miles without stopping. Hours went by before we paused for a quick break to eat snow off of branches to hydrate.

"Ugh, I should have brought something to eat," Arrowette muttered mostly to herself. I hated to admit that the past few weeks I had grown accustomed to daily meals. My stomach was angrily awaiting tonight's portion that wasn't coming. Instead of dwelling on the growls rising from my midsection, I tried to think of what we were going to do when we caught up with a pack of soldiers, if at all. Surely they outnumbered us, and this would be familiar ground for them. The only advantage we had was surprise. That, and Arrowette's deadly aim.

"Have you had close interactions with Skevsurvian soldiers before?" I asked, trying to get a reading on what we were up against.

"I know that they have ears, and will hear us approaching if you keep opening your mouth." She snapped back.

Sora, you're doing this for Sora. And Sanders. I couldn't risk Sanders wandering off alone out of worry for their new friend, but I knew they would trust me to go in their stead. I hoped they could. Sora was capable of more than Manden gave her credit for, but she was still just a child. My chest tightened around my resolve. I could not fail her.

But I wasn't alone. I reminded myself that as shitty of a mood she was in, Arrowette was visibly worried about her friend, which was a noticeable difference from her regular shitty mood. And even though I still couldn't wrap my mind around why they cared about each other, a small part of me was glad to have support on my quest into the forest.

"Can't do anything about them smelling you though," Arrowette uttered under her breath.

That small, shrinking part of me ignored her, my attention caught by the clearing of the clouds ahead. It didn't occur to me until then that I was heading out of The Colds. After finding Sora, I could send her back with Arrowette and I could remain. I could find work in their fields, I could go back to street sweeping. Anything to keep me in the warm changing of the seasons. I could feel sunlight again. Would I go back for Sanders? They'd already expressed not wanting a life in Skevsurvia, but did they mean it? They were the kind of person who could probably be happy anywhere, but I wasn't sure if I would be happy without them. And then there was the healer...

I tried pulling my thoughts away from distraction and focus on the task I had set out to achieve, but the thought of never seeing Kaineres again left a hollow feeling in my chest. My lips pressed together out of frustration, the cracked skin on my lips pricking me uncomfortably. He was a witch—and possibly a murderer. Not that I was any better.

Although it felt slightly warmer as we approached the border, the sun wasn't there to greet us, as if it too knew we were criminals. Night had fallen. Arrowette held up her hand in a command to halt, not paying attention to the fact that I had stopped several feet earlier. About a half-mile from where we stopped, a large wall made of wooden logs stood along the border of Skevsurvia. It had some cutouts in the wood acting as small windows and lookout points for guards to peek through, but there was no sign of a gate.

Arrowette knelt on the ground. I scooted towards her and did the same.

"If they took her straight here, they would have taken her to a holding cell near one of the front gates." She said quietly. "Most Skevs are religious, and are super weird about spirits living in the forest, so they'll keep captives near the border until they know they're not *possessed*."

"So, we find the gate, and then what?"

"Then we find the holding cells that will be near the gate, or so I was told. I'm thinking we wait here for a while, learn the timing of the guards passing the windows, and find an opening."

"And what, jump through and hope there's no one on the other side?" I asked.

She huffed. "Well, what did you want to do? I'm all for parading you around as bait, but I'm trying to be cooperative."

We only had to walk parallel to the wall for a few minutes before we spotted the entrance. No guards stood in front of it, but it was closed shut to The Colds. We followed Arrowette's plan and waited, watching the timing of soldiers just long enough to make out a pattern, noting as their heads peeked through the windows and moved along on the other side of the wall. It looked like numbers were stretched thin, so finding an unoccupied window wouldn't be a problem. The problem would be not knowing what was on the other side waiting for us.

We crept forward as silently as possible, weeding in and out of shadows and behind trunks and bushes. Since the air was warmer, there was a bit more foliage to hide behind. We made it to the opening and as agreed, I hoisted Arrowette on my shoulders to grab the ledge. Whether or not she'd actually pull me up was a gamble I was willing to take. After making sure to step on my head, she climbed up into the hole in the wall and onto the other side. I couldn't hear any scuffling or shouting, but I was worried for the few moments I stood waiting under the window.

Without warning, the end of a rope smacked me in the back of the head. The rest of it was hopefully tied onto something secure, and I hoisted myself up towards Arrowette's waving hand. The other side of the wall was just more forest, with a dirt road extending from the gate. We were standing on the few wooden structures built. It was attached to the log wall, narrow and spanning the length of it. There were no soldiers near us, but I could hear voices underneath us.

"Benhi on the roof again? I swear that kid gets too bored for a post out here. Benhi! Off the roof and back to your station!"

Arrowette and I froze, and upon realizing that we were Benhi, we booked it off the building and found a nearby tree to hide behind. The gruff voice continued their conversation.

"Freezing gods, kids these days have no proper training. Did you see that fellow that came back without his helmet? You'd think he left his head in there the way he was going on about 'forgetting to pick it up.'"

I made eye contact with Arrowette, who nodded in confirmation. Sora was here, somewhere. We just had to figure out where she was being held. We scanned the long buildings. They all had some sort of windows in them, but most were blocked with tarps and blankets to keep warmth in. Occasionally, a soldier would walk out of a room to check the windows above, but when they returned down below it was fairly quiet. We could hear shouting a ways off in the distance, but I couldn't make out what was being said. It was dark, and thankfully the light from the torches they used to keep their walkways lit didn't reach us in the forest.

Arrowette held her bow in her hand, her quiver placed against her hip stocked with arrows. I too, had one knife in my hand, albeit feeling a little less confident taking on an entire station if it came to that. As we watched the wall, and the buildings, and the guards, my muscles screamed from the long journey only to be frozen in a crouched position.

Maybe it was the leg cramps getting to my head, or the lack of sleep was finally catching up on me, but I turned and whispered to Arrowette.

"You said they're superstitious of spirits? And they'll always keep prisoners in holding to check for them?"

She looked at me like I was actively being possessed. "If you pretend to be a spirit or ghost or something, they'll likely just kill you!" She hissed back. I shook my head.

"No, we just act like we walked through the gate—won't they take us in holding?"

She glared at me but didn't say anything as she thought it over. "That's a huge gamble that they'll take you alive at all." She said at last.

"Don't people ever visit the Kingdom? It's not under lockdown." *To my knowledge.*

"Not from The Colds! Who would believe that we just *walked in?*"

I pointed. "Him."

I had been watching Benhi from afar. He was several buildings down, but I saw the lad continually jump up to the window to drop rocks or twigs down to the other side and then leap off and try to stick the landing.

Arrowette exhaled a long, slow breath of frustration but put her bow back behind her. "This is ridiculous."

We became experts at weaving in and out of shadows, finding the softest dirt to muffle our footsteps. When we got closer to the boy, I looked for the crunchiest-looking leaf on the ground and stepped on it. He whipped his head around and placed his hand on the handle of his short sword hanging on his hip.

"Who-who goes there?"

"Aw, it looks like he caught us!" Arrowette said sheepishly. I groaned. She might be deadly with a bow but being coy was not her strong suit. Thankfully, the kid bought the act.

"How did you sneak through? Don't move!"

"The gate was open at little—we squeezed in." I lied. "We're just passing through— this is the way to Skevsurvia, correct?" I didn't need him calling for backup, so the less threatening we could make ourselves, the better. We were just two travelers. From The Colds. In the middle of the night.

He took a step closer, hands still shaking over his blade handle. "You—we're not to accept passage through these gates. Are you bandits?"

"Would we tell you if we were?" Arrowette chirped.
Gods kill me.

"No! Not bandits, we're just passing through, like I said. We got lost in The Colds and wanted to get out of those spirit-haunted woods." Emphasis on the last few words. That worked.

"Oh! I can't let you go anyway, I'm afraid. Don't trust that you're not, infected or something."

Arrowette turned to me and I shot her a warning glance to go along with the ruse. I held my hands up.

"You do what you must."

He unsheathed his sword for moral courage and steered us to a room a few doors down. There was no light inside, apart from the torch's light seeping in through the cracks in the wood framing. We were placed in a cell made of iron and Benhi closed the door shut, locking it with keys he pulled from his chest pocket.

"Ahem, ah, young lad," I coughed.

He whirled around from the doorway.

"As much as I would hate parting with them, I don't think your superiors would want us to have our weapons, am I right?" I was the epitome of innocence. Arrowette slammed her boot down on my foot as Benhi gave a nervous laugh and fumbled over to take our belongings through the iron door. He looked around for a place to put them and settled for merely placing them on a bench near the door. Out of reach, but only from in the cell. He looked around in the darkness a final time and slipped through the door, closing it behind him.

"What the *hell* did you do that for? Next time you offer up my bow I'll offer up your head to a hell-hound." Arrowette hissed on about how angry she was and how stuck we were, and didn't notice the arm sticking out from the cell next to us. My eyes were slowly adjusting to the dark, but didn't need light to know who it was as she spoke.

"Arrow?" Is that you? Sora poked her friend from behind, and Arrowette spun around.

"Sora! Gods of the hunt, I *knew* they had you here." She wrapped her arms through the bars and around Sora as best she could, and the two of them fussed over each other to make sure the other was okay.

"Sora, how often do they check on you?" I asked. "Is there a pattern? There weren't any guards outside the door." I was already planning our escape out of the cell and over the wall.

"Oh! There were guards lined up, but most of them are chasing after a guy that got loose."

"That's convenient," I muttered. "All that trouble for one guy—why are they taking people captive like this?" None of it made any sense.

"I don't know why they took me—well, I know why, but we can get into that later. They're chasing after that one guy because they think he stole something from them."

Soldiers pulled people from banishment and were surprised when they turned out to be bandits. It didn't make sense at all.

"Stole what?"

"This." Sora dropped her voice to a whisper, and from inside her shirt pulled out a small booklet. It was cased in worn leather and from what I could see in the darkness, the pages were yellowed and torn. I wasn't much of a reader, but it looked like something I would have given a street dog to play with.

"They had a mage in here—an actual mage, questioning everyone the soldiers brought in," Sora explained. "He wasn't here long, but his questions started getting strange, and he mentioned something about Kaineres."

"Kaineres?" My ears perked up as Sora continued.

"He asked about the exiled witch that was charged with the murder of the Aristian princess, and then he started flipping through pages of his book as he checked us out. It looked important, so I grabbed it."

"You just grabbed it?" Arrowette questioned.

"From his pocket—when he wasn't looking. Sanders taught me."

I bit my tongue at what I had said earlier to Sanders about having nothing to teach. I wanted Sora to explain further but I knew this was a conversation we could have outside a holding cell. "Hold on—we need to get out of here."

"She's bright this one." Arrowette leaned against the wall. "What's the next step of your masterly plan, Trick-bleeder?"

Ignoring the insult, I smirked, and from my own pocket brought out the ring of keys I snatched up from Benhi while he was busy taking my knives. "Who do you think Sanders learned it from?" I said cooly.

Up until that point, I thought it was just the three of us in the cell, but as soon as the keys jingled, the iron bars shook as two people shoved their faces up against them. Arrowette stifled a scream with her hands. They were in the same cell Sora was in—adjacent to ours—and they stuck their hands out in a pleading manner.

"Please take us with you!" The smaller one said. "We can't stay here."

In the few hours Sora had spent in their company, they must have become acquaintances. She patted them on the shoulder.

"Of course you both can come. Arrowette, Rune, this is Desjin and Dyrus. They were also taken by the soldiers in The Colds. Skevsurvia is the last place Desjin wants to be, on account of them stealing from her well-known father and all."

I held up a hand to quiet her as footsteps walked by. I waited for them to pass before lowering my voice to Sora.

"Most of the guards are out chasing someone else?"

She nodded. I tugged at the beads in my hair while thinking. After listening again to make sure there was no one outside the door, I started unlocking the iron gates, freeing both cell blocks. Arrowette rushed over to her bow and strapped on her quiver, counting each arrow. Sora tossed me my knives and waved her hands at me for the keys. The keys unlocked the bench as well, which contained weapons taken from Desjin and Dyrus—two matching curved cut-lasses.

"Okay—" I whispered. "There is a window in the border wall above us that is just big enough to climb through. It's a drop, but if you roll as you hit the ground you should be fine. Sora—take this—don't land on it."

I handed her one of my blades, seeing as she wasn't carrying anything. The door to the holding cells wasn't locked, and thankfully the hinges were well-oiled. I went first, knife in my hand and back to the wooden wall, looking anywhere for a sign of soldiers returning. The coast was clear, or at least what I could see in the firelight. There were torches right above us, and we were going to be in plain sight, so we had to move fast.

I waved the others on as I jumped up and hoisted myself up on top of the flat roof. The others followed suit, and we sneaked to the window. Desjin was about to climb through when a shaken voice called out from below us.

"Stop where you are!" On the ground, Benhi held out his sword, his other hand rising to his lips preparing to whistle. His hand froze in front of his mouth, eyes locked on the end of Arrowette's drawn arrow.

"*Don't* make a sound." She commanded. She jerked her head to the group to get moving. Desjin hit the ground behind us with a thud, and then a skid, and knocked on the wall for Dyrus to follow. I helped lower Sora down onto Desjin's shoulders and turned back to Arrowette.

"Go," I said, still not entirely sure I wanted to go back into The Colds. She looked at me for a moment and then called down in a hushed tone.

"She has wicked aim with a knife. Blink and you'll have steel through your eye." She lowered her bow and climbed through the opening. She hadn't seen me use a knife like that, but I appreciated the bluff as Benhi licked his lips in fear, eyes darting from my face to my blade. I couldn't help but feel bad for the lad. This was obviously the last place he wanted to be. I was still debating with myself if this was where I wanted to be. Overcoming the shaking boy below me would be no contest compared to a monster, but it would mean never returning to the commune in the giant tree. Arrowette roughly knew the way back, but I wouldn't have the same luck if I tried on my own.

The weight of my beads suddenly felt heavy on my sternum. I had never been so close to the life I wanted, but on this side of the border, it didn't seem like much of a life.

I spoke calmly as I backed up into the window legs first. "We're just spirits, releasing ourselves back to the forest."

"I—I don't believe you," Benhi answered.

"Good. Don't trust anybody, kid." I dropped down, the steel knife barely missing Dyrus' face as she caught me. As soon as my feet hit the ground we were running.

"I think we taught Benhi a valuable lesson," I mumbled as we wove through the trees heading south.

"I think we *traumatized* him!" Sora heaved.

As we kept running I looked over my shoulder at the wooden wall fading into the forest behind us. I clenched my jaw at possibly losing the easiest opportunity I would be given to start fresh in Skevsurvia. When I looked forward again, my eyes noticed the outline of the stolen book in Sora's pocket. I wasn't sure what came over me, but I wanted to stay—I needed to make sense of all the strange things that were happening. My thoughts were racing faster than my legs. What were Aristians doing with wickeds—why was Sora taken prisoner—what importance did that little book hold? The knot in my stomach grew and it wasn't from hunger. The fact that people were looking for Kaineres most likely meant trouble for him—and I wasn't sure why that concerned me the most.

CHAPTER FOURTEEN

Kaineres

I cursed as the pot of liquid sputtered and sent droplets of sizzling oil onto my face and neck. The brewing mixture was almost finished, and the owl pendant was fully warmed under the firelight. Bandin rushed out of the medicinal tent, looking for an update. The finding spell wouldn't be as powerful as I would have liked, but with ingredients so low there was not much I could do to enhance it. I cursed again, this time at myself for not heeding Manden's warnings about the low stock of supplies. Sanders was out in the fields gathering more berries and herbs at my request, but we didn't have time to start fresh. I prayed that the energy in the pendant would be enough.

I took the necklace and dipped it into the bubbling mixture, coating the stone charm in the oils and herbs. I thanked the gods there was no wind to interfere with the spell. Holding out the glistening pendant by the string I breathed the words of a lost item's finding spell. Carefully keeping my arm straight, we watched the amulet closely as it started to swing outwards, but only in one direction. It kept swaying outwards as if reaching for its owner. Bandin wiped his hand through his white beard and silently mouthed a prayer to his gods. My chest tightened at what

I had already guessed but was now confirmed. Sora was being taken north. Manden was going the wrong way.

Bandin tilted his head to me in question. I thought for a moment.

"Rune and Arrowette are already on their way." I looked around the camp at the remaining people. "We don't have scouts to spare to go after them until Manden returns, we need to focus on getting her and the rest of the scouts back. She'll know what to do."

He nodded and went to find someone to act as a messenger. I looked up at the quickly darkening sky and headed back to the medicinal tent.

I didn't know how Manden did it. Protecting and caring for her family all while leading a commune in one of the most inhospitable environments. Fear gripped my heart at the thought of something happening to either of them. Any of them. If Rune returned with my niece safely, I don't know how I would ever repay her. Not if, when. I had to stay positive. As aloof and cold as she tried to appear I trusted Rune, and Sora was ready to head out into The Colds years ago.

I sat down at the desk only to immediately get up and toss my guts out onto the table. The pressure in my chest started to build and my throat tightened around the feelings still violently shaking their way through my body. Panic grew around the possibility of losing the only family I had left. I had to do something useful other than stirring oil over a fire. I couldn't lose them again.

Again?

I wiped the bile out of the corners of my mouth and steadied myself against the table. I had never been separated from them before. Maybe it was the uncertainty that drove me into a state of alarm—or the past few nights of nightmares. I rubbed circles around my forehead, trying to calm any racing thoughts. The terror and dread subsided only to guilt.

I only wanted Sora's birthday to be exciting—*fun*. Like mine was when I was her age. I had wanted the same thing. A game. Toss-ball no less, with my friends in my guild. I let it grow out of hand tonight, I overdid it again—I took too big a risk and now everyone else was facing the consequences for it. My eyes welled up. I had to *do* something.

They would be okay. Everyone here had survived much worse. They would return, and life could go on as usual, with higher safeguards put in place by Manden, naturally. In a while, they would all return home. Or would they? I felt useless, sitting here stirring old energies and confirming information Rune already knew. Rune...

Rune wanted nothing more than to cross the border into Skevsurvia when she first arrived. What would have changed her mind since then? Did I try at all to make this place more welcoming to her? Did I push her too far to learn magic after everything she's probably been through? I dug my nails into my hair as the wave of fear crashed over me again, threatening to drown out every good feeling forever.

"Kaineres?"

I looked up from where I had knelt on the ground to the entrance of the tent, where Sanders stood with a concerned expression on their face. They crouched down in front of me and put their hand on my shoulder.

"Sora will be okay. I just know it. Rune and Arrowette will stop at nothing to find her. Arrowette was in the army and Rune has faced her share of soldiers and monsters." They offered up a soft smile. "They'll come home."

I managed a nod to them, thinking to myself that the camp might not feel like home to everyone. Instead, I asked, "How is the rest of the commune?"

Sanders bit the inside of their cheek. "Tense. Worried. Not only about Sora but about the majority of the scouts out looking for her."

I sighed. I didn't know how Manden did it, but I was going to try. I braced myself against the legs of the table as I stood up, surveying the damage my stomach had done to the wooden surface. I would clean it later. I gently brushed the spiraling thoughts aside as best I could to make room for a long inhale. I held the fear, and the guilt, and thought of the words to say to ease everyone's nerves. I could do it. I needed to do it. It was the only aid I could offer in the moment.

I followed Sanders out of the tent and into the bitter cold. People had gathered near the entrance to the maker's tent, where Celeste raised her hand to me, expectantly. In passing, I thanked Sanders for their encouragement and walked towards the group—other members of my new family. I felt comfortable in this, somehow. I could step in and be the leader they needed in Manden's absence. Keep the peace until they came back. Until they all came back. And they would. Or I would march into the forest and bring them back myself.

—◊—

Rune

After we were certain we weren't being followed, we stopped near a large fallen tree to rest. I stretched my leg out on the log, trying to massage out a painful lump in my thigh that had formed while running. Desjin gathered snow to share with Dyrus. Arrowette took her bow off of her back and stretched her arms out wide.

"Sora," she said, "what in every realm of hell happened to you? You had everyone in the commune scared shitless."

Sora yawned. "It all happened so fast. I went after the ball, which had rolled farther than I thought, and when I got to the creek I couldn't see them passing by on the other side. The soldiers, I mean. Suddenly, they had jumped out of the fog and over to me. I tried to fight them off, but there were too many of them. I left a bunch of deep scratches on their faces though." She took off her boots to start rubbing her feet. "Anyway, the soldiers put me on a mule they had with them and carried me off like cargo to their base. I met Desjin and Dyrus in the holding cell, and they were able to explain things to me."

We all looked to the two cellmates, who I could now see clearer, despite the darkness. Desjin was the smaller of the two, with lighter skin, bushy sandy brown hair, and big brown eyes. Dyrus had a larger but softer frame, slightly tanner skin with long wine-red hair. I could tell of the two of them Dyrus was quieter, as she let Desjin do most of the talking.

"Skevsurvia is adding numbers to their army." Desjin said. "At first, we thought they were taking people against their will, then we thought they were just hiring mercenaries, but now we see they're doing both."

"Sora's not a mercenary," Arrowette said questioningly.

Desjin shook her head. "They probably thought she was. They've been sending out groups of soldiers into The Colds to find criminals that were banished over the years. They're offering them money to return and fight for the Skevsurvian army."

I snorted. "Are they still hiring?"

Arrowette shot me an irritated glare before turning back to Desjin. "Why are they building up their army all of a sudden? Did they have a plague?"

Desjin scuffed their boots into the dirt. "No, it's because of disunion rumors... The war rumors?"

The eerie silence of the forest crept in around us as we all looked at each other. Dyrus spoke, her voice soft and barely audible over the gentle rustling of tree branches. "You haven't heard?"

"We've been stuck in the first layer of hell for a bit. There's not much to hear." Arrowette retorted, gesturing around her. Sora faced us, palm over her heart.

"They say the Alliance is gearing up for a confrontation with the Kingdom of Aristus." Sora said. "Skevsurvia has spies in the Kingdom—Aristus that is, and there's rumor that the King has refused to step down."

I breathed out slowly. The Alliance was made up of the Six Realms, all separate monarchies that all adhered to various of rules of order. The Realms all had their own cultures, customs, traditions—but they followed principle statutes set by the Alliance. One of those statutes being that at the age of sixty, the leading Ruler must step down and give the throne to their successor. Because of these rules, major disputes hadn't broken out in centuries. There was an assimilation of new thoughts and ideas with older traditions. It had been centuries since someone had challenged the order. There was no way of knowing the kind of devastation the entire Alliance could bring if they acted out in violence.

"They also think he's plotting something secret outside of The Alliance's knowledge," Desjin said slowly. "King Amos knows he'll face resistance if he doesn't relinquish the throne soon—they think he's fortifying his army for the cause."

The wickeds. That must be what he wanted them for. What he was using them for.

"What do they want with Kaineres?" I blurted out, ignoring a glance from Arrowette. Desjin and Dyrus both shrugged and shook their heads.

"Who—the exiled witch? We don't know what that's about. The mage at the holding cell wanted to know his whereabouts, or if we had seen him—but we're not sure why."

"He was a powerful mage too—I could see his tattoos." Dyrus chimed in.

"What's in the book?" I asked Sora.

She patted where it was on her person, in her shirt's inside pocket. "I don't know. It was closed when I took it, and I think it needs a spell to open it. I'm sure my uncle can figure it out."

I straightened up and tightened Sanders' hood around my body. "We should get going. The sooner we get you back, the sooner we can call in the other scouts. Your mother might be halfway to the Southern border by now."

We walked on through the night, Sora occasionally assuring Desjin and Dyrus that they would be welcome members of the commune. Manden would be thrilled to have more scouts. I just hoped none were lost in their search for Sora. We wandered in the dark for a few hours longer than we should have, but eventually stumbled across a marker that Arrowette and I had left on our journey out.

When we got closer to the thickening fog, I was pleased that I was finally familiar with the ground underfoot. The inconspicuous Marks left on pebbles and the roots of trees led us back to the camp just as the sky was illuminated softly by the hidden sunrise above. The clouds above us were a warm pink and cast a rosy film over the rest of the campsite.

As tired as we all were, Sora broke into a sprint as the fog cleared and we stepped onto the dirt path that wove around the giant tree. Someone must have seen her because a loud wooden rattling sound vibrated through the air, alerting the rest of the commune.

"Sora!"

Kaineres was running down the pathway around the tree, looking just as exhausted as we did. He wrapped his niece into a tight embrace and then checked her up and down for wounds.

"A-are you hurt? Are you cold? Do you need anything?"

Sora brushed her sleeves off and smiled like she had just taken a stroll around the camp.

"I'm *fine*. Although I'm worried Manden's not going to let me leave camp again. Where *is* Mum?" She looked around as people started to approach us, but no Manden in sight.

"She's alright, she's on her way." The healer exhaled a shaky breath. "She took a troop out to look for you, thinking you were being taken South. We sent a few messengers out to bring her home."

"I told her, but no one listens to me!" Arrowette made her presence known and readily accepted the doting and fussing made by the surrounding commune members. Sora cleared her throat and gestured to the bandits behind me, who were still taking in the splendor of the giant tree.

"This is Desjin and Dyrus—they helped us escape from the border hold!" Sora explained.

Arrowette made a face at me that seemed to express that she didn't recall their assistance in escaping. I let a smile slip and watched as the crowd of people rushed over to them, asking about Dyrus' weapon and if Desjin had faced monsters before. The head cook mentioned something about a meal and led Sora and her friends to the other side of the tree, where no doubt there would be feasting in the dining hall to celebrate their return. As my eyes followed them, I met the healer's weary gaze, and I wondered how long he had been staring at me with his bloodshot eyes.

He held out his hand, and I awkwardly accepted it, squeezing his fingers in acknowledgment. Suddenly I was pulled into him as his arms wrapped around me. I stiffened at first at the abruptness, but let myself sink into the warmth of his chest as the scent of cedarwood swirled around me.

"Thank you." He whispered into my ear. While his voice was barely audible, the softness caressed something within me that sent a shiver down my neck.

"You don't have to thank me—"

"I know, I know. You require no commendation. Regardless, thank you Rune."

We slowly pulled back to observe the state of each other. It would have been no different than peering into a looking glass. Purple stained the corners under his eyelids, his face had paled, and his hair was slick with sweat. His double pupils roved over me intently, as if closely examining for any new scrape, bruise, or cut.

"You didn't worry about me, did you?" I teased as I slipped out of his hands. He returned them to his pockets and sighed.

"I had no doubt you could hold your own against a group of unlucky soldiers." His lips twitched upwards into a small smile. He did another once-over, making sure I wasn't going to fall to pieces when he turned around. "I was, however, a little worried you wouldn't come back." He dipped his head in parting as he turned and walked towards the dining room. I stared after him, squeezing my own hand.

"Me too."

All the torches in the communal hall were lit and even though mealtime was typically held in the evening, cooks brought out what they didn't get to serve last night. It appeared that everyone at the camp was too busy or nervous to eat. Sora was beaming from ear to ear, telling everyone about her first adventure away from camp. The head cook had made her favorite meal—stiff bread made from milled crickets. I wondered what Sora would think of bread made from barley or wheat.

The door burst open and in rushed Sanders, followed by a mob of scouts. Black hair filled my line of vision as Sanders threw themselves around me.

"You're back!" They exclaimed, taking their coat back off of my shoulders. "I hope you don't mind, my dear Rune, I'm *freezing*."

I reached for a slice of bread to hand them, but they had jumped around the table to Sora to check on her, squeezing between Ivon and the other scouts. Arrowette must have come down with something from the forest, because she kept clearing her throat. Ivon leaned over and gave her a peck on the cheek, which seemed to satisfy her enough to return her attention to the food.

The door opened again, this time to a sunken-eyed Manden. The ends of her short hair were coated in ice, and she was still wearing her snow-covered coat. She looked around the room and settled her gaze on Sora. She let out a long exhale and wiped something out of her eyes. Noticing her mother, Sora jumped out of her seat. She met open arms with her own, and the rest of the commune pretended to go about their business as the two cradled each other.

The slice of bread was taken from my hands, and Kaineres sat down in the seat next to me with a grunt.

"I would have never eaten this as a child." He said as he took a large bite. I rolled my eyes and snatched it back from him.

"Somehow that doesn't surprise me. I can only imagine the kinds of foods you dined on. Spiced fish deboned in front of you? Cuts of rare game?" I joked, taking my own mouthful of the brown loaf.

He snickered to himself and reached for a slice. "I ate *potatoes*. It was a medicinal guild, not a noble house for gods' sake." He passed me a wooden cup of some sort of mead and clinked it with his own. "To your future success as head-scout."

"Oh no, I don't want that. Manden wouldn't do that, would she?" I never craved any sort of leadership, especially over other people's lives when I could barely keep myself alive. He grinned and nodded across the table.

"If it came to it, I'll bet Arrowette would take your place of honor. She's has a sense of humility that befits a leader." He served me other offerings from the table, and then himself. I finished off the bread and dove into the assortment of steamed vegetables and nuts. We ate in silence, both of us watching the reenactment of Sora's capture. Sanders went off-script a few times and had to be redirected, but since they weren't there I still had to give them credit for their enthusiasm. Manden was introduced to Desjin and Dyrus, and after hearing their embellished contributions to Sora's rescue, she introduced them to Twig as her newest scout members.

Kaineres ran his hands through his hair and over his eyes. "I am going to be in my chambers sleeping for the next week, and if anyone gets injured they can help themselves to the contents of the medicinal tent." He yawned and got up to leave, making sure to say a few words to Manden and Sora on the way out.

At the mention of sleep, every bone in my body cried out to be horizontal, stretched flat on my bed in the magically warmed barracks. I followed Kaineres out the large wooden door and down the path. Sweet, sweet slumber called my name from the blankets as I entered the tent, but I paused when I heard Sora calling for her uncle.

In the moments of reunion and relief, I had almost forgotten about the grim situation the rest of the world was in, and what Kaineres might be in too. I hesitated at the threshold, the warmth of the inside melting the tips of my fingers as they brushed against the canvas. Turning around I saw Sora run up to her uncle and produce the small booklet from her pocket. She gave it to him and explained what had happened with the mage. His eyebrows furrowed in confusion as he took the small leather-bound book from her. He tried ineffectively to open it with his hands, but the cover was stuck shut on the pages.

They exchanged a few more words, and Sora went back inside the dining hall. With the witch still looking at the book in his hands, I stepped into the barracks. The hair on my arms stood on end as the fingers of a strong breeze brushed up against the canvas ceiling, rippling the material above me. A chilly reminder that there might still be unfinished business out beyond the cover of snow and trees. I sat on the edge of my bed, untying the laces of my boots and freeing my aching feet.

The wind howled on outside, an eerie presence in the otherwise ethereal morning. As I surveyed the shelter around me, I realized just how much I had begun to look forward to lying down in my bed. The nervousness I felt around some of the commune members had faded. Even Arrowette was just a pebble in the bottom of my shoe. If she wanted away with me, she would've already done so. My fingers threaded through the soft fur blanket I was sitting on as I thought of all the pelts I had seen traded to people of the upper city for half of what they were worth. Maybe Manden was right in wanting to build a life out here.

My muscles almost purred as I stretched out my arms and legs and walked to the storage chest to switch out my pair of socks. I pulled open the drawer and paused, peering into the cavity. There was no one in the tent but me, but I glanced around out of habit to make sure no one saw my eyes start to glisten.

A smile tugged at my lips, and I swapped out the worn woolen socks, giving a thoughtful pat on the head to the beast now guarding my drawer. I closed it gently and made for the soft fur blankets and the dry mattress I had been awaiting all morning.

I combed through my messy hair with my fingers as best as I could, keeping the beads in to give me something to fiddle with as I drifted off. They were comfortable—familiar. Feelings I was starting to associate with the commune. I'm sure I looked foolish sleeping with a smile still plastered into my face, but I couldn't help thinking about how different my life had become in the past few weeks—all the things that I looked forward to. The texture of cricket bread, the bickering between the scouts in the middle of the night, a sly smile on just half of his face... the warm grain patterns in the small wooden horse in my drawer.

Chapter Fifteen

Kaineres

A vile stench tainted the air and stuck its putrid fingers down my throat until I gagged.

Later had slipped my mind in the chaos of everyone returning—and the chance of falling so deep into sleep that not even my nightmares could wake me. I grimaced at the mess that had seeped into the wooden grain of my desk and raised my tunic over my nose. I grabbed one of the rags from under the workbench and soaked it in a bucket of water that was sitting nearby. Bumps on my skin rose as a sudden chill whipped through the tent.

"Manden sent for me, I hope you don't mi—*nghu*—*what in hell happened in here?*" Rune tightened her scarf over her face and scanned the room for the source of the assault on her senses. I draped the rag over the table, hoping the water would penetrate the grime in the grooves.

"It was a rough night," I said through the fabric of my shirt. I grabbed the cloak lying on the workbench behind me. Rune, not needing any more instruction, led the way out of the tent in a hurry. It was morning, the sky not quite as pink as it had been yesterday, but still golden in hue. I had slept all day and most of the night, my exhaustion finally serving me well for once. By the color in her face, Rune seemed to have similar luck. I gestured over to my chambers. The hut wasn't heated, but it would suffice until I could get a better clean of my workspace.

Twig had called for a scout meeting to discuss the news Sora brought with her, so I planned to keep my questioning with Rune brief. She fidgeted with the little blue beads at the ends of her hair as she surveyed my room. There wasn't much to look at. A desk covered in strips of paper I was drying, a fireplace that needed to be lit, and a bed—which both of us plainly avoided by standing on either side of the circular room.

"Comfy." She sniffed as she leaned her back against the block wall. I cleared my throat and retrieved the item of interest from my pocket. I placed it on the end beam of the bed frame. The size of the book was laughable in comparison. Its weathered edges and torn leather almost threatened to slip in between the cracks and notches in the wood. I busied myself and placed a few logs on the fireplace. I could feel Rune watching me as I did so.

"I don't know what it is or what it means, if that's what you're about to ask," she said.

I sat down on the floor and patted the space next to me as an invitation. "I figured it would be a slim chance," I said, taking a piece of flint and igniting a small fire in the kindling. "No back-alley traders interested in spell books?"

She made her way over slowly to join me next to the growing fire, holding the book in her hand.

"Is that what this is? A spell book?"

"Of... sorts. It definitely needs a spell to open it. I see no reason someone would glue every page together if they had no intention of using it as a fire log." I fed dried leaves into the fireplace until I was satisfied with the size of the flame. "Even as taboo as magic is in Aristus, There exist numerous magical resources—tools and references for magicians. Most are found in magical guilds or in households who employ a witch or mage, but some—some that hold historic value—are kept in libraries of note."

She flipped the book over, examining both sides at I continued.

"A great library in Elynchester held copies of some of the most notable books and scrolls written centuries ago by some of the most extraordinary and ruthless magicians. Years before I was born, news broke that it was raided, and books were scattered about the continent by bandits and merchants who did not know the worth of the objects they traded. The majority of the stolen inventory is presumed to be lost, but to a witch who knows what they're looking at, they could have stumbled upon something most priceless indeed."

Faint crinkles stretched across her temples as Rune squinted her eyes at me. "And do *you* know what you're looking at?"

"I believe this is one of those books. How it fell into the Skevsurvian mage's hand, I don't know, but he must have known what he was doing if he was reading from it. He opened it, somehow, and *that* is why I'm seeking your help."

"My help? After one lesson you're ready to risk setting flame to an ancient artifact?" She forced a small laugh, her lower lid quivering with an emotion I couldn't read.

"I doubt we'll be setting fire to anything—the worst that could happen is it doesn't open." I gave her a half smile. I hoped failing to open it *would* be the worst thing, but something in the back of my mind told me there was much more at stake.

I placed her other hand on the book. "Hold it intention-ally."

She looked at it warily, as if worried it would surely burst into flame once she focused on it, but she nodded and held it out in front of her.

"Can you feel anything?" I asked her, studying the curious expression she made. Her eyes were serious as usual but her lips twisted ever so slightly to the side. The skin of her lips was a bright pink hue from the cold, and her scar appeared both smooth and textured at the same time. Dangerous curiosity wanted to imagine what her mouth would feel like against my own.

She eventually shrugged and put the book down on the floor. "I feel strange leather."

I shook my head. "Do you feel any magical energy?"

"What would that feel like?"

"Well, what does it feel like to use magic?" I asked.

Rune paused. "It doesn't really, it just happens. Other than a sting from wherever I cut—I know, I know—but it's what I knew." She tapped a finger on the leather cover. "What *should* it feel like?"

I thought about it for a moment. "Maybe nothing... to you."

Her grey eyes narrowed as I worked it out aloud.

"See, when a witch uses magic, they feel the energy pulsing through them—I feel energy pulsing—a physical sensation with every spell I cast. I feel it *using* me as a catalyst for its purpose. I act as a host, but for a moment, simply giving space and direction. You might not feel it because... nothing is coming and going. You create it, you carry it with you. The world's energy is your energy. That's what makes you magic."

My thoughts carried themselves away with this realization until Rune brought me back to the present with a question I had been asking myself since Sora handed the book to me the morning before.

"How do you know what kind of spell it needs?" She steadied her gaze on the cover as if instructions would appear if she looked hard enough.

I rubbed my hand through my beard and made a mental note that I desperately needed a shave.

"That's the intuition I was hoping you'd be able to provide. An insight into what kind of magic it calls for. I sense magical energy present. But I don't know what to do with it. I can tell it *where* to go, but I need it to tell me where it *wants* to go."

She picked it back up again and closed her eyes. Her chest rose and fell steadily. I could picture the imaginary clouds of steam coming out of her nose and rising to the roof of the room. Her mouth twitched to the side again, and I felt a smile creep onto my face as the bridge of her nose crinkled in the most adorable way.

"It... it's trying to give me something." She said. "I feel a push, like it wants to... replace my space? Does that make any sense?" She opened her eyes and looked at the book as though it had insulted her.

"It does..." I replied, racking my weak memories for any drip of information I might have once known. "It does... it—"

It clicked. A memory, from long ago, me as a youth hearing about the history and application of such spell books. Spell books that were the recipe for a spell themselves. Rune gently placed the book into my open palm and allowed me to examine the binding.

"I think the lock is a key," I said, making mental notes of how worn the cover was, how simple in construction, how there was a stain in the corner that was barely visible...

I could feel Rune's large grey eyes staring at me, eyebrows slightly raised. "Ah yes. What a sensible thing."

Ignoring her mockery, I slammed my hand on the top of my knee and rose to my feet, causing Rune to jump a little.

"Sorry—I think I have it—what kind of spell it requires." I smiled to myself at the years of training slowly coming back to me.

Rune stood and brushed remnants of ashes off of herself as someone knocked on the door. I opened it to Arrowette, eyes wide as she glanced between Rune and me. A presumptuous grin spread across her face.

"Oh. I'm sorry, am I interrupting?"

"What do you want?" Rune leaned against the doorpost with her hands across her chest and ice daggers in her eyes. Arrowette's voice glazed the air like butter on a warm cake. Rancid Butter.

"I know you had an eventful past couple of days—and I'm sure you're reminiscing on the near-death experiences, but this is genuinely a desperate look for both of you."

"What do you want Arrowette?" I repeated the question through gritted teeth.

"Twig's called for that meeting to start. Although, Rune, since there wasn't anything you saw that I didn't, I doubt anyone will notice if you're too busy practicing your charms on the healer. I heard that you only had your very first lesson not so long ago..."

"Enough, Arrowette. You've left your message, now go." I narrowed my eyes at her and reminded myself that she also aided in Sora's safe return.

Arrowette turned around on her heels and clicked her tongue. "Alright then. Although, the more I think about it, you two might be a practical pairing, seeing as you're both some of the most wanted criminals in the Kingdom. You can bond over the blood on your hands."

"Watch your tone," I growled. I owed Rune more than my life for rescuing my niece. Regardless of Arrowette's assistance, I refused to allow her to drive a wedge between Rune and this commune. "Sora might still be a scout but one word from me, and Twig will have both of you scheduled so far apart you won't be able to spew your poison on her in passing."

She spun around with annoyance—and perhaps real-ization—plastered on her face, but I had already closed the door. Even in the dull firelight, I could tell Rune's face was as flushed as my own. I ran a hand through my hair and sighed.

"She's rather adept at crawling under someone's skin," I murmured.

Rune raised an eyebrow. "Like she's not throat-sleev-ing Ivon whenever the two of them can fit into the same shadow."

I grimaced at this new knowledge. "Well, Ivon is at least respectable, so I doubt she'd feel any embarrass-ment for that."

Rune snorted and wiped a loose hair out of her face. "I'm so sorry to have dampened your reputation."

My gut sunk at my miscommunication. "No-*no*—not you, *me*—I know people talk. The stories that have prob-ably been shared. I'm sure you know what I've... Anyway, I hope it comforts you that no one really listens to Arrowette's gossip." I gave her a sympathetic look as she studied my face.

Finally, she let out a breathy chuckle and opened the door. "I've fucked much worse," was all she said.

I released an anxious breath I had been holding in and made sure the book was in my pocket before following her out the door. I only made it a few steps before my senses hit me.

"The fire!—I'll meet you there, I need to put it out," I explained.

"Oh okay—" Rune replied behind me as I hastily made for the door. *Bile in my desk and now I'm leaving fires to spread.* I had been growing more and more forgetful the past few weeks. It was unlike me.

Inside my hut I grabbed a large wooden bowl of ashes and poured some over the fireplace, smothering the tiny remaining flames. I shook my head at my thoughtlessness and straightened out my tunic. She was dust. Dust that I simply needed to blow away from settling on my mind.

Only she wasn't dust. She was the person who marched out into a hellscape to save my niece—not to mention she did so accompanied by one of the most slippery people I had ever met. She was someone who made enduring this wasteland worthwhile, someone I looked forward to seeing every day. She was literally magic—and even with my title stripped from me, my witch's heart yearned for it.

Maybe it was the heat on my cheeks, but the air outside felt colder than usual. I didn't put up my hood for it was such a short walk to the planning tent. It buzzed with chatter as scouts talked over each other. I walked in and surveyed the room. There was no sign of Manden, but Twig was sitting in her usual stool, surrounded by a handful of his scouts perched at the round table, including Desjin and Dyrus. Rune stood to the side and leaned against a post. As I met her eyes she quickly found something else to focus on.

Twig motioned for me to join him at the table, and I took the open seat next to him as he waved the noise down in the room.

"Shut your teeth traps!" Twig shouted. "First order of business—Sora, congrats *again* on becoming a scout, my apologies for the next several moons of perimeter checks." Sora placed her chin in her palm as the tent filled with sympathetic laughter. I had spoken with Manden about keeping her on as a scout, and she only budged when Twig suggested Sora could be scheduled for routes close to home. I gave it a week before Sora fought for longer hunts.

"We're all glad you're safe and sound, not without thanks to Rune, our newest members, and Arrowette: who knew your inability to follow orders would save the day?" A few more laughs echoed around the tent as Arrowette stuck her tongue out at him and placed an arm over Sora's shoulder.

Twig continued, his tone growing serious. "Now, it has come to my attention that there is news from the North. Big news. Desjin and Dyrus are both from Skevsurvia. Ladies, Tell us what you know."

Desjin looked around the room as she spoke. "There is word of a possible war on the wind. War between the Alliance and the Kingdom of Aristus." The room went deadly quiet. "King Amos has refused to step down as King, and Skevsurvian spies have cause to believe he won't go peacefully. They think he's building up his army for the disunion."

A few scouts muttered under their breath about the captured Withins, and all I could see were the faces in that horse-drawn cage, being dragged to a fate more terrifying than The Colds. Desjin waited for the murmurs to settle before she continued.

"As of right now, that's all we know. Oh—and Skevsurvians are looking for um, what's his name again? Right—Kaineres the witch."

Everyone in the tent turned to look at me. The corners of my mouth twitched into a nervous grin. "Ex-witch," I said softly, staring at the knife marks in the table.

"Ex-witch, sorry." Desjin nodded. "They're taking people in and asking about the witch who killed—you know. Anyways, we don't know *why* though. Maybe it's in that book."

Twig cocked his head. "What book?"

I procured the leather spell book from my pocket and placed it on the table. "It's an ancient spell book that requires a spell to open it."

"Can you get it open?" Twig asked, staring intently at the dull mess of leather and paper in front of him.

I massaged the back of my neck. "I'm going to try. I need a scout's eye —maybe even a maker's eye to help."

Twig nodded and shifted his attention to the scouts. "Okay, after the meeting we can talk further. So—for the rest of you here now, conflict might be coming. We need a plan."

"No we do *not*."

Manden spoke sternly from the entrance to the tent, hands on her hips and eyes shooting killing shots between Twig's unkempt eyebrows. Twig grit his teeth prepared to fight.

"We can't keep having this conversation. Twig—you are going behind my back on this, and it's going to stop." Manden stood firm.

"I'm holding a very public meeting. I'd hardly call that treason."

Manden's face was twisted in anger. "We exist as a commune. Not a rebel plant."

"I'm trying to make a plan *for* the commune!" Twig's voice broke, but he rose to his feet. He held out his hand and pinched his fingers together. "Skevsurvian soldiers were *this* close to our camp. They *took* Sora. We're not a far journey from them, they'll be back."

Manden's lips curled into a small snarl, but she let Twig continue.

"If war does break out, we will be in their marching path. Fog or not. We need a plan."

The next few minutes were silent. Scouts looked anxiously back and forth between Twig and Manden until Sora broke the tension.

"Why won't the King of Aristus step down? Isn't fighting against all five other Realms a certain loss?" She tilted her head.

"There might not be anyone to take his place." It was Gwenna who spoke, seated across from me with her hands folded neatly in front of her. "The throne must be passed on to a blood heir. I don't believe he has any left. Even if the Alliance allows for an exception, it's likely Amos won't."

"The princess was his only heir?" Sora never lived in Aristus, and there was no reason to tell her until now about the tragedy that fell upon the Kingdom to the South.

"No," I said, feeling every set of eyes shift back to me. "She wasn't. But she was first in line. She would have taken the throne about five years ago." I brought my hands onto the table to rest on them as I spoke, needing some kind of barrier between me and the weight of the air around me. "On the night I was to become a mage, she died in an accident of my own making. I didn't know she was there—I didn't even know who she was, but that's not important right now. What followed in the years after that night only made that mistake all the more grave."

Gwenna, gods bless her, finished the retelling for me. "A lot of people thought it was an intentional attack. The rebel movement was forged that night and took it upon themselves to plan the downfall of the rest of the ruling class. Not without reason—King Amos and his leading nobles are known for being cruel to their lower-born subjects and unjust with their punishments. But some of the rebels were—and are—just as violent. They wanted blood for blood. About seven years ago, rebels snuck into the castle, and..." Gwenna's voice softened and she looked to Twig, who swallowed hard.

"Rebels trapped the remaining heirs of the bloodline and burnt them alive." He said quietly. "The oldest was not more than twelve."

Children. The remaining heirs were only children. It filled me with rage and added to the heaviness of the burden I carried. My tragic and terrible mistake was the first drop of rain in a storm that brought so many innocent casualties. I remembered the day the news finally made it to the commune. My knees buckled under the grief in my chest. There were still scratch marks on the wooden floor in my hut where my nails dug aimlessly at my own pain. Sora was only ten at the time. For moons I could not erase the image in my head of my niece's fear, staring down columns of fire with nowhere to escape. I still carried so much anger and nowhere to put it.

Sora gasped, and Desjin and Dyrus covered their mouths, eyes wide. Some of the scouts stared at the ground, likely part of the rebel movement at one point.

"They weren't all like that—the rebels," Gwenna added. "The majority just wanted peace, and a few twisted people made sinister decisions for the entire cause."

"And now the entire continent is going to run Aristus through because no one can take King Amos' place? How is that fair?" Arrowette huffed.

"It's not like he didn't have time." I was shocked to find Sanders sitting in the rear of the tent, having been quiet the entire meeting. They glanced around the room. "You know, to, 'produce' an heir. His advisors held these banquets and balls to find him another wife after the Queen passed. The news spread about town that he was too heartbroken to find a companion, but I don't believe it fully. I had friends in that particular business say his bed was always warm and that he confessed in secrecy that he never truly cared about the Queen to begin with."

A fleeting feeling of repulsion passed through me, but I ignored it. Small conversations broke out amongst the tent, and people chatted about the King, the threat of war, and what kind of devastation would erupt if all six Kingdoms engaged in battle. Manden cleared her throat.

"It is highly unlikely that all the other Realms will take the sword against Aristus. They could barely be bothered to lift a finger during the separation of Whelms." She thought for a moment. "We will make a plan for defending the camp. We will train everyone in it, not just the scouts, on defense methods. Kaineres will strengthen the sound barrier and Celeste will ensure everyone is armed with what they're comfortable using." She put her hand on my shoulder and leaned over me to examine the book. "Kaineres, you do what you must to open that book and find out why they're looking for you. Then I need you to get busy restocking all of our necessary supplies."

She faced Twig and enunciated her words carefully, as if speaking to a child. "Twig. Can I trust you to ready your scouts for *defending* the commune?"

Twig dipped his head. "Yes ma'am."

Manden narrowed her eyes at her head scout before jerking her head towards the tent door. "Sanders, come with me. We need to relay this information to Celeste and her crew." Sanders shot up and hastily followed after her, shooting an anxious gap-toothed smile at Rune before they left. Rune had been stone-faced the entire meeting.

"Kaineres," Twig turned to me. "You said you need a scout's eye?"

I pushed the book towards him. "Do you know what kind of leather this is?"

He gave it a once-over and shrugged. "I just kill em'. I can't really tell them apart once they've been skinned and dried." He moved out of the way as Bandin leaned over and picked up the book, stroking the soft cover with the palm of his hand. He nodded in the direction of the maker's tent.

"Yeah, Celeste would know," Twig confirmed.

Not wanting to waste any more time I excused myself and made to leave the room, only stopping at the opening to invite Rune along with a subtle wave. She did a quick scan of the tent before following me and looked up at the ceiling as she passed through the scouts—probably to avoid Arrowette's cheeky grin. When she got to the threshold, I held the flap open for her but she reached for one of her knives and held it by the blade. As scouts started to chat, Rune stood up on her toes and bopped the handle of her knife onto the tent canvas above her. The vibration sent the droplets of water formed on the inside pooling onto Arrowette's head.

Rune smirked to herself as a slew of curses and laughter trailed after us. I couldn't help but grin myself, wondering how I ever kept sane before she arrived. The comic relief brought me out of old and taunting memories.

"Good eye," I said to her as we walked to the maker's tent. She flipped her blade around and fit it back into her leather holster.

"The calculations didn't need to be that precise. She has a big head." Her words were tainted with humor, but her face was solemn and cold. She was a rebel at one point. It was clear that the blood-stained mark on history caused by the violent radicals of their cause was not one she was proud of.

I knocked on the large wooden beam at the entrance of the maker's tent. Manden and Sanders were already inside, along with Celeste and a few of her crew members. Celeste waved at us to come further into the room. A metallic scent hung in the air along with strong notes of musk and wood.

"Manden just gave us the news. Give me word of what you need and I'll see to it that it's made." Celeste assured me. I dipped my head in appreciation.

"I was actually hoping you'd be able to identify *how* something was made." I handed her the spell book. She tried opening the pages like I had done, and turned it over and over in her hands, feeling the spine and cover.

"Do you recognize what kind of leather they used?" I asked.

"It's not horse. Or any large livestock." She said with one finger placed in between her teeth in thought. "Look at the grain, the pores. The hide is very delicate. For the age it most likely is I'm surprised it has kept its shape." Her eyebrows furrowed together in concentration. "I think they made this with rabbit hide but removed the fur during the tanning process. Extremely delicate skin. What is the significance of knowing the animal?"

I accepted the book back from her and silently thanked my gods that the animal we needed wasn't extinct. "In order to open it, you first *use* it to cast a spell. It releases the magic used to bind it shut, freeing the pages to be turned. If I'm right, I only need to do this once. It should remember the hand that cast it. The spell is likely of a revivement nature, although to what extent I'm not certain. We discern and obtain the kind of animal used to make it—in this case, a rabbit, and use the spell stored in the book to revive one we find."

"How *dead* should it be?" Rune asked. "Can we take a carcass from the kitchen, or does it need to be freshly dead?"

"It will regain life and breath, so if we want to achieve this task humanely, it should be 'fresh'. It should still have the body that can sustain life."

"I'll see to it someone brings you a hare from the next hunt," Manden announced as she exited the tent, squeezing Celeste's arm as she passed. After thanking Celeste for her insight, Rune and I left the maker's tent and headed back toward our side of the camp.

I stopped short of the medicinal tent. "Rune…"

I waited for her to turn around.

"Yes?" She sniffed from the cold, her nose painted red from the chill.

"I can say the incantation, but I'd like you to try casting the spell—for the book."

She bit the inside of her cheek. "I wouldn't know what to do."

"I'll show you. Tomorrow, we can practice during your next lesson, if you're up for it. I promise I'll go easy on the history and focus more on application."

She gave a halfhearted smile in return but nodded her agreement. I knew she was uneasy about using magic. I wasn't sure if it would discourage her completely if I told her I felt the same way most days. That some magic still felt too wild to wield, too strong to force into the parameters of what I thought was possible.

Inside, I spent too many hours cleaning out the dried bile from my desk, only stopping to join dinner when I was satisfied with the result. The history brought up at the meeting left me uneasy and unusually bitter, so I ate quickly and returned to my hut to find a distraction.

Back in my chambers, I turned my attention to the spell book and what we needed to do. As I worked out a plan in my head, I cleaned up the sheets of paper drying on the desk. They were thicker than I would have liked, and writing on them would undoubtedly be a pain to manage. I held them for a minute wondering if I should start all over, scrap them, and reform them again. After ten years, I still hadn't perfected making paper like I was used to writing on at home in Aristus but I had always hoped that one day I'd catch on. I sighed and rested the messy stack back on the table. I'd fit them into my logbooks in the morning. At the moment what I desperately needed was a lit fire.

I leaned out of the window to grab the shutters but paused before I pulled them shut for the night. Above me, the clouds had parted to reveal a rare sliver of sky. The clouds only ever parted at night, but even then it happened so infrequently. An almost full moon beamed down on me, and I rested my arms on the sill to watch the night. I wondered what my gods thought of me. What they knew.

Out of the corner of my eye, I caught sight of the spell book where it rested on the table. My eyes blinked repeatedly at the newly formed words that appeared on the cover, barely visible in the moonlight. Fearing the clouds would submerge the sky again, I grabbed it and held it out into the air, my eyes straining to make out what was written. It was another language, but one I once knew. Crudely cramming together broken memories, I fumbled through a translation. It wasn't word for word in the common tongue, but it would do. There were instructions written into the binding after all.

I opened a cabinet under my desk and pulled out a small vile of ink and a quill. I scratched out the inscription onto one of the papers I made and cringed at the effect the rough surface had on my penmanship. It was better than nothing, and I couldn't trust my mind to remember things. I looked back up at the clouds making their way back over the face of the moon, dimming the light to a small blur. I bowed my head to the sky, an ember of hope sparking in my chest that my gods had the smallest ember of hope in me. *One day I will make it right*, I vowed, closing the shutters to allow the soothing darkness to engulf the room and cocoon me in its promise of rest before a new day.

One day I will make it right.

Chapter Sixteen

Rune

Kaineres and I walked through the fog, gathering small herbs and mushrooms we found along the ground.

"What does the sound barrier cover?" I asked. After a particularly rowdy discussion between some of the scouting members the night before, I couldn't help but wonder if the noise attracted nearby creatures.

The witch grunted as he yanked a large root from the ground and shook off the dirt. "It works in tandem with the fog that borders the camp," he said. "Fog and snow muffle sound naturally, so I draw on those principles and amplify them with magic."

"It works both ways, though?"

He nodded. "It's a risk that Twig and Manden were willing to take. I'd say it's become necessary, considering how wantonly boisterous everyone tends to be after a few poorly-fermented tonics."

"I like it. The noise. It feels less like..."

He offered me a smile. "Like living in the middle of nowhere?"

"I was going to say like living in exile. But yes, it also brightens the environment a bit." I knotted the top of my supply bag and attached it to my belt.

"You truly survived on your own out here for multiple years?" His large figure was shrouded in grey as the clouds filtered between us, but I could detect the sympathy in his voice.

I didn't realize how much time had passed until Sanders brought it up one night. The days passed quickly and slowly all at once.

"I wasn't always alone. There was time spent with other communes and partners in the past. Although one could argue that it took some additional effort surviving those interactions."

Kaineres placed another root into his bag and closed the top. "From what I heard, you and Sanders reconnected not long before we met."

"Not long at all. Had I known they were out here, I would have spent my days looking for them. But Sanders has a habit of showing up right when you need them, so we were sure to stumble upon each other eventually." I smiled to myself, remembering my friend's hay-covered head in the MistView barn. It was a fitting place to reunite, considering I first met them in their master's stable back in Flatkeep.

Noting each other's full bags, we changed course and headed back toward the camp. Kaineres would occasionally pick bark off of trees and put the pieces in his pockets.

There were so many questions I had for him. He was the first magician I didn't feel threatened by. After completing my scouting duties, I found myself offering my company to the healer more and more. Being with him felt like the most natural thing in the world.

"How did you make a finding spell? The one that led you to Manden and Sora?" I asked.

Kaineres readjusted the satchel on his shoulder and looked skyward to trace his memories. "When I was first banished, I was able to take a bag—this bag, in fact—with me. A dear friend of mine equipped it with any ingredient he knew I could craft spells with. Spells that would increase my chances of... not perishing within the first few months. Even with the supplies, I was woefully unprepared. I was hungry, wounded, and quickly running out of ingredients. I finally had the pivotal idea of crafting a finding spell. It would lead me to the thing I needed most. It drew on my desires, my state of being, my environment. A complicated ordeal that took about two moon cycles to put together. I had leeches attached to my arms for days at a time."

I shuddered at the imaginary suckling feeling that crawled along my skin.

"Ha—that's exactly how I felt. It worked though. I felt an internal pull. A strong pull that led me through the forest, through the fog—and directly into Manden's camp. The look on her face is one I'll never forget. I'm sure she feels likewise because my face was at the end of a spear." He chuckled, lifting a hanging vine out of the way for me to pass under. "I explained how I got there, and that I was a healer. M's ears perked up at that of course. But it wasn't until we swapped life stories that we knew we were family. The physical resemblance made sense then. I had no idea she existed, but she knew who our father was. She didn't seem to care that I was enemy number one of the entirety of Aristus."

"Well, it looks like you're famous in more than one Kingdom." I reminded him.

He looked up at the treetops and bit his lip. "Yes, I'm not sure what I did to deserve that honor. I suppose we'll find out later today, if the hunt goes well."

Back at the camp, we dropped off the supplies at the medicinal tent. The inside was spotless. Kaineres must have broadened his deep cleaning of the desk to include every corner and surface. Not that it was ever particularly dirty or disorganized. The witch seemed to have a place and purpose for everything.

His lesson this morning was just as orderly. A brief description of what I was to do followed by clear examples and instruction. He had provided two bowls of water, one hot and one cold. I was to transfer the heat from one bowl to another, practicing energy transfer. I amazed myself that I was able to do anything at all, although I ended up heating up both bowls, which was not the object of the lesson. Kaineres was impressed anyway and said he wasn't sure how to adjust the spell to account for my magical nature. I had never done any magic without scarring for it, so in my mind I accepted it as a success.

Despite the training, I still didn't feel ready to open the spell book, especially with the hourglass running. Kaineres already knew the spell and knew how to cast it. It felt like too much of a gamble for me to try and fail.

"Kain," I started.

"Kaineres." He said bluntly, but he looked down at his boots with an expression I couldn't see.

"I'm sorry—I didn't mean—" I don't know what compelled me to be so informal. He had just become so much easier to talk with.

He cleared his throat as if clearing away the moment in time. "It's quite alright. I'm fond of the name, genuinely, but it's not one I deserve." He offered me a weak smile, his eyes heavy with the weight of his sentence.

I had heard of people who, along with their banishment, were stripped of their name. Sometimes it was out of respect of who they used to be, and a new name kept people from speaking poorly of the person they used to know. Other times it was a matter of dishonor, taking every last thing a person had, including their name. I had a feeling in the witch's case it would probably be the former reason, but it didn't make it any less hurtful.

I debated whether or not I should tiptoe on ice I couldn't see the thickness of, but I let curiosity win.

"How did it happen—the accident?" I asked hesitantly. It was confirmed at the meeting but he was obviously not a revolutionary. It didn't make any sense as to why he would be able to get close to the princess in the first place.

He ran a hand through his hair and leaned back against the workbench. I took a seat on the desk in front of him, taking care to not squish the bags.

"To be honest with you I'm not entirely sure." He started rolling back his sleeves, exposing the tattoos on his thick forearms. I made a conscious effort to not stare at them, cursing myself for remembering how they felt wrapped around me.

"Every year,'" he proceeded, "there is a ceremony granted to some of the guilds in the upper city to congratulate a select few becoming mages. On the night I was to advance, I performed in front of the King and his nobles in the royal courtyard. It's frankly just a night of entertainment for nobility, but the guilds still view it as a chance to honor their most learned students. My attitude towards the event has always been—like the event itself—complicated." He lifted an eyebrow in thought while tracing over his markings.

"Anyway. I performed a spell of my own creation. It was risky, but I had been practicing for months. Maybe it wasn't enough time."

"You can create your own spell?" I asked.

"Anyone can. Spells, Potions, Sigils... Most people don't because, like I said, in doing so you take certain risks. Although it's rare to create a spell that hasn't been done before—magic has been around for ages. The very world was crafted with it. Most magicians are just relearning knowledge that was lost. The spell I made was what led to my advancement. My mentor saw what I had done, and went immediately to the King to request my placement in the ceremony. I doubt the nobles knew what they were looking at, if they couldn't feel it." He made slow, swooping gestures with his arms.

"I was able to harness all the power and energy of an entire space. Every magical trait held within an item or surface or person, I could hold it contained, bound by my mind and body. It looked beautiful, to be sure, but it was dangerous, and had the potential to change the way the upper city saw magic. I performed it publically just like I had practiced in private..." He drifted off and dropped his hands. After a few seconds, his mouth curved into a somber half-smile.

"I didn't know who she was." He shook his head. "I mean, I knew her, but I didn't know she was *her*."

My eyes narrowed as his words started to make sense only to him. "Who? The princess?"

He covered his face with his hands. "She was the *princess!*" He mumbled, dragging his fingers down his cheeks. "I had seen her before, in the city—even in the forest where I practiced. I never spoke to her, but I wanted to. I had no idea she was the King's daughter. There was a place set for her at the ceremony, but she didn't show up until I was in the midst of casting the spell. I saw her, lost my concentration, and..." His throat bobbed.

"That's all I remember. I've put pieces back together over the years, but nothing that really explained how it all went wrong. I remember coming to on the stone floor of the courtyard with soldiers gathered around me, I remember my mentor pleading for my banishment—as a replacement punishment for being executed right then and there. I remember my friend sneaking me the bag of equipment and trying to explain what happened. But all of it's fuzzy and all of it makes me physically sick. Especially knowing what it led to. I can't help but feel such guilt for all of it."

"But you had no way of knowing what would have happened—it was obviously an accident! You should have had a trial." My anger burned under my cheeks at seeing him this disheveled.

His hands massaged the memories from his creased temples. "I should be grateful I'm alive at all. My mentor had the merit and weight in the court to give me my life, at least. But I was stripped of my title as a witch, and I was never to take his name."

I wasn't sure what significance that held, but by the look in his eyes it meant something to Kaineres. I reached out and took his hand. "You don't deserve to be out here. You're not a murderer," I said softly. "I know people who do deserve this. And I know people who kill with intention. And you are not one of those people." I swallowed down the bile that had crept its way up my throat. I knew all too well the shame of a mistake you could never undo.

I suddenly felt the heat of his hand in mine. His thumb brushed over my fingers and the hair on the back of my arms stood up.

His voice was quiet, but heartfelt. "Thank you, Rune."

"I'll call you whatever you'd like me to call you, but I'd gladly speak good of both Kain and Kaineres." I met his russet and green eyes, glistening and framed with red. Blood surged up my cheeks and heat started to pool in my center as the distance between us closed. His dark lashline blinked away tears and revealed a steady intensity that sent ripples through my chest. His stare burrowed through me his focus wained from my eyes to my cheeks to my lips...

Suddenly feeling all too sentimental, I gave his hand a firm squeeze and hopped off the table, looking around for anything to do. Out of the corners of my vision, I saw him smile and rub his hand. He stood up and started unpacking the bags with me, pulling out a booklet to write down his new inventory.

"What did you think of the lesson earlier today?" He asked, the mood in his voice forcibly lighter.

"Oh, er. Listen, I know for some twisted reason you'd like me to do the spell, but..."

"Twisted?" He laughed. "You just said you could tell I don't have murderous intentions."

"Yes, I said you weren't a murderer. You could still be a sadist." I jabbed. "Anyway, I appreciate the misplaced confidence but I really don't think I'm—"

"—Ready?" It was Manden who interjected. She stuck her head into the tent and held up a bundled blanket, spotted with deep red. The rabbit.

Kaineres took the bundle from her and turned to me. "The sooner we can begin the better. I'll put my sadistic urges aside for the greater good." He balanced the rabbit in one arm to reach for his cloak, but I grabbed it off the hook on the wall and draped it over his shoulders for him. He bowed his head and stepped outside, holding the tent flap open for me with his back.

"The two of you make quite a lovely pair."

I didn't realize Manden was still outside.

Kaineres cocked his head and forced a smile. "What can I assist you with, M?"

"What are the chances whatever you intend to do goes poorly? Do you need extra hands? Or space?" She looked around the campsite as if imagining little fires spread everywhere and deciding which area would be the easiest to repair.

Kaineres walked past her and bumped her shoulder. "The camp will be fine, everything will be contained." He waited until we were a few paces away before lowering his voice to me. "But let's walk out a fair distance just in case."

We set up on the north side of the camp, where we could avoid people walking to and from the kitchen and scout tents. The fog played along the borderline of the camp next to me, acting almost like a wall to the outside. In front of me, Kaineres had placed the bundled-up rabbit and the book, patting the ground flat beforehand.

"What do you make of this?" Out of his pocket he withdrew a very thick piece of paper. I took it from him and tilted my head in question.

He lightly traced the cover of the spell book with his finger. "It bears an inscription, but the words are only visible under moonlight."

"How efficiently necessary."

"Yes, it's typical of older works to have an extra challenge thrown in. On the back of the page is the original, the one you're looking at is the common tongue. I had to translate it from another language, and I reworked the words a bit so it follows a similar rhythm."

"Which language do you have to say it in? If you need to say words at all." I questioned while looking at what Kaineres had written. Fortunately, I was able to read every line, recalling all of the reading lessons my mother made me sit in on with some of the more learned servants. They had taken discarded children's books and taught themselves how to read, passing down their knowledge at my mother's consistent pleading. There was once an age when I enjoyed spending time in a book, but as I grew, finding the time for it didn't seem worth the effort.

Kaineres rubbed his hands together for warmth. "It depends on the spell. Some should only be said in the language in which they were written and written *for*. Sometimes the power is present in the meaning, in which case the language you're familiar with is favorable because it's the one you know how to *feel* with. I've read over the words a great deal, and I speculate that this might be a meaning-driven incantation. I've also theorized that the rest of the book will appear written in the language it was opened with. At least, that's what I would do if I was creating a magical spell book."

"Well, we can only hope the ancient spell masters were as generous and foreseeing as the great Kaineres."

"You think I'm great?" His brazen smile was surprisingly white, considering he was so full of shit. I rolled my eyes in disapproval but couldn't stop the smile from spreading on my own face, gods damn him.

"I thought you said time was crucial." I barked at him.

Still wearing a smirk, he shifted himself onto his knees and took a few deep breaths. "Read it for me, if you don't mind?" He asked. "If I'm performing the spell, you can act as my scribe for the day."

"I think I'd rather be drained dry for my magic," I mumbled under my breath. His eyebrow shot up but before he could say something I cleared my throat and read the text.

"Vessel to fill, Quickest before you still,

Eternal moonlight guide you, New earth hide you,

Force that binds, Breath that finds,

Creature that lies, Creation you rise."

Kaineres closed his eyes for a moment, working the spell silently in his mind. Then he rolled up his sleeves and started to dig.

He didn't use a shovel or a rock, but his bare hands. His fingers scraped back the dirt and kept working downwards, the veins over his wrists and forearms bulging with each handful of dirt removed. His cloak slipped to the side, revealing a thick neck starting to glisten with sweat. Once the hole was large and deep enough to fit the rabbit's body I shook away my distraction and uncovered the rabbit from the tarp. I held it out to him, its fragile body already starting to stiffen. Kaineres took it gently, whispering the words of the spell.

"Vessel to fill, quickest before you still."

He placed the rabbit in the ground and looked up to the clouds.

"Eternal moonlight guide you."

He stood, inhaled long and slow, and with a forceful exhale, shot his hands up to the sky. The clouds directly above us swirled around and around, as if a gust of wind had driven them away. My hair whipped around my face as the gust kept coming, directing the remaining clouds up, up, up, until finally the night air poked through a hole in the grey cover. I didn't hide my awed expression as I saw the sky for the first time in a long time, the moon bright and full, beaming down on our small exposed patch of the world.

The witch collected his breath and sat back down, shaking his head at the energy the display took from him. I said nothing as I watched him work, seeing magic in a way I never had before.

"New earth hide you." He covered the rabbit with the top layers of dirt around us until it was fully enveloped in the ground. He dusted his hands together to shake off the excess and picked up the book.

"Force that binds," his hand stroked the spine of the book, and then the small mound where the rabbit lay, "breath that finds."

He rested the book on top of the mound and retreated his hands to rest on his lap.

"Creature that lies, creation you rise."

I waited for a moment, listening, but there was no indication that anything happened. No noise, no movement, no weird glowing.

Then, the book fell over. The wind had died down, and the ground was relatively flat, but the book slid down the mound of earth and lay there. Maybe that was it? Kaineres and I exchanged a glance, questioning each other on what to do next. Maybe it wasn't intended to revive the animal after all? Or maybe it was stuck? There wasn't much Kaineres did for the 'breath that finds' part. I leaned in. The witch hummed to himself, but did nothing to stop me as I blew a puff of air onto the buried corpse.

My hands hovered over the pile of dirt while I debated whether or not to help dig it out. Rabbits dig, right? Maybe that's why the spell called for a rodent? I wondered if it would know to claw its way out if somehow it did resurrect. My answer came and I withdrew my hands, still sitting forward to watch the dirt start to wiggle. Little paws poked out, pushing away clumps of earth with thin white claws. *Strange.*

"Were its claws that long when we put it in?" I asked, mostly to confirm that Kaineres saw them too and it wasn't a trick of the moonlight. He slowly furrowed his brows and tilted his head. As soon as the rabbit found its footing outside the hole, it quickly squirmed the rest of its body out. It breathed violently, its small ribcage expanding and contracting, shaking loose any dirt still clinging to its fur. What was left of its fur. The soft brown pelt started to shed along with the dirt, revealing pale skin that speckled. Speckled like a river trout.

"It certainly didn't have scales," Kaineres whispered, eyes widening at the ghostly vermin shaking in front of us, scaly and gripping the dirt with its cat-like nails. It sat there, almost buzzing, its beady red eyes looking at everything and nothing at the same time.

"Well now what do we do wi—" I was cut off as it darted for my leg, sinking its still-rodent-like teeth into my thigh before I could move. "Gods of the wick!" I cursed at it, yanking it out of instinct and tossing it aside. The creature hit the ground with a small thud and then sprinted away into the fog.

Kaineres had jumped next to me, his hand on my thigh to check the bite. Immediately my thoughts flooded with how large his hands were, how good the firm pressure on my legs felt. But I pushed all the swarming thoughts of his hands on my bare skin aside to focus on what the hell we just accomplished. "It's fine. Its teeth were small, so it barely went through the material." I nudged him aside as I checked the damage on my pant legs.

"I've never seen a rabbit attack." He muttered, utterly bewildered. He stood and helped me up.

"That thing is not a rabbit."

We stood and looked into the fog for a moment, both reflecting on the creature we just released—*created*—and released into the forest. I must have contorted my face because the witch tilted his head at me.

"What is it?"

I rested the palms of my hands on my blade handles. "I'm not sure whether I want to tell people about this or let it be a surprise for Twig to stumble upon on the next hunt."

Kaineres let out an exasperated chuckle. "Twig could probably use a change of pace out here. I'm sure he'd appreciate bragging about discovering a new species of monster." He laughed again, and I touched his arm.

"A new species of monster." That's what we did. We created a new species of monster. Kaineres looked at me like he had the same thought, his mouth suddenly a thin line. He walked over to the book on the ground near the loose pile of dirt.

"Let's see if this was all for naught." He picked it up, and gently ran his hands over the cover before pulling it open. It obeyed, and his fingers thumbed through the thin yellowed pages. I heard a sigh of relief and walked over to look at the ancient book.

"There wouldn't happen to be instructions to, I don't know, raise creatures of the realms of hell to this earthly plane, would there?" I said over his arm.

He snorted air through his nose. "Well that might explain the influx of monsters lately. Won't Manden be thrilled." He closed the book, keeping a finger in between the pages just in case it didn't reopen. "Skevsurvians might be getting creative in their added defenses."

"But what does that mean for you?"

"I'm not sure. I doubt they want my expertise in creating said monsters, because other than tonight I have no experience with such matters and I'd prefer to never have to do it again." He shuddered. We both left the pile of dirt where it was and went to inform Manden. Even though there wasn't much to be done about it, she'd at least like to know where the monsters were coming from. She'd find a way to get a leg up on the situation somehow.

"Well, well, well," Kaineres hummed. He had opened the book again and was scanning the pages as we walked. "It looks like the ancient spell masters were indeed as, what did you say, generous and foreseeing as I, the great Kaineres?" He held open a page, and I read the words *Cunningly Curated, Enchantments for Order of Disorderly Manners*, in the common tongue. Whatever the hell those words meant.

"Is that a direct translation?" I asked skeptically. The witch found the words I was reading and laughed to himself.

"I strongly doubt it. But even more impressive that the meaning has retained form while the phrases have been reworded so elegantly. A nice touch." He brushed his fingers over the page with a new fondness. "I've missed reading. Although this won't be much of a story, I'm actually looking forward to learning something new again.

"The Dead Queen's grave you two! What the hell was that?" Manden shouted as she stormed towards us. "You didn't tell me you were going to blast a beacon of clouds into the sky! Hope to your gods there aren't more soldiers prowling around."

Kaineres held out his hands in apology. "I doubt anyone could have seen it from outside camp. The fog's too thick." He gestured all around us.

Manden cursed under her breath and ran her hands through her hair. "Did you at least figure it out? Cook was hoping to have that hare back."

"Er..." Kaineres flashed an incredulous smile. "I don't think Cook wants it back now."

He explained everything to Manden as we retreated to the medicinal tent: the spell, the monster we *made*, and what it meant for the commune.

"Will it stop then?" Manden finally asked. "Can they make more monsters without the book?"

"Their mages likely have the spells or enchantments memorized. All we've done is inconvenienced them, and by we I mean Sora. I don't believe this means the end of new monsters."

Manden stopped near the entrance to the tent, chewing on the inside of her cheek in thought. "Well, at least we know where they're coming from. I'll talk to Twig about it."

"You're not going to mention the rabbit, are you?" I asked. Manden raised her eyebrow at me for a moment before understanding what I was asking. She belt out a laugh—hearty and dry.

"I knew you'd fit in here. A word of warning though—if he sees it odds are good he'll try and keep it as a pet."

I made a face and rubbed the spot on my leg where it sunk its teeth. Manden laughed again and strode away for the kitchens as Kaineres and I went back inside the tent. The witch left the spell book open on the table as he hung up his cloak. From his pocket, he drew a match and used it to light a lamp filled with some kind of oil.

"God's of the wick, eh?" He said over his shoulder. I found my usual seat on his workbench, grimacing at what I had shouted earlier. He continued. "I forgot, is that gods of brush fires, or..."

I sighed and adjusted my own cloak, trying to lift my butt off the table as the material caught around my neck from sitting on it. Kaineres stepped over and grabbed my waist, lifting me up in a fluid motion. I pulled the cloak loose and the witch set me back down and stepped back, waiting for my answer. I could feel my face flush, but I hoped that in ignoring it he would too.

"They're the 'gods of candles lit' formally, if they deserve any formalities at all."

He leaned back on his desk and raised his eyebrows. "Well. That's a very nonchalant attitude towards the deities of your birth."

"And I suppose I have so much I owe to them," I said flatly.

He crossed his arms across, looking around the ceiling of the tent. "Now let's see... gods of candles lit, that's a rare alignment, isn't it? Born on a moonless night?" He smiled wryly as he spoke, the nerve of him.

"Still-born. Or they thought I was. And Mother lit a candle to guide me to the gods of death since there was no moonlight, but I woke up."

"You woke up." He enunciated each word, sounding very much like his sister. "Sounds to me like you were chosen by the gods."

I scoffed. "All that superstitious bullshit to then only belong to messenger gods."

"And what's wrong with that?"

"Why belong to deities at all? They can't do anything except delay death for sleeping babies."

"I'd say messenger gods are some of the most influential."

I bit my cheek and looked at the ground. "Not in my experience."

His gaze softened. "You know, we were born on opposite cycles of the moon."

I lifted an eyebrow but stayed intently focused on the floor.

"I was born under a full moon, not a cloud in sight," he continued. "Talk about superstitions. My mother was *convinced* I was going to be a Within, especially given my fascination with magic. My father was a mage's scribe, so he would have been thrilled either way."

"Do you believe all that stuff?" I asked. "That gods really care about people in their charge?"

He held his chin in his hand for a moment, the small wrinkles near the edge of his eyes twitching as he narrowed his gaze.

"I do. I've seen too much of the world to think otherwise."

I swallowed. "You've seen too much of your world to think otherwise."

"Maybe that's true," he hummed low and thoughtful. "But regardless of which gods people belong to, I believe that it's up to each person to define themselves. I get to decide who I want to be, and that shouldn't be dependent on what divine hand guides me. I will also be the first to say that my life has been far more influenced by messages than by moonlight. Although that book certainly pulls on the rankings."

He dipped his hands in a basin of water on the floor and cleaned off the rest of the dirt still caked under his fingernails. My eyes wandered around the tent and landed on the spell book's open page. Under the strange heading I saw earlier, different enchantments were written out along with their ingredients. A sleeping spell, a mirroring spell, a stiffening spell, and an enchantment that removed the sound from a person's voice. Each spell had the potential to be quite unsettling, depending on what the author considered *disorderly manners*.

Twig's muffled voice came from the outside of the tent. It sounded like he was calling for some of the other scouts.

"Shit. I'm on duty." I hopped off the table and exited the tent, saying over my shoulder, "Good luck with the book." I thought I heard a 'thank you' in reply, but I kept marching towards the barracks. The book was open now, and the witch would surely dive into it straight away to find out what it had to do with him.

As I started my perimeter check, my eyes surveyed the mound of dirt and scattered claw marks in the earth. I wondered where in the pecking order a mutated hare would fall in a world of wolves and snakes. I massaged the mark where the rabbit bit me and hoped that there weren't even more threatening creatures being created—monsters that attacked just to attack and leave their victims half-melted into the ground. I knew where we fell in that pecking order and wanted to stay far away from it.

CHAPTER SEVENTEEN

Kaineres

For weeks I combed through the spell book cover to cover seeking anything that tied me to the Kingdom of Skevsurvia. Any moment I could afford some privacy, I read line after line of knowledge I at one point in my life already possessed. The refresher of information was beneficial, and to have it written down and at my fingertips was nothing short of divine providence, but based on the contents there was no reason I held any significance to the mage.

Tonight I was back in my hut, sitting cross-legged in front of the crackling fire. I had spent the earlier part of the day restocking ingredients and planning out potions to make ready for future use. The book pressed on the back of my mind the entire day, poking my thoughts out of the way, fighting for center focus. I gave in after dinner and went straight to reading it through for the fourth time.

It didn't make sense to me. I thought for certain there would be long-lost knowledge written here, and while some of the spells' contexts were archaic at worst, most of the information kept here was commonly taught at magical guilds or academies. Why make it so difficult to open the book itself? Perhaps the Skevsurvians weren't making monsters at all—there wasn't a spell, story, or ingredient related to them.

I rubbed my eyes as the subtle threat of a headache presented itself—pressure blooming behind my forehead. I flipped through pages of spells for tightening and charms for luck, glamours for trickery and trances for focus. A *Charm and a Half for Buttering Someone Up, Potion of Sightlessness and the Antidote for the Reverse...*

A *Turn of Phrase of Findings.* Odd. A spell I had already seen on the second page. This kind of book didn't cater to many mistakes or misprints. *Wait a minute...* I flipped through the pages again to another mention of the same spell. This couldn't be a mistake. I placed a leaf in between each mention of the findings spell and took turns studying the differences between each of them. They were all written the same way, but were under different headings and on different spots on their pages. The last one was the first spell mentioned on its page, the first one was second, the middle—third. I shook my head at the thought that the order meant anything. But I wanted to at least see.

There it was again, that pull. A whim of something only part of me wanted to do. *This is mad.*

I sat there for a moment with my face twisted in silent argument with myself. *It won't hurt to try.* And no one was around to see how foolish I'd look. I sighed and prepared my fingers on the edge of the paper. I turned in the order they appeared on their respective pages. The last one, the first one, and finally the middle, sitting right in the center binding of the book. I squinted my eye at the pages as absolutely nothing changed. There. A waste of excitement.

Another urge—to close the book. I might lose my access to the pages entirely. With most of my time spent stocking supplies, there was no time to open the book again with the revival—er—*recreation* spell. And even if I could convince myself there was, I was morally shaken from what I did to the first poor rodent to do it again. Still, I felt my fingers move to the cover and slowly turn it over, shutting the soft delicate leather over the yellow body. *Hells Ascend. I could ring my own bloody neck for that.*

I took a deep breath. I would make Rune do it. The opening spell. I knew she could. I would give her access to moonlight and she could do the rest. My fingers found the leaf that marked the last enchantment and pulled it open.

"Thank the gods," I muttered under my breath. The book remembered. Without thinking, I found the leaf marking the first enchantment and opened it. "Here we go again, I guess." Lastly, the middle page. The book fell open and flat across the ground from years and years of age and use. I removed my hands and stared in disbelief at the words I was expecting, but no longer saw. In their place, new words had formed—a different text.

I bit the end of my cheek to keep from smiling as I read on. Magic. Tucked away in a subtle pattern was a new list of instructions for new ancient spells hidden from common-place and silent for years and years. I read on.

Not spells. The corners of my smile dropped. My breath caught in my chest and my gaze hovered over the little black ink markings before me.

At once the distance between where I sat in front of my fireplace and the shallow icy footprints of monsters past disappeared, and there I was in the middle of The Colds. Frigid air coated the inside of my mouth and neck and froze the blood that pumped in my veins. Wind howled around me, swirling into my ears and breaking down every wall and catalog I kept in my head. My lungs were stuck in an endless exhale. Pouring out, out, until there was nothing left of me to give but a shadow of what a breath might have looked like if it could take form.

The fire crackled, jarring me and bringing me back into my hut. I still felt the chill of the floor from my legs and saw the shadow of the words looming in front of me, staring back at me from the page. This ancient magic recorded here was no enchantment, nor potion nor spell, but a curse. A curse I had only thought of for fleeting moments before deeming it desperate or impossible.

A curse. A *Curse of Binding.*

The headache was in full force now as pain reverberated inside my skull with each pounding echo of my heartbeat. I placed a hand on my chest to steady my breathing as I read on. "A deep and powerful magic... A trickery of space and time... Caused by a spell that harvests energy from another life constructed by a derelict hand... leading to the spell turning in on itself into a curse. A curse of binding..." I gulped, beads of sweat now fully formed on my brow. "...Binding the two energies together into one."

I never had a derelict *hand.*

My fingers moved from my chest to my temple, rubbing the sides of my face in an ill attempt to soothe the storm clouds in my mind. *I practiced for months. I never pulled energy from a living soul in that courtyard*—Unless the energy pattern was not one I would have recognized. Unless the compulsion that beckoned to me that night was not the pressure for more power, but the unwitting curiosity of a princess...

I buried my head in my hands and begged myself to remember anything. Anything at all that felt like my true memory, not a replica of a thought that was clouded by... *hers?* Did I really trap someone's soul in mine all these years? Was that what this even meant? Repulsion bubbled in my core. I felt sick. I skimmed the rest of the page, which only led to another brutal wave of nausea.

I stood up too quickly, ignoring the cracking my back and knees made from sitting too long. I needed fresh air. I needed to think. Or not think. *Wouldn't that be a dream.*

A dream. All those dreams, all those nightmares...

I didn't bother to grab my cloak. Let the bitter air calm me down. The walk to the bathing chambers was a blur of boots crunching and breezes nipping at my face and neck. Each pointed end of the overhanging tree branches felt like thin pointing fingers, nodding along with the wind with their prescient knowledge of who I was and what I'd done. *We knew the whole time*, they seemed to say.

Inside the chambers, I closed the door behind me and lit some of the scattered candles for light. The basin had already been filled with water so I stripped, set my clothes to the side, and stepped into the bath. The initial temperature difference burned, but I sat for minutes not doing anything but feeling the heat of the water penetrate my skin. The candle wax melted and dripped slowly as time passed. I thought about the horror of being a wick stuck deep inside a candle, a string unseen and therefore forgotten, trapped in layers of fat and oil.

I stared at the surface of the water, at the ripples created by the subtle movements in my chest while I breathed. The bathing chambers used to be the best place to clear my head, but now my mind felt as cloudy as the water I was sitting in. The markings on the wall flicked back and forth in the firelight, the etched gods almost dancing around me. One of the scouts had carved the images years ago, just like they had carved some of the embellishments in the dining hall. They were the first person I couldn't save.

The ingredients I had brought with me in my leather satchel had finally run out, and I was still getting used to making do with the plants I found around the camp. No potion was strong enough for their pain, no enchantment powerful enough to save their gaping wound. They died in the medicinal tent, the first of many. I still felt negligible, calling myself a healer. I didn't know what else to call myself. I wasn't a witch anymore, and I wasn't a fighter. Not a scout, not an artisan, not much more than a person who knows how to throw together a few ingredients and make a salve.

I let my body slip deeper into the water, the warmth of the bath holding me in an embrace I rarely felt. How was it possible, to hold another soul in my own body and not know it? Not that I would have noticed right away. Nothing made sense and my memory was as sliced and bruised as my reputation. But now...

My heartbeat was deafening as it pulsed through my ears. This might have explained the headaches, and the ghost soreness, and the nightmares. The memories? They're all mine, right? The guilt—for what I had done, for my mistake—was that mine? All this time was I carrying the emotions of someone I wasn't? Does that mean her soul is still reachable?

I groaned and tried to sink lower, but my foot slipped on the floor of the stone basin. My back slid down the side and my face plummeted underwater, not before hitting the back of my skull on the edge. I found my footing and my arms grabbed the side of the basin to raise my upper half back into the damp air. I flung my hair back out of my face and wiped my eyes clear. When my vision returned, I saw Rune, wide-eyed and at the door to the chamber, a crumbled-up rag and a bar of soap in her hand.

"Are you...alright?" She asked hesitantly. What might have been concern on her face was wiped away with a smirk. "Just going for a swim?"

I plastered on a smile as best I could but the edges of my lips quivered. "The water's lovely. Care to join me?"

She saw through it. "I didn't mean to interrupt." She turned, but I held up a hand to stop her.

"You're no bother at all. Guilds typically share a bath-house, so I'm used to people walking in and out when I'm trying to clean up. I'll hurry out so you're not waiting. I'll have all the sediment cleared, of course." I didn't know how long I had been wallowing in my own filth.

"No-no, it's okay. I don't mind waiting, you—you'll what?" Her eyebrows furrowed as she processed what I said.

"The basin, I'll clean it before I get out."

It wasn't scheduled for a cleaning just yet, but not want-ing her to literally sit in mucky waters of my own making, I reached my hands in front of me and then into the water, steering my focus on feeling everything in the water but the water itself. I said a spell that was refreshed in part from the spell book and lifted a cloud of sediment out of the water and into an empty bowl nearby.

Rune's face bore the same awed expression she wore when I had cleared the sky of fog the other day. In that moment it was all I could do but burst from the joy of seeing her excited by magic instead of wary of it. She quickly coughed her amazement away and assumed her typical stoic appearance.

"Magic has its charms." I winked, a fleeting feeling of childish pride swelling in my chest over the possibility of impressing the living statue in front of me.

"Charms. Clever." She placed her rag and soap on a ledge carved into the wall and turned for the door, stopping be-fore her hand touched the wooden frame. "Are you alright though?" She wasn't referring to the slip.

I ran my hands through my hair and wondered how much I should tell her. If I should tell anyone. Although if anyone understood the weight of impossible magic cours-ing through my very spirit, it would be her. "Meet me at the medicinal tent, when you've finished bathing. Please. There's something I want to ask you."

"Of course." She said quietly. With a nod of her head, she left the chamber to wait outside.

I got out of the basin, dried myself off with a spell, and then put my clothes back on, underneath the dancing shadows of carvings. I stared into the face of the goddess of the moon, her blank expression empty and whole, flickering and frozen, and realized I had felt like that for a long time.

Chapter Eighteen

Rune

I bathed quickly, barely tending to my hair afterward, which I regretted immediately after opening the door. My clothes were warm from resting on the heated shelf—the witch must have charmed it before he left because the effect on the shelf faded as soon as I had finished dressing. I bundled my cloak around me and made for the medicinal tent. I suspected Kaineres had found something in the book, based on his grim state. He seemed like he was taken captive by his own thoughts. He looked utterly grim.

I shook off the image of his pained face emerging from the surface of the water and took a deep breath before entering the tent. The healer sat at his desk, the ancient book closed in front of him with leaves sticking out of the sides. He had slicked his damp hair back, but a few rogue strands rested around his darkened eyes. He gestured to the workbench where I took my seat and leaned back on my arms, waiting for his question.

His breathing was slow and purposeful, like he was counting every breath. His eyes stared blankly forward, a glaze cast over his double pupils.

When he finally spoke, his tone was soft and unhurried. "If you did something terrible, but it was never your intention, and you're not certain how you even did it, what kind of responsibility would you hold yourself to? Would you do all you could to make it right?"

"I..." My fingers clenched the sides of the table as my face paled. "What do you mean?"

His few seconds of silence were enough to unnerve me, but I held my tongue down with my teeth until I drew blood, warmth flooding my mouth. Was he talking about the accident? His accident?

He continued. "For years I thought I had murdered the princess. That was the belief everyone held and thus what I was told."

I swallowed the blood in my mouth and relaxed my jaw. Kaineres pressed his eyes into the base of his palms.

"What if that's not true?" He mumbled. "Is there a fate worse than death?"

"Kaineres, what are you talking about? What did you find?" It was the book, I was certain, but the hair on the back of my neck rose and pricked my skin.

He sat back and looked at me, dark storm clouds swirling under his eyes. "There is an ancient curse. A binding curse. If a person tries to harvest life energy from another person, and there is too much force between them, the magic can transform into a curse, binding the two energies together. Intertwining their souls into one body."

"And... this is what happened to you?" I tried to piece together what he was implying. Two souls...

"I'm not sure, but the more I think about it, the more this cycles through my mind it—it makes sense."

"Were you trying to harvest, er, life energy that day?"

"No, of course not. I was delicate in keeping out of people's energy, that's what the difficult part of the spell was, not that anyone but a magician would notice." He was up on his feet now, pacing the small length of the tent. "But

I felt a pull, and I followed it, and my curiosity turned into disaster. No—not my curiosity...” An expression came and passed across his face, like wind whipping through a field and leaving it in stillness a moment later. Whatever it was, he shook his head clear of the thought. “I’m not sure what happened that night. But the book mentions a binding curse. That is what the Skevsurvians want with me. That’s why that mage had the book, I’m convinced of it.”

“Okay.” I paused, analyzing everything the witch told me, trying to catch up to where his mind was racing. “Let’s say you’re cursed. You’ve somehow *bound* the princess’s spirit to yours, and the Skevsurvians know this. Why would they want you?”

“I’ve been questioning that myself. It’s a very old and sinister curse. They probably want me held accountable for it.” He stopped pacing. “Or... or they think it can be undone and see to it the princess takes the throne. She’s the last heir, King Amos would have no choice but to step down.”

“*Can* it be undone?” Bringing back to life a person who had been dead for a decade seemed just as impossible as a soul being swallowed by another body.

“Here.” He picked the spell book up and turned to a page. There it was, spelled out in ink. A binding curse, followed by cautionary warnings and... a possible antidote. Or, at least wording that implied a counter-spell existed.

“Can you do this? Here?” Free himself from the princess? I busied myself by putting my hair up into a top knot to hide my concern. I imagined Kaineres, trying to split himself in two and my chest tightened. What was left of the princess anyway? Where does a soul go with no physical form?

“No. I wouldn’t try here, I have an idea of where to start, but I would want another professional’s opinion.” He chuckled sourly.

“So what are you going to do?”

"You never answered my question." He narrowed his eyes.

"Even if I did it wouldn't be up to me, would it?" I eyed him back.

"I value your opinion."

"Why?"

He opened his mouth to say something, but changed course and wiped the stray hairs out of his face. The witch massaged his jaw, tendons in his neck flexing and relaxing. I bit my lip again as he spoke.

"Knowing what I now know, I can't just stay here and ignore it. If there's a way to undo this, I have to try. I owe it to the Kingdom, I owe it to my guild, and I owe it to the princess."

"What about you? You were slapped with a life sentence for a crime you didn't commit."

"She's still gone because of me and I've been eating myself alive with guilt ever since. And her not being *dead* doesn't make things any better. But it does give me hope I haven't felt in a long time. Blood-curdling horror, and hope."

I thought about it for a moment. "You mentioned a professional opinion. You're not going to Skevsurvia, are you?" If he was set on it, then maybe I could go with him. Convince Sanders to come. We would make it out of The Colds after all.

"I don't know who I can trust there. No. I'd go back to Aristus. I'd find my old guild. I have a good friend—Marcus. He would know what to do, and he would help." He straightened himself and walked over to the tent entrance. "If I'm bound to the princess, there must be a way to reverse it—to free her spirit from mine. Curses are rarely permanent. If we can work through the potentially messy details of getting her body back, she could recover... resume her title, take over the throne, and the Alliance should be satisfied."

On his fingers, he counted out the points he made as he convinced himself. "That brings peace to an unsettled realm, and hopefully to her. It also will ease the tension in Skevsurvia. They'll stop creating more unnatural creatures and the commune will be safer for it. Thank you, Rune, for sitting with me in this."

I gulped down an uncomfortable mass of phlegm that had accumulated out of stress.

Kaineres nodded curtly to himself. "The more I think about this, the more it's clear that I have to make an effort to undo this. I'll go to Aristus, find Marcus, and repair the damage I caused. First, all we have to do is convince Manden." He said with a subtle smirk, which was quickly smacked off his face the second he opened the flap to the outside.

Manden, arms crossed and eyes cold tilted her head towards Kaineres. "You're not going to have much luck with that first step."

The healer groaned as he squeezed by her. "This camp gets smaller and smaller. How much of that did you hear?"

"Enough. And I'll tell you right now your plan is as well thought out as a bridle for a Reptiscis. What in hell makes you think you won't be killed the moment you step past the border wall? The majority of Aristus believes you dead anyway. You should keep it that way."

"M, I—"

"Don't 'M' me. You could be bound to the bloody sun gods, but if you think that leaving this camp will bring about anything but more death, you're not as smart as you look."

"This could prevent war from breaking out." Kaineres spoke just loud enough for the tents next to us to overhear. I hopped off the table and stood awkwardly at the entrance of the tent, eyes flickering between the two of them.

"So?" Manden threw her hands up, her oversized sleeves billowing around her forearms. "We have protective measures in place. We'll be ready. But not without a healer. You leave us, you risk more than just putting yourself in danger. You've lived here for ten years, can this truly not feel like home to you? Are you so desperate to leave your family?"

People had stopped what they were doing to listen, or did a poor job at pretending to busy themselves. Scouts came out of the barracks, cooks were poking heads out of the kitchen, even the subtle hum of Celeste's grinding stone had stopped. Twig walked over, hands out between Manden and Kaineres in an attempt to play political peacemaker.

"What's the ruckus for? And if there's going to be a fight I place my bets on Manden, sorry Kaineres." Twig chuckled, nervous laugh lines stretched across his freckled face.

The witch huffed. "There's no fight. I have no desire to run away, Manden, and that's the reason for going. I cannot in good conscience run from this. Someone is *trapped* in my soul and I can't just live like this forever. I don't wish to leave you, but I must make an effort to undo this."

Twig's gimmicky smile was replaced by a bewildered expression. "Someone is trapped in your *what*?"

Kaineres ran his hands through his hair. "The night I... *thought* I killed the princess, it turns out I put a curse on her instead. On us. I bound our souls together. That's what the Skevsurvians think—that's what is written in that spell book, a description of that curse. But there is possibility of a way to undo it and it might bring her back. It could restore her life."

Twig's bushy eyebrows lifted wrinkles into his forehead. "If she's back, she would replace Amos—that would stop the disunion before it began! She'd be a fresh start, a new ruler. This could change Aristus completely!" It was clear he was thinking aloud all the motivations of the abandoned rebellious movement.

"And it would leave us without a healer when we're already vulnerable with all the extra threats running wild." Manden's face was twisted in anger, but there was something soft and exposed in her eyes.

"He'll come back, won't you, Kaineres?" Twig's eyes were glistening and looking around at the camp, giving away the plan he was concocting in his head. "We'll be right for a few weeks. Think of it this way, when Kaineres gets his princess to take over the high seat, I bet high house favors for us won't be hard to come by, eh?"

Manden was red in the face. "Oh yes. *If* Kaineres makes it to the border and *if* the princess comes back to life and *if* she's made queen, I'm *very* certain her first rule of order will be to pardon a camp full of war criminals and thieves. Her people will praise her for that kindness."

Either Twig did not hear the sarcasm in her voice, or chose to ignore it.

"Yes, her people! Her true people and not just the noble shits that Amos caters to. She could be the solution we've waited for, but skipping the whole bloodshed part! A peaceful solution is right in the midst of our camp."

Manden crossed her arms across her chest and turned to Kaineres. "Who's to say she's going to be in a right state of mind when she's brought back? *If* she's brought back? Who's to say it's possible to undo this so-called curse anyway? Who's to say it won't *kill* you in the process?" She wiped something out of her eye as she continued to glare at the witch, who sighed with a heaviness growing on his face.

He pushed past Twig and wrapped his arms around Manden, who uncrossed her arms but stiffened in denial. Kaineres lowered his voice. "It's the right thing to do, M."

She cursed under her breath. "This is why I prefer criminals."

More of the scouts had moved closer from their sulking in the thresholds. They whispered back and forth, catching each other up on the conflict. Gwenna stepped forward and put her hand on Manden's shoulder as Kaineres withdrew.

"Manden, if it's true, and the princess is still alive, this might indeed be a step in the right direction for the whole of Aristus. She might have a kinder hand than her father, she might bring about some needed change, or at the very least settle the discomfort of the other Realms. Increased numbers or no, the commune just can't manage all the monsters at the rate they multiply."

Manden huffed and looked around. "She might be worse. She could be bitter about the last ten years, if she even remembers anything at all!"

Kaineres brought a hand to his chest. "Even so, if there's a way to unbind us, I can't just keep her prisoner forever. Living like this is madness. I... I have this feeling that she won't be like King Amos. I have reason to believe she has a kinder spirit. I think the people we care about have a good chance at a better future with her as ruler."

"So now it's your job then?" Manden's voice was firm but a lingering tension made it clear she knew she was losing the argument. "Why take on the burden of revolutionizing an entire Kingdom? Who made it your responsibility?"

"In a way, this is my responsibility." The healer's voice cracked, and something sputtered in my chest. "It's not a disaster I caused with intent, but my hand was still in it. I have the ability to change the course of what happens next—to aid the people I didn't know were suffering under my feet for years. I want to *better* things. For them, if nothing else. It was my responsibility the day I swore a witch's oath—to use my knowledge and strengths for the betterment of the Kingdom." He gestured to his chest. "Oh, and did I gloss over the theory that I might have a *soul* trapped inside of me?"

The raw emotion in his voice cut a cord inside my center, untethering some deep feeling of longing that had been trying to surface. I swallowed the rising heat, silently pleading for it to settle as I watched Manden search her thoughts for something else to say to get Kaineres to change his mind.

When she couldn't find anything, she clamped down on her refusal. "No."

"No?"

"No, I will not let you go. I will not let you abandon us." Her knuckles were white with contained rage. "I'm done with this conversation. I'm sorry for the predicament you're in, but it's too late to do anything about it now. If you leave us stranded I will never forgive you Kaineres. And this goes for everyone—" Manden swiftly turned to the gathered crowd and made her demand clear. "I don't give a shit if you have nobility strapped to your heartstrings or tendons or your liver. Consider abandoning post a death wish."

She bumped into Twig's shoulders as she removed herself from the scene, a warning not to broach the subject again. I was surprised there wasn't steam rising from her footprints as she carried her hot anger through the crowd. A few sympathetic expressions were exchanged, but the group quietly dispersed, leaving the healer alone in the middle of the pathway.

As Manden walked off, Kaineres' face remained twisted in resignation, clearly caught between the weight of the Kingdom that hated him and the family that needed him.

Chapter Nineteen

Rune

My nightmares consisted of Kaineres being ripped apart at the seams—his flesh melting off his bones and his muscles torn away from their tendons by an invisible force. His knees indented the dirt where he was hunched over, clutching his chest in agony. The witch's tortured eyes met mine white with fear, the emerald green hue almost glowing. He tried to call out for me but when he opened his mouth, all that escaped was a terrifying chorus of high-pitched screams.

The wind was as restless as I was. The tent fabric above my head rippled so violently that it snapped me into consciousness. I blinked open my eyes but could see nothing but darkness. Even the oil lamps kept outside the barracks had been blown out, submerging the entire camp in a tar-black night.

"*Dead Queen's unmentionables*, I can't sleep like this," Ivon muttered from his bunk. "It sounds like Twig is practicing his drumming on the ceiling."

Something hit the ground with a thud followed by boots scuffling across the floor.

"Where are you going?" Arrowette yawned.

"Somewhere with solid walls. I'd rather sleep in the dining hall than put up w—" Ivon's voice was cut short by another ferocious gust of wind that rattled the structural posts of the tent.

As the other scouts shuffled off of their mattresses to follow suit, I groggily pulled my boots out from under my bed. My eyelids were still heavy from the nightmares so I didn't bother messing with the laces. It would be a short walk to the dining hall.

I wrapped the blanket around my body and slowly trudged out of the tent, feeling my way around with my hands. As I stepped outside, I was immediately assaulted by another gust of wind that almost knocked me over. It was just as dark in the open air, and twice as cold. I bit my cheek and hurried in the direction of the giant tree.

The branches above me shook back and forth, scraping against the constructed rooms in the tree like cat claws on a wooden beam. Even inside the trunk, I doubted I would get any sleep.

Eventually, my vision could make out basic figures in the darkness, and I reached my hand out for the door handle to the dining hall. Solid wood punched into my knuckles as the door swung open.

"Oh! Rune—is that you?" Sora's voice barely met my ears before being swept away. "The older scouts beat us to it—there's no space left." She leaned into my ear as the wind picked up again. "I'm going up to Manden's room. Arrowette and Ivon are trying to sleep on one of the tables; there might be room to squeeze in with them." Sora disappeared to find one of the ladders and left me shivering near the door.

Trying to share a slab of wood with Arrowette sounded as warm as a blanket cut from ice. Sanders had been given lodging near the top of the tree, but as the currents in the air wove through the branches, I didn't trust my footing on the rope ladders that Sora had a lifetime of practice navigating. Instead, I made my way up the path towards the bathing chamber. The warming enchantment was subtle, but it would be much less miserable than back in the barracks.

The storms in The Colds were always merciless; a terrible beast in their own right, but something about this one made my pulse pound in my ears.

Before I could make it to the chamber, the howling of the wind increased in pitch, like the escaping steam from a teapot. My pace faltered as I realized the ringing in my ear wasn't just from the wind.

Another shrill cry broke through the barren canopy and reverberated around me—the hungry shriek of an animal who had just spotted its prey.

Warning bells rang out from the other side of the camp. Doors burst open as scouts jumped onto the scene. There was a monster somewhere nearby, but with no light to see it—

In the distance, someone called out frantically but the words were lost to the chaos of the storm churning overhead. I begged my eyes to adjust further to the absence of light, but I could see nothing but vague shapes fading in and out of view.

More screaming followed a screech so foul, it sent searing pain down the canal of my ears. My legs instinctively froze in place as a cold bead of sweat dripped down my back.

Scouts retreating from their perimeter duty were finally heard loud and clear.

"Aherrons!"

The frantic pounding of boots on gravel stopped abruptly as the commune became an open feeding ground for the massive predatory hunters circling overhead.

I willed my chest to breathe small breaths and I clutched my knuckles tight to keep from shivering against the painful chill of the air. The windstorm, however, made it increasingly difficult to keep still as it whipped my loose hair around my face and shoulders.

In the corner of my eye, a cluster of scouts huddled closely together with a large wooden plank over top of them, slowly inching toward the shelter of the dining hall. It was a risky and bold move, but standing out in the open felt just as vulnerable.

I grimaced as two talons emerged from a blur of shadow and pierced the shield like a hot knife in soft flesh. Arms reached out from the giant tree trunk and pulled the group into safety while the Aherron struggled with the makeshift shield. Screeching violently in frustration, the moth-winged beast shook off the broken slab and hurled toward the door.

I could see its silhouette clearer than I had ever been able to before. It was mostly a blur of silent wings and lethal claws, but its curved beak was almost serrated, with one long prong at the tip to better slice into flesh and tear it clean from bone.

After forcefully clawing at the thick surface of the door, the beast flew off impatiently moments later—but not before grazing someone's hand through a large crack.

Muffled cries from the injured scout were lost to the wind rushing past, almost pushing me back. I couldn't remain still for long. I needed to get out of the open but fear cemented my loose boots to the ground.

My attention was caught by an unnatural shiver of movement in the bushes at the edge of the campsite. As the Aherrons screeched excitedly from somewhere above the tree, a large slim figure emerged into my limited view.

The sinister sound of bones cracking tickled my ear. The long shadow slithered across the pathway, the ground hissing underneath its scaled belly.

Shit. I silently cursed myself for abandoning my blades underneath my bed. Not that I would have been able to wield them—the humming noise above me threatened to sink impossibly sharp talons into my neck.

I stood directly in the path of the Reptiscis, defenseless and unable to move. I was the perfect meal. Its wavering hiss sounded almost laugh-like, as if it knew it had me cornered. Its tail coiled behind itself, readying for an attack. I bit down hard on my cheek as I contemplated which monster would bestow the quicker death, and braced myself to run.

The reptile barreled toward me, but before it could clamp its wide fangless mouth around my skull, it smacked into an invisible barrier that sent it reeling backward.

"Rune!"

The healer's voice was right behind me, but when I swung my head around in surprise he wasn't there.

The Reptiscis collected itself and braced for another attack just as large hands wrapped themselves around my waist. The snake lunged again, but the invisible hold on me pulled me out of the way. Suddenly, I felt an arm wrap under my legs and I was lifted skyward.

"Hold tight—I've got you." A near-invisible Kaineres carried me away from the furious reptile and across the camp with long strides. I peered through his shoulder at the snake, now confused and angry.

Screeching grew louder and more frantic as one of the Aherrons closed in on its unsuspecting target. As quick as lightning flashing across the sky, open claws swooped down and pierced the soft underbelly of the Reptiscis, hauling away a large chunk of its body.

It recoiled from the blow, writhing on the dirt as another blur flashed overhead and clawed at the scales in the snake's back.

Kaineres' boots pounded into the gravel path, sending small rocks scattering as he raced us closer to his hut. One of the scout's tents was nothing but a torn tarp clinging to large pieces of broken bed frames.

I clung tight to the healer's broad shoulders as he shoved his back into the door of his hut, stumbling over the threshold with me still in his arms. We broke apart as his momentum hurdled us onto the bed and over the edge. A slew of curses shot through my teeth as my knees hit the floor. Kaineres was already up and closing the door behind us. There wasn't a fire lit, but the solid walls kept my body safe from the wind chill.

I crawled over to where the witch collapsed on the floor near the end of the bed frame, his body still eerily see-through. My chest pulled tight against my shirt as I heaved. My head still reeled from the fear of being cornered, knowing that if I had been alone, tonight would have been my last. Any words that could express how I felt died in my throat. I leaned against the witch, hoping he would know how grateful I was for his hasty rescue.

Outside the screams of the Aherrons cut through the storm, but no other sound of destruction was audible. Kaineres prayed quietly to the gods of the moon for protection over the rest of the commune. His voice was soft and earnest, and I couldn't help but feel a twinge of warmth in my stomach at his sincerity.

In silence, we waited for the long midnight hours to pass. Kaineres occasionally peered out of slats in the shutters to check for signs of anyone injured or stranded outside. I let the back of my head hit the edge of the wooden board as a shudder passed through my chest. Guilt started to weigh heavy on me for how senseless I had let myself become. The camp felt like an impenetrable haven when it was truly just a commune in the middle of the wasteland. Nothing was safe. No one fully out of danger.

I had never observed Aherrons near a camp of people. While it was uncertain whether or not they would return, it seemed unlikely that they would forget such a promising feeding ground. Depending on how much of the Reptiscis filled their stomachs, I figured it was only a matter of time until they threatened the commune again.

Deafening thunder shook debris loose from the thatch roof, coating my bare face in an itchy layer of dust. Before I could raise the sleeve of my arm to brush myself clean, soft hands gently caressed away the dirt from my cheeks. I couldn't see his face clearly, but I could feel the witch's gaze trained on me even in the dark.

No words were passed between us, but the shaking of his hands and the deep breaths he forced to a slow told me he was just as nervous and tired as I was.

I leaned into him, grounded by his solid frame and steady exhales. The warmth of our bodies seeped into each other, an invisible fire cradled between our ribs that braved the icy cold around us.

After the storm had settled, we were stirred alert by a knock at the door. Kaineres gently lifted my chin from his shoulder and I wiped the scar on my lips where saliva dripped from my mouth. The witch rose slowly, looking hesitant to open the door as if he wasn't sure who or what would be on the other side.

He did not breathe out a sigh of relief when he saw Manden's paled face, solemn and grim. He opened the door wide for her to enter, but she stood in the frame, a bundle of bloodied blankets in one of her arms.

Her usual confident tone was gone, replaced by a trembling softness. "You believe going to Aristus will stop the monsters." The statement was more of a question.

"Who is injured, M?" Kaineres' voice was barely above a whisper, his focus darting from the blankets to the giant tree behind her.

"Do you really think that releasing the princess' spirit—stopping the disunion—will halt the creation of new abominations?"

Kaineres only nodded.

Manden clenched her jaw and let out a broken breath. "Then go."

"What happened? Was anyone lost?"

The air was cold and tight in my throat as Manden caressed the crimson-stained blanket. "Selmine, from the kitchens, and Piper, from the scouting crew. There was nothing to be done. It was instantaneous."

My gut twisted. I didn't know Selmine all that well, but Piper was an older scout who always found the time to point out identification Marks to me. She had a small burn mark across her nose, and always wore her long grey hair in a braid. I saw a future version of myself in her—if I was lucky enough to live that long.

Manden cleared her throat. "Ivon is injured—his arm is in bad shape. And Sora's ankle is likely sprained from where she fell off a ladder, but they'll recover."

"Where are they—I'll see to them right away, we have to make sure—" Kaineres was already searching through the shelves mounted on the wall of his hut, but Manden shook her head.

"Bandin is tending to both of them in the dining hall. You can see to them when you're ready. Kaineres, I need you to seriously think about this journey South. You need a sure-footed plan. Trekking through the Colds will be even more dangerous now but I can't... I can't lose any more people."

Kaineres stopped still with wooden jars held in his palms and pain creased in his brow.

"I can't go alone, M."

I was a fly on the wall until that moment, when the tension in the air shifted weight and their gaze fell to me. The wooden beam of the bedframe suddenly felt too rigid against my back. I wanted to sink right through the splits in the wood, sink into it like resin and tuck myself away from what I knew Kaineres would ask of me. I opened my mouth to say something, but like usual, I couldn't find the words to form.

Manden clicked her tongue.

"Fine. You can take Rune if she wants. Know that this is generous of me, considering she's pulling her weight and then some as a scout." She mindlessly kicked her boots on the door frame, shaking clumps of dirt off the soles. "Bring Sanders as well. Celeste has enough hands right now. Desjin and Dyrus are coming along fine as replacements, respectively, although Dyrus might be needed in the kitchen... Hm." She shook her head free of settling emotions and cleared her throat. "That's all I can spare, but I won't send you out alone. Just... make certain this is the right course of action. For everyone."

She tugged the blanket closer to her blood-soaked torso and retreated back to the dining hall, her posture sunken from exhaustion. I couldn't see Kaineres' expression as he watched his sister walk away, but he stood in the doorway until the cold sent a visible shiver down his back. He closed the door gently, turning around to lean on it with a slow exhale.

I shook my head at the question he didn't need to ask aloud.

He sighed and dropped the jars into a pile on his desk. "I know Aristus isn't where you want to be, but there's no one else I'd rather have by my side."

"No-no, you misspoke." I waved a finger. "Aristus is where I'm *wanted*. As in a fugitive."

"That makes two of us," he said with a false smile spreading across his face.

"So you want to make it a package deal? My head will pay for the celebration the nobles throw and yours will be the main course they feast on." Going back was suicide for both of us. More than he knew.

He walked over to retake a seat next to me on the floor. His hand took mine in his gingerly, as if he was afraid to break it. "You lived in the shadows for years dodging capture. The best person suited for this undertaking is you. I know I'm asking a lot, but I trust you. If not for me, then the rest of the commune. I don't know how many attacks everyone can take before everything starts to fall apart. I'm going, and I need you with me."

There it was, the knot in my stomach. I sighed and felt his thumb brush up against the top of my palm. I wasn't going to let him wander in The Colds alone. I had selfishly hoped Manden would have fought back a bit more, but her will was worn down by her one soft spot. The health of the commune and the life of her daughter would drive her to fist-fight the gods. I bit my cheek and hoped my soft spot would get me out of this. In my staying back, maybe Kaineres could still change his mind. If I needed to I would drag every capable murderer and thief from the corners of hell to bolster the camp's numbers and chances of survival. And my last sliver of weak luck was the only other person as attached to the commune as Manden.

"I'll have to ask Sanders."

Chapter Twenty

Rune

This is how the gods punish me.

"You're serious?" I ground my molars together to keep my jaw from dropping.

"If what you say is true, then of course." Sanders was sitting on a low-hanging branch outside the room they'd been given—a room built into the middle of the giant tree, which they shared with a few other commune members. Other than hearing the chaos, they were safely boarded up from monsters that prowled the camp the night before.

I stood on the ground, leaning against the branch as I explained all that happened. "No pushback? I thought you loved this commune. You turned my ear when I tried to get you to leave the first time."

They shrugged. "I do love it here, but it just seems the decent thing to do. For the honor of Selmine and Piper..."

Great. Not only will I be traversing through the first layer of hell again, but both of my companions are guided by moral compasses. I tugged on my faded blue beads as I thought of something else to say. Sanders hopped off the branch and dusted themselves off.

"This could work out for everyone," They said. "The princess can be freed, Kaineres can prove himself innocent, and you might be pardoned!"

I forced down a lump in my throat. "I'm not getting my hopes up for that. But... it would be nice for Kaineres to get his life back." I meant it. In the hours since Manden had agreed to let him go, Kaineres had a new air about him. He was confident, he was calculating, and he was hopeful, even in the wake of all the destruction. He was also tirelessly nervous, but he used the anxiety to his advantage. He had already instructed Bandin to take over his duties as healer since Bandin had experience with making healing salves and potions. The witch had a spark in his eyes that I wouldn't dimmer, even though my thoughts about returning to Aristus were nothing but storm clouds stirring my own anxieties.

"Does he know? What happened?" Sanders asked quietly.

"No. And he doesn't need to. Please, don't—"

"Of course not. I won't say a word of it." They held their hand to their heart, a silent promise. One I trusted them to keep. "I think Kaineres would understand though—more than anyone."

"No. He has enough on his mind right now." A weak excuse, but an honest one. Sanders shrugged again and wrapped their cloak further around themselves. A part of me wondered how much influence the weather had on their keenness to leave for the city. They weren't haunted by any burning transgressions. The guilt and fear that boiled in my core would warm me all the way to the Southern border and straight into the grave.

Readying for the journey only took about a week. I helped Kaineres collect more supplies, and once the medicinal tent was fully stocked Kaineres guided me in enhancing the potions. I made the majority of them myself, and he said my handiwork and intention were enough to give them added potency. It was a lot easier than I thought it would be, the difficult part being choking down the anger I felt about every wrong thing I knew about myself. Every wrong injury of the past that happened in vain.

With Manden satisfied with the state of how things were to be left, she agreed to let us leave as soon as possible. I enjoyed my last real meal and observed the communal hall one last time. It reminded me of when I was younger, sitting in on the rebel gatherings, listening to their stories and laughing at the crudeness of their jokes. Back at the barracks—which was now one giant tent—I fell asleep quickly, the surrounding scouts feeling a bit more like siblings than strangers. My nonsensical dreams of monsters and snowstorms kept me in a trance until Sanders knocked on the wood of my bed frame. It was time to leave.

It was early morning as far as anyone could tell. Kaineres waited for Sanders and me in front of the medicinal tent. As they said their goodbyes to the commune, I slipped past the growing crowd and into the maker's tent. Celeste was sanding down what looked like the beginnings of a short bow, but stopped and wiped her hands free of dust as I entered.

"I was going to wish you off in a moment. I can get sucked into my work," she said, arms dancing in the air as she spoke.

"Oh, it's alright, I was actually looking for you—to return these." I drew the hunting knives from their holsters and held them out to her. "I know these are important to you. Chances of me returning are slim; I think you should have them."

She shook her head in refusal, but her expression was warming, her eyes glued to her father's knives.

"Please," I pressed. "I know what it's like to have little to remember someone by. There are other weapons for me."

Her lips pressed together, then melted into a beaming smile. She took the knives gingerly and laid them on a strip of leather on her worktable.

"Thank you. You will take these in exchange. A trade." She walked over to another table and picked up the cutlasses that Desjin and Dyrus came with. Celeste had obviously done some work on them; their handles glistened and the edges were visibly sharp. They were larger than the hunting knives, but they had the same curved blades, although not quite as harsh a curve as a sickle. I would need to adjust the straps on my legs and get used to the weight, but I felt a little more secure walking through The Colds with two swords.

"If you're leaving today," Celeste began as I practiced turning the cutlasses over in my hands, "I'm afraid I won't have time to make sheaths for you. Desjin and Dyrus didn't have any on them."

"Will they mind?"

"Dyrus is helping me with my work here and has made clear her dislike for fighting. I don't think she'll miss hers. And Desjin has expressed an interest in a bow akin to Ivon's. You'll need some protection guiding the healer through the woods. I think the cutlasses suit you." Her onyx eyes glistened. I knew Sanders would miss her. Most conversation around dinner was filled with the things they watched her build or fix, and the stories they heard about her life and trade.

We exchanged bows of appreciation, and I stepped out of the maker's tent, leaning the cutlasses against the log outside to adjust the leather straps of my holsters. The blades thickened at the end, but the metal handles hung on the leather loops in such a way that I could still pull them out quickly if needed. I would have to get used to them banging up against my legs as I walked.

Kaineres sauntered over, cloak flipping about behind him dramatically. He glanced down at the metal flanking my thighs.

"Not a word, witch." I shot him a glare as the humored expression grew across his cheeks.

"Sanders told me you were going to give Celeste her father's knives. She will cherish that gift."

I waved him off and slid one of the swords through the harness loops. "In a way, they were hers first. I'll swipe another good set from someone else I'm sure."

"I have no doubt."

"I'm still surprised Manden's letting you—us—go through with this," I said while working on the other leg.

"She does tend to keep a tight leash. But she means well. In recent years she's actually become a lot more open. Softer. I don't know all of the details of her upbringing—even after a decade together she's kept some secrets to herself. But I know she's trying. For as stern and impassive as some people paint her, my sister is really quite gentle."

I stood, adjusting to the new weight on my thighs. "In my experience? People who make great efforts to be gentle are the most rigid. Unwavering in their desire to be calm and centered all the time. Especially when they care about someone. Love makes the heart brittle."

"Sometimes. But it can also make the heart bend." There was a tenderness in his voice that I turned around to avoid.

In front of me stood the magnificent tree. I took it in one last time, the ends of its branches extending into the fog above and beyond. There was a small pang in my gut, and I swallowed down the feeling that I might miss this place. I would do whatever I could to protect Sanders, and I would feel too guilty if I let Kaineres wander around in The Colds and perish, but the nerves under my skin were about as wrecked as the ones apparent on Manden's face. She was hovering over Sora, probably worried her daughter would disappear with the three of us.

I finally caught sight of Sanders rounding the pathway from behind the tree. They were carrying a large sack full of supplies that the kitchen crew had given them. More than Manden had allotted—no doubt a result of either Sanders' or Kaineres' persevering charm. Most of the commune was out saying their farewells; even Arrowette was sulking near the entrance to the communal hall. When the news spread of our journey to Aristus, she was furious she missed the opportunity to volunteer herself as guide back to the high city. Sora was the only one who convinced her to give up trying to turn Manden's ear about it.

The commune was bustling, everyone comfortable with making a little noise now that Kaineres had reinforced the sound barrier. It felt so casual, so relaxed. It felt like something a home might feel like.

"You'll be well prepared for weeks to come." Kaineres told Manden, gesturing to the Medicinal tent. "Bandin knows where to gather ingredients and I've left detailed records of various potions and tonics even Twig could make." He lowered his voice and held Manden by the shoulders. "If everything goes well, I'll return when I can. This place is still a beacon of life. It was before I arrived, and it will be so when I'm gone. You should be proud of what you've created." He pulled her into a hug, Sora squeezing in the middle of them to join. Around Sora's neck was a charmed hounds-tooth necklace.

"Get out of here before I change my mind." Manden pulled back, arms crossed tightly over her chest. "It's a shame you didn't inherit our father's cowardice."

Kaineres narrowed his eyes. "Neither of us did."

I said my farewells to some of the scouts. I politely de-clined a bottle of Twig's self-made tonic, but accepted a shiny crystal from Ivon, who claimed it was charmed for sure footing. I received the warmest goodbye I could have from Arrowette, which was none at all. Bandin and Gwenna offered me hugs, Gwenna leaving me feeling a little unsettled by her curious expression, but I ignored it and turned to the head of the commune.

"Thank you, for everything." I wasn't very good with words, but it was just as well. Manden shared my bluntness, and patted my shoulder.

I grabbed the teary-eyed Sanders by the arms and nodded at Kaineres, who slung his worn leather bag over his shoulder and bowed his head to the tree, whispering something under his breath. The three of us walked south past Kaineres' hut, into the forest, and into the fog.

Earlier Kaineres had mentioned he had a plan for weaving our way through the woods, but Sanders wasn't there for that conversation.

"How are we going to get to Aristus?" They asked. "I've spent months in The Colds wandering in circles, and there aren't enough Marks to tell you where you're going."

Kaineres nodded. "We're going to need a finding spell."

I winced as I recalled the finding spell he told me about. "Please no leeches," I murmured.

Sanders' eyes grew wide, but Kaineres chuckled. "No, not for this one." He said, holding his hand out to me as I gingerly stepped over a fallen log. We were still deep in the fog, and the three of us walked close together to keep visuals on one another. "That spell was more abstract, pointing me to something I didn't know I needed. This one will be easier to craft because where we're going is a physical location, and I already know it exists."

"How do you cast it?" I asked. Now that we were back in the thick of the woods, we needed to be careful about how much attention we attracted.

"I have most of the ingredients, but there's one we'll need to pick up on the way. It's a magical item, but one that I know a certain commune already possesses."

"You've been to other communes?"

"Not exactly, but I've met people who have. Celeste was the one who informed me of this particular place, and it's not terribly far from us. They've collected for themselves a large variety of useful magical tools including an eye—infused with magic—from a bird of sight like an owl or a hawk. I know they'll have more than one to spare since the spell they use it for is rumored to be quite impressive."

Sanders narrowed their eyes. "What do they use it for?"

"The item can be used for any sight-seeing spell. We'll use it to see a path to Aristus. They use it in a nontraditional manner. They've found a way to charm the eye to keep themselves hidden, which makes it a difficult first stop for us. The whole camp is—"

"Invisible!" Sanders covered their mouth. "Sorry—*invisible*." They brought their voice down to a whisper. "The eye we need is in MistView."

"Yes." Kaineres grunted as his foot caught on a protruding branch. I grabbed his arm to help him steady. He squeezed my shoulder in thanks, the warmth of his hands lingering even between gloves and clothing.

As we walked, the fog started to ease, and the ground became clearer. After only minutes of travel, the swords at my sides were already bruising my legs from their constant banging. When we stopped for the night, I would need to do some serious work on my holsters.

Sanders was still curious about the spell Kaineres had in mind. "When we get the eye, what will you do with it then?"

The witch dug around in his satchel and pulled out an old silver compass. "I'll attach it to this. My friend gave me this in his limited knowledge of The Colds thinking it would help direct me, but the ancient magic of the forest interferes with it. It's rendered useless." He held it out to show it, and sure enough the thin metal arrow pointed not north, but spun limply as Kaineres shook it. "But," he stated, "When paired with the eye, along with a magical enchantment of my own, it should point to where we need to go."

"What's our plan for entering MistView?" I asked, thinking back to the encounter with the small city moons ago, Sanders and I barely escaping from flying arrows. "I hardly think we'll be welcome."

"We, er, had a bit of a poor introduction," Sanders explained.

Kaineres raised an eyebrow. "You broke in?"

Sanders nodded. I shrugged. Kaineres cocked his head to the side. "You stole something?" He teased.

"That's kind of the natural order of things out here," I bit back, but the healer only smirked.

"And that's why I wanted you to come. They're not going to hand over their magical treasure kindly, and we don't have much time to negotiate. I was hoping you'd use your talents for the good cause." He stared at me for a beat too long as he helped me over a dead bush, his eyes narrowing playfully. Hell should claim me for how much I liked it when he looked at me that way.

We walked on until the fog cleared, right as the ground dropped and we were on the top of a small cliff side. Bare bushes were scattered about, and I vaguely recognized the edge of the cliff. This was where the Reptiscis attacked, and where the scouts found us. I wondered for a moment who it was, as I never thought to ask. I imagined Bandin letting loose cans of sleeping gas, and Arrowette making a fuss about dragging our bodies back to camp.

We descended the small cliff and headed in the direction we thought the invisible town was in, stopping to collect undisturbed snow for water when we could find it. Hours passed and eventually we stumbled upon Marks on a tree—the same Marks I had seen before entering into MistView territory.

"S, you recognize this area?" I asked, looking around for people out on patrol... and creatures. Sanders tilted their head to the side as they looked above. I pulled my scarf higher over my nose and jerked my head for my companions to follow me. I tried to remember the lad with the rabbit and where he had gone. There were no Marks deep into the territory, but I would recognize the two trees when I saw them.

Sanders saw them first and tugged on my sleeve. I followed their pointed arm to the tall thick trunks with Marks on each, a secret wooden door. With no recent spell cast to it, even my magic wouldn't open it, but Kaineres' intense expression led me to believe he had an idea of what spell would transform it. Before Sanders could walk past me to the twin trees, I caught them and waved Kaineres over to hide behind a bush. Not large enough to hide us fully, but it kept us from being completely exposed.

"We need a better plan than just barging in there," I whispered. "We don't even know where the eye *is*."

"No..." Sanders hummed, "But I have a good idea where it might be." They reached into their pant pocket and pulled out the small embellished coin purse. "It would probably be where I found this."

Kaineres' brows pushed creases into his forehead. "Their locking mechanism is undone by *stonewall dust*?"

That meant something in his world, but now wasn't the time for a lesson.

"S, can the three of us sneak in and out of wherever you found that?"

They nodded, but pursed their lips in such a way that I felt no reassurance.

"And Kaineres, can you get us through that door? Or make the door—however that works?"

The witch procured that know-it-all half smile. "With the aid of that stonewall dust, I can get us in and out of anything."

As expected, Kaineres knew just what the trees wanted to hear, he even said it like the boy had—whispered the spell to each trunk, and then Sanders tossed some of the magic dust onto the large wooden door that grew together. We were through, and my focus on keeping them safe on our hunt was honed until we rounded a corner behind the wooden barn.

On the outer wall of a house was a wanted poster with my picture drawn on it. Well, it had my physical description on it and a picture of someone that looked like it could be me. My lip scar was clearly visible and this drawing included a scarf. It was more detailed than the posters I had seen nearer to Aristus. That day when I was found here with Sanders, they must have known who I was. I halted too long and Sanders turned around.

"You don't have to come with us." They mouthed.

I shook my head. Neither Kaineres nor Sanders was armed, aside from a small pocket dagger Sanders kept as a last resort. I wouldn't let them come to any harm. Unless I drew more attention, and that would make things worse.

Kaineres squeezed my arm. "We'll be in and out of here, hopefully before anyone sees us. If we make it back through this door, they can't see us leave unless they pass through it too."

I drew my cutlasses from my holsters. If we were going to make it through without being caught, I couldn't have the metal clanging on my legs as we snuck about. We trailed

Sanders around the backside of the small wooden structures, stooping low under windows and stopping when we
heard voices on the other side. It was still late morning, and
the commune was up and about.

We turned down a skinny alleyway with no doors or
windows, but it led to a flat dirt road. The main road. We
hid behind a large crate as people passed by, talking about
the cold or the monster that had come close to camp. On
the other side of the road were more wooden structures,
people going in and out carrying tools and food.

"It's too busy," I said, my voice a harsh whisper.

"Maybe we just time it right. That building over there is
where we need to be." Sanders pointed around the crate
to a stone building at the end of the road, a thick smoke
stack rising from its chimney. I could barely see it without
sticking my head out of the alley, so I didn't get a good look
at it. I weighed our options as people walked closer by, not
noticing the three of us pressing our backs into the faint
shadows of the alley behind the crate.

I gave one of my swords to Sanders. I'm sure the witch
had magic up his sleeve that he could use in a pinch.
Kaineres grabbed my arm firm, his eyes wide in warning.
I shook him off and directed Sanders.

"Give me the signal when you have the eye and I'll meet
you by the door out of here."

"What signal—*Rune!*" Kaineres hissed under his breath
and reached for me, but I pushed off the wall in a burst of
energy and in an instant I was running through the street.
I received mostly bewildered looks from people confused
about who I was and what I was doing, so I let my scarf dip
past my chin in hopes of grabbing more of their attention.

"It's *her*! She's back!" Someone cried out, and it wasn't
long until I had a trail of angered townspeople on my footprints.

My path was blocked quickly by a group of men and women armed with various tools. No arrows yet, but I wasn't going to try my luck. I dashed for another alley with crates and hauled myself up to the tops of the buildings. The roofs were also made of sturdy wood, but they were slick with sleet and snow. *Ivon your crystal better work.* I kept a steady pace, using the ice to my advantage when I could slide across, and using my cutlass to dig into the wood to give me something to hold onto. Rocks smacked me in the shoulder and legs as townspeople ran underneath me, throwing what they could find. I prayed that they wouldn't find anything sharp.

I had a good rhythm going, bounding from rooftop to rooftop, until I came to the barn. It was too tall for me to jump onto it, and the pitch was too drastic for me to climb. There was a crowd at the bottom, and someone had grabbed a ladder. A man climbed his way up the building I stood on, an ax in his mouth and a net in his hand. I backed up and saw a smaller crowd of people on the other side of the house. *At least most of the town is here.*

"You're gonna pay for what you've done, and it looks like I'm gonna get paid for bringing you in!" The man laughed a ragged raspy laugh that could've been mistaken for a cough had he not been smiling. His shirt was worn, but woven into it were the colors of a noble house of Aristus. My stomach churned harder as I held out my cutlass to keep him distanced. My legs burned from keeping myself balanced on the icy rooftop, and my knees wobbled with each step the man took towards me.

I glanced from right to left at my shrinking exit points. The man in front of me might have been nobility once, but he was no foot soldier. I charged him, my eyes on his feet. He swung his ax and missed, and his body flung to the side along with it. He tried to secure his footing but his boot hit a patch of ice and he slipped backwards off the roof and onto the gasping crowd.

My momentum brought me off the roof, and I tumbled onto the ground with a thud and a clumsy roll. Spitting dirt out of my mouth, I scrambled to my feet amidst a cluster of townspeople, who grabbed my arms and cloak. I tore from them, swinging the dull side of my sword around to knock their hands back. I jumped on a small wheeled storage cart to gain access to the other row of houses, and barely made it up before another ladder slammed against the side. Pairs of people ascended the ladder after me, and nets were being thrown this way and that, with no particular aim. I leapt and slid from roof to roof, stopping as I approached the stone building. I couldn't lead them there. I turned around to a wall of people on the roof and on the ground below, nets and chains drawn.

Chains? I cursed and spat on the roof. My exit points were nowhere to be found.

"Why don't you turn yourself over easy now, and we'll promise not to drag you by your hair the whole way to Aristus, hm?" Said a man in front of me. He too wore the faded colors of a noble house. I wondered for a second what crimes he would have had to commit to get banished from his House.

I inhaled, long and slow, wishing I had asked Kaineres for more than two magic lessons. I think I felt it, the magic in me, or maybe it was fear. Either way, the feeling was strong and one I had felt before, during a spell I had cast before without knowing how. I thought of the first lesson the witch had taught me, and while we didn't cover much, the knowledge was there. I exhaled, feeling the warmth inside me. It burned my chest and dried my throat. Steam escaped my nostrils in stacks. I inhaled again, drawing the air deep into my belly.

The man was close to me now, so close he prepared to cast his net. I felt the heat rise in me again, and I let it burn, I let it coat the inside of my throat and I let it scar my tongue. I thought of the leaf, blowing in the wind, the energy that propelled it forward just long enough. All I needed was long enough.

In a wild surge of released breath, flames shot from my mouth and nostrils, shooting forward and searing my lips. I blew it straight into the wall of people in front of me, and they scattered, screaming and ducking away from the fire shooting over their heads. It was just a small burst, but enough to grant me clearance through the crowd and over to the next building.

What's taking them so damn long?!

As if on cue, I heard a high-pitched rooster call pierce through the screams of the crowd behind and below. Sanders. I dug my cutlass into the wood and pulled my-self over the top of the roof and slid down to the side of the building. I was in a mad sprint towards the barn and the door I knew was behind it. I skidded to a halt as an arrow landed in a wall inches from my face, then I charged again in the direction of the barn, making my movements erratic as the arrows pelted the ground and walls nearby.

As the door came into view, I saw Sanders and Kaineres running from the outskirts of the town. Sanders whistled again and waved me on, using their other hand to throw the dust over the door. It opened, and the three of us jumped through, followed by a herd of townspeople.

"I hope to hell you have it," I yelled out of breath as we ran, the words painful and raw as my throat vibrated. Kaineres bent down every so often as he ran, gathering handfuls of dirt. Unlike the last time Sanders and I ran from the MistView commune, the people were not letting up on our trail after knowing who I was. They were going to alert the entire forest with their shouting.

Between dodging trees and branches, I shot Kaineres a confused look as he picked up handful after handful of dirt, until he turned on a whim and faced our pursuers. He threw his hands in the air and shouted an enchantment, at once scattering the dirt into a thick cloud-like mass. It was almost impossible to see through, and it fanned out in the direction he threw it in, hiding us from view. We kept running with the cover behind us until we were sure we had lost the crowd.

Safe from pursuit, I collapsed on the forest floor and started coughing. They kept coming, wave after wave of breathless heaving. Kaineres handed me a canteen he pulled from somewhere in Sanders' bag. I chugged it back, the cold water soothing the charred insides of my mouth. He knelt beside me, encouraging me to drink all of it, assuring me we would find more. I did as he said, and drank until my lungs were too worn out to scream in pain. I nodded my head in thanks and as the healer rubbed my back, subtly checking me over for any wounds. His eyes landed on my mouth and nose and went to retrieve something from his satchel. He came back with a salve and didn't wait for me to ask what it was before removing his gloves and applying it to my lips. It stung, but I sat still and let him work. His fingers were gentle as he delicately painted my lips with the pads of his thumb. The relief was intoxicating.

"Easy. This should speed up the healing process and keep the skin from scarring." He said as he returned the salve. Pulling out a different vial, he uncorked it and brought it to my lips. "Drink."

The liquid was viscous, but soothing, cooling the burning sensation in my throat.

He looked like he was about to ask what happened, but I coughed and repeated myself.

"You have it, right? The eye?"

Kaineres gave a curt nod and gestured to Sanders, who held out the small round eye, its iris yellow and sparkling.

"The rest of the compass doesn't require much, so I should have it prepared and working by morning. We can rest for now. Make a proper camp and take the time you need to heal while I work. Then, we'll be on our way to Aristus."

I gulped but didn't say anything about how after the last encounter, Aristus was the last place I wanted to be.

CHAPTER TWENTY-ONE

Rune

Kaineres spent the night working on the compass, visibly nervous about taking it apart and putting it back together. *Mastery over machinery is not a skill I've honed,* he admitted.

With a little help from Sanders, the two of them were able to put it pack together and Kaineres cast the final spell to make it function. The metal needle spun around, making clicking noises until it slowed and swayed to point in one direction. Whether or not that direction was Aristus would be something we'd have to discover in time. It was our only clue where to point our boots, so we followed the magic compass.

We spent the days walking and the nights taking turns sleeping and watching. I lit most of the fires, as I had more experience working with the moist conditions the ice and snow left. We had a tarp just large enough to cover a small shelter of angled branches. The three of us huddling close together underneath it created enough warmth between us. Kaineres cast enchantments over us while we slept to keep our scent hidden from monsters in the area. They must have worked, because the next day I would see the occasional paw print in the dirt near our camp.

To save time, we walked right past Marks and straight through commune territories, although we didn't see anyone for days. We did come across a Birthless in midday, but I made quick work of it with my cutlasses. The swords proved harder to throw than the knives, and I almost lost one of them to a small creek when my aim was off, but I was able to retrieve it after the second throw stuck.

"You know, they make weapons specifically for distance fighting." The witch teased.

"I value versatility." I countered. "For instance, you make a good travel companion because of your healing knowledge and your potential to act as bait," I emphasized the last word, but Kaineres only laughed.

"I'm so appreciative you see value in me. It gives me the strength to try and survive this unbinding spell."

His words settled uncomfortably in my gut. "There's a chance you won't?"

He pursed his lips in thought. "Curses are rare. I've only undone a few in my lifetime, but they were of a simple nature, so they make for a poor comparison. I have my theories about how to rectify this, but it would be foolish to ignore all possibilities."

Another reason to avoid Aristus and forget about the curse altogether. I wouldn't dare say it aloud though. It was clear Kaineres had made up his mind, and a part of me envied his resolve and character. I thought about what I would do if I was given the chance to fix my past mistakes. I would probably be too much of a coward to do anything. Although, if I truly was a coward I supposed there would be nothing to fix. Too many of my mistakes have come from moments of reckless bravery. I had a feeling the witch's bravery stemmed from days and weeks of careful, calculated planning.

Even with the thin needle assuring us we were heading in the same direction, The Colds played tricks on my mind. It felt like we were walking in circles. The same mangled tree crossed our path three times, but the Marks we eventually stumbled on told us we were, in fact, crossing territories.

"There's a river up ahead," Sanders reported, backing away from the symbols carved in the low-hanging branch. They squinted into the distance, suddenly very serious. "Hell's Tongue."

The witch rubbed his growing beard. "I don't remember a river. How great is it?"

Sanders blew air out of their lips in a heave. "Personality-wise? It's got a bit of a temper. As for its size, it's fairly large to try to cross without some kind of boat, although people say it shrinks as it gets closer inland. If you don't remember it that's probably where you crossed it. The smaller creeks in The Colds stem from it, but if there's a Mark for it, I think it's the main body. It has rapids that are too quick to freeze over. If you're not careful it'll drag you under and you won't come out again until it's carried you halfway down the river."

I hummed with amusement as I realized their participation in idle gossip was proving to be very beneficial.

"Well then," Kaineres said, "let's be careful."

We heard it before we laid eyes on it. The roar and rumble of water splashed in and out of itself as it snaked through our path. The air picked up into a foul breeze and the hairs on my arms were pricked up and painful. As we grew closer, I could see Hell's Tongue for what it was. An icy bath that welcomed warm and cold-blooded creatures alike to wash onto the wake of their eternal sleep soaking wet.

"We should walk the length of it until it's safer to cross," I said more to myself than my party. I surveyed each side of the river. On the bank, rocks were slick with ice.

"That could take days though, maybe weeks," Sanders said loudly into the mist, holding their arms up to block the spraying water from hitting their exposed face.

"We can't afford to lose that much time. The spell on the compass will wear off eventually." Kaineres was pacing the upper bank, his eyes narrowed questioningly at the water as if he wasn't sure he could trust it. I could answer that question with certainty.

"As your *guide*, I strongly recommend finding a safer crossing point. We can't swim across those rapids."

"No, but that's an idea."

I followed the witch's pointing finger to where Sanders stood several horse-lengths away on a large, flat rock formation at the edge of the water. It was one of many. Some small, some large, poking their faces out of the water like natural steps taunting anyone foolish enough to use them as such. The formations were mostly smooth aside from small dips and chips in them, which offered places to stick your foot or hand into should you need stability. It was still a shitty excuse for a bridge, and there was a large gap between the two middle rocks where the rapids gushed through.

"Sanders!" I ran over as my friend reached their foot out and balanced between two rocks. They only whipped their hair back and held out their hand.

"Come now, Rune, my dear. We'll waste too much time wandering around if we don't cross now, and the quicker we get out of The Colds the better."

I took their arm to help them back to the bank, but they were surprisingly strong for their little frame. I was lunged forward onto the rock beside them. The squishing of mud behind me told me Kaineres wasn't far behind.

"Fine." I gave in. "We'll cross over into our deaths here."

I looked at my new path, now jagged and grey and freezing cold. A gateway to the second layer of hell. The dark rocks were almost lost under the roaring trail of water that gurgled by them, but I pushed my weight onto another one and felt my boot hit the hard surface. I clenched my teeth as water gushed over my ankles and occasionally splashed up to my calf. I sloppily tied my cloak into a knot at the bottom to keep it somewhat dry. Kaineres, helped on to the first rock by Sanders, had fashioned his into a very large and clunky shawl.

"This is a shit idea," I yelled over the water.

The three of us slowly made our way across the river. I surpassed Sanders to make sure the rocks were stable enough and wouldn't shift under our weight as we stepped on them. The middle proved to be as tricky as it looked. I waited until a large surge of current rushed past before making the jump onto the other stone step, landing sharply on my ass as my boot slipped. A slew of curses flew out of my mouth as I clung to the rock, digging my nails into the crevices to keep me from being swept away. After ensuring I was going to remain on the rock, Sanders burst into laughter, their cackle diluted by the whitewater rushing past.

I waited for an opportunity to stand and rubbed my aching tailbone, the sting exceeding that of the icy water now soaked into my clothes. My teeth chattered hard enough I thought it would chip a tooth.

"Can you manage this?" Sanders lifted their bag of supplies off their shoulders.

I nodded, as words wouldn't come out as anything other than indistinguishable chattering. I caught the bag with a very polite grunt, shooting a glare at the witch who bit his cheek in humor. Most of the rocks on my side of the river were far more forgiving and rose higher out of the water. I gingerly made my way across to allow Sanders to make the jump in the middle. Showing off, they made the landing and remained upright, grinning so smugly I knew I wouldn't hear the end of it.

Kaineres, having the longest legs of the three of us, didn't have a problem crossing the gap but his knuckles were white as the drifting snow as he gripped his satchel. I made my way to the bank, one slick step at a time. Making a mental note of which rock was loose, I shouted the information back at my party. One of the last rock formations to cross was wide and slanted, with a thin shimmer of ice on the air-exposed surface at the top. I used it mainly to push myself off of and fell gracefully on my ass again, barely missing the sharp metal of my blades. I was close enough to the bank that I could pull myself out of the current and onto land, my entire body shivering and numb from the waist down.

I tightened the bag around my shoulder and turned to Sanders and Kaineres, still inching their way across. Sanders reached the slanted stone. Swallowing back a wave of shivers I braced to shout a warning, but the words didn't come fast enough.

My warning a second too late, Sanders' boot hit the sheen of the ice and slipped into the water, the current pulling their weight sideways off the rock. Their arms frantically scratched at the stone's smooth face but there was nothing to grab onto and in seconds their head disappeared under the dark water.

"SANDERS!"

My heart fell into my stomach as I stepped into the river, my eyes desperately scanning the path of the water to see where they were taken. I braced to jump in after them but a force knocked me back and threw me out of balance. I fell backward onto the wet bank as Kaineres dove into the river. In my lap was the satchel he threw, along with his bundled up cloak. I scanned the dark channel as the current curved around more stones, splashing up against fallen logs and branches. My legs felt like solid ice, but I forced myself up from a crawl to a bumbling sprint alongside the river's edge.

It was just river for too long, there was no sign of either of them. My heart pounded in my chest and my stomach threatened to drop out of the bottom of me. I couldn't lose them both. I couldn't.

Pebbles and dirt sprayed out in every direction as I continued sprinting down the bank, refusing to acknowledge the speed at which they were being hurled downstream. The swords clanged against my side over and over again. Just when my legs were going to give out from underneath me I saw a figure in the distance, clawing its way out of the river.

Kaineres heaved as he dragged Sanders up onto the bank, gagging for air over and over as his body shook.

"*Kaineres!*" I skidded to a halt on my knees beside them, dragging them both further up the bank and onto dryer land.

We found an area with enough brush to keep the wind chill down and laid Sanders on the healer's half-dry cloak. Their body was ice cold and limp, and blood trickled from their forehead where they must have hit a rock underwater. I removed my gloves and pushed aside the clumps of wet, dark hair stuck to their cheeks and face. Kaineres removed his own gloves and tossed them aside, his hands shaking violently. He pointed to Sanders' shirt.

"T-too c-cold." He breathed out.

I understood, and eased them out of their sopping wet clothes. Kaineres dug through the supply bag and pulled out a worn blanket. He tightly wrapped it around Sanders to preserve any warmth they had left. I threw my arm around my friend and held them tight, listening closely for any air coming through their nostrils or ajar mouth. I would be irreversibly pissed at their gods later, but for now I was relieved that Sanders was breathing. I exhaled an exhausted sigh into their chest as I heard rhythmic pumping. Slow, but steady.

"Wh-what are you doing—how are you doing th-that?" Kaineres pressed his hands against Sanders' cheeks, their neck, their forehead.

"*Doing what? What do you mean?*" I looked up from my friend's shoulder as the witch took my hands with his own and placed them over Sanders' head. They weren't warm, but they were warming up. Not nearly as frozen as they were seconds ago.

"They're warming up—you're warming them up," Kaineres said, continuing to remove the rest of Sanders' wet clothing—their boots and socks—with shaky fingers.

"I'm not doing anything—I don't know—"

"Whatever it is, don't st-stop. K-keep pressure on their chest like you were." Kaineres tossed the wet clothing to the side and took off his own, the wrinkles in the fabric already starting to freeze stiff. He tugged at my mostly dry shirt, gesturing for me to take it off and wrap it around Sanders' exposed feet.

I did so, and removed my ice-cold pants and socks to keep my legs from losing all feeling. After a few minutes of holding tight to Sanders I felt their face again, and noticed that they were indeed warming up.

I turned to the healer and held out my arms. "Kaineres—"

All he did was nod, shivers taking over his whole body. His face was paling to a dangerous shade of purple. I sat in his lap with my arms wrapped around his chest and he leaned his weight into me, resting his head on mine.

"Th—thank you," he sputtered out.

"Shh. Just focus on breathing." I wiggled an arm out and pressed my palm against his chest. His usually tan body was sickly white, and I tried not to stare at the unique markings on his chest I hadn't noticed the night in the bathing chamber. In between his pecs was a tattoo—the same rust-red color as the ones on his arms—in the shape of a singular eye.

What had caught my attention, however, was not the tattoo but the strange purple markings just underneath his skin. They almost looked like veins or lightning fanning out in all directions starting from his midsection, but were thin and faded. His whole body convulsed at a small gust of wind that ripped through the brush. I returned my attention to keeping him warm, pressing my body into his. His heartbeat thumped in my ear, a beat that felt solidly reassuring.

"*Thank you*," I said. "You... You didn't hesitate a moment."

"I d-didn't know if—if you could swim." I felt a short laugh rise through him, but when he exhaled it turned into another shiver. "It feels like dulled fire—in the best way," he murmured, placing his cold hand over mine. Even after near death, he concerned himself with assuring me. "They'll be alright."

"And you?"

"Don't you worry," he whispered. "I take my duty of monster bait very seriously."

The panic that was frantically pulling at my lungs slowed a bit and sunk down into my gut. I let out a long breath and drew back from Kaineres when his skin started to feel warm. I told him to watch Sanders as I went to find wood for shelter and fire, my cloak awkwardly tied around my waist like a poorly fashioned skirt. The combination of wet skin and a lack of suitable clothing had me clenching my jaw in freezing misery, my magic blood the only reason I could still stand. I was only gone a few minutes, and I made sure to stay within earshot in case I was needed. Most of the surrounding wood was damp, but I found enough small branches to make use of.

Kaineres set up the tarp while I built the fire. Even though the light was a literal beacon in the environment, we placed scraggly branches over the tent to blend it in with the surroundings and for added insulation. The spot we ended up in was secluded enough. I didn't like how close we were to the river, but the vegetation around gave some extra cover. I hung all our clothes over the fire for hours until they had dried completely, using my body heat to warm Sanders in the meantime. After we clothed Sanders back in their warmed outfit, Kaineres put his dried clothes back on and then resumed staring in every direction except for where I sat.

"You can look," I said quietly, putting my layers back on. "I don't mind."

The firelight glowed red against his cheeks as his eyes met mine.

"Are all of those from out here?"

It took me a moment to realize he was talking about the scars that scattered across my body. Red and pale-white jagged marks marred all of the places I had been scraped, stabbed, and cut.

I chuckled low and sourly. "Not all of them."

His expression was soft and worn from more than just physical exhaustion. Something I too felt, and had been feeling since being exiled. Perhaps even before that. I glanced over to the bundle next to me. Sanders was still resting on a pile of our cloaks, every once and a while muttering something nonsensical. We couldn't travel with them like this, and I wasn't sure how long they would need to recover. The injury to their head wasn't severe, but how the cold would exacerbate it was concerning. I looked across the fire to Kaineres, whose quick thinking and rather reckless act had saved my closest friend. I owed him for that. Probably more.

"I was born to a lower-class servant in Flatkeep," I said quietly, my voice still hoarse and raw. "My sister, Rena, was born a year later." I scooted close to the fire, sticking my boots out allowing the heat to sink through the leather to my frozen toes. Kaineres shifted his cloak around himself, his eyes locked on me as I spoke. "I showed signs of being—unusual—early on. My mother and the few other servants who knew kept it hidden from people outside the house as well as the masters that lived there. It was my sister who gave us away."

"Your sister... is a Within too?" Kaineres slowly tilted his head to the side in intrigue.

"Her powers were stronger than mine—she had been tending the garden for years with no issues, but one day in the middle of Summer, her fingers coated everything with a thin layer of frost. Mother didn't know what to do with her. She was terrified something was going to happen to us, or someone would take us away. Her fear was warranted, of course. Not a week after my sister started accidentally killing every plant she touched, the master of the house found someone looking to pay a great deal for wicked blood.

"I exposed myself, against my Mother's wishes, in hopes that they would take me in Rena's place. My naivete had us both dragged out to markets and drained for vials of blood in exchange for services and favors to the master's house.

He wasn't particularly skilled, so we became his primary source of income. Rena would often get sick from it, and Mother shirked her duties to keep our wounds clean from infection. One day, a witch came to market from one of the noble houses, needing magical blood for a healing potion for a child. She was seeking an animal, but was pleasantly surprised at finding my sister and me instead. Rena had already been cut and drained a few times that day, so she was near blacked out. My master gave the witch my blood claiming it was my sister's because she was more powerful, and he received a hefty payment in return."

"Which house?" Kaineres asked sharply. His brows were creased in anger, but I shrugged.

"I don't know. I don't remember. The coin purse the witch used had a symbol on it, but I don't know which noble House is which. And it wouldn't matter. They all send their magicians to market for things like that." I glanced over to Sanders, who was still curled up in a ball, their chest rising and falling.

"Sanders was the one who warned me the soldiers were coming. Foot soldiers had passed by Sanders' portion of town looking for my master, and the 'corrupted' wicked he offered. Something had gone wrong with the spell. Instead of curing the child, it had made the illness worse, and the child developed a fever that wouldn't resolve. The noble House alerted the authorities, and Aristian soldiers were sent after Rena to prevent her blood from being used again. No one would believe that the blood was mine." My fingers found the beads at the end of my hair. The beads that I had given Rena after I found them at an artisan's stall in the market. The first thing I had ever stolen, just to make her smile. I gripped them tight, thumbing over their smooth surfaces.

"They ripped her from my arms and slit her throat on the cobblestone to make a statement. My mother was heartbroken, and never the same. My master was barred from selling wicked blood in the market, and I left the house to become a street sweeper. Every day after, whenever I cleaned the street I swore I always found more traces of her blood. Pooled and dried in the crevices between stones. Stained in the grain of a wooden stall post." A soreness swelled in my throat behind my tongue, cracking my voice. "It should have been me."

"No."

Kaineres was up and over the fire, grasping tight my hands in his as he sat next to me. "It shouldn't have happened at all. Not to your sister, not to you, not to anyone. It wasn't your fault. There—there are greed-driven cowards walking around with witches' titles. Those vile wretches will rue their actions, if not this life, then the next—"

"You don't know that. No one *knows* that. It's just something people tell themselves to lessen their grief or their consequence. No *one* will pay as much as I have." Hot tears were starting to fall down my cheeks and burn my face.

Kaineres took off his gloves and gently wiped them away as they fell, his eyes still fixed on mine. His voice was solemn, but it cradled me in a tenderness I let myself sink into.

"I'm sorry Rune. I'm so sorry." His own eyes glistened as his palms pressed gently into my cheeks, holding the weight of my sadness in his hands. "It's not your fault. Aristus has been consumed by greed and fear for so long it's seeped into the very magic that once established it. You have every right to be angry and hurt. I'm angry about what's been done, and by the gods I'll do everything in my power to make certain you're never hurt like that again."

He brought his forehead to mine as I sobbed. Pent-up grief washed over me and past my eyelids as I released it—felt it, for the first time in a long time. It strained against my throat and clogged my nose as I surrendered myself to it.

"I know it doesn't bring your sister back. I know it doesn't take any pain away from the past, but I will not leave you alone in your grief."

Tear after tear fell from my eyes and onto his hands. His thumbs gingerly brushed my cheeks. I wasn't sure how much time had passed as I broke apart in his hands, but his gentle grasp on my face never wavered. A cavity of guilt threatened to swallow me whole as his kindness surrounded me. He never once asked if I deserved it in the first place. It *should* have been me instead of Rena. It was my blood. My crime. I just didn't know how to explain to him how much more there would be in the world without me in it. And I was too tired to try. The heaviness that pounded in my sinuses and drenched my back in sweat was crippling, and his hands were so soft...

After my tears started to ebb, his thumb slowly tilted my chin. His lips were cold as he softly kissed my forehead. I closed my eyes as the exhale from his nostrils sent shivers down my spine.

"Rune, I so desperately want to change how the world sees Withins, change how the world sees magic. But for now, I'll be whatever you need me to be. Even if it's just someone to cry on. My hands are here to hold you whenever you need them." He brushed another tear away and pushed back a loose strand of my hair.

There it was, the softness is his gaze—sure and unmoving, but kind and endlessly patient.

Steam drifted up between us. I felt it, hot on my skin.

"Your fingers!" I sharply pulled back to examine his hands, now bright red from burns. He shook his head and moved his hands out of my reach.

"They're fine, Rune. It's alright. I was freezing my ass off a minute ago, and I prefer this. This doesn't hurt me." He smiled at me but I could still see enflamed streaks left by my tears on the back of his hand. "You don't hurt me."

The lump in my throat rose higher. "I'm sorry—it's the magic..."

"Hey, shh—You don't need to apologize." He furrowed his brows in sympathy and grabbed the sides of my face again. "You never need to apologize for existing as you are. Your magic and you are not separate entities. You *are* magic, magic *is* you, and the rest of the world covets and fears what they do not know. They do not know you and will never get to, and for every wrong thing I've done in my life I don't know how I've avoided the punishment of not knowing you. The day you walked into my realm of hell I knew you were going to change the life I had settled for."

The tears had stopped falling, but the insides of my nose burned as I tried to breathe in through the congestion. "I don't remember walking into anything the first time I came to camp."

"Oh no, you were very horizontal. That sleeping gas really knocked you out. I was speaking metaphorically." He smiled and pressed his nose to mine.

After a few deep breaths he released my face, but his eyes still examined me like a healer. I looked over to make sure Sanders was still breathing and that they weren't shivering in the cold.

"Thank you," Kaineres said softly. "For telling me about your sister. I know memories like that aren't easy to retell."

I wiped the sides of my face, steaming from the harsh winter air. "Thank you... for listening."

The corners of his eyes creased. "I'll gladly listen to anything you have to say." Kaineres added a handful of kindling to the small fire, the fresh streaks on his hands parallel with his tattoos. He was—in every way—marked with his dedication to serve, marred with his intention to care. "Rest, Rune. I'll keep watch. On the camp and Sanders. Try to sleep, please. Keep them warm."

I rubbed the remaining wetness out of the corner of my eyes and curled my body around the sibling I chose for myself. I listened to the sound of their breathing, their exhales deep and uneven like the current of a distant river.

CHAPTER
TWENTY-TWO

Rune

Wind howled through the bare trees like the whistling snore of a long-slumbering beast. I clung to the pile of branches I collected for firewood, using them to shield my face from the frigid air. The forest was still eerily dark, but I was relieved to see Kaineres' spells were working on our campsite—from a distance, I could hardly notice the faint glow of light.

Upon approaching our setup I laid the branches down in a pile and hovered over the flame, adding the driest wood methodically until I was satisfied it wouldn't need constant tending to. Sanders was still sleeping, but woke briefly during the night to sip on warm water and a few mystery ingredients from the healer. I let both my companions rest as much as they needed, happy to concentrate my time patrolling or keeping the fire going. Bringing my knees close to my chest, I was tempted to close my eyes for a moment, but Kaineres stirred across the fire.

He was leaning against the trunk of a tree, the exposed roots curving around his body like some ornate armchair. He smiled softly, and as my face started to flush I hoped it wasn't visible from where he sat.

The wind kicked up a flurry of leaves and frost into the campsite, my hair and scarf whipping in every direction as the air dragged its icicle fingers across my face. Sanders seemed unbothered in their sleep, surrounded by the small shelter of brush and tarp I had built for them. I grit my teeth together and braced for another gust, muttering niceties under my breath.

The witch laughed low and unevenly. "We could always share body heat. I wasn't near conscious enough to enjoy it the first time." He patted the ground in between his legs with a grin that was far from clinical.

I could feel blood rush to my face as warmth came over my cheeks, and I hoped that the redness of my nose made it seem like it was from the cold.

Kaineres saw through it and waved his fingers in the air. "You're a tad warmer, no? *Magic.*"

"Oh go fuck yourself." I bit the inside of my cheek as the edge of my lips twitched up at his amusement. Damn him.

"I'd prefer to keep most of my blood flow directed to my heart right now, but once we get to city limits I'll think about it."

"Will it be warm in the city?" The thought interrupted the heat growing in my abdomen. I hadn't thought about what season it was. When I was first exiled, I counted the days and kept track of the moon passing when I could see it, but there was no point in looking forward to a Spring season that wouldn't reach me. I lost count a few months in.

"Well, as the fates would have it, I suspect winter is just starting."

Of course the witch would have kept track. I grumbled my most insincere thanks to my gods for the ironic timing.

Kaineres gave a sympathetic shrug. "It will still be warmer. The activity of the town and all its people will make it feel a little less like hell. Who knows, we may even catch a glimpse of the sun as we emerge."

We sat silently for a few minutes, each of us quietly watching snow float its way to the ground, sometimes veering off path to dance with the wind before settling into the dirt. Occasionally Sanders would tighten the blanket around themselves in their sleep, or softly mumble something incoherent. Kaineres leaned his head back against the trunk and looked up at the grey sky hovering so close above us.

"It used to be my favorite time of year." He sighed deeply, breathing out a cloud of steam through his nostrils. "The end of Autumn melting slowly into Winter. The progression is so beautiful, so delicate. Every other change of season always seemed so sharp to me in contrast." He let his hand drop and combed through the cold earth with his fingers. "They didn't seem to blend into each other with the same softness. I've always admired Winter's ability to embalm everything in a natural slumber—both patient and relentless."

I couldn't keep the small giggle in my throat down.

"What?"

"Only you would romanticize the most lethal season."

"I can romanticize *every* season. Winter just so happened to woo me in return."

"Is it still your favorite?"

His fingers stopped roaming through the dirt. He brushed his hands together to the side, shaking off the clumps that stuck to his nails.

"It was the transition that I loved. The part of the natural cycle that brought rest, and waiting. There is no cycle here. No rest either. It's not the same. The commune was a safe haven for me, but these woods never felt like home. The day I was banished it felt like my soul was ripped apart. I guess in some ways it was. I'm not sure if I'll get that back."

I pulled my eyes from him and studied our surroundings. The tops of the trees scraped together as wind rummaged through them. The fire between us flickered on silently—as if it too was wary of the surrounding woods shrouded in snow and uncertainty. I watched as the light danced, its chaos rhythmic and nourishment steady. The witch's gaze on my skin was heavy and hot as he watched the fire burning through the reflection in my eyes. The excitement in my stomach decayed into an uncomfortable aching. I didn't know why I felt like I needed to tell him that I had more in common with the freezing night air than the flames he kept his focus on.

Any warmth in me would burn through anything good anyway. There would be nothing left but char and ash and smoke that carried the smell of what was and what couldn't—married together in unholy disaster.

"Rune?" The lower register of his voice sent the blurred visions scattering.

"Hm?"

The corners of his lips twitched upwards as he repeated himself. "I asked if you knew what you wanted to do—if this all works out."

"What do you mean?"

Kaineres ran a hand through his hair. "I mean, if all goes to plan, and you're hailed as a hero for freeing the long-lost princess, what will you do?"

I hadn't thought about it. I hadn't thought I'd ever be in the position to. The chances of being free from banishment were less than slim. Chances of being any kind of hero? Nonexistent.

"I... don't know."

"You don't think this will work?" Not accusatory, a genuine question.

"I... don't know enough about what we're walking into. A lot has changed since we've been away. There's no way to know. Even if we can free the princess..." *There's no way to know how she's going to feel—what she's going to do.*

What I didn't say out loud, Kaineres seemed to hear. Or maybe he had been thinking the same thing. He sat back to lean against the rotting trunk that groaned to support his weight. The witch crossed his arms across his chest in thought.

"I'm not sure what she remembers, or what she's seen—through me, if anything. I feel like if she has, she's seen enough... to know."

Clouds formed in his eyes, a haziness drifting over the moss covered logs. The stark green weeds climbed their way up the trunks of his ever-brown forests, grasping at anything they could take hold of.

"Are you scared?" I asked.

He let out a sigh, and I was worried for a moment that I had only pushed him deeper into his thoughts. Slowly his eyes met mine.

"Would you be?"

Of course. Maybe. A younger part of me was scared of everything. Yet the idea of something going wrong—being pulled apart at the seams and shattered into a million different pieces never to be recovered again offered a kind of twisted solace.

"I don't know. Yes. Scared of what, exactly?"

"You asked me." Kaineres tilted his head to the side, a small smile returning. Good. At least he was out of his head a bit. I wouldn't press him—

"I'm scared of the uncertainty of it all," he started. "I rely on things being planned out. Structured."

"Really?" I widened my eyes in false bemusement and in return, he threw a small piece of ash-touched kindling towards me.

"*And* this isn't something I can well plan out. At least not the refractory variables."

"Refractory variables..." I repeated in humor to myself. "No, there really is no organizing the refractory variables is there?"

The witch shook his head, his lips framing his gritted teeth in a smile. "I just don't know for certain how this is going to work. *If* this is going to work. I don't even know how I did it in the first place—the curse, anyway. The binding would have taken an ungraspable amount of power that I didn't know I possessed. And that was at the height of my practice—I was minutes away from becoming one of the most learned mages in the kingdom. For the past ten years, I've barely been doing scribe work."

"But surely that knowledge doesn't just leave you?"

"It can. Just like any other skill, I suppose. Skills build up but they can also break down. Let's say everything does work—the undoing, the unbinding spell. Shaye is free again. What then?"

"What then," I repeated, hoping the ruler we unleashed and set on the throne wouldn't be just as cruel and power-hungry as her father. *Shaye.* He said her name like he knew her. I guess he had, in passing—in mystery. I thought for a moment about who he might have been, who he was before.

"Did your eyes always, erm..." I gestured to my own, but stumbled on the wording.

"No. Side effect of the curse, I suppose. As well as the purple markings you saw. Didn't have access to a looking glass for months after I was first exiled though, so you can imagine my surprise when—" He froze, his eyes narrowed and staring at something beyond me.

My hands found the handle of my cutlasses and I turned my neck around slowly, straining to see out of the corner of my eye. There was nothing but hazy forest, snow drifting all around covering everything in a fresh film of white. Everything but a small patch of dirt a few horse-lengths away. Instead, the snow settled in mid-air, as if resting on something invisible.

Not invisible—translucent. As if whatever stood there consisted of poorly made glass. A creature. The only parts not entirely see-through were a heart pumping blood that faded into nothing, and some kind of digestive tract.

An Eerree.

I turned on my heel and faced it, stumbling backward over the fire and onto Kaineres. His hands rushed to my sides to steady me as I pressed my body into his. My eyes flashed to Sanders, who was just a bundle of blankets. I hoped it would give them enough cover. I felt Kaineres try to move out from behind me to get to them.

"Stay close to me," I whispered, my eyes glued to the heart floating towards us. It crept ever closer but stopped on the other side of the fire. Its visible insides hovered over where I had been sitting, the heat rising from the flames distorting its shape even more.

"What is it doing?" Kaineres breathed out.

I searched the cloudy air around the figure to get an idea of how big it was. I pressed further into Kaineres' chest, pinning us to the tree.

"Looking for its size."

Eerrees had terrible vision, although that didn't usually stop them from hunting something they thought was similar enough to their shape. Only the most recently replaced organs were visible, so it was hard to tell which ones they still needed. This one was larger than both me and Sanders, but it might think Kaineres a worthy resource.

"Is this the scenario where I act as bait?" The witch whispered coyly in my ear, although I could feel his heart pounding against my back.

"*Shut up and stay low.*" I hissed. My arms were growing heavy waiting for the monster to make its move. I dared to rest the tip of my sword on the ground in front of me after it was clear the Eerree was taking its time. It must've been weak, carefully picking its prey. It stood there for minutes before I realized it would be a waiting game.

"It's not going to strike yet," I whispered.

"Why?"

"It doesn't know how big you are for certain. And it's not strong enough to take on both of us."

"You get all that from a few floating glossy organs?"

"I get that from almost losing mine. Just stay put behind me. Safest bet is counting on it losing interest."

So we waited.

Kaineres eventually wrapped his hands around my waist to let me sit further back into his chest. I spread my legs out over his to hide them while trying to ignore how exposed I was in his lap. My gaze was on the Eeree but my focus was starting to wane to how his hands felt around me. I wondered how his skin would feel. *Fuck.*

After scattering the thoughts away with silent curses, I noticed that the Eeree was growing bored. After pacing around the campsite twice, it made its way deeper into the forest, its tracks erased by fresh snow.

I brushed off the snow that had collected on my legs and chest and shivered at the freezing moisture that snuck its way through small gaps in my clothes.

Slowly Kaineres' arm squeezed gently around my ribcage and pressed my back to his chest.

"Hold on just a moment." His voice was barely audible over the wind-carried leaves dragging across the icy dirt.

He leaned us both back against the tree, and his legs switched places with mine, pushing mine together with his. I ignored the quickening thump in my chest as I felt him on every side of me, wrapping me in body heat that soaked through our clothes.

"Here." He gently took my head in his hands and angled me away from him, exposing my skin near the collar of my shirt.

The hairs on the back of my neck rose as he pulled back my scarf and pressed his lips to my nape. He inhaled, and as he breathed out slowly, warm air from his lungs washed down my back and deep into my spine. My eyes fluttered shut at the feeling, and gods curse me I let my head press into his left hand, while his right was braced against my stomach. He held me for a few long breaths, each one sending streams of warmth down my body. It was all I could do to keep from melting into him completely.

He leaned even closer, his lips grazing the back of my ear.

"I can't breathe for the both of us." He lazily wrapped my scarf back around me.

"What?"

I heard the smirk in his voice. "You shouldn't hold your breath like that."

"I—why are you doing that?" I turned my head around to look at him.

"Because you're cold. And consequently the warmer you are, the warmer I get. But I can stop if you're not comfortable."

"I didn't say that..." I wasn't about to admit how fucking good it felt either. He chuckled at my stubborn and transparent response and continued to blow hot air on my neck, my ears, my cheek...

He shifted in place behind me and a soft moan escaped my mouth as I felt how firm he was against my lower back.

In a fluid motion, Kaineres grabbed my legs and swung me around, lifting my ass with his hands to help me straddle overtop his lap. His double pupils flickered their focus across my face, jumping from my lips to my eyes in silent request. I nodded, and let his fingers take my chin.

His thumb gently grazed my bottom lip as he held me steady and drew himself closer. I felt the heat of his breath as our lips met, cold and cracked. He pressed his kiss into me, soft, but unyielding as his hands glided their way behind my neck and into my hair. I leaned into him and let my eyes close, the beating in my chest exposing me.

He withdrew slowly and looked me over, the russet in his eyes twinkling. He was beautiful. I felt the corners of my lips twitch, a smile I let surface. Kaineres kissed me again, this time ravenously drawing my hair into his fingers like he was afraid the wind would carry me away. The hairs of his beard scraped against my chin as his jaw widened to take more of me. He moaned low and hungry, the vibrations flooding my throat. I grabbed the vest around his neck and pulled him towards me until I lost my balance and I fell backward. His hands around my head caught me, and slowly let my head rest on the ground. He brought his body above mine and I felt the weight of him push into my chest with each ragged breath that escaped his mouth into mine.

My hands wandered up around his neck and over his broad shoulders, my nails catching on the fabric of his sleeves. Each kiss from his lips was more ravenous—needy. I could feel the tip of his tongue dance on the edge of my teeth. I bit down slightly, just a tease, and that was enough to send him pushing forward into me, all over me, his hands still firmly gripped in my hair and around my waist. I let another moan escape, low and guttural, as I wrapped my legs around his. I couldn't remember the last time I had been touched like this, kissed like this, and even in the middle of a frozen wasteland all I could think about was how much I wanted it. How much I wanted him.

Kaineres groaned and pulled back sharply, his eyes shut tight, as if in pain. I scanned his face and a panic froze my pounding heart. I leaned forward, my legs still wrapped around him as I ran my hands over his body, searching for wounds—an arrow, a blade, a talon. He opened his eyes for a moment and then winced again, turning his head to the side. I gently grabbed his face, my peripheral vision scanning the area for anything unusual, a monster, a bandit in the bushes—

Kaineres took my hands in his and let out a slow breath. "It's alright... It was just..." He sighed and forced his gaze to meet mine. His face was contorted with conflicting emotion. I could still see the desire, the trust, but beyond it was something I couldn't name. He looked tired. He looked defeated. He looked like he was going to throw up.

And he did.

He moved my hands out of the way just in time to toss the contents of his stomach onto the icy dirt next to us. Steam rose from the pile of brown bile sinking into the ground as Kaineres hung his head over it, expecting another wave. I slithered my legs out from behind him and withdrew from any possible splashes and waited. When it looked like the worst of the nausea was over, I handed him a cup of the water we had heating next to the fire. He washed his mouth out and spit. After brushing dirt over the mess, he cradled his head and groaned. I waited for yet another wave, but he shook his head again and laughed. The laugh sounded forced, or one that resulted from too much exhaustion.

"Kaineres?" I was hesitant. "Are you alright?"

He ran his hands through his hair aggressively, itching at the back of his scalp like a deranged dog. He was silent for a long pause, staring at the ground while I waited for his response. As if trying to shake away haunting thoughts, he jerked his head to the side.

"You know I haven't joined with anyone in ten years? I haven't so much as *touched* another with any trace of want in a decade." He looked up at me, eyes rimmed with red. "Not that I'm supposed to. As a condition of my exile, it is tradition that I remain *chaste* should I ever hope to be reinstated in the guild, which, if you'd ask anyone, is highly unlikely!" His voice cracked with years of pent-up emotion. "All—*all* this time, I've thought it was just my guilt that's kept me from people, some desperate obsession with *honor* that caused me to push people away. But it's just *her*." He bit his lips and let out an exasperated sigh. "It's *her*."

I tried to wrap my head around what he was saying. "Wait—she. I thought her spirit is dormant—"

"I don't know! I don't know, but I have these feelings that I know aren't mine, but I carry them. I feel them. I feel so much, all the time, and I'm so exhausted. And you stumbled into camp and I was finally hopeful. Hopeful you were someone I could know, and trust, and touch, and feel and every time I get close to you I feel like heaving my guts out."

"You're pretty easy on the eyes yourself," I said sarcastically, much harsher than I meant to.

"I—" A flash of hurt ran across his brow that made me regret saying anything. I didn't know why the mention of the princess made me so defensive around him. Kaineres put his hands on his chest. "I don't know what she sees. I don't know what she hears or what she senses. But I know she's bound to me in more ways than I can understand." He adjusted his shirt collar, looking for something to do. "Once I free the princess, I free myself."

I turned from him to stare into the fire. The crackling of kindling was louder than normal. The earth crunched behind me as Kaineres shifted in place.

"I wasn't lying when I said you would be the best guide out here, but I withheld sentiments I wasn't sure you were ready for." He said softly. "If everything works out, if we achieve what we set out to do, I'd like you with me. I know a magician's guild might be an uncomfortable place for you, but there's a good chance I won't be reinstated, no matter what I do. We could travel. I could take you to Elynchester or Periv or anywhere else you'd like to go. I want you with me, Rune. I want to feel everything you make me feel, unhindered."

"I don't like how you keep saying *if. If* everything works out. Why are you taking a risk like this?"

"I can't live with myself if I didn't try to undo this. Shaye is trapped, but I'm realizing that so am I."

I turned back to him to see him watching me with a deliberateness that stirred something in me. The deep breaths I took to help calm my heartbeat barely made a difference. An unsettling feeling was growing in the place of desire, but I did nothing to wipe off the taste of his kiss lingering on my lips.

A well-timed blessing, Sanders stirred under the blankets and shook us both out of our heads.

"Mmmnnn. Rune?" Sanders mumbled into the blankets and started blinking open their eyes. I rushed to their side and placed a hand on their face. The color of their cheeks was starting to return to normal.

"I'm here, S." I brushed the hair out of their eyes as they continued to blink awake, taking in their surroundings. It was almost morning, and the fog above the treetops had a subtle orange glow.

"The guards..." They propped themselves up on their elbows. They started piecing together words quite sleepily. "I... had a dream I was a rat. Not... a real rat. I was still me but rat size. And all my friends were rats, and we lived under the floorboards of a giant palace. Maybe it was a normal size palace, but it was giant to us, because we were rats. The guards let out a giant dog... maybe a normal-sized dog... but it chased us all through these tunnels. And..."

They yawned, eyes finally adjusting to the soft light of morning and fading fire. I sighed in deep relief and pressed my head to theirs.

"I'm glad you're feeling better. S."

Sanders scrunched up their nose. "What's that smell?"

Kaineres and I exchanged glances between ourselves and the covered pile of vomit on the other side of the fire.

Kaineres stood up and shook the snow off his legs. "I think it's my turn to gather more kindling." Without another word, he bundled his cloak around his face and trudged off. My eyes did not leave his form until the clouds passed between us and he vanished into the morning.

CHAPTER TWENTY-THREE

Kaineres

We had been walking for days. The compass pointed ever onward, giving a direction, but not a distance. Between Rune and Sanders, the Marks carved in the trees exposed helpful information, but other than a few hostile communes there was not much else we could avoid. Rune and I made quick work of any monsters that saw us through the protective enchantments. She never complained about her swords, but I could tell she was frustrated with how long it was taking her to get used to them. I wished I was more aid to her. The majority of my magic and potions were focused on healing and defending, not opposition. Although I would boldly admit Rune fared well on that front by her lonesome.

We hadn't talked much since I almost vomited in her mouth, and I was thankful Sanders was feeling in better spirits as they were filling most of the conversation. I found myself at a loss for words. I wasn't sure whether to be angry at myself or the imprisoned princess—if I had reason to be angry at all. The vast blankness of the scenery and the frigid cold gave way to a host of bitter thoughts that cycled in my mind over and over again. When the anger subsided, the wretched guilt set in. Guilt for the curse, guilt for the state of the Realm, guilt for the shadow of rejection in her grey eyes when I shoved her aside.

In front of me, strands not confined to her braid twisted and twirled as Rune led us through naked branches and over frost-covered roots. I couldn't detect any irritation towards me, but she remained silent—an intricate statue of undetectable emotions, hand carved by what I could only imagine was her stubbornness to survive against odds.

At the end of the second week, we started to run into more people. Desperate bandits, mostly. With one of us always on watch at night, it deterred people enough from attacking us while we slept. We were close to the Southern border, and even Sanders kept volume low as we kept a watchful eye on our surroundings. It wasn't until we came to a series of Marks carved into a tree that the silence was broken.

"We're almost there," Sanders hummed, their hands picking at the scores notched in the wood. "I think I recognize these. A few more miles this direction. We should make a plan before arriving near the border wall."

"And we need to be careful about who sees us," Rune added, her focus darting all around. "I already feel like we're being followed. Lighting a fire tonight is risky."

"Then we don't," I said plainly. There would be soldiers going in and out of the border gates and I would do everything I could to keep Rune from them. We locked eyes and I gave her a reassuring nod. "We camp with no fire. We might not get sleep but we should rest our feet. Finish the last of our reserves, and map a way in. Once through the border wall I can get us to the guild."

Rune set up the usual shelter of branches to keep us hidden while I cast enchantments to muffle our voices and smells. It was freezing without flames to keep us dry, but Rune's body heat kept Sanders and me comfortable as we cradled her between us.

Sanders must have been comfortable enough to fall asleep because they started snoring a few minutes after we laid down. Rune snuggled her head into the crevice between my arm and chest and I closed my eyes at how good she felt beside me. She wouldn't sleep. Neither of us would. The fog above the treetops carried a distinct and unshakable heaviness.

"How much do you think the city has changed?" Her voice was barely above a whisper.

"I don't know. Ten years is a long time."

And there was such little information that made it to the commune that I had no idea what was even left of the life I was cast from. We were firing arrows with our eyes closed.

"Did you mean it?" Rune asked. "When you said you wanted me with you?"

I leaned over and kissed the top of her head. "If Aristus has no place for us then we'll find somewhere that does. If that's what you want."

She turned to me and placed her arm over my chest, igniting a delicious burning underneath my skin. "I'm sorry for snapping at you. I... I'm just not ready for what might happen to you if..."

I took her hand in mine and brought it to my lips. I kissed her gloved knuckles, inhaling the leather and scent of charred wood that lingered. She laid her head back down on my shoulder and started tracing the outline of my beard lazily, sending shivers down my back.

"You've spoken about the other Kingdoms like you've been. Have you seen them? In person?"

"Not all of them. I learned about them growing up, and once I became a witch I did travel to Elynchester and eventually made it to Periv. They're both beautiful, each in their unique way. Nothing like the Aristus you know."

"Hm." She exhaled slowly. "Traveling sounds... lovely. Seeing the world as it is, just to see it."

I had always just one driving force since my banishment. Two, if you count survival. But I wanted nothing more than to get back home with my family and rebuild what I had lost. But at that moment, I ached to take Rune with me. Once I granted myself my own freedom I would take her with me and I would show her the world.

The trees rustled above us as a breeze drifted across the sky. It carried an eerie disturbance to the already uneasy night. All was quiet but for the howling wind and a distant chorus of wailing. Rune tensed in my arms at the faint sound of collected dispair—voice layered over voice of lament and blood-curdling despair. It sounded like it stemmed from the city, or perhaps the ghosts of the banished long past.

Dry bushes directly behind us snapped. Before I knew what was happening, Rune climbed over top of me and out of the shelter, slamming her body into and struggling with something on the ground.

"*Rune!*" I shot up and squinted my eyes to try and see the dark figures rolling around in front of me. Sanders woke up and was on their feet instantly, pocket knife in hand.

It was a person, and Rune fought with the assailant on the forest floor, each grappling for the other's throat. I couldn't cast a disarming spell without it hitting Rune, but as she kicked away the bandit's raised staff she gave herself the upper hand. The man yelled in frustration and fear as Rune brought one of her swords against his neck, pinning him to the ground.

A puzzling combination of excitement and embarrassment rose through my chest as I marveled at her intensity. Watching her grind someone into the ground stirred something in me, and I physically wiped my face with cold hands to hinder the wild thoughts racing through my mind. *Keep it together.*

"Get off—nngh—*please!*" The bandit's hands cut into Rune's blade as he tried to raise her sword off his neck.

"What the *fuck* were you trying?" Rune hissed back, pressing further into his skin. He winced as the skin of his palms spliced open. Any desirous thoughts wading through me turned taut as I worried she might actually kill him.

"Rune..." I said low, creeping towards them.

"What do you *want?* You were following us." She hissed again.

"No—not long—I—"

"Rune." I repeated slowly. "He's disarmed."

"Your compass!" He squeaked out. "Your compass works! That's all I was going to take—I swear!"

"Give me one reason I shouldn't separate your head from your shoulders."

"*Rune.*" I reached out for her, but Sanders grabbed my arm and put a hand up, telling me to wait.

The bandit cowered underneath Rune's stare. "You're going to Aristus—I—I'll tell you how."

"Why the hell should I trust you?"

"I have no reason to lie—I swear! I swear on the gods of the hunt." He showed his arm bearing a thin metal chain with beads and symbols dedicated to his gods. Rune said something under her breath I didn't catch, but it sounded characteristically caustic.

"Fine. Make it quick and I won't make carrion of you."

"The logs. The clean cut logs... point to the burrows."

Sanders perked up. "The tunnels still exist? I thought they were discovered and filled."

"N-new tunnels. Burrows. Smaller but they lead right under the army's wall. It's the truth. Follow the logs." He closed his eyes and recited a prayer as Rune contemplated what he said.

"Fuck off." Rune released her pressure on his neck and the man scurried out from under her, holding his bloody palms against his stomach. He left his wooden staff where it lay and ran off into the woods.

Rune wiped the blood of her blade in the dirt and turned it over in her hand a few times, debating whether or not to put it back in its holster. An exhale of relief forced its way out of my chest as I knelt down next to her.

"You weren't really going to kill him, were you?"

Sanders stretched out their soreness. "She's all talk. She just knows how to get information out of people. It's a hound-eat-hound world out here so it won't be the last time he gets a knife to his neck."

Rune remained silent as she massaged her jaw. It was too dark to see her expression clearly, but her mind was anywhere but here.

"What tunnels, Sanders?"

"People once used a tunnel system to aid people banished in The Colds. They would sneak out food and weapons to the other side. Everyone who knew someone over here used it, not just rebels. When I last left Aristus, the army had been tipped off about it and they filled the holes. Only a matter of time before new ones were made I suppose. Do you think he was telling the truth?"

Rune scoffed. "No. But we might as well look for the logs since it's the only information we have."

We silently packed up our supplies and used the compass to walk alongside the Southern Border. The daylight started to illuminate the mist above us, and we finally stumbled across the logs sometime mid-morning. The 'clean cut' logs the bandit spoke of were trees that had not fallen naturally, but had been chopped down. Like giant Marks in the forest floor, pointing to Aristus.

Sanders led us south with Rune in the rear, swords drawn and ready for miles. My heart ached to see her so exhausted—always on alert.

"Shh." Sanders raised a hand. They used their fingers to signal back to Rune something she understood, because the two of them crouched at the same time, pulling me down with them. I tilted my chin above the brush and saw a stone wall far in the distance, akin to the stone surrounding the King's Courtyard. Also in the distance was a troop of equine soldiers, lacking their nauseating cage of captured Withins. Crouched low to the ground, we waited for them to pass on down the wall.

Sanders made more signals to Rune, and she tapped me on the shoulder to follow them. The last clean-cut log was pointed directly at another large tree, still upright but curiously covered in dry foliage. Sanders pulled a blanket of branches to the side to reveal the entrance to a large burrow, just big enough for a person to squeeze through on their stomach. *Please no.* I cast a desperate glance toward Rune, who simply returned a sympathetic grimace and tightened her scarf around her mouth.

"We've come this far," Sanders whispered. Then they crawled into the burrow head first.

Rune gestured to my satchel. It wouldn't fit alongside me. I gingerly gave it to her and she fashioned it to her person as I ran my fingers nervously through my hair. *Gods of the moon preserve me.* My head started to throb. Never a good sign. My heart quickened its pace, and air I wasn't ready to lose escaped my lungs, leaving me gasping for more.

Hands softly caressed my waist and untied the cloak clinging to my neck, then drifted lower to unbutton the sides of my vest. I closed my eyes and allowed Rune to pull the tight material over my chest and tuck it away into the bag. Breathing came a little easier with just the loose tunic, even if it was freezing.

"It widens a bit," Sanders called back, their voice muffled by their own body blocking the sound.

I gave Rune a squeeze on the arm and shifted down to my stomach, inching myself forward and into the hole in the earth. It was too dark, too damp, too much like crawling into my own grave. I focused on my breathing as I crept forward on my elbows, cold dirt scraping all sides of my body as I dragged through. Rune wasn't far behind me, and she gave me a reassuring squeeze on my leg.

I wasn't sure how far we had to go, and I desperately hoped that no one was coming towards us from the opposite direction. A few minutes in my head was screaming in pain; the smell of musty dirt and stone tugged on long-logged memories that only surfaced in waves of panic. I couldn't piece them together, but images flashed in my mind of crawling through tunnel spaces, dark and dismal. We were going to trap ourselves in here—suffocate underground. I shut my eyes tight and kept wiggling forward inch by inch, closer and closer to an exit we didn't know was there.

The burrow did eventually widen a bit, but not enough to get up or even sit. We belly-crawled onward, the dirt fading into patches of brick and stone as we got closer to the city limits. The skin on my elbows scraped through my sleeve on the jagged floor, but it gave me hope we were almost there.

"*Ouch!*"

In front of me, Sanders suddenly stopped. "I think... we're across. This looks like an exit."

Tears filled my eyes as Sanders pushed through a wooden slat to the other side, streaks of light dripping into the burrow and kissing my skin with greed, touching every inch they could reach. *Light.* I grabbed Sanders' hand as they hoisted me out into the open winter air, brisk but entirely divine. Any aching in my head had subsided to the warmth of sunlight and I felt the rising anxieties melt away in the brightness of the day. I turned around and let the tears fall as she emerged, hand over her eyes and smiling.

Not smiling—laughing.

Rune, with dirt on her face and cuts on her arms laughed into the sunlight, casting a spell on my heart that ripped me open from the inside. Her joy was a blanket of ice and I could only marvel at how softly it settled into my chest. There was such a coldness to it, a harshness in her gravelly tone that somehow seemed to wrap gently around everything it touched, cocooning me in my own warmth like a glove to a hand.

I reached for her, pulling her up and out of the tunnel and into the empty alleyway in which we stood. She drew Sanders into an embrace, and they in turn yanked me towards them. We held each other, sunlight streaming directly above us, anointing us with the rhapsody of being alive, our breaths echoing like rhythmic music in each other's ears.

"I hope I'm not interrupting something."

Our attention snapped to a man at the end of the alley, leaning against the side of a building wearing a magnificent crimson coat. The lifted sleeves exposed deep red tattoos on his dark skin—bands on his middle fingers connected to bands on his forearms. Silver jewelry dangled from his ears to his jaw, and while his face was twisted into a stern expression, he had a gleam in his eyes.

"Honored to be the first to welcome you back to civility, rotten heathens."

CHAPTER TWENTY-FOUR

Rune

"Marcus." Kaineres let out a breath and walked slowly towards the stranger. I released the grip on my swords as the two men pulled themselves into a tight embrace. Instead, I quickly raised my scarf over my nose and pulled the hood of my cloak over my head. In the exhilaration of feeling the sun on my skin again I completely forgot where I was.

Kaineres held the man's face in his hands as he repeated his name. "Marcus. Why are you here?"

"I was about to ask you that same question. What in the name of your gods are you doing? You get spotted by the wrong person and you're dead on sight."

"I know, I'll explain everything—we need a place to talk. A safe place."

The other witch let Kaineres go and examined us. Sanders, bless them, positioned themselves casually in front of me. Marcus made a tight line with his lips but nodded to Kaineres. He reached into his cloak and retrieved a tiny vial.

"This will only last long enough to get to my house."

"House? What happened to the guild?"

"It's not safe for you. We can take turns explaining everything later. Here."

Kaineres took the vial and uncorked it, gesturing for us to join him. He sprinkled it over Sanders, who disappeared right before my eyes.

"Sweet Mother!" They grabbed my arm with an invisible hand.

Kaineres sprinkled the dust over me, the same way he had that day in the woods. The tingle sensation was familiar, but still bizarre. Lastly, he covered himself, and the three of us were nothing more than human Eerrees—transparent enough to see through, but not perfectly clear.

"You'll have to keep quiet, and keep to the shadows," Marcus said as he waved us behind him. "I can't look behind me in order to avoid suspicion, so don't fall behind."

With that, he was off—his long legs carrying him swiftly through the empty streets. Why were they empty? Wherever the burrow led was definitely part of the lower city—near Flatkeep and the marketplace. But it lacked the usual chaotic energy of people cramming into each other every which way. The run-down buildings were abandoned, and parts of the town looked burnt. The wooden shingles of rooftops looked more like the bottom of a fireplace—covered in soot and ash.

The air was cold, but it hadn't yet snowed in the Realm, so we didn't worry about leaving footprints. As Marcus turned down streets that were more crowded, he started walking down alleyways to avoid people passing by.

Aristus was just as dreary as it was when I was exiled. Grey cobblestone streets and plain plaster buildings erected with no real order—winding and weaving all the way up to the main street towards the castle. Marcus took us through tight pathways close to buildings and under awnings until we finally reached a cluster of homes near the upper city. He opened up a small wooden door leading to some sort of basement or cellar and gestured for us to climb inside.

The basement was not much larger than a horse stall, most likely built for storage. Marcus closed the door behind him and touched it in three spots until it made a clicking sound. A locking mechanism, perhaps. He rubbed his hands together furiously until his palms started glowing from the friction. He pressed his hands to the low ceiling above us and chanted something that transferred the dim light from his fingers to where he placed them on the plaster. I couldn't see their face, but I knew Sanders' jaw was gaping at the soft glow that remained on the ceiling—as if it was merely a curtain someone had lit a candle behind.

"Now," Marcus grunted as he found a place on the floor to sit, "is the part where you explain everything."

Kaineres pulled the magic powder off of himself, becoming visible again with a sweeping motion of his hands. "I will, but first I must ask—how did you find us?"

"I could feel you beneath the city." Marcus said, and taking in Kaineres' expression, added, "I charmed the length of the city walls to alert me when you passed through. I wanted to be the first one to get to you, in case... well. Be glad it was me."

"Immensely. Why are we not at the guild? What happened?"

"King Amos happened." Marcus shook his head. "The night of your banishment the King and his court tightened their fists around the use of magic. The majority of guilds were shut down, most witches and mages were stripped of their titles unless they belonged to the noble Houses, and the markets were cleared of every item and ingredient known to contain magic. South Society Guild, while not shut down, has been heavily guarded by soldiers the past couple of months. I don't know the reason behind the sudden reinforcements, but right now it's not somewhere you can show your face. Even if it looks as unkempt as it does."

Kaineres patted down his scraggly beard. "What's this business I'm hearing about regarding the disunion?"

"King Amos is acting as though he's found some kind of fault in the ordinances. News is he won't step down because there is no blood heir to take his throne. Not even a nephew or niece. I... don't know how far information spreads, but I assume you know about the assassination years after you—*left*."

Kaineres only nodded.

"Well, for years following he's held a remembrance in their honor—all the children. It's tomorrow, actually. You couldn't have come at a worse time Kain—Kaineres. Each year the King goes deep into the retelling of their deaths, and always brings up the princess. No one has forgotten and King Amos seems just as heartbroken as the day he lost them. He refuses to replace them, but he's already past sixty years of age. The Alliance doubts his sincerity. To be honest, so do I."

"That's why I've returned. It's a long story, so I'll condense where I can." As Kaineres began his retelling of the events leading to our journey, Sanders and I started to fade back into view. Still feeling all too exposed, I willed myself to blend in with the surroundings, hoping I could enhance the enchantment just by focusing my energy on it. It worked to an extent. I was partially visible, partially see-through. Like how a Skevsurvian might envision a ghost. Marcus didn't seem to notice, as his eyes widened at Kaineres' tale.

"Niece? What niece?" He ran his hands over the top of his smooth head in confusion.

"That's a longer story. But yes, when my niece returned, she had this." Kaineres reached into his satchel and removed the delicate spell book. His friend gently took it into his hands and tried to open it to no avail. "Said she swiped it from a Skevsurvian mage. Took me weeks to open it."

He went on to explain the contents of the book, including the description of the binding curse. Marcus sat motionless with his hands over his mouth, staring at the little leather-bound bundle in front of him.

"Her body was never found." He finally whispered. "Oh Kain-eres, did you know?"

"No, of course not. I mean I had mindless musings about the possibility but nothing would ever confirm it. Until this." He put the book back in the satchel and rubbed a hand through his hair, still freckled with dirt. "I have an idea on how to undo it, but I wanted your opinion, Gustan's as well, if he'll see me."

Marcus stared at the floor. "Gustan has passed on. He... I know that night broke both of you, but I hope you know he tried everything he could to spare you. It was never his wish to cast you out."

My chest cracked at the emotion that washed over the healer's face. They were talking about a world I knew nothing of other than the fact that Kaineres wanted desperately to be a part of it.

Sanders tugged on my sleeve. I looked down at my arms that were slowly appearing and a panic crept into my lungs. A cough forced its way out of my throat and morphed into a fit of dry heaving.

Sanders asked if there was a well nearby, and Marcus, still honed in on the witch, pointed in the direction I could find one. The door's lock disengaged with a swipe of his hand and I rushed out, my cloak still pulled over my head. I threaded my beads through my fingers and briskly stepped in the shadows to where the well was. *Shit.*

It was in the middle of the street, and there were too many people. I grabbed tight to my throat and begged myself to stop coughing, muffling the noise into my scarf as best as I could. I found an overhanging ledge and sank beneath it, squeezing behind a tall hedge bush still orange from autumn.

I shouldn't be here. I can't be here.

The dryness in my throat calmed down, but I was frozen underneath the ledge, terrified that someone would spot me trying to return to Marcus' house.

Kaineres trusted him. He trusted him as a friend and also trusted him to help undo the curse. I wouldn't be any help at all. I did my part. I guided him through The Colds. We made it out alive. He didn't need me anymore. Marcus would help him free the princess and he would prove his innocence. He could go back to his guild. His life.

But he wouldn't be able to find me again. Would he want to? Where would I go? I couldn't stay in Aristus. I could always go back to the commune. Without the compass? Without Sanders? No shitty powerless god could untie the knot that threatened to tear my gut apart. My hands cradled my head as the panic ripped through me, hitting every soft point and open wound I thought to be frozen. I went from having nothing to having everything in a matter of days and I walked both of them right out of the only place we could be together. I clenched my tongue until the pain seeped around my mouth.

The sun moved slowly overhead into the afternoon and took away the shadow I hid in inch by inch. I laughed through my nose at the irony. Years of my life, begging to see the daylight only to cower from it when it drew near. Some rogue rebel.

"Rune?"

Kaineres ran past the hedge concealing me and headed for the well. He was wearing a different set of clothes, but he was still far too exposed. I pushed off the wall and ran after him.

"Hey—you shouldn't be out here." I grabbed his arm and tugged him back into the alleyway. Relief flooded his face as we locked eyes.

"You shouldn't be either. You've been gone too long I was worried something happened. Sanders is getting a change of clothes from Marcus. He might have something for you too, just to get into something clean." He put his hand on the small of my back to guide me towards his friend's house. "Marcus agrees with me on my theory to reverse the curse, and he'll help any way he can. We need to lay low though, people are already gathering for the Remembrance."

I balked.

"Rune?" His voice was too soft, too concerned.

"When can you do it?" I pushed. "If Marcus can help why are we waiting?"

"That's where things get complicated. I need to be where it happened. Where time and space remember."

"Remember what? Why can't you do it somewhere safe?" It didn't make sense. And the longer we waited the more at risk we were to lose everything. The longer we waited the more the past would barrel back to me and ruin everything.

He turned towards me, his confusion masked by an exasperated smile. "I thought you were anxious about what had to be done, and now you want to rush into it? What happened?"

"No, it's not that—"

A soul-wrenching sound pierced the air around us. Anguished echoes from the night before, but much clearer and distinguishable for what they were. Screams of distress and sobs of desperation floated above the rooftops and into the alley.

Mourners—gathering in the streets. Noblemen. Court members. Parents. I watched them pass by from the coverage of the alley, mother's weeping and cradling bundles of firewood wrapped in cloth—soft linens with playful patterns. Those who didn't have bundles carried unlit candles and small objects. A toss ball. A slingshot. A wooden figurine.

The wailing continued to grow as the mass of grievers walked on down the street towards the large gate to the upper city, where in the distance I could just make out a poster displaying the marred face of a girl.

Their sobs rang in my ear and rattled through my thoughts, tearing down my defenses and leaving behind something broken and empty. I didn't feel the gust of wind that blew my scarf free from my face.

"Rune." Kaineres looked through the alley, past the mourners, to the gate where the poster hung, corners flying in the wind. "What were you banished for?"

His eyebrows furrowed and I winced at the way he brought his gaze to me. My sternum cracked around my heart as the skin of his neck flushed and his eyes reddened.

"Please don't—don't look at me like that—" *Please.*

"*What were you banished for?*" His voice cracked with anguish and his eyes flashed with rage that wasn't entirely his own. The deep green of his eyes burned a hole through me as his double pupils narrowed. Vibrant. Emerald. Trapped. The same deep green eyes filled with terror on the other side of the glass.

"I didn't *know*, Kaineres." Tears were streaming down my own face now. I didn't care if they seared right through my skull.

His large chest caved with each jagged breath he released. His voice leeched out through clenched teeth as he paced towards me. "Every rebel that passed through the commune said it was a *calculated,* and *deliberate* attack. How could you *not know?*"

I shook my head. "There weren't supposed to be children. It—it was the council chambers. Our intel told us it would be a meeting. Not... I truly didn't know."

"Oh, just the adults then? Th-th-that makes it better. Doesn't m-make you as much of a *murderer.*" He was panicking, but his words cut deep.

"What did you expect then? Huh? You knew I was a member of the rebellion. There was a *fucking bounty* on my neck. You found me in *The Colds*—You had to have known I wasn't perfectly innocent."

"You're right. Come to think of it, I-I'm not sure I know you at all. Convenient of you to spare me the gritty details of what kind of dirt work you did for the heroic cause." He wiped his face with his palms, the streak marks from my tears still visible on his hands. "How do I know you're not lying? Th-that you didn't come all this way just to finish what you started? *You,* wanting to get as far away from Aristus as possible somehow didn't need much convincing to come back with *me."*

The gutting sobs in the distance tormented me from every angle—gnawed at me from the marrow in my bones.

"Is it her?" He could barely breathe out the words. "Is that all you wanted?"

"*Kain—*" My throat burned.

"Why not kill me off then? Why drag it out?"

"*Kaineres* please—*I came only because of you. I wanted to keep you safe.*" Each word scorched my tongue and sizzled out of my mouth, breaking the chapped skin on my lips.

"Safe from *whom?* You, Twig, each and every rebel, after all you've taken your goals have never wavered. I will not let you take her. I *will* make it right."

Before I could force any more sound out of my throat, the witch turned for the house and left me standing, mouth burning, chest cavity exposed and raw, in the middle of the alleyway. My knees gave way to the burden I could no longer carry and I stumbled back out of the shadows and into the street.

The warm winter sun gently slid its fingers across my face and the singe felt like being thrown into a fire lit by a lover. The softness stung more than every deep cut from a blade and I felt helpless as I stood in the daylight, bloody and bare.

My throat burned. My ribcage felt like it was filled with boiling water and hollow at the same time. A trail of crimson dripped from my scarred lip and down my chin. Through blurred vision I saw Kaineres disappear through the cellar door in the distance. I sank to my knees, alone, staring at nothing and feeling everything. My blood dripped down my chin onto the grooves in the cobblestone. As the crimson seeped into the dirt and mortar, the final strand of what was left of my resolve snapped, myself along with it.

A shout that didn't quite reach my ears vibrated across the surrounding plaster walls, followed by the thundering of footsteps. I didn't draw my swords as I was surrounded. Maybe I was too tired. Maybe it was because I knew there was nowhere left to run. Maybe in my core, I knew it was what I deserved.

Hands gripped my arms and a rope was placed around my neck and back, and as I was lifted skywards I closed my eyes to block out the sun.

CHAPTER
TWENTY-FIVE

Rune

The open wounds on my cheeks snagged on the ground as I was dragged by my ankles. The thick metal chains that bound my hands together dug tight into my wrists. A metallic flavor coated my tongue and leaked out my lips as they smashed against rough stone steps. My cutlasses were confiscated along with my belt, outer shirt, and cloak and once we descended to a lower level of the prison hold, I was thrown inside an iron cell. I grunted as the end of a steel-toed boot hit the back of my head.

"Filthy Trick-blood." An Aristian guard spat on me, kicking me further into the cell to strengthen the message.

The door clanged shut, exacerbating the pounding ache in my skull. Keys rattled before a large bar was placed in front of the iron-barred door as an extra layer of precaution. The guards retreated down the narrow hallway and exited through an old wooden door we must have come through. The prison hold was a spiral structure just outside the castle walls. Down the dark stairways and musty hallways were small cells, divided by either iron bars or slick stone walls. The thick scent of mold acted as a cold press on the inside of my inflamed nostrils.

I sat up slowly as specks of light flared across my vision. My state was a mess, but Rena's beads clung bravely to a few strands of hair. The soldiers knew who I was. While the riot dragged me over to the prison, people went into great detail about what every layer of hell had in store for me. But I should have been dead already. Unless the court nobles wanted to get creative with their punishments. Frozen wasteland wasn't torture enough. I guess they wanted to look me in the eyes as they killed me.

I looked around. Not that there was much to look at. There were no lights of any kind. Not even a window. I had no idea how much time had passed since Kaineres left me near the well.

I knew it wouldn't sound good, no matter how I explained it. But it truly was an accident. An unforgivable, irreversible misstep. Whose fault exactly, I never found out. But I was the one caught.

Buried memories trickled back, revealing the months of planning, the secret meetings, the information gathered from servants inside the castle. We knew every Court member's schedule—every meal they ate, every dance they threw, every visitor paid for time spent under sheets. Every meeting held with the King. Every meeting, always held in the Hall of Assembly. It was a moonless night. The lights were out. They had always been prone to secrecy. I thought nothing of it.

I had been practicing for months. Using my own magic. Embracing the fire that boiled up woven from rage and grief—and bringing life to it with a slice of my wrist. Mentors shoring me with confidence. 'Sweet vengeance, straight from your own lips' they proclaimed. 'What better judgment, than to wipe them out with the very magic they drain in the streets'. The assembly hall had been filled with old scrolls and records from previous gatherings held. Only when the piles of kindling erupted with flames did I see their faces.

In my horror, I slipped off the side of the building where I perched and tumbled down into a garden bed surrounded by castle guards who only saw the fire from a distance. They didn't listen to me scream, begging them to go back. And when they did it was too late.

I released a breath that came out in shudders. With my layers stripped, it was freezing in the hold. My body ached from being hauled down the stairwell—from dragging myself through a burrow like a vermin—from the weeks-long journey through a barren hellscape. My spirit dulled from the violent return to loneliness. Despite it all, I hoped Kaineres could free himself. He deserved that much. He deserved the life he wanted. A healer. In a twisted, selfish way I almost coveted the time I thought he might be a ruthless killer. Then he wouldn't have had to stoop so low to be near me.

There were no swords to grab, no knives to unsheathe, even my fists were chained together, so I did nothing when I heard scuffling on the other side of the cell.

"Are you a wicked?" A voice. A quiet voice. A young voice.

"Yes."

I willed my eyes to adjust to the darkness, but the only things visible were figures of shadow. A few in my cell. A few in the cell next to me.

"*Kasey, do it.*" Someone whispered.

I heard a small grunt, and then from the corner of the cell, a small dim light started to grow from a young boy's arm where he had bit himself open. He was covered in bite marks and clotted blood. In his tiny pale hands, he held out the light—flickering over his skin like a jar of fireflies. Around him, huddled together, were groups of people—all different ages with long scars in their forearms. All of them wickeds. The wickeds the King was collecting.

"Where did they find you?" The young quiet voice belonged to a girl much younger than Sora. Her palid skin was pulled taut by chains tightly strapped to her arms and legs. "The streets or the banish lands?"

"I... The streets. I guess." Pain stuck a pin in my stomach as I examined all the faces—shivering, scared, numb. "Is this all of you—of us?"

The girl shook her head. "There are more in this hallway, in other cells behind the stone walls. Kasey is one of the only people who knows how to make light."

It flickered weakly as the boy narrowed his eyes in concentration to keep it glowing.

"Do you know what they're keeping us for?" I asked. These people didn't look like criminals. They looked like captured prey.

"Not really. The soldiers come to bring someone in or to take someone out. They're using us for something but we don't know what. Sometimes they take a whole group at a time. They won't kill us all at once because they need it fresh." It meaning blood. "But they usually go in order of who they brought in, so you don't have to worry about being taken right away."

I wasn't sure that was the silver lining. "They want my head for multiple reasons, so they might have me cut in line," I said mostly to myself.

"I knew it." A woman shifted from against the wall. "Your face. You're so much older now."

I focused my blurry vision. When Kasey's light flickered over her face, I could just make out the woman's soft jaw and long brown hair that must have once been beautiful. She looked to be around Manden's age, early forties.

"I was a member of the rebellion, you see," she whispered. Her voice solemn. "Look at where that wretched man has driven us."

She was talking about the King, but I knew there were two sides to a war.

Pity—and a faint glimmer of hope not meant for me—twinkled in my chest. My fate was cemented, but I could give them something to cling to.

"The King can't hold the throne forever," I said.

"There's no one left under the law to take his place." The woman scoffed. "And every person who claims to share his bloodline has been proven wrong in court or *mysteriously* disappeared."

That didn't surprise me, but I continued. "There is one left. Ten years ago, the Princess Shaye Aristus was never killed. It's... complicated to get into, but her spirit is about to be set free." And not at the cost of the witch, I hoped.

The wickeds exchanged incredulous glances with each other.

"If all goes well when her spirit returns to life, she will be able to take her place as the Queen of the Realm. How differently she will rule is anyone's guess, but it's enough a reason to not give up all hope." It felt like utter rubbish as the words left my tongue. I sounded like Sanders, and probably looked ridiculous saying such things with bruises on my face and blood trailing down my neck. But if there was a way to raise some of them out of despair, I wanted to do it while I had the chance. But everyone's faces just grew more concerned.

The woman sighed. "Even if what you say is true, King Amos won't let it happen. He's made it clear he has no intention of stepping down, even with the threats from the Alliance."

"He'll have to, even the court nobles have to follow the order of the Alliance." As I said it I felt foolish. The nobles were under Amos' thumb.

"Even if they *wanted* to, it wouldn't happen." The woman pushed back. "If somehow the princess returns, and it would take an act of the divines to make that happen, the King would kill her the moment he has an opening to."

"Surely he wouldn't want to lose another kid? She'll be his only kin left!" Even if the amount of heartbreak over the rebel attack was drawn out, that's not something someone would willingly put themselves through just to maintain power.

Again I was met with faces of concern. The woman shifted onto her knees and placed her bound hands in her lap.

". . .You don't know." Her voice sent a chill down my spine.

Kasey's light flickered out as he turned his head toward the woman. Darkness scattered away all the sight I had of the damp cell. The woman spoke in hushed tones as if she was afraid of which shadows could hear her.

"The night we planned the attack on the King and his court, somehow word was leaked to Amos. There was a last minute change of plans, and he canceled his meeting with the court in order to prepare a gift to the children. A... a book reading, I was told. Late at night. He ushered in every child that was his own and that shared his bloodline. Some of the Courtiers' children too. They huddled quietly in the Hall of Assembly waiting for the King to return with a storybook. We were never notified of the change. The only person who knew who the attack would target was Amos Aristus."

The air around me grew colder. The sound of labored breathing was the only noise that carried through the cell. And in the darkness, the only color I could see was the shade of green being overtaken by white-hot flames.

I didn't want to believe it. It didn't make sense. The amount of cruelty, for what? A few more years of ruining cities under your orders? To make the enemy seem that much more heartless? Surely more than just *he* knew about what happened that night. Would it matter if it did? For the right price?

It was difficult to reach my beads with the way my hands were bound, but through searing pain, I re-threaded them through my hair and tucked them behind my ear. Memories unraveled as I put pieces together. Princess Shaye would have to be a better leader than her father. Even her spirit broke at the loss of her siblings. I could feel her anguish through his tears as he—

Kaineres. There would be no one to warn him. The King might not even let the unbinding happen—he would kill Kaineres the moment he set foot in the courtyard. I stood, and without my strength to balance me, my knees buckled and my back slammed against the iron bars. *Shit.* I stood again, bracing myself against the cold iron.

"Kasey—do it again." The little girl said.

"—I'm trying!"

I was finally about to stand upright, and I wasn't worried about the blood I lost as most of the wounds had already clotted dry. Teeth chattering, I took heavy steps over to the cell door to figure out the locking mechanism. Even if it was foolish, I had to try something. Groaning underneath the weight of all the magic I did not know, I pushed my head against the iron bars of the cell door. The witch didn't ever produce spells that packed a punch, so there was nothing I could even mimic that would help. *You can't heal a door open you fucker.*

Clumsily, I groped my hands along the side of the frame to feel for hinges. Maybe if those were struck hard enough...

I felt warmth on the other side of my hands. Like breath. Was that me? I paused as soon as I reached the top hinge and gave the metal a sturdy wiggle.

With a squeal from rusted metal, the bar against the door clanged to the ground. I backed up and fell on my tail-bone in surprise. The hinges squeaked as the door pushed slowly inward.

The flickering light from Kasey's magic lit the cell again, and in the doorway stood a shaggy-headed figure wearing a cheeky gap-toothed grin.

"Damn, Rune, you should try this magic stuff out sometime."

I choked back tears and threw myself into Sanders' embrace. They really did know how to get themselves out of anything.

"How did you do that?" I whispered. I wasn't sure how they got in or if the guards were still stationed outside the door at the end of the hallway.

Sanders pinched their eyelids together in an attempted wink and jingled a little embroidered coin purse holding the remaining stonewall dust.

"I mouthed the phrase Kaineres used when he unlocked a chest in MistView—where they hid the eye. I only knocked out one set of guards just outside the door and I don't know how much longer they'll stay out, so we better hurry."

Sanders rushed to open the rest of the cell gates, and I pushed past the wooden door to find two guards hunched over each other, one with a visible welt on his forehead. *Well done, S.*

There was a window ajar where Sanders must have snuck through, and I let out a sigh of relief when I saw that the window let out fairly low to the ground—near the forest on the south side of the castle wall. The prison hold must have been built into a hill, with main access from the top. Where the captives would go, I wasn't sure. But I had to get to Kaineres before he walked right into the end of a sword.

After Sanders had freed every cell in the hallway, we squeezed through the window and lowered ourselves down with a chain of the captives' clothing—offered up and tied together. With the help of the older Withins, we were able to get those who were weaker and smaller to the ground safely. Sanders ushered them all towards the cover of trees towards the South and grabbed my hand for us to follow.

"Wait—" I tugged back. "We need to get Kaineres. He's in trouble."

"How do you mean? Marcus is sneaking him into the courtyard with a disguise." They took the last remaining bit of stonewall dust and sprinkled it on the iron bars. I wiggled my hands out when the lock on the chains loosened.

"Take me to the courtyard. I'll explain on the way. We have to reach him before he's seen."

As I ran and told them everything I had heard, I tore off the sleeves of my undershirt and fashioned them around my head. It wasn't as thick as a scarf, but it would have to do to keep my scar from being noticed. Not that I was all that unassuming given my lack of clothing and the damage on my skin akin to battle scars. But I just needed to reach the witch in time.

We ran through alleyways and under low decorative trees—We had made it past the walls of the upper city and the stark contrast was sickening. Beautiful buildings, art mosaics in the street, the scent of food wafting through house windows. As we drew closer to the Castle Courtyard, low hums of horns caressed my ears. The remembrance must have started at dawn—the sky was a gradient of deep blue and yellow, the sun barely peeking over the horizon line.

A few people shouted their offense as Sanders and I pushed through the tightening crowd, frantically searching for a familiar head of dark, grey-speckled hair. We were too short to see over the bustle of people, and I pulled Sanders aside to stand on the ledge of a large planter. A few mourners swat their hands at me to get down, but I didn't move until my eyes landed on the back of a deep red coat.

"*Marcus!*" I sprinted, knocking drinks out of hands and leaving trails of disgruntled Noblemen behind me.

Marcus turned on his heel, eyes wide. "What the *hell* are you doing here? I now know who you are, and if you think—"

"—*Marcus, he's in danger. Kaineres is in danger.*" Please listen to me.

"He's in a disguise—he'll only reveal himself at the right moment."

"He can't—the King will kill him, he killed them all, he—" Heat rushed up my throat again. *Not now.*

Sanders caught up to us. "You were right Marcus, when you said you didn't believe his grief was real. It's not—he'll do anything to keep things as they are. Amos doesn't want the princess to return."

Marcus shook his head in disbelief and confusion. "I—I don't even know where he is right now, I thought he would look too recognizable next to me."

A collected gasp followed by sporadic shrieks came from the center of the courtyard. *No.*

"*Wait!*" I pushed through the crowd to find him in the center, having thrown off his cloak in dramatic form to gain attention.

Guards surrounded him instantly, although their expressions were questioning. As though after ten years he truly was hard to recognize.

However, on the raised dais near the center of the courtyard, a man looking no older than fifty stood slowly from his seat, eyes glaring and mouth twisted in shock. King Amos.

Before I could run out, Marcus held my arm back. "Wait—it might be okay."

Kaineres scattered dust around him, collecting more gasps of terror from the crowd. When he spoke, his voice echoed throughout the courtyard.

"Your Majesty, King Amos, I come before you to right a wrong from many years ago."

King Amos snarled, but held out a hand to stop the guards from attacking. His voice was steely and unnaturally cold. "How could you possibly redeem yourself from what you took from this Kingdom? From these people? How dare you expose yourself on this day of sorrow. How dare you still live while her blood is on your hands."

Marcus held me firm as I tried to pull away. I needed to get him out of there.

Kaineres bowed his head low and held his hands high. "The offense that happened the night I was banished was not a murder, but a curse." He waited for the shudder of the crowd to settle before he continued his plea. "One I did not intend to cast. It was never my intention to take the princess from you. But I announce myself here, today, in an effort to undo this tragedy. I shall unbind the magic keeping us as one, and I shall free her soul to rebuild herself from her ashes."

The King raised an eyebrow, obviously contemplating what the witch said, seemingly not as confused as everyone else around him. After too many terrifying seconds, he waved his guards at ease. His gaze darkened.

"Show me."

The healer inhaled deep, steady, and intentional breaths sending billows of steam rising upwards. He guided his hands one at a time over his chest then down his arms, intimately, almost like a dance. With steady breathing and the motion of his arms, his body shifted forward, resisting something. Then I saw it. Energy pooling on his chest and swirling around his hands with colors I had never seen before, feeling very much in front of us and also very distant. The morning sun added its shimmer to the growing mass of winding energy and illuminated the courtyard with streams of pale color, like the light cast from stained glass.

Beads of sweat formed and dropped from his face, and his eyebrows furrowed at the tension he held in his hands, in his spirit. Although jaws hung open, there was not a sound made in the crowd as they watched the exiled witch cast his spell—separating himself and surrendering a piece of his soul to time and space around him.

And time and space remembered.

At our feet, from cracks in the walls and crevices in the cobblestone, rubble and ash swept by and started to swirl furiously around Kaineres as he pushed and pulled the magic through his person. Even the King had to steady himself on the dais to keep from falling over in the sudden gust of wind that had picked up.

Kaineres screamed under the weight of it all and my heart froze. I pulled free from Marcus' hand only to be blown back along with everyone in the courtyard. A loud banging sound—like the cracking of a boulder off a mountainside pierced the air, and from the ground I could see two figures lying in the center of the courtyard.

Slowly, everyone surrounding them recovered from the blast, wiping their faces in awe and disbelief. I crawled forward on my knees, trying to find the rise and fall of his chest.

Get up. Please get up.

The witch's body released a shudder, and he gingerly lifted himself up from his elbows. Next to him, was the body of a woman with night-black hair. Kaineres reached for the cloak that had been tossed aside and placed it over her bare skin, shielding her from the cold.

The King and his guards stirred in the background, observing the scene in front of them. The King's eyes were wide as he glanced between the witch and his daughter. He snapped his fingers.

"Kill him."

"No!"

The guards drew their bows, but instantly a cloud of thick smoke materialized and overtook the courtyard. Someone gripped my arm and yanked me sideways, pulling me through the crowd now screaming and darting in panic. Before I was dragged out of the smoke, I felt something tingle over my body. When the morning sky became visible, my arms were not, and the invisibility charm settled over the rest of my body by the time I was pulled past the castle gates.

CHAPTER TWENTY-SIX

Rune

Marcus' house was tastefully decorated on the inside, but there was no time to take in details as bags were being thrown on tables and vials of potions were pulled off of shelves by invisible hands.

"Here." The voice of Marcus retrieved a few articles of clothing out of a wardrobe and threw them onto the table. He must have been talking to me. "Don't put them on now—they won't be affected by the enchantment."

"Neither will the bags."

The relief I felt at hearing the healer's voice was overwhelming.

"I don't have any more invisibility enchantments left. Everything is at the guild." Marcus collected what he needed and the two leather satchels buckled themselves up. He passed one over to where Kaineres spoke, and the bag tumbled around a bit in the air before being hung on an invisible shoulder. "We can't stay here," Marcus continued, "They'll know it was my cloaking smoke. We have to retreat somewhere."

Sanders joked hesitantly. "I've been meaning to pay Flatkeep a visit for memories' sake."

"Actually—that's not a bad idea," Marcus said as all the oil lamps dimmed and shutters slammed shut. "Flatkeep has long been emptied after the raids. And it's far in the lower city so it'll take a while before any troops can extend their search down there." The door swung open. "Quickly—before the enchantment wears off. Keep the bags and clothing under your current shirts if you can. It's the best we can do for now."

We walked as fast as possible, following the sound of each other's footsteps, taking the same shortcuts we did yesterday. Gods. It was only yesterday. Every bone in my body ached and every muscle burned from the windstorm of events tossing me around.

"Everyone still keeping up?" Marcus called from behind me. We were in the lower city now, and I knew my way around the familiar streets. "We'll find out soon enough won't we?"

My shoes reappeared first, which was alright since it kept me from tripping over loose stones and debris from the ransacked homes. By the time the rest of the enchantment wore off, Sanders was waving us inside an old shopfront that was boarded and abandoned. It once belonged to some type of herbalist. The humid smell of mold growth permeated through the air. There was no light, other than the silver streaks of sunlight that poured in through cracks in the vaulted rooftop. On every wall, there were wooden shelves and glass jars. Most were broken and all of them were covered in dead plants or mildew.

With a gruff sigh, Marcus set his bag down on one of the only wooden tables that was merely tainted by dust. I untucked the bundle of clothing from underneath what was left of my shirt and shivered at the cold air that replaced it. We were all visible now, but I could've felt the weight of the witch's gaze on me if I had my eyes gouged out.

"What is she doing here?" His tone was low, and eerily calm.

Sanders rushed to my defense. "She saved your life you numb-ass."

"*Marcus* saved my life. *You* on the other hand—" He took a step towards me but Marcus held out his arm.

"I only had the smoke cover ready because she gave me a warning. I think there's something we don't know."

Kaineres bit his lip, but he wasn't nearly as angry as he had been the day before. There was something clearly different about him; something had shifted since the unbinding.

Marcus turned to me. "I explained everything I knew, Kain-eres explained everything he knew. I think it's your turn."

I gave a curt nod. "S, how safe is this place?"

Sanders walked over to the front door and put the lock in place—a simple plank of wood across the door frame. "This entire street is abandoned, but no one came in here even when it was occupied. The owner had left it to rot, quite literally. But there are rooms attached to the back that should still be furnished, if a little dusty."

It would have to do, considering our lack of options. My feet begged me to get my weight off them so I opted to sit on another table, pushing aside broken jars and damp record books. I threw on the thick wool sweater Marcus had lent me, and I was reminded of how efficient clothes could be at keeping warmth in.

Kaineres cleared his throat.

I was about to meet his eyes but nerves won and I glanced at the floor instead. I had no proof of what I was about to tell them, but all I needed to say was my piece. If Kaineres wanted me gone I would go. With Marcus at his aid, he would be able to flee from Aristus if the time came. I exhaled a bitter breath and recounted everything I heard and experienced during the night.

I didn't examine their faces, but I could feel stares turn into sickened expressions as I went on. I told them about the wickeds—caged, bled, and discarded for use. I told them about the woman and the girl, and Kasey. I told them about the rebellion. What it was for. All that was taken from us. The restitution we wanted, the change we needed. I told them I was young, and scared, and angry. I told them about what happened on this night years ago, and the flames I cast, and the kindling that caught, and the faces I didn't expect to see. I told them what the woman revealed, about Amos' greed and unquenched desire for things to remain exactly as they are.

I told them I was still a murderer. I told them I still cast the spell. I told them I still remembered their faces, and that some of them were the age my sister was when she was slaughtered in front of me. I told them that every day since then, I've wished I could undo it, that The Colds were the only place frozen enough to numb the memories. I ...

I couldn't see out of my eyes as the tears filled up, but when I went to wipe them away with my sleeve I brushed against a hand that gently touched my face. His thumb caressed my sunken eyes and wiped away the hot droplets forming. A streak of sunlight kissed his face, his striking russet brown eyes his own.

Kaineres wrapped his arms around my waist and lifted me up into a tight embrace, his chest solid and warm and the comfort of him seeped into me as I hugged him back. I buried my face into his neck as he held me closer.

"I shouldn't have left you," he whispered into my hair. "I didn't want to. I. . . I should have believed you from the start."

"You were right to be angry. I still walked into that night with the intent to..." To kill. To get even. To send a message. Like a dog trapped in a corner, biting for blood.

"It's what you knew. I understand why. I wasn't angry, I was... hurt? Surprised? I felt so many emotions take over. Never before had I felt her pull so much of my will like that before. I'm so sorry." He pulled back to examine my wrecked face and I suddenly felt embarrassed for the state I was in. "I should never have left you. Could you forgive me, Rune?"

I wiped my eyes with my sleeve and dipped my chin in response.

Kaineres smiled softly and kissed the top of my forehead, his beard tickling my eyebrow. "You're positively divine." His playful smirk returned, and I beamed at how good it felt to see him smile.

"If you think I'm pretty now, just wait until I have a bath."

He laughed. "I thought blood and dirt were part of your allure."

I wrapped my arms around his neck as he planted a kiss on mine. On the other side of the room, I noticed Sanders' bewildered expression and Marcus staring intently at the discarded jars of mold on the shelving. I brushed away the tension in the room with an awkward laugh, and Kaineres set me down on the table.

As he stepped back, I took all of him in. His broad frame was seemingly lighter, and he held his head higher off his shoulders. The smile in his eyes was captivating as he looked at me with single pupils in each eye—no specks of green to be found. He did what he set out to do, what he promised. He freed himself from the binding curse that had weighed him down for ten years. He had freed the princess.

The princess.

All of my senses snapped back into place. "The princess—King Amos is going to kill her!"

Marcus rejoined the conversation and dug through his satchel as he spoke. "Since there were so many witnesses, it's highly unlikely he would do anything drastic right away. That doesn't mean she's not still in danger." He pursed his lips to the side in thought. "We should still make an effort to come to her aid."

"What do you suggest we do? Hell knows what kind of state she's currently in." Kaineres' eyebrows furrowed in concern. "And the Realm is at risk if anything happens to her—the threats from the Alliance, the Withins, the gods-damned cities collapsing."

Marcus pulled out opaque glass bottles and handed them to Kaineres. "I know. But we need to be sensible. Look at us. We're in no condition to help anyone."

Of course, he was right. While I was the only one still caked in blood and dirt, the rest of us were tired, bruised, and everyone but Marcus had days' worth of sweat and grime built up. Kaineres uncorked the bottles and sniffed, his eyes fluttering as he inhaled. From where I stood next to him I could smell the floral aroma waft through the air and cut the scent of rotting wood and mildew.

"You brought soap?" Kaineres chuckled.

"I brought the essentials." His friend crinkled his nose. "And all three of you have gone nose-blind."

We all agreed on cleaning up and resting as much as we could. We would need clear minds and energized muscles for the trip back to the castle, through blockades of soldiers, and then approaching the unknown state of the recovered princess. Sanders mentioned there might be a well in the basement of the herbalist shop, and sure enough in the storage cellar there was a well that still held water, along with a bucket to draw it with.

The water was just as dirty as we were, but Kaineres and Marcus cleared out the debris until it was as clear as creek water. In another room on the main floor, Sanders found a tub to clean and fill, while Kaineres and I worked on heating it to a comfortable temperature. 'Just like the bowl of water in the woods' he said, and although it was much bigger I was able to use my own magic to heat the entire tub. I was getting used to it. Magic. Not being afraid of it. Instead, I started seeing uses for it everywhere. Energy, manipulated and shaped with intention. It felt natural.

The soap Marcus brought was ridiculously luxurious, and as I sank under the water I giggled—gobsmacked at the contrast between the moment and every other day of my life. I didn't sit as long as I would have liked to but I didn't want to hog the tub so I scrubbed myself as clean as I had ever been. When I got out of the water, I tried using magic to feel the water droplets on my skin and repel them downward. It worked slightly, some of the wetness remained but I was pleased enough with the progress I had made.

I bundled myself into fresh clothes—I could've kissed Marcus on the mouth for how good they felt, if a little large. My leather belt once again came to the rescue to hold up the long pants to my hips. He even brought a comb—why he had one, I wasn't sure, but I worked through knots until my hair could be braided easily. I refrained from immediately putting on my worn leather boots. Let my feet breathe for a few seconds.

I was just about to exit the small washroom when a reflection caught my eye. The image was hazy and spotted on the rusty glass, but as I moved closer I could tell it was a woman. In a looking glass.

I touched my face, my lips where her scar was. I blinked her eyes and I furrowed her eyebrows together. The resemblance she had to the girl on the poster was minimal. Just the scar, pale skin, and brown hair remained. But she was older now. She had lived through a few layers of hell and died a few times too. She grew some. She loved some. She wasn't as nervous to love a little more. She smiled at me. A weak, tired smile, but it was all I could muster for us. And it was enough, for now. There were still more layers of hell to visit, but I wasn't really nervous about that either.

A rapid knock came from the door and Sanders peaked their head in.

"Uh, sorry to bother you dear, but is the toilet chamber free at the moment?"

I excused myself from the washroom and looked around for a place to sit that wasn't going to make the bath worthless.

"Psst." Kaineres waved me over from the steps leading to the basement. I set down my dirty clothes and boots and tiptoed around the debris towards him.

"What is it?" I whispered.

Gods help me, his crooked smile was perfect. "Would you like to see something practically paradisaical?"

I had no idea what that meant, but he looked eager to show me so I let the witch take my hand and lead me downstairs. In the basement, there was a backdoor. Dead vines clung to the chipped wooden frame caked in mildew.

"Open it," Kaineres whispered.

I struggled a bit with the handle until the hinges creaked in obedience, and I let the air rush out of my lungs as I took it all in.

Life and growth all different shades of green flooded my vision. A greenhouse—sunken into the ground and overgrown with whatever plants could thrive. The thick, foggy glass ceiling was covered in specks of color as vines stretched their way to the top. The temperature was warmer than the cold breath of winter outside, and the humidity clung to my face and neck like a scarf. It was as if someone bottled early spring and gave it a haven to sit timeless. There were dead plants in large ceramic planters, but out of the broken soil grew new ones, chaotic and climbing high.

In the center of the calm chaos there was a little wooden desk and chair, mostly untouched other than a film of condensation that permeated the grain and caused it to split. The sun's light gleamed through the glass ceiling as it made its way overhead, bathing the small forest sunken in the lower city. It was breathtakingly beautiful. A kind of beauty I thought I'd never see again.

I turned to share my excitement with Kaineres, but when I met his eyes he just stood there grinning, looking over every inch of me with desire in his gaze.

"Should I gift you a garden?" He closed the door behind him and leaned against it. He had traded his faded tunic for a long-sleeved shirt of sturdier material. It must have belonged to Marcus because Kaineres' broad frame pulled the fabric tight against his chest, arms, and stomach. His dark hair was still damp from his bath, and the slick strands were teasing my fingers to come and comb through them. I swallowed. He smirked.

He uncrossed his arms and stepped towards me. "Once we're on the other side of this, I have a few ideas of where we should go first."

I let him take my hands in his, acutely aware of every place our skin touched. Heat burned from my stomach as I was immersed in his scent. I inhaled sharply as he stroked his thumb across the back of my palm.

He tilted his head to the side and cooed. "What's wrong?"

The nerve of him.

"I don't think you know what you do to me." I choked out.

He chuckled softly and brought my hands to his lips. The warmth of his breath made the hair on my arms prick up.

"Whatever do you mean? Surely I haven't done anything to melt the frozen statue before me." His eyes flickered from my eyes to my lips—for just a second. "But now that you mention it, there's no telling what I wouldn't give to see you crack."

My heartbeat picked up pace and my breathing turned shallow. The next words I shot at him were through gritted teeth. "Or, you know exactly what you're doing and you revel in being an ass."

He feigned a blow to his ego. "I've seen you stare down monsters without flinching. This leads me to believe such an effect on you seems unrealistic. Are you accusing me of witchcraft?"

My lips pinched together to keep a smile from spreading, but the witch beamed back at me, the corners of his eyes creasing with laughter. I memorized his face. Every plane, every line, I wanted to hold him in my mind the way he held me. Intentionally, firmly, naturally. Kaineres noticed the shift and furrowed his brows.

"I swear I didn't bewitch you."

I laughed, shaking my head at his concern. "No—it's just—It's been such a long time since I've... cared for someone like this. Like you. And you're naturally a kind person, I wasn't sure if you knew how I felt or if you felt similarly..." I was rambling, but words didn't fall off my tongue the way his did. "I was terrified something was going to happen to you. I want you, Kaineres, and I—"

His lips pressed into mine softly—fervently, and the tenderness relieved a weight that haunted me. It was beautiful and it was terrible and it gave strength to a weak part of me and it weakened something I thought was strength. I leaned into his chest and let a gentle moan escape my throat. His hands wrapped around my ribcage and with my eyes closed I felt him swing me slightly around. I still needed more of him. I let my tongue slip delicately behind his chapped lips.

In an instant my back was pressed against the door to the greenhouse and his hands were holding my face as he kissed me again, fierce and wanting. I melted into his mouth as his fingers held my face against his and he kissed me over and over again, like an animal untethered and wild. I kissed him back, breathing him in and intoxicating myself with the faint smell of sweat and his musk.

Warmth pooled down my chest and into my center—lost in the tangle of him and still desiring more. My hands drifted lower to fiddle with the leather belt around his pants. He let out a breathy laugh into my mouth as he untied the belt with ease and went back to running fingers in my hair, letting out my braid and grabbing fistfuls of damp hair into his hands.

I was crushed between the planks in the door and the weight of him, soft and solid all at once. He grabbed my waist and tugged me closer, the bulge in his trousers pressed against the gap between my thighs. My hands found the bottom of his shirt and I pulled it upwards, clumsy and impatient. In a fluid motion, he pulled the fabric over his shoulders and tossed it aside, baring his wide chest still stained with lightning.

"Will you take me?" His words were barely audible as he breathed them into my neck. In response, I pushed him towards the chair leaning against the desk next to us.

He removed the rest of his clothes and hastily set them down as a barrier on the cold seat. As he sat down, I removed my pants but before I could tear off my shirt, he grabbed me and pulled me into him. My legs sprawled out around him, I was painfully aware of his thick cock nestled between my thighs. I kissed him again, my tongue dancing around his mouth while he peeled off the rest of my shirt. The cold air hitting my breasts sent a shiver down my back, but Kaineres lifted me up by my ass and brought his mouth to my nipples, covering them with the heat of his lips.

I ran my fingers through his thick hair, pulling tight as he continued to draw circles around my nipple with his tongue. An urgent moan escaped me when I felt the tip of him slide right underneath me, and I ground against his arms, begging him to lower me just enough. His mouth released my chest and kissed his way up my neck, still holding me captive just out of his reach.

"Fuck you." I cursed into his hair as he brushed up against my entrance—now soaking and throbbing with need.

His words tickled the back of my neck. "I told you I'd wait until we reached the city, didn't I?" The witch chuckled at my impatience as I tried to push myself down onto him.

Damn him to any layer of hell that would take him. I begged. "Please."

With one hand on the back of my neck and the other around my waist, he positioned himself right underneath my opening. I froze in anticipation, but he squeezed my hip in response.

"I have you, just relax right onto me."

He whimpered as I slid down the length of him. My mouth gaped open at how thick he was—at how fucking good he felt. His brows furrowed together in desperation and pleasure while I adjusted to his length.

"That's it love, ease onto me—*Fuck*, you're perfect."

I clenched around his words.

"Oh?"

My teeth clamped down on my bottom lip from embarrassment, but his smile curved upwards in cruel delight.

"—and here I thought you needed no commendation..." He brushed his lips to my ear and whispered, "But this can be our little secret." He tightened his grip around the back of my neck and waist and pulled me down further onto him. A gasp escaped me that melted into a shaky moan at his fullness. He stilled to let me adjust, but my hips started bucking, eliciting a wicked smile from the witch that made my mouth dry with desire. "Perfect indeed."

He grabbed my hips with his hands and matched pace with the motion of my hips, grinding me against him with slow and steady movements. I braced my arms on his shoulders and intertwined my fingers in the hairs on his neck. My gods, he made my body feel things I hadn't felt in years, if ever. The room was silent but for the squeaking of the chair and our breaths, ragged and rhythmic.

"Come on," he said, low and breathy. "Fuck me how you want to. That's it. Use me."

I kept grinding into him, gradually picking up pace as he hit a sensitive spot inside me that sent shivers down my spine. He bit his lips as he watched me pleasure myself on his cock, his gruff whimpers echoing in the room as I tightened around him.

One of his hands slowly trailed up my side, over my breast, and wrapped around the base of my chin. His thumb brushed against my bottom lip and he ever so gently pulled my chin forward.

"That's it, Rune, fuck me just like that." He held my chin steady and locked his gaze on mine.

His eyes were his own now, single pupils surrounded by deep russet hues swirling with longing and emotion that was all his to feel. I lost myself in his focus as I felt a wave of pleasure rising. I kissed him hard as it rushed through me and his groans reverberated through my throat as I pulsed around him. He gripped the back of my neck and held me against him as I continued to sink deeper into the feeling—his sweat, his skin, his fullness. I shut my eyes tight just wanting to capture the moment, remember it breath for jagged breath.

His pulse thundered into my ear and I clenched tight around him until his breathing staggered. He tried to control the groan that escaped with a forced laugh, but I could still feel him throbbing inside me. I lifted myself until his tip almost slipped out and I slammed right back down again, wetness leaking down his inner thighs.

He clenched his jaw. "Someone's quite bold, aren't we?"

I would have laughed back at him had he not startled me by picking me up and flipping me around. My stomach slammed against the wooden table. I yelped at the cold, and with a swift motion he moved the clothes from the chair onto the edge of the table. He shifted his weight against me until I was trapped between him and the wooden plank, his hands placed dangerously on my hips.

The tip of his hard cock teased my entrance as he rocked back and forth slowly. Viciously. My lips throbbed in anticipation as he continued to drag light pressure up and down my wet opening at a cruel, leisurely pace. I needed more.

"I knew you were a fucking sadist," I ached, trying to sway my hips back against his hands holding me in place.

"Do you want me to stop?"

I didn't need to turn around to know he was smirking. He had me right where he wanted me and I craved every second of it.

"Kaineres, *Please.*"

"Please, what?"

"*Fuck me, witch.*"

I cried out from surprise and relief as he thrust himself deep into me, sending my mind spiraling in circles. His fingernails dug into my flesh as he fucked me so hard I thought the table was going to collapse and myself along with it. The wood creaked underneath our weight but he wrapped an arm around my stomach, holding me in place as he continued to thrust his hips back and forth, the swing of his balls overstimulating me each time he slammed into me. I choked back a cry as I felt heat start to boil in my stomach. Delicious pain started to sear in between my legs and I wanted more of it.

"*Gods*, Rune—" Kaineres choked words out between grunts. "You feel... incredible." His thrusts became more frantic as the tension between us started to build. "Where—do you want me?"

"Don't move." *Please don't move.* "Right here."

With a few final blows from his hips, he groaned as he came—his hands still wrapped around me, pulling me into him. The intensity dulled some of the sensation, but as he withdrew I could feel drops of warmth leak out and drip down the inside of my thigh. I thought I was going to pass out from the pleasure, and my knees started to buckle.

Before I could brace myself, Kaineres scooped me up into his arms and sat me down on his lap, the wooden chair cracking in protest. I let my head fall onto his shoulder as he caressed my hair and kissed me softly on the forehead. Our chests shuttered heavily from exhaustion and the thick air that cocooned around us. His fingers guided my chin up and brought my gaze to his.

"Call me Kain."

I kissed him, wanting very much to stay just like this. His arms around me were warm and safe, sturdy and soft at the same time. I couldn't remember the last time I felt this content—this *alive*. Through fluttering lashes, my eyes sleepily tracked the specks of dust dancing in the streams of light pouring into the greenhouse. A vision I thought I would only ever see in dreams.

Our hazy moment together was cut short as the door to the greenhouse opened and shut closed very quickly.

"*Sorry!*" Marcus' muffled voice apologized from the other side. "I was definitely interrupting something that time."

Kain groaned in exasperation as I chuckled into his neck. "At least it's not Arrowette." I reminded.

"Subtle gifts from the gods."

I remembered what he said about the vow of chastity he took. The vow he just broke. "What of your title?"

He sighed softly. "That's all it is. A title. I was too concerned with the honorific for so long that I failed to remember why it meant so much to me in the first place. I fell in love with magic and the wonders it could bring. That hasn't changed, and if anything, has been reignited. I would much rather tour the world with you, magic stirring in our wake than sit alone behind a desk reorganizing scrolls."

"But you love reorganizing scrolls."

Kain laughed through his nose. "I never said I didn't," he clarified. "But I would still rather be with you, regardless if I am a witch, ex-witch, scribe, or outlaw."

"If you wish to stick with me, the latter is most likely."

He playfully squeezed my thigh. "Good. That makes things much more interesting."

After noticing the bumps on my arm from the chill, Kaineres retrieved my clothes from the floor and dressed me back up. He took his time with each article of clothing. Pulling my arms and legs through the sleeves of the fabric leisurely and intentionally, his fingers caressed every inch of skin. Whether he bewitched me or not, what he was doing was unquestionably magical. And I loved him for it.

We lingered in the vibrancy of the greenhouse, sitting on the ground, listening to the steady beat of heartbeats and exhaled breaths. The squeaking and creaking of glass panes twinkled overhead as wind brushed over the roof, playing music for us as we sat amidst the vines. Music that lulled me into a peace I was learning how to relax into.

The looming threat that surrounded Aristus still poked the back of my mind, but I clung to the remaining intimate moments with the healer as tightly as I could.

When we finally rejoined the others in the herbalist shop, we ate small portions of food Marcus had brought—dried meats and bread—and although Marcus complained the whole meal, the rest of us drifted into bliss with every bite. A small benefit of the hellish conditions my body endured—I hadn't had a fertility cycle in years. A part of me wondered if my body was broken forever, or if it would return to normal given enough time and food. I didn't really care.

There was a generously sized bedroom off the main floor, and thankfully it wasn't as overgrown with mold as the shop was. There was only one bed, however, and it would barely fit three of us. Marcus strung up a blanket he brought and expressed he would sleep better in a hammock than huddled tight on the bed with us. So we rested our bodies as much as we could afford. Even after the day we had and the threat of soldiers after us, sleep beckoned my eyelids closed from where I lay between Sanders and Kain. My body warm, my heart full. Still, I couldn't help but notice the witch's breathing seemed stiff—tense. I leaned over and kissed his cheek.

"We'll find a way to her," I said softly.

He squeezed his hand around my arm, the burn marks from my tears like the streaks of water on a windowpane. How we would find the princess, we'd have to figure out tomorrow, and quickly. Not just for her sake—but for the Withins, for the lower cities, and for the rest of the Kingdom who didn't know the kind of monster they served.

CHAPTER
TWENTY-SEVEN

Shaye

Morning filtered through sheer curtains; the warm hues of the fabric cast murals of tangerine, amber, and gold against plaster walls. Specks of dust floated in and out of light's reach, shimmering and fading in midair. It was quiet but for a muffled trickle of water coming from beyond the large arched windows. I squinted in the glow, my eyelids heavy and my vision taking its time to focus. My. . . vision.

I was. . .was I? Yes... I could see that I was lying under a canopy of delicate lace that hung from the ceiling and softly framed the large circular bed near one wall of the room. Soft as the edge of a feather against bare skin, sheets layered around me, wrapping me in comfort—aside from a thin band of coolness around my wrists.

Where am I?

I turned my head to the side and saw bookshelves filled with fictitious stories and volumes of romantic poetry, cloth-bound and covered in dust. Over a pastel desk was an ornate-looking glass covered in necklaces and scarves. The bedroom was beautiful, in the way a headstone of a cemetery might be. Carefully curated, untouched, and left as a kind of tangible memory.

A wisp of hair fell over my cheek and tickled my nose. My hair. I wiggled my face back and forth to feel more of it, the thick ends poking my skin and causing trembles to cascade down my neck. I flexed my toes and kicked out my legs, stretching sleeping muscles back to life. I went to scratch my stomach, but my arms were tied back by restraints. Steel cuffs, attached to a chain, attached to a metal bar on the wall. *What in Hell?*

I yanked harder, rattling the iron chains over and over again in frustration. *What in all Hell?!* I thought about calling for help, but I wasn't sure who would answer. I shut my eyes and replayed everything I remembered.

I felt myself scatter, untethered... and then, I was bound again. But it was different. It felt right this time. It felt like falling back into place after losing your bearings from spinning out of control. It felt like me. I woke up in the courtyard... naked except for his cloak.

Kain! Where was he? What happened to us? Where did they put him? I yanked on the cuffs again. My memories were hazy, like stories told from the perspective of an un-trustworthy narrator. I wasn't sure which memories were mine and which were his, and the longer I tried to pull them apart, the more confusing they became. But they were still mine to recall.

I groaned at the metal digging into my skin. Did no one know who I was? Did I look different? But I was placed in my old room, in my old bed. They had to know. Something seemed off. Almost Unsettling.

The grand set of doors to my left swung open. I jerked my head around to face the intruder, and when I met his eyes my chest tightened uncomfortably.

My father calmly closed the doors behind him and leaned against them, looking at me with relief on his face but wariness in his stance. His face looked vaguely older, but the rigidness of his body was the same as when I was young. His dark hair was pulled back into a small top bun, and he had swapped his beard for a thick, styled mustache. Around his neck was the symbol of his leadership—a solid silver band.

"You're awake at last." He put a hand to his chest. "I was so worried the—*change*—would frighten you."

I dug deep in my throat to find my voice. "Why am I chained up?"

Amos made a face that made him look like he was suffering from a nauseous stomach. "It was for your own safety. I had no idea how you would react to the events of yesterday."

So it had been a day. I had half a mind to ask about Kain, but I needed to get out of bed first.

"I'm alright, Da." I gave him a weak smile. "I'd love a change of clothes, though." I was wearing a set of tight-fitting nightclothes that the chambermaids must have put on me. I couldn't wait to get into something looser.

"All in due time." He said softly.

Why the fuck does time have to be due?

I pulled against the restraints trying to sit up, but they were too short. "Da, why not? I'm okay now, truly."

My father simply shook his head, his taut expression cold and distant. "It's for the best. You were possessed by a great deal of magic. Magic messes with people's heads—their emotions, their memories..."

"I'm telling you I'm stable! Please—the cuffs hurt!" My jaw clenched at his refusal, but he stood firm.

"It will give me peace of mind while I try to deal with the matters at hand. I can't spare guards to escort you at the moment. You will stay here where you're safe." The king opened the door and slammed it shut with him on the other side.

"*What?* What matters at hand? What are you doing? Where's Kain?"

A lock engaged in the double doors. My throat vibrated as I screamed. He couldn't leave me here forever. Unless he had no intention of unlocking me at all. I gave up lashing out against the chains and tried to think. Amos had always been cold, but never cruel. At least, I didn't remember him that way. He had his prejudices...

My heart skipped a beat when the foggy memory of the caged Withins crept into my mind. Whatever reason he had for collecting Withins couldn't be a noble one. His fear of magic was no doubt reinforced by the rebel soldier, Rune. Warm tears flooded my eyes and my nose clogged. I would never get to say goodbye. My brother, my sisters, my cousins. All taken from me, all at once. She deserved to rot in hell. But that didn't mean that every magical person needed to suffer.

Through blurry eyes, I looked down at my chest and stomach the best I could. My body did feel different than I remembered. Like it had aged along with me when I reformed. I had already passed maturity when the collision happened, but now it felt older, softer. My stomach and hips were fuller and my hair was longer. As if my ashes grew with me, and the body I wore now matched the soul of a woman. How old was I now—thirty years or so? A decade of my life, erased. No one's fault but mine. I needed to find Kain. I needed to tell him how sorry I was, for everything.

I was about to scream out again, for who or what I wasn't sure, but before the cry could build in my chest the doorknob wiggled. The lock clicked, and the doors creaked open slowly. I had every intention of giving Amos a piece of my mind, but he didn't enter the room. Instead, an older woman, maybe in her sixties, slipped in and closed the door behind her.

She was beautiful. Her long white hair was placed in a tight bun and her pink and freckled skin looked well cared for. Her smile lines around her mouth and eyes gave her a comforting and jovial appearance. Her frame was small and thin but she moved gracefully across the room towards me, her posture perfectly straight.

"Coretta!"

I remembered her name. She was my father's top advisor, and I saw more of her than I did him growing up. Coretta placed a key into each metal cuff around my arm and released me. I sat up and wrapped my arms around her, the first human touch in a decade and the first familiar face I was glad to see. She tugged me close and softly combed my hair with her hands, taming any flyaway strands with a press of her fingers.

"Oh precious Jewel, My *Princess*!" She cupped my cheeks. "You have no idea how relieved I am to see you again. Is this really you or a nasty trick?"

"It's me Coretta! I promise. I don't think my father believes me though."

Coretta twisted her lips into an expression I couldn't decipher, but she patted my hand and helped me off the bed. "We should hurry before he gets the guts to check on you again."

"You won't get in trouble for helping me will you?" The last thing I wanted was for someone else to pay for my mistakes.

Coretta made a puckering sound with her mouth. "To any and all rings of hell with the King." She whispered harshly to me. "My dear Shaye, there have been happenings going on behind these castle walls that not even I fully understand. King Amos is working against the good of his people—and himself, whether or not he wants to admit it."

"What is he doing?" I matched her hushed tone, but she just shook her head.

"I wish I could tell you everything now, but Amos expects me at his side momentarily, and we need to get you somewhere you won't be bothered. Come with me. Quickly."

Coretta led me by the arm through the eerily empty hallways. Some of the stone walls had been painted, some decorated with portraits of Queens, Kings, and Noblemen past. My memory of the castle was starting to unwind itself as we went into a different wing, past a few sets of rooms until we came to a large single door with ornate wood carvings overhead. Coretta unlocked it and ushered me inside.

"These are my chambers. No one will bother you here. Guards are stationed outside the castle or by the main exits."

"—Why?" I asked as I turned around the room, taking in the magnificent hand-painted mural on the ceiling.

"The King has ordered a search for the exiled witch that cursed you."

Kain. He wasn't taken after all. He was on the run. I grabbed Coretta's arm.

"Coretta, please, don't let Da hurt him—it was all a big misunderstanding, Kain is innocent. He's not a threat to anyone—"

The old woman collected my hands together and clenched them tight in hers. "*Alright*—Alright, I believe you. I will do my best to calm Amos' temper about this, but lately he hasn't been bending his ears to anyone." Her soft blue eyes turned gravely serious. "Shaye, your father is not well. I refuse to keep you chained up, but you must stay hidden. I had your chambermaids bring a few items for you to wear, but please stay here. I will be back when I can, although that may not be for a long while."

She kissed my knuckles and gestured to the neatly folded pile of clothes on the nightstand. "And stay away from the window, lest you be spotted by a patrol." She mentioned as she exited the room.

The lock engaged with a click and I was once again trapped in another room, albeit with a little more space. The mural on the ceiling boasted years of skill and practice—a hand-painted scene of a hunt. Men and women on horseback, hounds with white-tipped tails, and a fox running for the thicket. Coretta had painted it herself when I was only a child. Her ornately crafted furniture was painted as well, all different shades of cream and white that highlighted the deep crimson shades of her bedspread.

Walking to her nightstand, I immediately picked out a new set of clothes to wear so I could squeeze out of the nightclothes. I chose a loose-fitting gown with soft, twirl-able material and tapered long sleeves. The sage green fabric complemented the olive tone in my tan skin. I spun around in the dress and let it tickle my legs as I moved. The plush layered rugs in Coretta's room were too squishy to condone shoes, so I let the pads of my feet explore the ground beneath them freely.

I felt alive again. Truly alive, no longer a shadow revealing itself in limited conditions. I jumped onto the bed and sank into the inches of quilts and blankets, letting pillows cradle my head. I sent up a prayer of safety to Kain, wherever he was.

Turning over to my side, I stared toward the window, currently covered in a set of ruby red drapes. They were gorgeous, with patterns of silver stitching embroidered on the edges, but I desperately wanted to see what was behind them. What kind of commotion was caused since the unbinding? Commotion enough to warrant troops of guards and soldiers stationed around the castle. *He brought me back. Why was that so threatening?*

Before I could sit and think better of it, my bare feet were sneaking me to the window to get just a glimpse of the outside. Coretta's room was on the east side facing away from the city so there was likely nothing to look at anyway. If my memories were correct, it would overlook the forest from the top of the steep cliff on which the castle stood. But just in case things had changed...

I peeled back the curtains and as I suspected, there was not much to see other than a raised cobblestone path that encircled the entire building, and then a drop-off to the tops of trees in the background. There was also a lively garden bed beneath the window whose occupants had managed to survive all the way till early winter. Only a few of the petals had shriveled from the cold. The window was on a slanted wall that faced another slanted room adjacent to it, and I could see an open window twin to the one I peeked through. From what I could tell, there were numerous bookshelves inside.

The library!

The faintest and fondest of memories leaked into my thoughts. Growing up I spent hours and hours in the many small libraries the castle contained, reading my days away and slipping out to read further into the night. Books that my father would have had my hide for if he caught me bringing them to my room. I squinted my eyes to get a good look at the shelves—to see if any of the titles awoke anything else from the shadows of my mind. I giggled to myself, noticing a few copies of an erotic play once performed by a traveling theater guild. Then there was a whole shelf of dull glossaries filled with maps, probably, and...

My eyes narrowed at the peculiar little book that at first glance blended in, but the longer I looked became more and more unlike the rest. But I had still seen it before. Hadn't I?

Footsteps approached coming up the cobblestone path and I ducked under the window sill. When I was certain they had passed by, I peeked back over the ledge. A pair of castle guards, back turned, were walking the other way. I couldn't tell if anyone was in the library across from me, but I needed to get a closer look. Pushing on the glass, the window swung open silently, thanks to the gods the hinges were recently oiled.

Cold air smacked me in the face and neck. *Great goddess' bleeding tits, it's freezing.*

I snuck over the ledge, over the garden bed, and into the open library window. There was no one inside. The double doors to the hallway were closed, and no lights or lanterns had been lit. Even the center fireplace was out cold. There were bookshelves on every wall, surrounding a comfortable set of couches and chairs facing the fireplace. I highly doubted anyone would venture here if there was truly a ruckus caused in Amos' impetuous panic, so I grabbed a stool and perched atop it, reaching for the pale leather-bound book on the top shelf.

As soon as I touched it the hair on my skin stood up, and I had to bite my cheek to keep myself quiet as I slipped off the stool. I was still getting used to my balance, I suppose. I knelt right there on the ground and studied the small, delicate, and obviously old book in my hands, identical to the one found by my—by *Kain's* niece. A sister to the ancient spell book the Skevsurvian Mage had. A sister to the ancient spell book that contained the secrets of the binding curse. But why was this here?

Even the Court mages—if there were any left—didn't possess an extensive knowledge of history, especially when it came to ancient magic. And the King would certainly lose his shit along with the permanent stick up his ass if he knew this was here. Unless... Coretta was right, and he was hiding something even from his advisors. I tried to open it, and of course, the cover didn't budge. *Shit, how does this help me now?*

I glanced around the room, ransacking my brain for any bit of information that might help me. It was quite possible it required the same spell as the first, but there was no way to tell. And even if that was the case, there would be no rabbit and no moonlight available. My hands gently pet the delicate hide.

There would be moonlight tonight though. And as long as Kain was safe, wherever he was, I could wait. I could at least uncover the text magically etched in the cover and see if this was truly the twin to the ancient spell book in The Colds. I had a terrible feeling that it would shed light on secrets Amos had been keeping, and whether or not Kain was the only one in danger of him.

— ◊ —

Kain

The first rewarding sleep I'd had in years was interrupted by a loud banging coming from the front door of the shop. Rune was out of my hands and through the bedroom door before I could adjust my eyes. The deep slumber had our minds playing catch-up with our bodies as the rest of us stumbled after her.

Rune didn't have her swords, but she found a broken glass bottle and wielded it like one in substitution. She signaled to Sanders about how to approach the threat on the other side of the jiggling door but before their plan could materialize, I heard mumbled voices on the other side of the wall.

"*Someone's already in here!*"

"*What? This place should be abandoned.*"

They sounded familiar. Ignoring Rune's stern hiss, I removed the plank and swung the door open to reveal three dirt-covered rogues.

"Gods of the moon, Twig—" The freckled scout fell tumbled inside along with Gwenna and Bandin. "—What are you doing here?"

The three of them scuffled around to get their bearings and walked further into the shrinking herbalist shop.

"Is this all of you?" Sanders peeked their head out the door once more before closing it and replacing the plank barrier.

Twig slammed his ax down on the table along with a few tattered cloth bags full of supplies. "Can I say—before we get into this—that you people are ridiculously difficult to track?"

Rune's eyes widened. "It was *you*! *You* were the ones following us. I knew that bandit wasn't the only one." And she lost precious hours of sleep from tossing and turning, thinking at any moment we would be ambushed.

"And it was *you* that night!" Gwenna startled me; I could already see her winding up her wrist to yank at Rune's ear. "*You* are the rebel girl whose attack—"

"She's alright, Gwen." I stepped between them, putting my hands up in defense. "It's not what it seems. Apparently King Amos is responsible for more atrocities than we realize."

"Surprise, surprise! Heinous Anus once again proving himself to be devoid of humanity." Twig stretched his lanky arms out until his shoulders cracked. "I knew there was more to the story. But it's fun to know one of my top scouts has been a celebrity all this time."

"Oh please don't call me that." Rune groaned softly. I wasn't sure which infamy felt worse for her—being a despised murderer or a relentless rebel heroine. She made it clear she didn't want to be either. I shot her a look of sympathy.

"Say, Kaineres—" Twig squinted his eyes. "You're looking a little different. One might say you're lacking your usual *spirit*."

Only Sanders laughed. Gwenna cursed under breath and Marcus continued to look very confused in the background of the conversation.

"So you heard?" I said, eager to get to the details of why they tracked us down.

Gwenna nodded curtly. "Even while keeping to the shadows, news spreads like sickness in the streets. I'm sure Manden is going to be awfully glad you're still alright, Kaineres."

I caught the apprehensive glance Bandin sent to Twig.

"Is she okay?" I asked. "Is the commune safe?"

"Oh sure, sure." Twig rested his back against the wall. "I mean, Manden is going to scoop our eyeballs out with sticks when she sees us again, but the commune is in good hands."

"She doesn't know you're here?" I ran my hands through my hair. "Scooping out your eyeballs is the least she'll do to you," I added under my breath.

"Eh. I had a feeling things weren't going to go smoothly when you returned." Twig explained, finally. "And Gwenna told me she knew who you were." He gestured in Rune's direction. "I didn't know if maybe you were going back to kill the King."

"I'm not killing *anybody!*" She crossed her arms tightly over her chest. "I came to keep Kain safe." And she had, despite my making it difficult.

Twig used a dirty fingernail to pick something from his teeth. "And it looks like you've done a wonderful job. However, are the soldiers gallivanting through the city looking for a lost pet? Ah, I thought not. I guess Heinous Amos doesn't like his gifts returned. You'd think a doting father would reward the person risking their life to bring his daughter back from the dead unless..."

"We've already pieced this together, thanks."

"So?" Twig threw his hands up. "What's the plan? What have we mapped out, where is the princess, and how long are you going to stay hidden away in this..." He sniffed the air. "What is this place?"

Marcus spoke next, clearing his throat and waiting until all eyes turned towards him. "I am going to assume you are more *friends* from The Colds. I'm also going to assume you were at one point in time, members of the rebellion uprising."

"If by 'one-point in time' you mean currently, then yes. Didn't want to miss out on the fun, see. King Amos is why most of us were banished, excluding Bandin. Ensuring Amos is off the throne is as good a chance as we'll ever have at leaving those gods-forsaken woods."

Marcus bit his cheek. "Alright then. Well, the Princess Shaye was taken somewhere in the castle, and because so many people saw her return there's not much Amos can do about her at the moment. That doesn't mean he still won't try something nefarious when the timing is convenient. He's probably waiting until people look the other way. Right now he has soldiers sent after Kain-eres. Er, *Kain*. It's going to be difficult to find the princess and give her a warning... If she's stable enough to receive it."

"Ah." Twig stroked the very patchy beard on the tip of his chin. "Two hens in the fox den then."

"No." While her tone reminded me a bit of Manden, I was slightly impressed with how much rebel slang Rune still recalled. None of it made any sense to me. "I don't like the idea of using anyone as bait."

I scoffed. "You used yourself as bait in MistView."

"That was... different. There's more at stake here. If any-one gets caught and they're not a Within, I guarantee the soldiers have their bows aimed to kill. Amos won't take another risk with banishment."

Twig stood back up with a grunt. "That's the difference between us then, isn't it? Amos can't take another risk but we can. I sure can. It's no different than walking into the fog knowing there's a monster somewhere inside. Look at you—you've got an ex-witch, a framed murderer with magic blood, a scrappy loose cannon, and a..." He squinted his eyes at Marcus, trying to tell what he brought to the table.

Marcus rolled his eyes. "A mage."

I whipped around. "A *mage*? Why didn't you tell me—"

"—*Head*mage."

My mouth dropped open into a bewildered grin at my friend's news. "Marcus they made you Headmage—that's magnificent! I—"

"Can talk about it later." Gwenna cut me off. "I agree with Twig. We'll help in any way we can. That's why we came here. I know the layout of the castle. I can tell you where the princess will most likely be kept. It'll be safer for you to use the servant passages so I'll draw up a map as best I can."

Bandin smiled reassuringly and clapped me on the back. I silently hoped he had briefed someone else about the heal-ing salves and potions that the scouts would likely need. But right now my focus was set to the task at hand.

We tentatively agreed to go through with an old distraction tactic and let the scouts draw off the guards to take them on a chase away from the castle. The rest of us would find a way into the castle and track down Shaye. Although Marcus had run out of invisibility enchantments, he said he had something else that would make us slightly inconspicuous. Gwenna drew a rough map on the back of an old record sheet. She hovered her face close to the paper as she wrote out directions for us to follow in and out.

Gwenna bit her lip. "I don't know how you'll get behind the upper city gates. Even with foot soldiers distracted, they won't move the stationed guards from their posts near the entrances."

I furrowed my brows. "What about the tunnels?" I tilted my head to Marcus for confirmation.

The Headmage shook his head in confusion. Maybe he had forgotten about it in the past decade.

"Near the guild—the tunnels," I continued, "Similar to the ones we crawled out of on our way here. But larger."

Marcus shook his head again slowly. "No, I don't remember any tunnels. I think you're getting your memories confused."

I wiped a hand over my mouth and replayed old hazy images that I was certain were mine. "Maybe. No, there are tunnels near the guild that lead straight under the upper city and into the castle. I remember."

The room grew quiet as I paced back and forth, massaging my temples and chuckling impatiently. I didn't want to summon another headache but I wasn't thinking clearly. "It was boarded up and hard to see through, but there was a door that led to a storage bin on the outer wall of the guild. That's where I would go to... practice... magic."

"Kain," Rune gently touched my arm. "Have you ever been in the castle?"

No. I hadn't. So why did it feel like I had? And why would I sneak around to practice magic when every person in my life encouraged me to do it?

"These... aren't my memories," I whispered, like a heartfelt confession. "She... practiced magic."

Crumbs of the past, from a spirit that wasn't mine, settled in my recollection. I was a child—a girl—sneaking through dark dirt hallways out of boredom, stumbling across a boarded-up grate. Tugging the grate aside, I squeezed through a board that wasn't nailed down properly and stood on a storage barrel to peek over the plaster wall. Even with a large hedge in the way, I could faintly see through stems and leaves to the small courtyard below. There was the soft trickle of a fountain, the murmuring of voices, and I saw another child—a boy, swirling liquid in a glass without even touching it. It was ...me. But so was I.

I knew when the mages held class. I was there at every lesson I could afford to slip away and listen to. To spy on. For years. I recreated the same techniques, and it never took me long to master each step. I caught on quickly. Everything made sense.

I was no longer a child. I was at that excruciating age of being a woman, but too young. It was harder to sneak around when there were more responsibilities and more expectations and magic was a thing to be used but never understood. It was dangerous. Amos was furious every time I asked to learn more about it. But even with living off of drips of condensation outside the glass, I reveled in it. I was great at it.

I was forbidden to go. Locked away in my room, watching from the window as nobles got drunk off of cheap wine with expensive labels. They wouldn't even understand what was happening. But I would. For months I saw him practicing in the woods—from a distance. And this was my one chance to see him up close, to talk with him, to ask him what it felt like.

It beckoned me. The dais was even set for my arrival. Amos was the only one who knew I wasn't coming. So I wouldn't look out of place if I snuck out again.

I knew he was casting the spell as soon as I set foot into the courtyard. I could feel it—the shift in energy. I had never been able to feel it before. Casting magic was breathless—easy. Meanwhile, this felt like a tug on my soul and I craved more of it, I wanted to swim in it. Purples, blues, and greens danced across my vision and dared me to step closer, to give in a little to it. Just a little piece of me, and I could feel the magic surge through my veins like it was a part of me.

Because it was. I wasn't afraid of it, even when I stepped too close. Even when I heard the crack, even when I saw the terror in his face and my heart shattered until it stopped. Even when it pulled me apart at the seams, I wasn't afraid. It still felt like me.

It was only when my severed spirit was put back into a vessel I didn't know—a body that wasn't mine—did the pain start.

"*Kain!*" Rune was holding my head in her lap as I came to.

In a panic, I sat up, heaving out the rest of the stolen flashbacks. "*She's a Within.*" I choked out. "*Shaye is a Within.*"

"What? How do you know? What happened?"

Marcus handed me a cup of water, and the frigid temperature coating my tongue helped bring me back.

"Her-her memories—they make sense—in a way. That's-that's why the spell went awry. There was too much energy because she *is* magical energy." I wiped the hair out of my eyes. "Shaye is a Within, and I think Amos knows."

"Shit." Rune breathed. "Amos won't kill her—he's going to use her."

"No he won't." I lifted myself off the ground and held out my hand to Rune. "We're going to get to her first."

Twig and Sanders cheered until they were scolded by Gwenna to keep quiet.

Twig waved her away. "That's the spirit!" I ignored his wink. "We've got nothing to lose and everything to gain. Every day I'm barely surviving, adapting to the realms of hells that seem to fight over which one gets a hold of me. My view from here is, I'm going to die anyway. I might as well take a long shot at something good while I'm still kicking."

While Sanders passed out dried fruit and meat to commemorate the moment, my nerves ran cool at what we had to do next. My gaze fell on the Within next to me, smiling softly and shaking her head at Sanders. My muscles tensed. I *did* have something to lose. I didn't want to put Rune in harm's way again. Not after everything she'd already been through.

I placed a hand on the small of her back. Icy grey eyes met mine and I gestured to the back room in silent request. She followed.

I closed the door behind us and kept my voice low. "Rune."

"Hm? Are you alright?"

"Ah—yes. I don't feel all that honorable for exploring a past that wasn't mine to explore, but I'll deal with the ethics of it later." I held her softly by the shoulders, her body heat seeping into my fingers. "You don't have to come with us."

She tilted her chin in concern.

"I—I don't want you to think I'm expecting you to. I know there's a history of people making choices for you, and that's the last thing I want to do. The closer we get to Shaye, the more at risk you are. You could stay behind, and when this is all over, I'll come back for you. I promise."

Rune pressed her hand against my cheek, relaxing my nerves and warming my thoughts.

"I told you I would keep you safe," she answered softly. "I still intend to do that. And the gods know I won't let Sanders make reckless decisions without me." A smile spread across her cheeks and my heart thundered. She could melt The Colds with that smile. "You asked me what I would do to make something right—if I had done something terrible, even if I didn't mean to. I didn't answer because I wasn't sure there was anything I could do to make up for what happened. But I can do this. I can protect the last Aristus. And that's a choice I want to make."

I wrapped my arms around her and buried her head into my chest, memorizing the feel of her body against mine. She held me in return, her fingers digging into my shoulder blades.

She mumbled something into my shirt that I didn't catch.

"What was that?" When I pulled back she laughed and I let the icy gravel of her voice cascade down my spine. "I said hell knows you need me for offensive maneuvers. If you get caught you won't be able to potion your way out of anything."

I raised an eyebrow. "You haven't seen all the potions I can craft."

"I look forward to learning under your hand in the future." She flashed her canines and hells claim me, I wanted to take her right then and there.

I growled in her ear. "You, my dove, have no idea."

CHAPTER TWENTY-EIGHT

Rune

"Are you sure this is going to work?" Twig squinted his eyes at me as Marcus painted the charmed paste onto my cheek.

It applied some kind of illusion that altered the appearance of the person wearing it. He had already dipped my hair in a liquid with similar properties, and my once brown hair was now tar black.

Kain answered for Marcus as he applied the same paste to Sanders. "You won't see a difference because you know it's an enchantment. If a stranger sees it, she'll be unrecognizable."

"Her scar won't be visible, and that's her main identifier," Marcus confirmed. His thumb placed the final swipe of paste on my nose. "We're working with the hopes that people will remember what Kain looked like at the Remembrance yesterday. It's much easier to make light hair darker, but the reversal takes time we don't have. We'll have to leave his as it is. I hope the change of facial features should be enough to let us slip through the cities."

"Are you certain you can distract the soldiers away from the guild?" I asked the scouts.

Twig scoffed. "Not only am I certain—I'm very much looking forward to it. Gwenna will stay here to keep a watch on the supplies while Bandin and I take in all the excitement. They may have tried to burn it down, but lower city is still home turf. We'll spin 'em' in circles."

The scouts were adept at overcoming obstacles and I had seen them fight off more than their fair share of monsters, but no monster was ever able to fire arrows at long distance. I hoped they were prepared for that.

I trusted that Kain and Marcus knew what they were doing, but it was a little unsettling walking out of the herbalist shop with only face paint on for cover. When I had asked why there were so many spells and enchantments that aided in illusions, Kain explained that the visual magics were surprisingly easy to achieve. 'People see what they want to see, and don't see what they don't know is there'. Even still, he warned that we couldn't linger in people's eyesight for too long because once one person saw through it it would lose its effectiveness altogether.

We didn't wait for nightfall after Marcus suggested the long shadows of sunset would help strengthen the illusions. While the sky was a dazzling orange and purple, we headed out towards the guild in groups. Marcus and Twig went first. Sanders had already passed by the guild yesterday so they knew where to guide Bandin. Kain and I went last, listening for a signal that would tell us there was trouble.

I wished I had my scarf—not for cover, but for warmth in the brisk winter air. It was strange that The Colds never felt like home. Even though the sun blessed the sky with radiant hues of orange and amber, Flatkeep looked dismal. Grey stone streets, grey stone walls, faded grey stone and plaster buildings. Even the structures made with bricks were stained dark. Only when I grew older did I realize it was a survival tactic. Willing oneself to fade into the environment—to look indistinguishable from the next house.

My master once served a noble House. When he saved enough coin and favors to earn a dreary old set of buildings in the lower city, he and his family sought servants of their own. Even while pretending to be a king of his parcel, he never bothered to add a touch of color to even the window sill. It was a cycle. No one figured out how to remove the target from their back so they just looked for someone else to shoot at.

And I was no different.

Posters of my face started appearing, detailed descriptions along with enticing rewards—coin, clearance, even favors from the King himself. *Wanted alive* the posters read clearly. As we wove our way out of Flatkeep, I caught a glimpse of the castle high on the hilltop. Even if I wasn't aware who was fated to be inside the Assembly Hall that night, I still don't know if I would forgive the girl who lit a match to kill. When I was young I asked my mother why our master treated us so poorly. Even after years of memories lost to time, her words echoed in my head. *People can easily become the villain in someone else's story by doing anything to be the hero of their own.*

Kain slipped his hand in mine and gave me a reassuring squeeze. How he had forgiven me so effortlessly, I'll never know. Sanders understood because we had such a long history together, but the witch hadn't spent enough time with me to know who I was. Maybe he knew who I wanted to be, and that was enough for him. I squeezed his hand back.

We walked on towards the upper city and my calves started to complain at the slight incline. At least I was comfortable—despite earning a few strange looks for my attire. Baggy shirt, baggy pants, and a belt that was becoming one of my most treasured possessions. As the buildings we passed improved in size, color, and condition, Kain's hand became slicker with sweat. The guild was close.

My face itched as the cool air hardened the paste. As I wiggled my nose a piece fluttered to the ground. Kain cleared his throat in an unnatural way as a warning that the paste wasn't going to last much longer. I felt incredibly exposed out in the open streets, and even more vulnerable without any weapons. Back at the commune, the scouts would practice sparring by hand, but I always tended to rely on my knife skills to get out of a pinch. The only thing I had on my person was a long glass shard from one of the broken jars in the shop. It gave me the occasional motivational thump when it hit against my leg from my inside pant pocket.

Kain's guild was directly off the main street, less than a block away from the grand walls that surrounded the high city. Behind the flaunted safety of the tall stone barriers were the dwellings of noble Houses and other societal members of importance. It wouldn't have surprised me if additional guards walked the streets, watching for any of us witless enough to cross over.

I recognized the red tile roof of the guild from one of Kain's descriptions. It was bigger than I thought it would be—there were low flat roofs all around, but the surrounding fence was broad and extended far back from the street entrance. It was a proper academy. Sure enough, there was a pair of guards at the front gate, and Kain moved his arm to hold my waist tight. We slowed our pace.

In the distance, a chicken cooed softly. I tugged his waist towards the alley and together we slipped out of the crowded street and toward the call. There was a row of tall hedges that braced against the large containing wall of the guild, and even with bare branches it gave us comfortable cover to slip between. We rounded the back side of the circular guild structure and finally regrouped with the others. Bandin handed me a damp towel and gestured to his face.

"This blistering cold is cracking the paint," Marcus whispered harshly. "It served its purpose in getting us here but it's of no use going forward."

We wiped off the remainder of the useless mask and took in our surroundings. The entire rear of the guild faced a small community garden that had obviously been neglected or forgotten about. Through the hedge, I could see dead weeds, naked trees, and large frost-covered pots. It was perfectly invisible. Against the tall ivory wall behind us, there was a worn-down storage shed well hidden by overgrown bushes. The princess' secret passageway.

Twig scrubbed his hands together and blew warm air into his torn shirt sleeves. "Alright kids, this is where we leave you. Give His Royal Illustriousness a sloppy wet stab wound from me, would you dearies?"

"We're trying to avoid him altogether." I reminded him curtly as I nudged him on the shoulder. "First step is to make it to the princess, and then get her somewhere safe." *And then we get as far away as possible.*

Twig gave me a firm pat on the arm and shook Kain's hand.

"Be careful," Kain said to the scouts as they braced to cause a disturbance.

Twig chuckled. "It's either we face soldiers or face Manden, and I think this would be a quicker death, don't you? But the commune is in good hands. Arrowette will whip any new scouts into shape."

"I'm surprised she didn't come with you." I mused out loud. I was certain the ex-soldier would have jumped at any chance to go back home.

Twig shrugged. "I offered. Said she didn't want to be caught traveling alongside rebel criminals. But I know she just didn't want to leave Sora, or any of them for that matter.

She's got a softer underbelly than she wants people to believe."

I knew the feeling. Bandin gave me a squeeze on the shoulder as the two of them slipped past. They wiggled through the hedges and strutted off towards the main street. Twig swung his ax back and forth casually, and I could only wonder what kind of mayhem he must have stirred in his prime.

They were out of sight for a few minutes before a loud whistle pierced the calm sky. Twig's high-pitched voice called out from a distance.

"The tricky ex-witch Kaineres! There he is! Soldiers! After him!"

The excitement carried over the tiled rooftops as thundering footsteps and panicked shouting shook the street. The chase was on.

Kain and Marcus cleared back the dead vines and branches with a touch of their hands. I made a mental note to ask him how to do that later. After yanking back thick boards with a metal prybar Marcus brought in his bag, the two of them revealed the grate on the top of a cellar door. The gateway to the tunnel.

It was well-rusted, but the two magicians worked together to pry the metal door free. Marcus counted down as he pulled the grate off silently, and when Kain threw his hands skyward the creaking sound of a hinge breaking sounded off somewhere in the sky above us. Sanders cursed under their breath in awe.

Before us was indeed a tunnel—dark, dirty, cold—but much more spacious than the burrow we crawled through on our way into Aristus. Kain drew his lips into a thin line.

Sanders and I nodded to each other, and they took my arm and helped lower me into the tunnel. There was a small drop into the ground, but I was glad Kain and Marcus would be able to stand up inside. Marcus was the last to enter, and he closed the grate overtop of him. The dying glow of sunset only reached a small patch of ground near the tunnel entrance.

Remembering the glow Marcus created with his hands and the shimmering Kasey produced from his, I rubbed my hands together and thought not only of heat, but light. I thought of igniting a fire right in between my hands, the friction like that of a stick against dry kindling. My fingertips warmed. My palms burnt. The tips of my fingers and knuckles began to emit a faint red light.

In the glimmer, I could see the whites of Marcus' eyes grow. "Is she—"

"—Shhh—let her focus," Kain whispered excitedly, his own eyes sparking with pride.

It felt good—magic. It felt natural. And other than a slight burning sensation in my hands, it came easier than I thought it might. My callused skin was teetering on a thin line between casting a light and igniting one. I forced away all thoughts of heat and focused solely on light and darkness. Contrast. Red and orange hues, blue and purple shadows, extending from my fingertips.

It wasn't as strong as the warm orange glow Marcus created in his basement, but it was enough light to lead us through the tunnel without the risk of a twisted ankle.

"Gods she's perfect."

I bit back a smile as Kain whispered to himself under his breath, but my traitorous body gave my feelings away as the light grew stronger. Sanders thought it was incredibly amusing and their laughter echoed through the tunnel.

"Sshh! S, we don't know where this leads. Do we?" I looked back at Kain and received a shrug in response.

Marcus dug into his bag for a compass nearly identical to the one Kain had. "We just need to keep going east and we should reach the castle. If there are any turns, we'll be able to set ourselves straight. Kain, do you remember at all where this tunnel connects to?"

"No, and to be honest I'd prefer to refrain from rifling through experiences that aren't mine."

Marcus sighed. "Ever the moral magician, he is."

We walked on through the tunnel, pausing every so often as footsteps shook dirt free from the ceiling. As we made our way further east, the tunnel started to look more finished. The protruding roots and dirt gave way to bricks and stone pavers. Old and rotted wooden beams were placed overhead suggesting the tunnel at one time had some structural stability. Sanders was either growing nervous or bored, as their melodic humming filled the space around us.

There were a few more tunnels that veered off to the right and left, but we continued eastward. I wasn't sure how long we had been walking, but a noise from the end of the tunnel startled me enough to extinguish the light in my palms. Sanders walked smack into my back with a gasp.

Using my fingers to brush against the wall, I continued tip-toeing further. As the tunnel curved sharply, so did the incline. We were going up. As we slowly rounded the corner, the noise from the other side grew louder—moans and grunts along with words I couldn't make out. Suddenly, a flash of bright light illuminated the long narrow chamber, followed by blood-curdling screeching. It sounded almost creature-like. I retrieved the glass shard from my pocket.

Another sharp turn, this time gifting us with small streaks of yellow light spilling in from the other side of a boarded-up door. Night had fallen which means it must have led somewhere inside. I signaled the group behind me to stay silent as I peered into a small gap in the wooden boards. Beyond a table covered in stacks of paper and scrolls, a sliver of a room appeared before my vision. I was a fly on a wall. A fly on a wall in a gods-cursed torture chamber.

My stomach contracted and threatened to force its contents up my throat. The metallic stench of blood finally reached my nose, but I could see it before I smelled it. In the center of the room was a large thick slab of stone with metal chains attached to all four corners. Bright crimson liquid shimmered in puddles on the slab and dripped onto the ground—where there were already dark stains deep in the porous surface.

Figures passed in and out of view. Court magicians—decorated with fine metal jewelry and intricate tattoos, wearing thick aprons and gaudy leather gloves up to their elbows. They exchanged few words with each other as they retrieved samples of bright red liquid from a spherical jar hanging from the ceiling. It looked like some sort of perverted chandelier; thick, viscous wine oozed down the inside of the glass as it slowly drained into vials. I already knew whose blood it was.

Kain startled me as his hand clenched around my elbow. Thankfully, my surprised gasp was drowned out by the opening and slamming of a giant iron door on the other end of the room. Two Aristian soldiers dragged a small body by chains on their arms. I watched with clenched teeth as they hoisted him up onto the slab and shackled his arms and legs. Tiny bite marks marred the flesh on the boy's arms as he struggled against the restraints in vain, sobbing between his panicked screams.

Fire burned my throat and steam ran out from my nostrils. Sanders puked.

"But they got away..." They breathed out.

I stepped back. There was only a failing door and a couple of wooden planks between me and the small Within screaming and heaving on the table. I could get to him before—

"No!" Marcus grabbed my arms and held me back. *"There's five of them and four of us—we can't take them on all at once."*

"But they're going to slaughter him!" Or worse.

"And they'll slaughter us next—we need to find the princess," Marcus bit back.

The boy's scream was muffled. I pulled out of Marcus' hands and peered back over the crack to see a witch lay the rotten carcass of a canine on the child's body—covered in dirt as if it had just been dug up. Sanders puked again.

My heart pounded. My hot blood ran cold. Kain looked at me with fear and rage in his eyes as he made the same connection. Skevsurvia wasn't creating monsters.

Aristus was.

As a court witch poured the vials of poached Within magic onto the fresh runes etched in his stomach, Kasey's scream was cut short. A flash of light blinded me and the foul stench of blood and rotten magic penetrated the room. When my eyes adjusted, Kasey was gone. The carcass was gone. In their place was a heaving, glowering mound of fur and bone.

A hell-hound. It was easily three times a man's size, and barely fit on the slab. It whimpered, then shook its head, then tried to stand. From the corner of the room, a witch was ready with some sort of long metal and glass tube. A needle, filled with a potion. They were going to sedate it.

There it was—our opening.

"Kain now!"

At my command Kain kicked the boards in with three solid blows, distracting every monster inside long enough for me to knock my full weight into the man with the sleeping potion. The glass shattered and the cries of alarm were soon overpowered by deep, menacing growls.

"*Move!*" Marcus yelled before sending a gust of glass debris flying toward the soldiers behind me. It gave me enough time to scramble out of their reach and back to Kain and Sanders, who were head-to-head against a set of furious magicians. Kain had some kind of physical shield up in the air, but the court witches used the vials of Within blood to their advantage, crafting a formidable cloud of toxic vapor. The peppery smell burned every one of my senses—my eyes watered, my nose couldn't draw air, my mouth choked on the gas.

The cloud suddenly dissipated as the witches found themselves in the jowls of the hell-hound. I remembered a familiar pain in my shoulder as its jaws snapped their spines one by one. The hound dropped their limp bodies on the blood-stained floor and bared its teeth at the newest target. I turned the glass blade over in my hand.

Marcus had managed to subdue the soldiers, and the witch I first attacked lay in several bite-marred pieces throughout the room. I held my hand up to the beast stalking my direction.

"Easy Kasey..." I kept my voice low and as soft as possible. Any remnants of the boy were replaced by the creature—a deadly creature that was confused, frightened, and pissed off.

The hound lunged forward with a snarl, smacking its muzzle on Kain's hastily constructed barrier. Sanders pushed us to the other side of the room while the canid shook its head furiously. We backed up to the iron door Marcus was busy unlocking, but the hound whirled around for another strike.

The strain of holding his defense barrier was growing heavier, and Kain's arms slackened underneath it. The hound lunged again and I threw the shard of glass towards it. It yelped as the glass cut into his nose, but the scratch was minimal compared to the size of him.

"Kasey..."

I couldn't find it in me to kill the sick animal prowling towards us. I had slain monster after monster in the forest, but that was before I knew... Even if he wasn't himself anymore, his eyes were too human...

My back pressed into Kain and he put his arms out in front of me, trying to lift another barrier. His voice was tense as he spoke through gritted teeth.

"Please believe me when I say I'm ecstatic you're developing a sense of empathy—but I can't stress how unfortunate the timing is."

The monster launched off its haunches and slammed into Kain's weak barrier, sending all of us tumbling through the door Marcus had pried open. He slammed it shut with the hell-hound snarling on the other side, scratching and biting at the door.

I stared through the metal, still piecing together what I saw and what it meant. What all of the monster killings meant. Every Within that was turned. Every Within I hunted. Every Within that died by my hands. How much innocent blood did my hands drain without me even realizing it? Cold remorse settled over me.

"I—couldn't do it. I..."

Kain lifted me up by the arms. "It's alright." He held me tight to his chest, and I breathed in the scent of him to bring myself back to the present. His heart was pounding just as loud as mine was. "I know."

Marcus reminded us that more soldiers might be coming and that we needed to continue further into the castle. The hallway stretched in front of us was empty, and Marcus retrieved the map Gwenna had drawn for us to try to make sense of where we ended up. We followed him down the pathway, but I couldn't help but think about the Withins in The Colds—lost and trapped in unearthly bodies, hungry, scared, and alone. As snarls and whines faded into the distance behind us, I wondered if dying might have been the more merciful fate.

CHAPTER TWENTY-NINE

Shaye

The flash of light illuminated the entire sky. Like a strike of lightning, a thunderous boom was heard a second after. I stuck my arm out the window. The sky was painted with mellow shades of dusk, but no rain. No clouds either, which was a convenient necessity for reading the inscription the ancient book hopefully contained. I kept glancing at the door, worried that Coretta would enter and scold me away from the window. When she returned briefly to bring me a meal around midday, I had barely made it back over from the library next door. I sat rigidly at her small dining table, hiding the book under my seat cushion hoping she wouldn't ask me to stand up.

She said she couldn't stay long and apologized profusely that she wouldn't be able to join me for supper, but I insisted I would make do with the leftovers. The silver platter of food turned my stomach into an empty well, and I only managed to save a piece of soft bread for dinner. Everything was perfect—it might have been coincidence, but Coretta brought all of my favorite foods. Hard cheeses, hand pies stuffed full of soft potatoes, glazed roots, and pitted cherries. I didn't bother to use the silverware, but towards the end of the meal I dirtied the fork and knife with a hand pie when I recalled the endless monologues Coretta could get into over manners.

I swirled half a cherry around in my mouth, wishing the cooks could have left the seeds. Everything was almost too perfect. After gulping the meal down in minutes I was left with practically nothing to do other than pace by the window, ducking when a patrol sauntered by. The day passed by painfully slowly and the lock on the door mocked me the entire time. I busied myself trying to piece together how I would tear the book apart. It was here for a reason—someone was using it.

The library on the other side of the wall was one of the smallest in the castle. Only royal family or court members used it. There was a good bloody chance the King would waltz in at any time to retrieve the book, but I took the risk hoping he was too busy creating hell for everyone around him.

Weather permitting, there would be moonlight. But there was no way to find a rabbit for the spell. Ideas fluttered in and out of my mind, cramming together and fighting for my focus. If I was in more of a hurry I would have been annoyed at myself, but the freedom to think my own thoughts and in my own time brought a satisfied smile to my face. I would figure something out.

Nightfall sank overhead slowly, but thankfully the moon faded into view early in the evening. It looked like a delicate pearl, sitting comfortably on a blanket of deep purple velvet. I took another peek out the window to see if any guards were stalking by before sitting down on the sill. The book was in view of the moon, so it should awaken the words just as it had in the hut.

I thanked my gods I was right. Once invisible words appeared in the soft hide of the cover. I wasn't sure exactly what the text said, but it looked identical to the one Kain had transcribed. It must be the same unlocking spell. My smile dropped. *Shit.* Where in frozen hell was I supposed to get a rodent?

Out of the corner of my eye, through the library's open window, I saw antlers hanging on the wall. It was a desperate thought, but I wondered what other resources the room full of scholarly valuables might hold. With the book in hand, I climbed over the sill, over the garden, and into the room, scattering freezing dirt on the carpet where I stepped.

The shelves on the walls offered nothing that would help me—a few empty glass containers, more antler decorations, and plants that were long dead but had been charmed to look healthy and perky. I groaned and slumped into a tacky leather-stitched armchair in front of the fireplace.

"Vessel to fill..." While risky, I knew speaking aloud would help steer my thoughts toward something useful. "Vessel to fill." Did it really have to be a rabbit? Kain used ancient magical knowledge combined with technical application. And it worked. But magic was so rarely so perfectly square. Magicians used rules to help them remember how to use it, but rules didn't contain all it could do. There was always another meaning. Magic so heavily relied on intention.

"Quickest before you still." That was anything alive, except for maybe an animal that was spooked stiff before it died. What else could it mean... Water? I couldn't make a creature with that. The crescendo of a song? Couldn't fill a vessel. A heart? That's morbid. So is *using a rabbit corpse.*

"*Ugh.*" I pushed myself out of the chair and tampered with the fireplace. It was fucking cold and I was too miserable with everything else going on to sit in an icebox. There were quick-fire starters placed in a small jar on the mantel, and when I added enough logs to the fire, the matches caught immediately. For someone who detested magic so much, the King sure used a lot of magical items in his home.

I placed the jar back on the mantel and almost knocked over an ornate glass teapot. A delicate vessel.

"Vessel to fill, quickest before you still..."

In a frenzied flurry of likely misguided optimism, I leapt over to the door and locked it from the inside with the turn of a bolt. As I sat back down in front of the fire with the teapot in hand, I prayed that Coretta would catch someone picking their nose or wiping their hands on their shirt. That would buy me time.

I rubbed my palms together. It had been a decade since I was able to cast magic with my own hands, but now seemed as good a time as any to start again. Books nearest to the hearth sagged in on themselves as I transferred the rigidness of their binding to the bricks that surrounded the fire. With the extra strength, the bricks easily expanded forward until I had made a sloppy imitation of a kiln. The insulated heat grew stronger, and I grabbed a pair of thick leather gloves hanging above the mantle.

"Vessel to fill..." With fire tongs, I carefully hung the teapot over the flame and rested it on a grate of cast iron. "Quickest before you still." I held it in the blistering heat until my arms grew weak—until sweat dripped down my brow and until the glass glowed an incandescent red. The glass started to lose its sharp edges as it melted, softened by the intensity of the fire. Taking it out with the tongs, I clumsily dropped it on the brick hearth in front of me.

"Shit!" It dented the side of the glowing glass orb, but I waited until I could touch the glass with my gloves before readjusting it. "Creature... creature. It needs to be some kind of bloody creature." The rabbit was the first animal that came to mind. The book cover was most likely rabbit hide, so that's what I had to work with. With the gloves and tongs, I pulled and stretched the softened glass into the closest structure I could get to a rodent. I pulled out four legs, fashioned a round head where the spout was, and coiled up the handle into a tail. Celeste made the entire artistic process look much, much easier.

My skin burned hot and my arms were shaking from the weight of the tools. Eventually, it did start to look like a rabbit. Coretta had given me painting lessons as a child in hopes I would take up the hobby. I was too impatient for slow-drying paint, but at least I knew how to craft basic shapes to assemble a very misshapen rodent. The glass cooled too much by the time I reached the ears, and its body was too stretched out from where it smashed on the floor. It looked more like a weasel as the tail uncoiled itself and dripped down. It was a creature, and the ancients would have to take it.

"Oh!"

Before the glass completely set, I pried a a poker into its back to create a small hole. It wouldn't contain much, but it was a vessel again.

I wiped the sweat off my face with the loose bottom fabric of my dress. Going back outside into the night of winter would be a blessing. Taking care to not drop it, I lifted the small weasel-like critter with the gloves and tiptoed it over to the window. It made contact with the ground with a startling hissing sound and steam clouded my vision.

"*Mother of Whelms*, ancient magicians were so needlessly and pretentiously excessive." I continued to curse the construction of such a spell while the glass figure cooled down. When it was finally cold enough to touch, I removed the gloves and cleared my throat. Now all I had to do was remember the words.

"Vessel to fill, quickest before you still. Eternal moonlight, er—guide you." I removed a plant from the ground and made room for the deformed rabbit. The sky was dark now and the moon and stars were shining overhead. "New earth hide you." I gently packed the sculpture in with the top layer of garden dirt covering it like a blanket. "Force that binds... *Shit* the book." I jumped back into the library to retrieve the soft leather-bound spell book and laid it on top of the burial mound, stroking the spine. "Breath that finds." I inhaled deep and concentrated on the meaning of the spell, the possibilities that could be unlocked with it, and the truth it needed me to find. I released it all into an exhale and blew it over top of the dirt. "Creation that lies, creature you rise."

I worried for a moment that I had mixed up the last two lines, but I had to bite my lip to keep from celebrating out loud as the dirt started to move. It *fucking worked.* I scrambled back to give it space as the creature poked its tiny nose out of the ground. I don't know what I was expecting to see, but I gasped in awe as a glistening silver stoat shook its way out of the hole in the garden. Its fur was celestial; its sleek sheen caught streaks of moonlight and sent them scattering in tiny reflections on the surfaces around it. It looked around at its new life of sensation, flicking its long tail and turning its small round ears every which way.

"Yeah, it feels great doesn't it?" I giggled softly to myself. The stoat didn't find it as comical, and it took a swipe at my hand before it scurried out of the garden and down the cobblestone path towards the forest.

"*Hey!*" I licked the bite mark to stop the blood from trickling down the top of my palm. I braced to chase after it, but another blinding flash of light illuminated the sky. Outside, I could hear the booming sound much clearer and realized it was coming from the northeast side of the castle, not too far from where I was. Nothing about it seemed natural, and I stooped down to pick up the only clue I had as to what Amos was trying to materialize. The book opened limply in my hands, the cover exposing a bookmark that had been shoved between a few pages.

Someone had definitely been reading this, and had already discovered what took Kain days too long to find. Using the bookmarks as guides, I flipped to a page in the middle. I flipped to a page in the front. I flipped to a page in the back. I didn't scour the words beforehand, but I knew that the text had changed from innocent recipes and theatrical enchantments to charms and curses much more sinister in nature. Now began the investigation.

Back in the safety of Coretta's lavish room, I sat on the ground and rested my back against the bottom of the bed frame. I flipped through the pages of twisted stories and terrible tools and powerful curses. None of it was particularly helpful because Amos could have used any of it to his advantage. Maybe that was enough to condemn him. The thought of him harming Withins for any reason made my blood boil and I shifted uncomfortably on the carpet.

As I continued to flip through the flimsy pages, a thin silver lace of thread fell out and into my lap. Another bookmark. My eyes danced back and forth between the words in front of me until I felt my heart sink into my stomach. I read it again.

As realization hit me, I couldn't find the air in my lungs and my mouth hung open, dry and cracking. The walls in the room started settling closer to me—the hunting mural on the ceiling shifted its target and the spears and spikes were pointing straight towards me. I was trapped again. My hands started sweating. I needed to get out. *Now.*

I ripped out the page and threw the rest of the book under the bed, scrambling to my feet trying to escape the tension in my chest. I ran for the door and turned the bolt. Thank the gods it undid the lock Coretta set from the outside and I pushed open the giant door. There was no one around, but I didn't double-check to see if anyone was coming as I sprinted down the hallway. I kept running and running, my bare feet vibrating with each step as they absorbed the shock of cold hard stone underneath. My long hair swirled around me as I ran, faster and faster to wherever freedom was. I couldn't think—I couldn't piece together memories fast enough—so I let my legs carry me through the castle where they wanted to go. Back to the escape.

I fled through the empty hallways, chipping my shoulder on corners too tight and snagging the fabric of my dress on bulky furniture. Tears started flooding my eyes as fear started to catch up with me. I wiped them away as best as I could with my sleeve as I rounded another corner, running—running—running, until my body slammed into something solid and sturdy that sent me tumbling back.

Brushing my hair out of my face, I sat up to see what the hell I ran into, and at my eyeline there was an outstretched hand—marked with rust-red tattoos and liquid burn marks. I trailed my gaze up the arm and landed on his face. His beautiful face. My pulse echoed loud in my ears as Kain smiled softly, his presence bringing every sense of familiarity and safety back to me. His voice sounded so different from the outside and sent a fiery shiver down the back of my neck.

"It appears the fates are set on us colliding."

I gingerly took his hand and he lifted me off the ground with ease. I didn't let go of him as the two of us looked at each other for the first time, each our own but still chaotically and intricately intertwined. His cheek creased from his tilted smile and my heart melted at the relief I felt. There was more color in his skin—warmth in his eyes. He stood taller, lighter, without the weight of my recklessness. He opened his mouth to say something, but I needed to tell him everything.

"I—"

My words sizzled and vaporized on my tongue as she stepped into view. Her hair was darker, but her cold face and scarred mouth awakened anger in me that I had not yet fully been able to feel until that moment. The tears that formed in my eyes fell down my cheeks, salt coating my lips as I cursed her to the deepest labyrinths of hell.

"*Don't you fucking get anywhere near me—*"

Kain wrapped my rage up in strong hands and held me steadily by the upper arms.

"Hey, hey—it's alright, she's not who you think—"

"*I think she's traitorous scum that has a lot of fucking nerve—*" My words were spat out through gritted teeth as their faces flashed before my eyes. I wondered how scared they were. How trapped they must have felt.

Kain bent down to bring his face to mine. "Shaye—she is not responsible for the death of your siblings. I promise. She's not going to hurt you."

His voice rang out in my head a few times before I understood what he was saying. The woman behind him just swallowed and stared at me with a sickly uneasiness. A witch from Kain's guild approached me slowly, patting Kain on the back for his attention.

"We need to move somewhere safer. Sanders?" The man conversed with someone holding a tattered sheet of paper, and the two of them waved us to a stairwell further down the hall.

Kain offered his hand to me again, but I didn't miss the look he gave the assassin as we followed her. Instead of climbing up, we entered through a skinny door on the other side of the stairwell that led to a cramped kitchen. It was a prep area the servants once used. Their stations must have moved elsewhere because the inside was covered in dust and the cupboards were bare aside from a few pellets of rat droppings.

As the door closed the door behind us, all of them released a collective sigh.

The map reader bowed their shaggy head low towards me. "Princess Shaye Heiress Aristus," they extended their arm outwards in a flourish that made their oversized sweater swallow their hands, "may I be the first of this lot to say what an honor it is to finally meet you. You have no idea how thrilled we are to see you still in one piece."

The assassin gave them a suspicious nudge with their elbow as I examined Kain's strange party in front of me. The other witch, tall and dark-skinned, looked familiar to me but I couldn't place if I had seen him before with my eyes or just in memories. The map reader—also vaguely familiar to me—rubbed the side of their ribcage and tossed a confused expression over to the cold woman as she furrowed her brows at them.

She... didn't look armed at the moment, but she also looked like someone who could arm themselves with a feather and place hair-thin cuts in dangerously precise places. She looked like an assassin. And there was no way of telling what kind of shit she had hidden in her ridiculously large pants.

Kain cleared his throat. "What Sanders meant, is that we're relieved to see you're doing alright. All events considered. We weren't sure how you'd feel after..." The unbinding. His eyes twitched as they looked me over, finally noticing the state I was in. My hair was a mess, my dress was stained with dirt and soot, and my face was damp from tears. Kain reached into his pocket for something, but the person named Sanders held out a piece of torn cloth and offered it to me.

"It's clean. Mostly. We were running for a bit so it might be damp—"

"...Thank you." I took the gift and patted my face dry. "Why were you running?" The situation caught up to me. "*Why are you here?*" I turned to Kain. "*Castle guards are out looking for you—they've been searching all day—If they see you—*"

"We know. But it was worth the risk." Kain leaned against the counter with a groan, stretching a sore muscle.

"Just to see if I was okay from the spell?" Knowing Kain, I would have believed it, but the expressions the rest of the group wore had me unsettled.

"To prevent you from suffering the next." The tall witch murmured under his breath, but Kain hummed a warning.

"Marcus,"

"She needs to know. She might not come with us if she doesn't."

"If I don't know what?"

The four exchanged looks as if they didn't think they'd make it this far in their plan to check my sanity.

The rebel assassin knelt down on the ground in front of me. Her voice was low and quiet, like footprints treading carefully in fresh snow. "Princess, there's something you need to know about King Amos Aristus."

CHAPTER THIRTY

Rune

Kain helped me explain the parts I couldn't, bless him. The five of us sat on the floor of the kitchen while a small window illuminated the space with stars and moonlight. The princess took everything in with tears in her eyes and a mixture of shock and anger pressed tightly between her lips. Despite all she had been through, she was strikingly beautiful. Her thick raven hair shimmered in moonlight as she gathered it into her hands and combed through the tangles. There was not a single blemish, scar, or cut on her dark olive skin other than surface dirt on her fingernails and soot on her neck. She was older than I thought she'd be—she looked at least thirty years of age, and the fabric of her dress artfully hugged the soft curves of her body.

It was only her emerald green eyes that suffocated my airways and kneaded the painful knot in my stomach. Thick dark eyebrows emphasized her accusatory stare as she examined me up and down, feeling me out.

"Princess, although my past actions are far from innocent, my intentions were never to take your family from you. My targets were the heads of corrupt noble houses that had been preying on weaker subjects for decades. It probably doesn't mean anything to you, but I give you my word." I bowed my head to her, internally begging for forgiveness underneath her condemning silence.

After excruciating minutes, she closed her eyes and sighed through her nose. "It's not impossible to believe... but you also must understand it's not easy to. I—" Her head jerked to the side in painful memory. "Crimes have been committed from every angle in the Kingdom. That much is clear. I do believe what you're saying about my father is true—his abuse over the Withins. After what he intends to do to me to keep his throne... it makes me think he'd do anything."

"What do you mean?" Kain said softly. We explained that she was in danger of being his next target, but we weren't sure how.

Shaye shook thoughts away and pulled out a crumpled piece of paper from inside her dress pocket. "Earlier today, I found another ancient spell book—identical to the one Sora stole in The Colds. Someone has been using it—Amos has been using it, I'm convinced—no doubt with the aid of one of the court mages. I ripped out the page that was bookmarked."

She unfolded the thin sheet of paper, releasing an undignified croaking noise from Kain's paling mouth as he took in the shredded piece of history. He visibly fought the nausea on his face and gingerly took the massacred artifact from Shaye. He cleared his throat of what I could only imagine was a long-winded lecture about the pricelessness of such an item, and focused on reading its contents.

His distressed face twisted into a horrified expression as he read it over again. And again.

"He's not just making monsters for his defenses." He said aloud. He met Shaye's eyes with fear in his own. "He's been trying to make himself younger."

Marcus cursed. "He can't do that. No one can do that."

Kain shook his head as he assembled the King's plan in his mind. "Maybe not in years, but in physical form. There are curses here to transfer life to someone else. Forbidden healing magic. If you call it *healing*. He's using the healthiest Withins and draining them to extend his own life."

"But even with powerful magical sources, the effect won't last. He'll still age and die as nature intends, he just won't notice himself growing older."

Kain ran his fingers through his hair. "Whatever he's doing now is probably just experimental. He knows it won't last—*unless*, the life he absorbs is 'that of his own'. That's why he didn't immediately kill me at the Remembrance. That's why he didn't kill Shaye when we first were un-bound."

Shaye clenched her fists. "He's going to sacrifice me to keep his fucking silver band. He's following suit of Whelms. He's making another Undead Realm."

Sanders cocked their head to the side. "Isn't the Queen of Whelms *actually* dead though?"

"Yes, but her entire Queendom loved her so much they vowed to never replace her. It was their choice. My father knows half of his Kingdom despises him. He's taking it by force."

"He may be trying, but he won't succeed as long as you're safe," I said with a certainty in my voice that surprised me. "That's why we came all this way. We've found you, and now we're going to get you out of here."

Shaye rose to her feet. "No—I can't leave. If I leave then he'll continue executing Withins and raiding lower cities. He needs to be stopped."

I stood to meet her. Her eyebrows narrowed in determination as I tried to explain our limited options. "We could barely make it in here to find you. It'll be tricky to go out the way we came, and we have no idea where Amos is."

"I do," she bit back. "There was a flash of light—like the one you described in the... earlier tonight. But this one came from the Northeast Wing. I think he's doing something there."

My breath stilled. "He's in the Hall of Assembly."

Marcus nodded slowly, bringing information to his mind. "The Hall has been boarded up and left untouched since the attack years ago. Like some kind of memorial. Amos is one of the only people allowed clearance. Not even parents can visit."

"And no one thought that was at all suspicious?" I thought out loud. Shaye cut me a deadly glance in response.

Kain rose to his feet and addressed Shaye. "We'll go where you want. I agree with Rune that it would be much safer to readdress this at a later time, but we're here now, and I understand the urgency." He looked out the window at the night sky. "If we help you reach the King, what do you plan on doing?"

"We need to expose him. People need to know I'm alright and the Aristus Realm can be passed down and out of his hands. The people need to know what he's done—to my siblings and to every Within. Some of the children lost belonged to court members and Nobles. They deserve to hear the truth. And whatever is in that Assembly Hall could provide visible proof of everything."

Kain nodded. "Then that's where we'll go. Although it's risky, the hallways were surprisingly barren. Shaye or Sanders can lead us through the castle undetected, and—"

A loud bang startled us from outside the kitchen door followed by a low growl reverberating through the stairwell. A creature sniffed at the foot of the door and scratched the wood with sharp claws.

"*Oh, gods of death take me.*" I cursed under my breath. I looked at the small circular window near the top of the wall. The kitchen was sunken into the ground so if we climbed through, we could sneak straight onto the dead grass lawn outside. "I can take us to the Assembly Hall from the outside," I said coldly. "There's a lot of us, but it's dark. We have a good shot."

The door burst off its top hinge and bravely hung onto the lower one. The hell-hound raised its paws and slammed into the door again, snapping the rest of it off the wall with a loud crack.

Marcus shoved his hands towards the window and it shattered open. "Still don't want to kill it? Then outside it is!"

He climbed out first, stepping up onto the counter and through the shattered window pane. I jerked my head at Kain.

"Kain, go—take the Princess." I raised my hands out to make myself a larger target for the snarling wolf. Its haunches were raised and its teeth were bared. I heard someone scramble out of the window, but I didn't dare take my eyes off the beast in front of me.

"*Kain, go!*"

He stopped trying to build a defense shield around me and followed Shaye. Sanders put something cold in between my waistband and my skin before crawling up and out.

"Not that you'll need it!" They shouted back in false confidence.

The tiny pocket knife was in my hand right before the wolf slashed its fangs out. In a blur, I cut across the tip of its nose again, sending dark red blood splattering against the white cupboards. It whimpered in pain and clawed at its mouth, giving me time to leap onto the counter and get pulled up by Kain's strong arms. My foot was barely out of reach before the hound snapped again, but only its head could fit through the tiny opening.

Kain whistled to Marcus and together they performed the same spell they had when they opened the loud grate to the tunnel. The witch and mage collected the growls and viscous barks of the hound and shot them off into the distance, alerting several soldiers in the process. The armed guards nearby sprinted in the opposite direction following the sound of the beast, meanwhile, the real hell-hound was growing bored of being stuck and retreated in defeat.

We were in a small vegetable garden outside the kitchen, where luckily there were large overgrown bushes still covered with dead leaves that gave us shelter to crouch under. We were on the west side of the castle and needed to climb further uphill to reach the Assembly Hall. The buildings hadn't changed much in the last eight years, and I hadn't forgotten the path I made for myself in shadows that night.

There were a couple of close calls near the various entryways to the castle—guards lined up with spears on the ground and with crossbows on watch towers. It was tricky keeping everyone in the same shadows, but when my foot slipped over a sharp ledge Kain held my waist tight against him. He let loose a relieved breath in my ear and quietly kissed me on the temple. I couldn't wait for it to all be over—the running, the fighting, the sneaking. I finally had something I wanted, and I was going to do anything to make it happen. I would restore his princess to her Realm and Kain and I could finally exist without the stress of survival. I would even admit to him that I was excited to learn more about magic.

From a distance, the Assembly Hall looked like every other part of the castle—grey stone construction with a steeply pitched tile roof. On closer inspection, however, it looked right shit. The tall windows that flanked all three protruding sides were crudely boarded up, and the dark marks from the long-doused fire burnt every corner and ledge it touched. Behind it was a fenced stone balcony, also cut off from the rest of the castle. It overlooked the sharp drop down the cliff and to the forest in the distance.

We were approaching it from the rooftop, hiding from watchtowers behind decorative spires and flags. When the coast was clear, I slid down the tile roof on my side, bruising my hip as it smashed along each ceramic plate. I dropped to the ground and softly cooed—a signal for them to follow. One by one they dropped, Shaye being the only one to lose her balance and tumble forward into the patchy grass. Ignoring Kain's offered arm, she brushed herself off and spat out a slew of curses of grotesque detail.

After we collected ourselves, Marcus pried a loose board off the window and we all snuck inside. I tugged at the string of beads behind my ear. Nothing about this place felt right. There was an eerie energy in the air paired with a low hum coming from all sides of the vast room. The ceiling was failing in several places and light filtered through large cracks, highlighting destruction and debris that hadn't been touched in years. As my eyes adjusted, my boot stepped on an ash-dusted book. My stomach dropped as I turned it over. A small lamb and frog danced together on the cover. A children's storybook.

The princess stalked over slowly with a haunted expression. Her eyes fell on the overturned book on the floor and her eyes glistened.

My voice was hoarse and nearly silent. "I promise I didn't know."

Her lip twitched into a snarl. "But you knew someone would be trapped here." She spoke only loud enough for me to hear. "And you burnt it up anyway."

Before I could respond, the low humming noise in the background grew into a deep, menacing growl.

Marcus clapped his hands and illuminated the floor with a soft blue glow—taking the streams of skylight from the ceiling and scattering them along the ground. The entire hall was dimly lit with hues of blue—like it was built upon glowing ice. The glow cast menacing shadows on the walls from the rows and rows of cages before us.

Giant iron cages blockaded the door to the castle. Behind each set of bars was a stirring, snarling creature. Shaye inhaled sharply at the sight of hell-hounds baring their multiple sets of fangs, Reptisci crackling from the inside, and the organs of Eerrees floating hauntingly in the center of their cages. There were monsters I had never encountered before, and each one looked more savage and bloodthirsty than the next. All of them were going to be released into the Colds or set on any member of the Alliance that would dare defy the King's Disunion.

Footsteps echoed through the hall, slow and relaxed, like someone taking a stroll about the forbidden parts of the castle late at night. The dim blue light cast a long shadow against the ceiling as he stepped out of the darkness from behind the cages, his face much too young to be sixty.

"It's quite past your curfew young lady." King Amos stepped ever closer to Shaye, hands casually behind his back. His posture was at ease, but there was something dishonest and threatening about his gaze.

The four of us sheltered the Princess, and while it offered little attack power—Sanders' pocket knife turned over in my hand comfortably and naturally. Amos tore his stare away from Shaye and eyed each of us down, a vulture deciding which tendon to tear out first. His eyebrow twitched at the sight of Kain.

"I'll admit I underestimated you, oh lost prodigy of Gustan Cre-Twelle. I thought you'd be more of a coward—halfway to Elynchester by now. Yet here you are, stringing along the other Cre-Twelle into your perilous mess."

As he glanced at me my knuckles around the knife turned white. "And *you* are much more difficult to kill than what you're worth. I should have known your wicked vitality would keep you alive even in banishment. Your return is my divine punishment I didn't slit your throat the night you were caught."

"—Is it true?" Shaye pushed past my shoulder to face her father. "You knew about the rebel attack, and you did nothing to stop it—*is it true you lured them here?*" Her fists were clenched and her canines bared in rage. Amos answered with a quiver of his lip, his face showing no remorse. Shaye cursed at him. "*For what?! For your selfish desire—*"

"Selfish?" Amos raised his voice instantly, his eyebrows crinkling inward. "You have no right to accuse me of selfishness when it was *your* wretched desires that led to your fateful destruction ten years ago."

Shaye's mouth dropped open in furious confusion, but before she could say anything else, Amos took another step forward. He was only paces away.

"*You* were corrupted by your obsession with vile experimentation and heretical teachings. Sneaking out—*you think I didn't know?* You think I didn't see my own daughter change before my very eyes? Your soul was convoluted with wickedness long before your body was lost. I—I was weak then, I was fearful. I thought it could be redeemed, reversed. But years later it haunted me. Like a shadow settling over the Kingdom, your spirit lingered the halls and I saw you everywhere. So I did what must be done."

"*You killed them Da!*"

"I SAVED THEM!" Sweat beaded on his brow as he screamed, his voice reverberating off the ceiling. "I was *forced* to bestow upon them a death kinder than life. Do not mistake my sacrifice for one of selfishness. This Kingdom is a burden upon my shoulders and I will do what I must to keep it safe."

"*Safe from who?*"

"FROM DEMONS LIKE YOU!" He spat on the ground, strings of saliva clinging to his chin as he glared at his daughter. "I know not what transgression I have committed against the gods to have *deserved* this—this threat of *evil* in my own line. But I was terrified it would continue. That you wouldn't be the last one. What Realm could be led by someone corrupted with such vice—such a destructive power? I saw a divine opening—a way to cleanse the line once and for all. To save them all from wretched futures."

"*You're a fucking murderer!*"

Kain held onto Shaye's arm as she lashed out at the King, who merely shook his head.

"You are not able to understand because your mind is already lost to the power within it. I will lead the Kingdom of Aristus into a new age, and its leader shall remain age-less, carrying the burden of protection and provision for centuries to come."

Shaye's voice choked out in sobs. "*You've been* slaughter-*ing your Kingdom—You've been using them like kindling for your delusional fire! You fucking hypocrite—you use magic every day!*"

"Only because I must. Once stability has been achieved I shall rid the realm of its disease. And your deliverance will be helping me in such a cause." He slowly raised his fingers to his mouth, preparing to whistle for his guards.

In my peripheral vision, I realized Sanders was no longer with us. In a panic, my eyes searched around the room while my head remained focused on the King. Behind where Amos tensed in front of us, there was movement in the shadows. On top of a caged Reptiscis, Sanders hung down and rubbed something over the lock. A piece of fabric—the cloth they had given Shaye earlier, now infused with subtle Within magic. They whispered the words to the releasing spell they knew and the cage creaked open.

The King barely had time to dodge out of the way before the giant snake barreled out of the cage and into the room towards us. I pushed the others out of the way as the reptile struck the ground where they stood. Its fang-less mouth hissed in anger and jerked around to find another victim. It sprung from its coiled body towards Sanders on the cage, but Marcus threw up a defense barrier that knocked it back.

Shaye ripped from my hand. She chased after her father, who was busy smashing apart a window to flee through. *Shit.*

I launched myself after her, but the Reptiscis slammed its tail down in my path, almost knocking the wind out of my lungs. Strong hands hauled me up and pushed his barrier against the body of the crackling reptile.

"Go!" Kain waved me off. "*We'll take care of it—without killing it—I promise.*"

"What?!" Marcus heaved and groaned in exhaustion from his position against the front of the giant snake, but I was already up and over the window.

I found the last of the Aristus family on the large balcony, dangerously close to each other.

"You maggot-infested, self-inflated, bile-spewing *traitor!*" Shaye was chewing her father out for every atrocity he committed, faulting him for endangering the Realm with the Alliance's threat of war. "You treat everyone who serves you as disposable fodder for your pathetic twist for control. You'd send out soldiers to fight and die in *your* name in a war *you* caused. You'd put the entire Realm in harm's way just so a throne contorts to the shape of your fucking ass over centuries? You disgust me. I am *ashamed* to be your daughter—"

Amos pushed her off in disgust, managing to put her between him and the stone fence overlooking the edge of the cliff. I snuck up behind him carefully, hoping neither of them made any sudden moves.

"A good King readies his Kingdom for all possibilities. If the Alliance wages a fight against my people, that mistake will take a heavier toll upon them than they realize. As for you, my daughter—the flesh of my flesh, the bone of my bone, a wretched curse has swallowed your existence and marred your purity." He grit his teeth. "You share no blood of mine."

Shaye swung her fist at him, but he caught her arm and held her tight as she struggled to pull away.

"You forget that it is *only* your blood that I require. Poor Princess, consumed by the magic, driven mad—jumped to her death to escape the wickedness within her."

Heat surged in my throat as he braced to shove her over the balcony. I screamed out for her, hot fire in my mouth searing the words into a spell. Amos released her arms with a pained cry and grabbed his neck. The thick silver band burnt his skin as it glowed a faint red, steam rising up into the cold night air. He grappled with it and unclasped the back, ripping layers of skin from his neck as he yanked the necklace off.

It clanged to the ground, still hissing. A ribbon of raw exposed flesh dangled from the King's neck, blood tricking down his chest and soaking his shirt.

Shaye scrambled to her feet but Amos caught her by hair—cursing her gods. They were still too far. Before I could reach them, the King retrieved a long thin blade from his pocket and raised it to stab her chest.

"No!"

As the knife left my hand I felt the metal handle brush against the prints of my fingers. It was so delicate, so small, so unlike the weapons I had to wield on the journey here. I had spent so much time adjusting to the weight of the cutlasses that in the panic, my aim was thrown off.

With the subtle, gentle sound of steel piercing flesh, the blade intended for his hand sank deep into his open neck, halting his sword above her chest.

His mouth gaped in shock and his body tried to breathe, only to send droplets of sputtering blood out from his mouth and streaming down his neck. His eyes met his daughter's as he grunted something incoherent and collapsed to the ground.

Shaye fanatically looked him up and down, slowly realizing what happened. As she started to collect herself, she knelt next to his body and held his sputtering chest. Bitter tears streamed down her cheeks and merged with the splatters of blood on her face.

After a minute his body went limp in her lap—green emerald eyes nothing but orbs of glass staring blankly at the sky.

"He's dead." She whispered flatly. Her eyes flickered to me, her expression grim.

"He-he was going to kill you."

She clutched his chest with her fingers. Her voice was solemn and almost silent. "Only if I let him."

Every nerve in my body was begging me to flee, but for some reason I was frozen where I stood. She was still too exposed here on the balcony. I couldn't leave her. I—

Dainty footsteps startled me, and I turned around to a thin older woman with paper-white hair. Her hands covered her mouth and I braced for her to alert the entire castle.

Instead, she merely cleared her throat and composed herself. Through the window after her came two guards, currently not armed. She waved them towards the dead King.

"Take the King's body to his chambers at once. Ah—ah!" She whispered harshly at the guard's concern. "Immediately. You can see he's quite ill."

The guards took Amos' body from Shaye, still kneeling on the ground. The only way off the balcony was through the broken window, so the two carried him carefully through as gently as they could.

The woman gave them final commands. "Lock yourselves in and wait for me. Speak to no one."

The princess lifted her head to the woman, wet streams running down her face. "Coretta, I—"

"Shhh, now. It's alright." The woman knelt down beside Shaye and tucked her head into her chest, soothing her long black hair. "It will be alright. Sickness like this happens all the time." She took Shaye's face in her thin fingers. "Are you hurt?"

Shaye shrugged but shook her head no. Coretta squeezed Shaye's hand and the two helped each other stand. I stood rigidly near the edge of the balcony, feeling invisible and naked all at once.

"I will take care of everything regarding the King's sudden... illness. My dear, your Queendom will need you to find the courage to take the reigns, but this is not the place to discuss such matters." Coretta kissed her on the head. "When you're ready, meet me in your father's chambers."

With a shuddering sigh, Shaye nodded and released Coretta. After the woman climbed through the window with much more grace than I thought possible, I was alone again with the Princess. The only Aristus.

"Shaye," My lips opened to speak but I had no idea what I would say to fill the gaps between us.

She furrowed her brows in bitter determination and feigned strength. Crossing the balcony, she met my eyes with a stare that dried my tongue against the back of my teeth. "It is not lost on me that you would so easily spare a monster that couldn't be changed but not a man who could be."

Her green dress whipped around her as she retreated into the Hall of Assembly and I was left in the dark embrace of winter, surrounded by a familiar loneliness. The wind blew my hair forward and pale blue beads tickled my ear. I let out a slow, steady breath that centered me as I watched its steam rise and dissipate in the breeze. After scanning the balcony a final time I turned back to the Assembly Hall to see what damage was done, leaving behind a bloody silver band that glistened under the stars.

Chapter
Thirty-One

Rune

The assembly hall was quiet, the blue light charm on the ground just barely illuminated. One of the caged monsters occasionally groaned or hissed, but the chill in the air encouraged everything to remain nearly silent.

I hugged my friend closer, their hair prickling my face. "I'm just glad you're alright, S. That was quick thinking on your part. But there were quite a few monsters to choose from. Why the snake?"

Sanders laughed and whistled a tired sigh through the gap in their teeth. "It was the scariest one. Also seemed the most pissed off."

And it still was. Even back in its cage and curled up into a tight coil, vibrant rage gleamed in its yellow eyes. The three of them had managed to trick it back into the cage with an illusion spell, but not before wearing themselves out. Marcus and Kain sat back to back on the ash-dusted ground, sweat dripping from their temples.

"Who was the lady?" Sanders asked.

"Coretta." I remembered her name, but I didn't know anything else about her.

Marcus did, and groaned as he rose to his feet to explain. "She's one of the King's advisors. It seemed like the princess trusted her though, so I think she'll be alright. However, speaking from a medical practitioner's perspective, that man they hauled in was *not* sick."

Kaineres groaned as he stood. "What happened?" His tone was inquisitive, but not accusatory.

"He—he had a blade. He was going to kill Shaye, and I was too far to disarm him. I took the only shot I had and it... well. I didn't mean to kill him, but I couldn't let him hurt the princess either."

Kain simply walked over to me and wrapped me in his arms, salt and cedar enclosing me on every side. I drank him in and let his words sink into the surface of my neck.

"It's alright, Rune. I believe you." He tipped my chin up towards his face. "Shaye is no longer in danger of her father. Messy accidents aside, we did what we came here to do."

The four of us walked out of the unlocked doors into the hallway, where one of Coretta's guards was waiting to take us to the King's Chambers. We were stiff and nervous the entire escort, but once we made it to the entryway in front of the King's large double doors the guard left us outside and at ease.

We waited outside of the chamber for hours, tailbones and backs aching against the brutal stone that covered the entire castle in hostility. Silence hung in the air—heavy and freeing at the same time. The worst was over for Aristus, but what became of us was entirely up to the soon-to-be Queen. My fate rested in the hands of a woman whose entire family died by my own. And I wasn't feeling good about it.

I didn't aim to kill the King tonight, but I also didn't feel the weight of regret I expected myself to feel. It was the weapon I had. It was my blade or his. His neck or hers. I made right on my silent vow to protect the princess from harm, and even now, I could admit to myself that I would do it again.

In the instant I released the knife I could see a future where Aristians thrived with her as their Queen. All Aristians. The elites, the civilians, the rebels, the Withins. It had been ages since there was a Within-born Noble. She could change the entire Realm for the better, and hope was something I could taste as easily as the blood on my lips.

Sanders disturbed the false peace with the question we were all asking ourselves. "What the hell do we do now?" They threw their arms across their chest, long sweater sleeves engulfing their hands.

Kain looked in the direction where Shaye was meeting with her advisor behind the double doors. "I suppose that's up for the future Queen to decide."

"Not to get ahead of ourselves..." Marcus cleared his throat. "But, on account of you *not* murdering the Princess—and instead putting your life at risk to ensure her safety..." He scratched the back of his bald head nervously. "Pending the lifting of your banishment of course, will you honor the South Society Guild of Medicinal Magic with your presence?"

That was a proper mouthful. Kain raised his brows at his friend's proposal and gave me a weak nudge with his shoulder. "Only if you make room for two."

Marcus pursed his lips. "I know the Headmage, so I think that could be arranged."

I asked the gods to spare me under my breath, but I was secretly interested in experiencing a life so different from the one I had been living. One where magic and I were the same. But the likelihood of it coming to pass...

Kain saw me bite my lip in concern. "What is it?" He whispered.

"My chances of redemption with the princess are slim..."

He gave me his reassuring half-smile. Sweat-dampened locks of hair that fell across his forehead swayed as he tilted his head. "I think she'll eventually come around. You came around to me, didn't you?" He pressed a kiss to my head that softened the piling anxieties and whispered into my ear. "Give her heart a chance to bend."

The large doors to the King's Chamber opened slowly. Through the ornate wooden frame, with cheeks still wet but head held high, Princess Shaye Heiress Aristus came into view. With guards and her advisor behind her, she looked regal even while covered in dirt and blood. All of us scrambled to attention, knees cracking from exhaustion as we stood.

She looked each of us over, softening her gaze on Kain as she spoke. "We have a Queendom to rebuild, and… I haven't been myself the past decade." Shaye caught herself smiling at her own joke due to Sanders' contagious giggle. "Anyway, even with advisors, I'm going to need support from people I trust. Will you help me?" Her request was directed to Kain more than anyone else, but Sanders bowed low in humble acceptance.

"We are at your service, my Queen." Then, after a short pause, they added: "You're on our side, right?"

Shaye let out another giggle and shook her head. "The main work will be to abolish the sides. There's no need for war, civil or otherwise. So our first mission is to stop the turmoil surrounding these walls. I've already called off the search for Kaineres and the escaped criminals, especially considering they're already in my hallway."

Her words were laced together with confidence and warmth. She spoke like a Queen. Like someone who had practiced the art of speech and persuasion, both exceedingly royal traits. From experience, peace was so much easier to talk about than to achieve, but something in her expression made it seem like she was the right person for the undertaking.

Coretta swallowed back a gasp of surprise when Sanders jumped forward and threw their arms around Shaye, but the princess laughed and hugged them back, seemingly eager for a friend after years of a different kind of banishment.

As she walked us to the main castle entrance, Shaye explained that messengers were sent out to the city, announcing the King's sudden deadly 'illness' and Shaye's willingness to take charge as Queen. The Coronation ceremony would be held as soon as possible, according to Coretta, who had excused herself to dismiss the Court witches from their heinous experimentation for King Amos. Shaye was adamant that every captured Within be released and given medical treatment for their wounds, as well as comfortable living arrangements. Even if that was the only thing accomplished tonight, it would have been well worth it.

Shaye paused at the castle's grand entry. As the doors swung open, the fabric of her dress danced around her legs and bare feet. Wind ran messy fingers through her hair and dried the remaining dampness on her face. There was a potency to the way she looked out at her lost Realm. She was a force to behold, a rising sun after years hidden in the clouds.

Marcus and Sanders walked on ahead of us, but at the silent request in Shaye's eyes, Kain and I remained on the steps in front of the castle door.

"Thank you. Both of you. I recognize that you both made sacrifices in order to free my spirit, and I will forever be in your debt for your bravery. Kain, I—" Her voice broke. "I'm so sorry for everything. Your ceremony, your title, your family, your banishment, it was all my fault and I never—"

Kain collected her hands in his. "After what I heard tonight, as painful and as confusing and as *freezing* as the past decade has been, if the curse was the only thing keeping you safe all these years, then I am honored to have played my part."

"But—but you lost everything—"

"I lost everything I had, but I gained everything I *needed*. I met my sister and my niece, I was able to bring some healing to a community that needed it, and I met people I don't think I could ever live without." His subtle glace in my direction sent blood rushing to my cheeks. "You needed safety and freedom and the only place you could find it was unconsciously wandering through the most dangerous part of the continent with someone who knows nothing about survival. Magic is funny like that." He winked in my direction, his smug half-smile plastered to his ever-enchanting face.

Shaye breathed easier and forced out a chuckle. "Well, I wasn't always unconscious."

Kain stood straighter, not having heard her quite clearly at first. "There you go, see—Wait. W-what do you mean by not always unconscious? How much could you see? How much *did* you see?"

Shaye's laughter cascaded down the castle steps as she guided him towards the courtyard with her hands. "We should discuss everything later, but right now I think the Headmage is trying to get your attention."

Kain's stunned expression was turned around to face Marcus, waving his hand at the bottom of the stairs in the distance, pointing past the courtyard. From where we stood on the hillside I could see through the courtyard and down the main street in the upper city, where three tired scouts sauntered towards us, arm linked in arm. A very excited rooster crowed as Twig raised his hands in triumph, followed by Sanders' own celebratory bird call.

"Rune." Shaye's low tone kept me from following the witch down the stairs. "I will not send you back into banishment. Regardless of your previous involvement with violent rebel attacks, you were also charged with a crime you didn't intend to commit. That doesn't absolve you of the assault you were planning on enacting that night."

She looked past me to Sanders sprinting full speed at Twig, Bandin, and Gwenna, leaping onto Twig's shoulders and sending them both barreling into the ground. "The Rebellion still exists, even in hiding, and they trust you. If peace is going to happen for everyone I need a voice to reach all ends of Aristus. But do not mistake the Realm's trust for mine."

I bowed curtly to the coming Queen, understanding the precarious position I was in, and also the possibility that came with it.

"However," she continued, "I meant what I said. For what you did to free me, and for Kain as well, you have my gratitude."

"I look forward to your reign as Queen." An honest admission. A complicated one, but genuine all the same.

Kain waited for me at the other end of the courtyard, his marred hand open and outstretched towards me as I neared. I gladly took it and held him firmly, finally feeling the sense of relief I had desperately ached for all those years.

"I hope you know you don't have to join the guild." He said as we walked the cobblestone path through the colorful buildings of the upper city.

It was still early in the morning, and the streets were empty and quiet. People not aware of the troubling and Realm-altering events of the night were sleeping peacefully in their homes.

Kain rubbed his chin, his beard thick from weeks of travel. "I'd like to make it clear that I would be beyond thrilled, but it's a choice that's yours to make."

"I've already made it."

"Oh?" His eyes sparkled in the changing hue of the sky.

My voice spoke with a confidence that felt good in my chest. "I want to learn more—about magic. About myself. From someone who knows what they're talking about. I can't wait for Marcus to teach me."

Kain's laugh pierced the quiet of the morning and with a swift motion, scooped me up into his arms and swung me in a tight embrace. "It's going to be everything you could ever want. Of course, we'll need to take various trips to places of historical importance, and they'll obviously need help reshaping that garden surrounding the guild. You haven't yet seen all I can do with potions, now that we have access to proper ingredients—"

He would have kept talking had I not kissed him, full and passionately on the mouth. His fingers wove into my hair and his arm pulled my waist into his chest. My heart seared with a blissful intensity—a flame inside me that felt like the most natural thing in the world.

As we slowly released each other, the sun peeked over the horizon line and illuminated our faces.

Like Autumn bleeding and melting into Winter with a slow but steadfast burn, where reds and oranges yielded to dark hues of grey and navy, so did the night fade to dawn—deep blues and purples dissolved into warm yellows and pinks. It was magical, suspended in the moments between two beautiful things—watching them collide tenderly, delicately, and all at once.

A smile brightened my witch's face as he gazed into the start of morning, admiring the transition. Feeling the duality of two spirits at once, and the breathtaking interlude that existed within them.

I was starting to understand. The beauty of it, the freedom in it. I could feel my soul step out of the fog and into the sharp contrast of who I was and who I wanted to be. Solid and soft, resistant and vulnerable, snow and flame.

I had been the hunter, forced to maim and kill for survival, spilling blood to save my own. I had been the hare, always running, never catching my breath, fearing each shadow and fleeing from every danger. But somewhere there was space between them, where the pounding of life in my ribcage was not a steady drum but a beat that rose and fell. Feasting on possibility and bending low into rest, a flame ever burning—bright as the sun above the city spires, beyond the tree tops, shining through golden lining over silver clouds.

Acknowledgements

If you enjoyed this story, credit is due to the amazing people who supported me throughout its conception and creation.

I am so grateful to my partner, Reed, for their endless support and encouragement. They gifted me the space, time, and baked goods to continue working on making this dream a reality. Their excitement for the story and characters kept me going during the long night hours of writing and editing. Without them, the unfinished draft of The Witch and the Wicked would still be rotting in a long-lost file somewhere.

A hearty thanks is owed to my found family for giving me the necessary push to finally get this work published and out into the world. They're the best band of rogueish misfits an outcast could ask for.

I'd also like to acknowledge The Nerd Fam LLC, for it was only by their marketing prowess that this story fell into the hands of the book-loving community.

MegKPart, you needlessly mysterious bitch, thanks for the art.

And lastly—thank you, dear reader. The world is filled with countless beautiful stories, and I'm thrilled you took a moment to experience this one.

www.ingramcontent.com/pod-product-compliance
Ingram Content Group UK Ltd.
Pitfield, Milton Keynes, MK11 3LW, UK
UKHW041127070325
455838UK00006B/212

9 798989 205004